AF269015

ANCHOR

ANCHOR

palm south university book 2

kandi steiner

Copyright © 2016 Kandi Steiner
All rights reserved.

No part of this book may be used or reproduced in any form or by any means, electronic or mechanical, including photocopying, recording, or by any information storage and retrieval system without prior written consent of the author except where permitted by law.

The characters and events depicted in this book are fictitious. Any similarity to real persons, living or dead, is coincidental and not intended by the author.

Published by Kandi Steiner
Edited by Betsy Kash
Cover Design by Kandi Steiner
Formatting by Elaine York/Allusion Publishing
www.allusionpublishing.com

EPISODE 1

Bear

"Well, so much for that plan."

"HAPPY TWENTY-FIRST BIRTHDAY, BEAR!"

I smirk at the chorus of screams from Skyler and her sisters when I open the door of the Omega Chi house. Skyler leans up to kiss my cheek as the rest of the KKB girls filter around her, filling the already-packed living room.

"Thanks, ladies."

"I'm going to get you so wasted tonight," Skyler promises, throwing me a devilish grin. I have no doubt she'll deliver.

Skyler is my best friend on campus and, as of last semester, officially my Little Sister in Greek life. The way every guy in the room is eye-fucking her right now, I know they all think I'm crazy for not trying to score with her. But Skyler and I have always just had an unspoken connection — love, but in a family way.

Spring semester is already in full swing, even though classes just started this week. We already made it through spring rush, adding just shy of twenty new brothers to our fraternity, and now those pledges are finding out exactly what it means to be an Omega Chi Beta. It's Saturday night and our house is wall-to-wall with brothers and girls from every single sorority on campus. Our alumni brothers are supposedly leaving us alone since we held our act together last semester, but something tells me they won't exactly be pleased with us in the morning.

It's only eleven and we've already had two noise complaints.

Oops.

"Come on," Skyler says, grabbing my hand. "It's time for shots!"

I don't have time to argue because she's already tugging me through the crowd, brown locks swaying behind her. We brush past the two beer pong tables set up inside and jet around the living room where a make-shift dance floor has been set up. The entire house is dimly lit, a soft glow on the dark wood floors. As soon as we reach the island bar in the small house kitchen, she scores two shot glasses and fills them with tequila.

Fuck me.

"To finally being able to drink legally in a bar but still drinking here, anyway, because it's way more fun." Skyler holds up her shot glass to mine, her long, soft brown curls falling over her shoulder. Her bright blue eyes are radiating with an infectious energy, amping up my own excitement. Birthdays have never been a big deal to me, but I guess twenty-one is kind of worth celebrating.

"And to best friends who know exactly what alcohol to give you so you don't remember what happened the next day."

We clink our glasses together and throw the shots back, the tequila burning the entire way down. Our eyes water and we both reach for lime slices at the same time, laughing.

"Should I be getting your autograph? It's not every day I take shots with the hottest new poker player on the scene."

Skyler rolls her eyes, sucking her lime slice dry before snatching up two red Solo cups. Several brothers are watching her, drooling, my Little included — but Skyler doesn't even notice. "Hardly."

"You can't even deny that after the tournament over break, Sky."

She chews her cheek, filling our cups from the keg. She drinks half of hers as she hands me mine. "I know. It just feels weird. I don't want to think about it right now."

I chuckle. "Fine. Let's go numb our minds with drinking games."

"Now that's a plan I can get behind."

We make our way to the backyard where several tables are set up. It's January in Florida, so for once, I'm not sweating. In fact, a few of the girls are wearing light hoodies and everyone is in jeans. It's one of the maybe five cold days we'll have before spring shows up again, and all the windows to the house are open, taking advantage of the cool air.

"Any news from your family?" Skyler asks as we scan the tables. I stayed with her all break, so she's well aware of the fact that I haven't heard a peep from my mom or my older brother since I wrote them the check after semi-formal last semester.

"Just Clayton. He's starting back up at school and says he's been sleeping over at his friend Mac's house a lot lately. He sounds good."

"You okay?" She turns to face me when she asks, probably to make sure I don't lie to her. This time, I genuinely feel like I don't have to.

"I am. Not even thinking about them." And it's true. Maybe I'm finally sick of their shit enough to where I refuse to let it weigh on me, or maybe I'm being selfish for once. Either way, I'm just excited to be back at Palm South — especially since we're just a few short months away from Spring Break.

Skyler smiles. "Good. Oh! I think I see a table."

She points to a half-empty table and I nod, following her toward it. We start gathering a few of my brothers and her sisters to play chandelier with us when a girl I've never met before pops up in front of me.

"Hi!"

Her voice is loud and perky, and my eyes widen a fraction.

Taking a second look, I realize there's a very long, very sexy pair of legs attached to the too-spunky-for-me voice.

"Are you the birthday boy?"

Her question catches me off guard, almost as much as her unique appearance. Her hair is just past her shoulders, jet black at the roots and faded into a deep purple at the ends. It's curled, falling similar to the way Skyler's does naturally, and she's wearing a thick pair of black frames. She's dressed simply in a black v-neck t-shirt and bleach-washed jeans, though they hug her in all the right places. Her smile is bright, curious, and unapologetic.

I can't for the life of me figure out why, but I immediately want to nail her.

My eyes flick to her plump lips.

Okay maybe I do know why.

I hold one finger up. "Guilty."

Her smile widens. "Thank fuck." Without warning, she wraps her arms around my neck and pulls her mouth up to mine. Her lips are soft and wet, and even though I have no idea what the hell is happening, I grip her small waist tight in my hands and snake my tongue into her mouth. She moans, her hands fisting at the back of my neck. I bite her lower lip as she pulls back, releasing it with a pop.

"They dared me to give you your first birthday kiss of the night," she pants, her eyes still on my mouth. When she lifts them again, I realize they're a bright green. "It was really going to suck if you were unfortunate looking."

"Does that mean you think I'm hot?"

She smirks. "I mean, I wouldn't mind giving you your *last* birthday kiss of the night, too, if that answers your question."

I can't say I'm not shocked by her honesty. Most girls play hard to get, or not interested, or whatever other fucking games they think make them seem like they're not easy targets. This girl is standing tall, eyes on mine, confident and sure.

And it's so fucking sexy.

Grinning, I lean in closer, brushing her hair behind her ear so I have easier access. My dark hands are a stark contrast to her pale white skin. "And what if I want more than just a birthday kiss?" I whisper.

She inhales a stiff breath, just enough to let me know I'm affecting her the way I want to. Then, she licks her lip and pulls away from my grasp. "I guess you're going to have to hope my friends have your interests in mind the next time I pick dare." She winks, turns, and rejoins a small group of girls across the yard. They all giggle and keep their eyes on me, but I can't take mine off of her.

"What the shit was that?" Skyler asks, sliding up beside me with two freshly filled cups. She holds one out to me and lifts the others to her lips, her eyes following mine to the group of girls still watching us.

"No idea," I murmur, taking the cup.

"Come on, let's drink." Skyler starts setting up the game and more people gather around us, but I keep my eyes focused on the girl with the purple hair until she finally turns to sneak a peek at me again. I hold her gaze steady for just a moment before her friends drag her back inside the house.

I don't even know her name, but by the end of the night, I'm determined to know her bra size.

It's almost three in the morning.

Skyler took off about an hour ago to meet up with Adam, her boyfriend in Alpha Sigma, but not before completely following through on her promise. I'm drunk. And that's an understatement.

Lacy is hanging all over me, licking up my neck and whispering what she wants to do to me. Had this been last semester, I probably would have given her a second round in my bed. She's cute — caramel skin and carefully-styled natural hair. She wasn't a bad lay, per say, but she was just a distraction for me during a shitty time. My mom had just asked me for money and I needed a temporary escape. But tonight, I'm celebrating. I'm not looking for a distraction.

I'm looking for a really long, really hard, really incredible fuck.

And I know just who I want to get it from.

"Excuse me," I say softly, grabbing both of Lacy's wrists in my hands to peel them off me. She pouts as I let them drop into her lap and make my way across the living room where only a few Zetas are left lazily dancing. The girl from earlier is leaning against our pool table, talking to one of our new pledges. He's a cool guy, but judging by the look on her face, she's two seconds away from yawning or completely falling asleep.

As if on cue, she covers a yawn with her hand, still nodding along with his words to make it seem like it couldn't possibly be him who evoked that reaction.

"Hey, Caleb," I interrupt, clapping him on the back. "Having fun at your first O Chi party?"

He's clearly about as sober as I am, because a shit-eating grin spreads on his face. "Bro, this is the best night of my life."

I chuckle. Caleb is a freshman, and after that comment, I'm a little scared for his pledging process. He has no idea what he's in for.

"Glad to hear it. Unfortunately, I'm going to have to pull the birthday card and steal this beautiful girl away from you." My eyes cut to the girl with the purple hair and she fights back a smile.

Caleb's face falls. "Wait." I cock one brow, letting him know he really shouldn't argue, and his shoulders deflate a little. "Yeah... yeah, okay. Happy birthday, Bear." He offers a reluctant smile before taking a long drink from his cup, leaving me alone with the girl I can't wait to get back to my room.

"Kind of presumptuous, don't you think?" She asks, but her eyes are already undressing me.

"Depends."

"On?"

I shrug. "On whether you let me take you back to my room or not."

She stares at the hand I'm now holding out toward her, seemingly debating her options. She could easily walk away, find one of her girlfriends and leave the party without so much as another word. But the way she's chewing her lip tells me that's not exactly the plan she has in mind.

"I'm only going back with you on one condition."

I wait, hand still outstretched as she narrows her eyes.

"I want two orgasms tonight. And not the kind I fake, the kind I can't hold back with. The kind that make my legs sore in the morning."

My teeth find my bottom lip, fighting back a smile. *Who the hell is this girl and where has she been hiding?*

"I'll give you three."

The left side of her mouth lifts just slightly as she looks confidently up at me through her lashes. Then, she slides her small hand into mine.

Tugging her through the remaining crowd, I lift her as soon as we reach the hallway. Her back is pressed against the wall right next to our founding brothers' class photo, her legs wrapped around my waist. I suck the skin on her neck between my teeth and she hisses.

"What's your name?"

"Shawna," she answers, panting.

"I'm Bear."

"Nice to meet you."

"Likewise."

Gripping her ass in my hands, I shove us through my room and kick the door closed behind us. Shawna is already stripping her shirt off as I drop her feet to the floor at the end of my bed. I follow suit, tugging my jeans and boxers down in one fluid movement and kicking them to the side. Shawna is impatiently naked and pulling at my shirt. She lifts it over my head and I take it the rest of the way, tossing it to the side.

Then she's staring at me.

More specifically, at my cock.

"Holy shit," she breathes. She reaches out, trailing her fingertips down the middle of my abdomen, all the while still staring at my dick. When she reaches my waist line, she pulls her fingers to her mouth, her eyes flicking back to mine.

I smirk.

The only light in my room is streaming through the window from a street light, but it bathes Shawna in a soft blue light, hitting every curve. Dropping to my knees, I run my rough hand over the smooth skin of her neck, her breasts, her flat stomach.

Wait.

Are those nipple piercings?

Oh, fuck.

Definitely going to have to play with those later.

"Round one," I growl against the sensitive skin of her clit, one side of my mouth quirked in a cocky smile. She smiles back, but her face falls into a soft *O* when I close the distance.

She's moaning, bucking her hips forward with each flick of my tongue. I groan, too, because she tastes so fucking sweet. Sliding two fingers inside her, we both exhale together, her at the way my touch feels and me at how wet she is.

Snaking my free hand up her stomach, I palm her breast, massaging it in time with her rolling hips. Shawna cries out, fisting her hands in my barely-there hair and pulling me closer. When I suck her clit between my teeth, I pinch her piercing at the same time and roll it between my fingers.

She gasps.

Stiffens.

Holds her breath.

And then she comes.

I'm pretty sure she's waking up every single brother in my house right now but I don't give a single fuck. She's completely unfiltered, moaning my name like it's the last word she'll ever say. When she steadies out, her legs still shaking, I stand and put my mouth hard on hers. She tastes herself eagerly, panting as I slip my tongue between her lips.

Her hands wrap around my neck and she lies back on the bed, wriggling her way up to the pillows and tugging me with her. The purple ends of her dark hair are highlighted in the dim light of my room, sprawled out on my pillows, framing her bright eyes and swollen lips.

I spread her legs with my own, hitching one up at my waist as I position myself at her entrance. Her eyes are wide, and I have to steady my breathing and remind myself to go slow. Judging by her reaction earlier, I'm not exactly the size she's used to dealing with.

Kissing her lips, I bite the lower one before moving down her neck to her collarbone. Then, slowly, steadily, I flex my hips and bury my cock inside her.

And she is so. Fucking. Tight.

"Oh God," she cries, digging her nails into my back. With any other girl, I'd pull out my usual line — *Nope, just me, babe*. But with Shawna, I have no words. I literally can't say a fucking thing because I'm focusing too hard on not busting after being inside her for less than thirty seconds.

But I hold out, adjusting my rhythm to please her without granting myself the same gratification — not just yet. And then, I give her round two.

And three.

And just for the hell of it, four.

Cassie

"**I'M JUST SAYING, YOU'RE** not living if you've never tried a finger in the ass before," Jess says with a shrug, not the least bit ashamed, just as I reach the small table in the middle of our campus coffee shop.

I blink, dropping my bag into the only open chair. "Well, conversation at Joe's has certainly progressed."

Jess smirks, waggling her eyebrows at Ashlei who just shakes her head. I try to fight back my own smile, but give up when Jess starts fingering her donut.

"Gross, J-Love!" Erin tosses her napkin and it hits Jess square in the nose, but she just laughs and keeps violating her pastry.

Cup O' Joe's is a small coffee house, dimly lit and walls peppered with local student art. The open roof and piping paired with the wood and rustic furniture give it a modern, hip vibe. It's one of my favorite places on campus to study, and I talked the girls into meeting for coffee this morning before my second class. Spring semester has already kicked off and we had yet to all be together outside of sisterhood functions, so I wanted us to make time to catch up.

Jess demonstrating anal on a glazed donut wasn't exactly what I had in mind.

"I think I'm with Jess on this one," Skyler chimes in. "I mean, I'm not saying it needs to get crazy. Just a little boop, you know what I mean?" Skyler and Bo crack up laughing while Erin covers her face with her hands. Ashlei smiles, but it doesn't quite reach her soft brown eyes. She seems off.

"I'm grabbing coffee. Anyone need a refill?"

They all shake their heads, holding up full cups. Retrieving my wallet from my Vera Bradley messenger bag, I take my place in line, scanning the menu.

It feels kind of strange being back at Palm South, especially after how my first semester ended. I shift at the thought of Clay and Paris, but shake it off quickly. Winter Break was my time to regroup. I opened up to my older sister about what happened – everything from losing my best friend to losing my v-card to a complete douchebag. Surprisingly, she had some pretty great advice. The best piece being that, at least for freshman year, I should just avoid boys in general and focus on myself.

So that's exactly what I'm doing.

No boys, no drama — that's the way it works. And I am more than looking forward to being drama-free.

"Excuse me," a smooth voice says over my shoulder. I turn in place, swallowing when I see the exotic creature the voice belongs to. "Just going out on a limb here, but are you by chance a caramel latte girl?"

My mouth is so dry. *Why can't I swallow? Is it hot in here? Oh God, I hope I'm not sweating.*

I'm *totally* sweating.

Of course, this creature picks the semester I choose to be boy-free to waltz up behind me in line at the coffee shop. His long chestnut hair is pulled back into a messy bun, giving me full access to stare into his glorious blue eyes. They're peppered with flecks of gold, and I'm sure he's some sort of god. He's just standing there, crooked smile beneath his beard, tattoos lining the muscles of his right forearm like a warning sign to the mortals. The way the sun is streaming through the tinted windows of the coffee shop illuminate him in a way that lets me know I'd be cursed if I touched him.

Probably dead if he touched me.

He clears his throat, cocking one brow. "Is that a no, or did I forget to put pants on again?" He chuckles, but I squeeze my eyes tight.

Do NOT think about him without pants on, Cassie.

"Sorry. I, uh, no." I shake my head, nervously reaching for a strand of my fiery red hair to twirl. "I mean, yes, I like caramel lattes, but no, you can't buy me one."

"Good thing I didn't buy these." He holds up the two cups in his hands.

I'm confused.

"I work here," he says, gesturing to the small stage on the book store side of the shop. A lone guitar is propped up against a tall metal bar stool and I stare at it a moment, blink, and then find his eyes again.

Of *course* he plays guitar. Of course he does.

"They give me a free drink when I play, and they accidentally made two cups. So, I have this extra one, and I figured it'd be better served in the hands of a pretty girl than getting cold at my feet while I play." He smiles, this time showing a row of beautiful teeth that make me forget how to breathe.

"Well, I appreciate it, but I can't take your coffee."

He frowns. "Why not?"

"Because you're a boy."

"That is a fact," he says with a soft laugh. It's a soothing sound, the sort of laugh that makes me feel like I can trust him.

I blush just as the girl in front of me leaves the counter and it's my turn to order. "Exactly. So, thanks, but no thanks." I offer one last smile before turning to place my order. I still feel him behind me, his godliness just radiating off of him, but I don't dare turn around. He finally chuckles, and I feel him leave, which allows me to finally release the breath I didn't realize I was holding.

I quickly pay for my order and rejoin the girls at the table.

"So, Skyler became famous over break, Jess watched a lot of porn, Bo ate shit trying to figure out how to ski and I suffered through a stomach flu in Europe, which wasn't half as bad as suffering through my mother when I got back home," Erin summarizes, lazily dunking the tea bag in her large beige coffee cup. "Ashlei, Cassie, you're the only ones left. What'd you do over break?"

Ashlei's chewing her straw, avoiding all eye contact. She looks tired, and I notice dark circles under her eyes that weren't there before break. I'm not that close with Ashlei, but even I know there's something she's not telling us.

"I just worked."

"Worked?" Jess asks, pausing with her cup halfway lifted to her mouth. "What are you talking about? You don't have a job."

"Well I had one over break," Ashlei spits back. She's definitely sassy today.

"Doing what?" Jess challenges.

"Bartending."

"Bartending," Jess repeats flatly.

"Well, I swore off boys forever," I chime in, trying to take the heat off Ashlei. She gives me a *thank you* smile, but Jess is still eying her. "Or at least, for the rest of freshman year."

"I like that idea," Erin says with a smile. "Maybe I'll join you in that initiative, G-Little."

"Speaking of boys, how weird is it that I have a boy-friend?" Skyler asks, sucking the last of her iced coffee drink dry and shaking the ice in her cup.

"Super fucking weird," Jess replies quickly. Skyler laughs. My stomach turns.

"Sorry to interrupt, ladies." I hear the voice and I don't even have to turn around to know who's standing behind me again, especially when every jaw at the table drops. "I just had to come over because, well, because your friend here has completely shattered my confidence."

I turn slowly, my eyes trailing up his god-like body until I meet his own blue pools. He bends down on one knee, bringing us face to face.

"You see, I didn't actually get that coffee for free, I bought it when I saw you walk through that door over there." He points, but no one's eyes move from his face. Rubbing his hand over his beard, he shrugs. "I had no idea what kind of coffee you drank, but I figured it didn't matter — I just wanted to talk to you." Someone sighs. My money's on Erin. "But then you totally shot me down, and at first I was going to let it go, but my mom raised me to always go after what I want and never stop fighting for it. And what I want right now is your phone number."

This is not happening.

Pulling his phone from his pocket, he holds it out for me to take, his eyes still fixed on mine. "Well, your phone number and your name."

"Her name is Cassie," Skyler says quickly and he chuckles, that same smooth sound giving me chills.

"Cassie," he tries it on, testing how it feels on his lips. "What do you say? Make my mom proud and give me your number?"

"Oh my God, give me," Erin says, snatching his phone from his hands. She types out what I can only assume is my number and hands it back to him. "Thank me later, baby G."

I try not to laugh, but fail miserably. He smiles in triumph.

"Well, I guess you can live to be a momma's boy another day..." I trail off, waiting for him to tell me his name.

"Grayson," he says, holding the hand sans-phone out to me. My eyes trail the tattoos. "Grayson Anderson."

Yep, even his name is one of a god.

"Cassie McBee," I reply, tentatively taking his hand. He lifts it to his bearded mouth and kisses it softly.

I'm *really* trying not to swoon, I swear.

"See you around, Cassie McBee." He stands with a wink and a half-wave to the rest of the girls before making his way back to the stage. I stare long enough to watch him strap on his guitar before turning back around.

And everyone is staring at me with a shit-eating grin.

"I hate you all."

"I'm sorry," Jess offers through a laugh, throwing her hands up. "The no-boy rule doesn't apply to boys like *that*."

"Neither does the three-dates-before-he-scores rule," my Big adds.

"Little!" Erin chastises Skyler, but we all laugh regardless.

My eyes find Grayson across the room just as he begins strumming out a soft acoustic tune. He smiles, one strand of his hair falling from the bun he's haphazardly tied at the back of his head. Each strum of the guitar calls attention to the muscles in his arms and I allow myself to stare for just a moment longer before snapping my attention back to the girls.

They're all staring, too.

Well, so much for that plan.

Jess

I THINK I'M IN heaven.

My feet are propped up on the dash of Jarrett's truck, Trey Songz is on the stereo, we've almost finished off a joint and I know in less than ten minutes, I'll have his glorious cock inside me.

Like I said, heaven.

Pinching what's left of the joint between my finger and thumb, I inhale long and hard, holding it in as I pass it back to Jarrett. His lids already low, he takes one last hit before extinguishing it in a half-empty bottle of Gatorade. I can't remember the last time I got high, but I know for a fact that it never felt this good. Maybe it's because Jarrett has better weed, or maybe it's just because Jarrett is involved — period.

With all the windows up, the smoke clouds around us, circling in new designs each time one of us breathes. Jarrett is watching me closely from the driver's seat, his eyes still hooded, his teeth just barely tugging on the flesh of his lower lip. Being away from him all break almost made me forget how fucking beautiful he is. Dark eyes, tattoos lining his arms, thick erection straining against his basketball shorts. I've never wanted him more.

"So now that you know about my boring ass Winter Break, what did you do?"

Jarrett smiles lazily. "Same old. Worked at the bar and surfed when the waves were big enough. I did spend some time with Spencer, too."

"Surfing buddy?"

"Kind of. She's trying to learn, but she's pretty new to Florida so it's like trying to teach a ten-year-old. She's getting better though."

I stiffen when I realize Spencer is a *she*, not a he. My mouth dry, I reach for my water bottle and try desperately to calm my racing heart. We're not exclusive, I told him I didn't want to title it, but he also said he didn't want to fuck anyone else. He didn't want *me* to fuck anyone else. And I haven't.

"Oh. Well, I'm sure she'll be just *fine* with you as her teacher." I try not to sound bitter, but I know I completely fail. I clear my throat, looking out my window at the soft waves crashing on the dark beach. When Jarrett's rough hand slides over my thigh and grips me gently at the knee, I chance a look in his direction.

One brow cocked, Jarrett looks amused — pleased, almost. *Asshole.*

"Are you jealous, Jess?"

I scoff. "No. Why would I be?"

He clicks his tongue, shaking that gorgeous head of his. "Shame. I was really hoping you were jealous."

"You're an ass!" I smack him across the chest but he grabs my wrist with his hand, pulling me over the console to straddle him. As soon as my knees settle on either side of him, he bucks his hips up, stealing my breath with the feel of him against me.

"She's the bar owner's daughter, and I'm not the least bit interested in her." Sliding both hands down my arms, he grips my ass firmly and rocks me against him, the friction making my eyes flutter. "You're the one I want, Jess. The *only* one I want."

My eyes are wide, my mouth just slightly open as I stare at him through the smoky darkness. I feel my heart tug, a sensation I'm far from used to. When Jarrett says shit like that, it makes me want to call him my boyfriend.

And I don't do boyfriends.

Not anymore.

"Good," I breathe. "Because I want you, too."

"Yeah?" Jarrett asks, tucking his hands into the back pockets of my jean shorts. He drags me up against the length of him, building the friction. "What do you want to do to me?"

Licking my lips, I lean in closer, biting his neck with more pressure than I intended. He hisses through his teeth as I softly kiss the same spot. "I want to ride you," I breathe against his skin, kissing his Adam's apple next. "I want to make you come with my name on your lips." Another bite on the other side of his neck. His hands move to my waist and he grips me hard. "And then," I whisper, dragging my tongue up his neck before pulling his earlobe between my teeth. "I want to take you to pizza."

Jarrett bursts out laughing as I sit back on his lap, waggling my eyebrows. The weed has settled in my blood, making me feel almost as high as Jarrett's touch makes me feel.

"God," he pants, still smiling. "That is the sexiest thing anyone has ever said to me."

"Did I mention there'd be... garlic knots?" I breathe the words in a sultry manner, biting my lower lip.

Jarrett groans. "Keep talking, baby."

I drag my hands down his chiseled abdomen before tucking one beneath the band of his shorts and palming his erection through the silky fabric with the other. "And," I continue, rolling my hips in time with my hand on him. "You can get whatever. Toppings. You. Want."

"Fuck," Jarrett growls. His hand flies to the side of his seat, reclining us back in an instant. He lifts me effortlessly, tossing me in the back and quickly following. Settling between my legs, he kisses me hard. "I think I just came."

"Better not have."

He smirks, but then his lips claim my own again and I no longer feel like joking. His hands are in my hair, pulling, tangling. His lips are on my neck, my collarbone, the swell of my breast. I arch my back and his hand finds the zipper of my shorts, tugging it down. His fingers snake beneath the harsh fabric of my jeans and he rubs me over the lace of my thong.

"Jesus Christ," he breathes, his forehead against mine. I can feel how wet my thong is and I know that's what he's noticing, too.

Pushing himself off the seat, he grips his shirt at the back of his neck and pulls it up and over his head. I follow suit, maneuvering out of my tank top and bra. Leaning up, I run my fingers down the middle ridge of his chest and abdomen before tucking my fingers in the band of his shorts. I push them down over his ass, his erection springing free. Taking him in my hand, I lift my eyes to his and lick my lips. His eyes are heavy, hooded with lust and a high I know I'm not experiencing alone. When I close my lips around his tip, he drops his head back, running his hands over the bald surface.

I grab his ass in my hands and pull him deeper into my mouth. He growls when he hits the back of my throat and I instantly grow wetter. Letting him take control, I reach up for his hands and move them to my hair, keeping my hands clasped over his. He's gentle at first, careful not to hurt me, but as his breathing shallows and his desperation grows, his hands fist in my hair. Opening my throat for him, he pulls me all the way down, my lips touching his base as I gag slightly.

"I fucking love that," he breathes, trying his best to slowly move in my mouth. When I gag again, he curses, pulling me back and grabbing my shorts at my hips. I lean back and arch up long enough for him to peel them off of me. A condom wrapper is ripped, he quickly rolls it over himself, and then he's between my legs, his tip at my entrance, his lips hard on mine.

Wrapping my legs around his waist, I use my heels to push into his backside, closing the distance between us. He fills me quickly and all at once. My breath catches and he groans as I drag my nails down his back.

Jarrett pumps slow and calculated, moving us in time with the slow R&B music crooning through the speakers of his truck. The closer we get, the faster we move. When he leans back on his heels, moving his thumb to circle my clit as he pounds into me, I moan in ecstasy. I'm close, so fucking close.

But then, Jarrett stops.

"Don't stop," I moan, wrapping my legs around him tighter.

"I need to hear you say it first."

I open my heavy lids, peeking at him through the smoky darkness of the truck. Or is that steam? Maybe both.

"I want you," I breathe, squirming beneath him.

"That's not what I meant."

I groan. "Then what?"

He smirks, his dark eyes ablaze. "You were jealous."

I'm panting so loud. "What?"

"You were jealous."

"No," I argue, but I'm quickly losing my resolve. "I wasn't. We're not exclusive."

"Oh?" he asks, pulling out until just his tip is still inside me before quickly slamming back into me. I cry out, an incredible sensation flowing through me. "Are you sure?"

"Oh God, Jarrett, just fuck me."

"I fully intend to. But first, I want to hear you say it." I lean up on my elbows, biting my lower lip as I gaze up at him. He simply cocks one brow, waiting. I still don't answer. He pulls out again, this time leaving me completely empty. I instantly crave him. "Say it."

"Fine," I mutter. "I was jealous."

"What was that?"

I purse my lips, trying to fight back a grin. "I was jealous, you ass hat. Now finish getting me off before I go find someone else for the job."

"We've already been through this, Jess," he says, shaking his head as he positions himself at my entrance. "No one can fuck you the way I do." As he slides back into me, filling me completely, his thumb mercilessly working my clit, I know he's right.

I come apart, crying out into the darkness of his truck just like I did the first night we met last semester. He follows shortly after, and then he collapses, his body deliciously heavy on mine. So much has changed since then, from me trying to fight him, to finally giving in, to now wondering if what we have is more serious than either of us are admitting. I shake my head, not wanting to think too much on it. We've having fun. That's what matters right now.

Our breaths still coming hard, Jarrett leans up, running one hand through my hair as his dark eyes devour my own. The way he looks at me completely immobilizes me. It's like he wants to lock me up in his room and never let me leave, like he wants to brand me, own me.

He smiles crookedly, biting his lower lip and planting one slow kiss on my mouth.

"Now about that pizza."

Bear

REACHING INTO MY BAG for my notebook, I let it drop on my desk with a slap and kick back in my chair. It's the second week of class, but since I decided to ditch the entire first week of class, being that it's syllabus week and all, I'm still trying to get in the swing of things. Omega Chi is a great fraternity to be in if you want to have fun. If you want to sleep, on the other hand, not so much.

The professor is already scribbling on the whiteboard as more students file in. She's odd — just as I would expect an art professor to be. She has wild curly hair and paint-stained overalls like she just came off the set of *She's All That*. I already know I'll struggle in this class, but it's a mandatory course for all Graphic Design majors, so here I am.

I'm debating sneaking in a quick five-minute nap session when Shawna walks through the door to the classroom.

Holy shit.

Sitting up straighter, I watch as her green eyes scan the room from beneath her black frames. Her hair is piled into a messy bun on top of her head and she looks like she just rolled out of bed in her yoga pants and tank top. Still, I feel an uncomfortable pressure in my jeans.

When she spots me, she blinks, almost as if she's unsure if I'm really there. Then, she smiles, and jogs up the stairs to my desk. I'm about to offer a *hello* when she throws herself into my lap, kissing me like we're alone. Her hands are on either side of my face, mine find her hips. If it were any other girl, I'd be weirded out or pissed or both, thinking she was under the impression we were dating just because we fucked. But, oddly enough, I'm completely fine with Shawna kissing me where everyone can see.

"Is this how you say *hi* where you're from?" I ask when she pulls back. She giggles and slides into the seat next to mine.

"I was just making sure you were still a good kisser. Sometimes when I'm drunk, I think guys are really great kissers and then they end up letting me down when I'm sober."

"Well?"

She scrunches her nose. "Yeah, you're still pretty good."

I can't help but smile at her. She's unlike any girl I've ever met before.

"You never called me."

"Well, you see, in order for me to call you, that would have required you actually leaving your phone number."

She blushes, but just slightly. "True. Tell you what — I'll give you my phone number, but you have to take me to dinner after class tonight first."

"Is that so?"

She grins wider and nods. "Mm hmm. I mean, I probably should have made that a requirement *before* I let you see my nipple piercings, but I'm not exactly a traditional type of girl."

"You don't say."

We're both smiling, eying each other, sizing the other one up.

I like this girl.

The professor calls the class' attention, so I lean over to whisper my response.

"Dinner it is. Where to?"

I've never watched a girl stuff a fat, chili and cheese covered hot dog into her mouth before, but it's oddly arousing. Maybe it's just because I'm stoked she ordered more than just a salad, but I'm just watching Shawna eat, grinning like an idiot.

"What?" she asks around a mouthful.

I shake my head, dunking a French fry into the ketchup on my plate. "Nothing. I'm just impressed."

"That I can eat a hot dog? What kind of weirdos do you usually take to dinner?"

"The wrong kind, apparently."

"So true."

Shawna winks, wiping her mouth with a napkin and taking a long pull from her soda before propping her elbows up on the table. "So, Clinton Pennington, AKA Bear, AKA birthday boy with a magical tongue — I never would have guessed you were an Art major."

I cock a brow at her tongue reference. "Graphic Design, actually. Are you an Art major?"

"For now." She smiles, her cheeks pushing her black frames up her face a bit. "Tell me more about you."

"There's not much to tell," I reply, feeling a bit uncomfortable. I don't really talk to anyone about myself other than Skyler, and that's just because she pries it out of me. Watching Shawna's lips press together, I have a feeling she and Skyler might have a bit more in common than I originally realized.

"Sure there is. What are your hobbies?"

"Sports, weight lifting, drinking, fucking."

"All the essentials."

"Exactly."

"What sports?"

"Football mostly, but I like basketball, too. What about you?" I ask, popping another fry in my mouth and leaning back. The small diner she picked only has five booths and they're a little too cramped for my liking, but I don't mind being closer to her.

"I love to draw and paint, and listen to live music."

"Favorite band?"

"Twenty One Pilots."

"Nice. I've heard a few of their songs."

"Careful," she warns me, sucking the fry salt off her fingertip. I'm momentarily distracted by her plump lips. "I'm a pusher. I'll talk your ear off until I convince you to listen to their album with me and then go to their concert."

"Hmm... dancing to good music with you all pressed up against me? Sounds terrible. Definitely don't do that."

She grins.

"Your turn. What's with the phoenix?"

Her face scrunches. "How do you know about the... oh." Shawna blushes a bit when she remembers exactly how I saw the phoenix tattoo on her lower back.

I just grin.

"It's my only tattoo, kind of a metaphor to live by, I guess. Rising from the ashes and all."

"How many times have you had to rise?"

She swallows, and I'm afraid I've maybe asked too much, but she still answers. "Enough times to know you never come back as the same person who went up in flames."

She keeps her eyes locked on mine a while longer before taking another drink of her soda. I'm studying her, noting the freckles on the apples of her cheeks, the chewed nails of the hand she's holding her cup with. Everything about her is so different than what I'm used to.

"So what's your family like?"

I stiffen, clearing my throat. "Shitty. Well, most of them. All of them, really, aside from my little brother."

Her mouth pulls to the side. "Shitty how?"

"Shitty like they're druggies, they use me for money, they told me I was worthless growing up and now they think I'm arrogant." I don't know why I just opened up about all that shit. I never tell people my family drama — Skyler is the only one who knows.

I wait for Shawna's mouth to drop open or her eyes to go wide, but she just offers a sad smile. "I'm no stranger to family drama, either."

"What do you mean?"

Shawna crosses her arms over her chest. "Definitely not first date conversation material."

"And mine was?" I ask, chuckling. She smiles, leaning forward over the table.

"I like that you opened up to me."

"I'm still trying to figure out why."

Her eyes fall to my lips. "Why don't we go back to my place?" She flicks her eyes back to mine. "Maybe you'll be able to hear yourself think better there."

"Good thinking," I reply, returning her smile. Calling the waitress over, I pay for our check and leave a cash tip on the table before grabbing Shawna's hand and leading her through the door. She's smiling wickedly at me, her green eyes curious yet challenging. And I know without a doubt that there will be absolutely no thinking going on once we make it to her place.

Cassie

IT WOULDN'T BE A new semester at Palm South without an Omega Chi party. At least, that's what everyone has been telling me all week. Since I bailed on Clinton's twenty-first birthday party last Saturday, Skyler is dragging me to their house tonight and I know trying to get out of it is pointless. But, I feel more prepared tonight, less in a funk than I was last week. Classes are picking up and so far, I've been drama-free.

Knowing who will be at this party, I just hope I can stay that way.

"So is it weird doing interviews for the blogs and stuff?" I ask Skyler as we walk toward the O Chi house. Kappa Kappa Beta and Omega Chi are on opposite ends of Greek Row, but it's a nice evening, cool without being too cold. The rest of the girls are already there waiting for us, but Skyler had a phone interview with one of the top poker blogs and couldn't reschedule, so I stayed back with her.

"A little." She shrugs. "Mostly I'm just annoyed by them."

"Really? Isn't it good exposure?"

"Sometimes. I mean, I like when they ask me about how I started playing or what my advice for new players is. But, most of the time, they'll ask me about shit that isn't relative — who I'm dating, what my diet is like, what lotions or hair products I use." She shakes her head, worrying her bottom lip between her teeth. "It just sucks. Because I'm a female player, they're less interested in my skills than they are in how I look."

"Wow. That is shitty."

She nods. "I mean, don't get me wrong. I know that looks can be used as a weapon. When I walk into a room of guys who don't know who I am, it's easy to fool them into thinking I'm a novice. I can flirt them into folding or hanging on when I have a good hand. But still, I just wish they'd stop publicizing it all over and start taking me seriously."

"They will one day, Big," I assure her, and I really know it to be true in my heart. Skyler is fierce, and even though I've never seen her play a game of poker, Clinton talks about how amazing she is all the time. "You'll see."

"I hope so, Little Nug." She winks at me just as we reach the Omega Chi house. We push through the front door without knocking and filter into the crammed house. It's insanely noisy, screams and music filling every room. I kind of miss the quietness of our walk.

Clinton scoops Skyler up in a crushing hug when we reach the kitchen, spinning her around as she pounds her baby fists on his chest. They're both laughing, and I can't help but notice how truly happy Clinton looks. I don't think I saw that big of a smile on his face at any point last semester.

"Skyler fucking Thorne! Keg stand. Right now."

Skyler laughs as he lets her drop back to the floor. "Done. Where's the keg?"

"Follow me," he says with a grin. Before we can exit, Skyler is scooped up in another hug.

"Damn, Bear. Not even going to let me kiss my girlfriend before you go stealing her away?"

Adam presses his lips to Skyler's as she giggles and I tuck my hair behind my ear, looking at Clinton instead. I am definitely not thinking about how good Adam's hair looks, or how his t-shirt is tight around his bicep muscles, or how his body wash smells the same as it did when I laid in his bed before Winter Break.

No, I'm not thinking about any of that.

"It's an O Chi party, Adam. Not Alpha Sig. My rules."

"Fair enough," Adam concedes, pecking Skyler one last time before smacking her butt as she scampers off. "Don't let me down."

"What? You're not going to hold my legs?" she asks, eyes wide and playful.

"Good point. I'll be right there." He turns to me as Clinton and Skyler make their way toward the keg near the kitchen. "Hey, Cassie."

I swallow a bit when he says my name, nothing but kindness shining in his chocolate eyes. He's looking at me like he's half-worried, half-expectant. Of what, I can't be sure. "Hey."

"Did you have a good break?"

"Yeah." I don't know why I'm making this so weird when it doesn't have to be. "I'm going to get a drink."

Without another word, I slip away and head in the same direction Skyler and Clinton had. Skyler's hands are already braced on the handles of the keg but I snake my cup in, quickly filling it before wishing her luck and heading off to find the other girls.

Jess and Erin are dancing in the living room, but I'm not quite on that level yet, so I wave at them before continuing to peruse the house. When I spot Ashlei and Bo in the hallway that leads back to the bedrooms, I make my way toward them.

"I told you I'm fine. Please stop worrying about me. I've got it under control, I promise." Ashlei's words catch in her throat when she sees me approaching, but Bo is still watching her carefully with a concerned look on her face.

"Hey girls," I say tentatively. "Am I interrupting?"

"No way, roomie," Bo replies with a smile. She cut her hair over Winter Break and I have to say it suits her. Her dark eyes and high bone structure are on prominent display. I didn't really get to spend much time with her last semester, but we're rooming together in the house this year, so I look forward to changing that.

"We were just talking about you, actually." Ashlei smiles and Bo waggles her eyebrows.

Oh no. This can't be good.

"Why do I feel like I should run in the other direction?"'

They both laugh, and I notice Bo hooking her pinky in the jean pocket of Ashlei's shorts.

"The Kappa Kappa Beta date auction is coming up. We think you should be one of the girls we sell."

I blanch. "Um, absolutely not."

"Come on!" Bo pleads. "You're the only redhead we have and you're smoking hot. I know you could bring in some big bucks."

"Bo is Co-Community Chair this semester, so she really wants to try to outdo last year's results," Ashlei adds. "It'll be fun, Cassie. Promise."

I sigh. "Are you going to badger me until I give in?" They both nod, grinning, and I just shake my head. "Fine. But you two owe me."

Bo squeals. "Yay! Thank you, thank you, thank you!" She wraps her petite arms around me and I pat her back in return.

"Don't worry, we'll pay you back in the form of shots on your first Spring Break." Ashlei winks, lifting her cup before taking a sip.

"That doesn't sound like fair payment."

"That's because you haven't been on a Spring Break yet."

"Touché."

Bo hooks Ashlei by the crook of her elbow, dragging her toward the living room. "Speaking of Spring Break, we need to sweat off some pounds. Let's dance!"

Ashlei tries to grab my hand, but I pull back. "I'll be right there. Just going to get a refill," I say, wiggling my empty cup in the air. Bo blows me a kiss and then they disappear into the crowd and I lean back against the wall.

I'm not sure why I'm feeling so off. I haven't seen Clay or Paris since I got back from Winter Break, but the wounds they inflicted still feel so fresh. Thinking of the talk I had with my sister when I was home, I push myself off the wall and head for the kitchen.

Don't let anyone else have that much power over your emotions, Cassie. College is an amazing experience, but it's up to you to ignore the drama and focus on the good. Avoid silly boys, ignore spiteful girls, and don't be afraid to have fun.

I think it's time for a shot.

It only takes me an hour to get into the party spirit. I guess whiskey will do that to you.

I'm already sweating from dancing with the girls, so I squeeze my way through the crowd to the back porch to get some fresh air. When the cool January breeze hits my skin, I sigh with relief, leaning my forearms on the railing.

"Water?" He asks, and I know it's him before I even turn around. My heart picking up speed, I turn at the hips and take the water from Adam's hand, offering a small smile.

"Thank you."

"No problem. You girls are fun to watch."

"Creeper."

He smirks. "Can't help it."

"I'm surprised you're not out there dancing with Skyler." I don't know why the words sound so bitter when they leave my lips. I don't care that he's dating Skyler. I'm happy for them.

Truly, I am.

"Sometimes it's more fun to watch." His eyes light with an intensity at those words, his white teeth blazing against his tan skin as he smiles wider. I quickly take a drink of my water.

"Congratulations on your rush. I heard it was the best Alpha Sig has had in a long time. Stole a lot of guys Omega Chi wanted."

Adam beams. "Yeah, thank you. I'm pretty stoked about it. The pledges are all really excited to be here and to make a great name for our fraternity."

"Must be your infectious attitude," I tease. Adam smiles, but it fades after a moment and he just stares at me. I feel naked with his eyes on me that way.

"Why didn't you return my calls over the holiday?"

I drop my eyes to my hands, picking at the nail polish on the fingers gripping my cup. "I just needed a break from everyone."

"Even me?"

"Especially you," I murmur, my chest tightening.

"What?"

I sigh, lifting my eyes to his again, somewhat thankful he didn't hear me. "It's nothing personal. I was just homesick, so I tried to focus on my family while I had them close."

Adam's brows are still furrowed, but he relaxes a bit. "Understandable." For a moment he just watches me, and I really wish he'd stop. "I was just kind of worried about you, you know... after the way the semester ended." I really, *really* wish he'd stop looking at me the way he is. "Are you okay?"

"I'm fine." It's not a lie, not completely, anyway. I was far from fine over break, especially after Clay took my virginity and then embarrassed me in front of the entire school. But being home with my family really did help, and now that I'm swearing off boys, I know I'll be okay.

"You know I'm always here for you." His hand touches my arm just slightly with his words and I shudder.

"There you are!" Skyler bounds out the sliding glass door and throws her arms around Adam's neck. His eyes are still on me, but his hands wrap around her small waist. "Come dance with me."

Finally tearing his eyes from mine, he smiles down his nose at her, nodding. "Whatever you want, Poker Star."

Skyler's blue eyes dazzle in the low light of the night as she turns to me. "Coming, Little?"

"Yeah. Just give me a second."

Skyler drags Adam inside and I lean on the railing again, focusing on my breaths. My skin still feels hot, despite the water and the fresh air. Once I feel I have myself together, I pull out my phone to check the time.

And I have two missed texts.

Both from a number I don't have saved in my phone.

– Okay, so I waited a few days so I wouldn't seem so desperate, but I'm tired of playing the "I'm not interested" game. Can I take you out this week? –

– ... Please say yes. –

I smile, biting my lower lip as I type out a response.

– Friday. Seven o'clock. Ralph's. –

If Grayson wants me to break my no boys, no drama rule, he's going to have to work for it.

First test — saving me from the creeps at the auction.

Jess

UGH. I'M FUCKING BORED.

Buzzed.

But bored.

Refilling my cup at the keg, I watch as Ashlei and Bo dance in the living room. Ashlei's long blond hair is sticking to the back of her neck, but she somehow makes sweating look sexy. I swear she was born to dance. It still hasn't left her, even though she stopped dancing back in high school.

There are guys all around them, but they've turned every single one down enough tonight that they're staying away now. They only have eyes for each other. Ashlei's hand is on Bo's waist and they're giggling, hands lingering, eyes flirting.

It really doesn't bother me that they're together. Honestly. What really fucking pisses me off is that Ashlei is one of my best friends and Bo is my Little and yet neither of them have told me about their relationship. I tried talking myself out of it, thinking maybe it was just a drunken kiss, but ever since we got back from Winter Break they've been inseparable. I can just tell, the way they act around each other, the things they say, the things they *don't* say. In fact, I'm not sure how anyone else hasn't caught on yet.

I've been spending more time with Bo lately, making sure it's one-on-one attention and not just sister events. She made it clear last semester that she wasn't going to take a Little until she got the experience of being one herself, so I'm trying to be better. Still, every time we're hanging out and she skirts around questions about her dating life, I get a little more irked.

I swear I'm going to explode on the both of them if they don't fess up soon.

Sighing, I take a sip of my beer and whip out my phone, shooting a text to Jarrett.

– This party sucks. I'd rather be with you. –

– Ditto. This professor assistants game night is as about as exciting as tweezing out my eyelashes. Shocking, right? –

– Don't worry. I'll make sure you have a good time tomorrow night. ;) –

Smiling, I tuck my phone back in my pocket just as Skyler slides up next to me.

"Have you seen my Little? Or my Big?"

I shake my head. "Last time I saw Cassie she was dancing with you, and Erin said she had to pee but that was like thirty minutes ago."

"Weird. Oh well. Did Erin tell you what the Social Chairs have been thinking for Spring Break?"

"I thought they weren't telling us until chapter next week?"

Skyler's blue eyes gleam as she rakes her damp hair off her neck. "They aren't, but Erin has all the inside knowledge now that she's on the executive board. And she heard the girls talking to the O Chi boys about Key West!"

I squeal. "Fuck yes! Oh my God, I haven't been since my parents took me when I was in high school. I was too young to drink then. Oh my God, this is going to be amazing."

"The possibilities on Duval Street alone make me giddy."

Frowning, I eye the beer in my cup. "I should probably start drinking vodka waters like now."

Skyler laughs. "Spring Break diet here we come!"

My phone buzzes and when I check the message, my mouth goes dry.

– I'm not satisfied with just tomorrow. Go find an empty room. –

I smile, but can't deny the little flip in my stomach. I love when he goes into sexy Jarrett mode. It's like there's a switch — sometimes he's just hot, funny Jarrett in presentable PA clothing. But when the switch is flipped, he's unbearably sexy, demanding, fire-eyed Jarrett in nothing but a tight pair of boxer briefs.

I personally prefer the switch flipped.

– Are you asking me to sext you, Jarrett Locke? –

– Was there a question mark in that last text? Find a room. Now. –

I bite my lip, a little turned on at the thought. Dirty pics and words in the middle of a crowded party? I can dig it.

"Be right back," I tell Skyler, pushing myself off the wall we were leaned against and heading straight for the bathroom. There are several in the house, but the best one is in the upstairs loft. By *best,* I mean *cleanest.* Using the bathroom in a frat house is like hanging out the door of a speeding car. You're taking a risk. My Big used to always say, *"Shots and squats, my dear. Do not touch that seat."*

Making my way up the stairs, I type out a text to Jarrett asking him what he wants me to do to myself. The three little dots pop up letting me know he's texting me back and my stomach tightens in anticipation. When I push through the bathroom door and find Erin with her head in the toilet, my excitement fades.

"Shit, Ex, what the hell?"

She heaves, but it doesn't sound like much comes up. Cursing, I fall to the floor next to her and scoop her dark blonde hair up, fastening it at the top of her head with the spare hair tie on my wrist.

"You're such a freshman right now."

Erin groans, leaning back on her heels and lifting her eyes to mine. They're red, rimmed with tears, and her entire face is a sheet white. "I'm so fucked, Jess. I'm so, so fucked."

"What are you talking about?" I shake my head, ripping a few sheets of toilet paper off and offering them to her to clean her face. "You're fine. Just drunk. Let's get you out of here."

"Jess, you don't understand."

I groan when I see the dirty text from Jarrett, telling me, in *amazing* detail, what he wants me to do to myself. Then my phone pings again, and it's a photo of Jarrett palming himself. His abs take up most of the picture, but just the sight of his hand wrapped around his thick cock makes me whimper. It's clear he also snuck off to a bathroom, and all I want is to be bad with him.

But, sisters first.

Fuck me.

"I understand just fine. Do you not remember me on Spring Break last year?"

Erin huffs, grabbing my wrist with force. "Goddammit, Jess, listen to me! I'm not drunk!"

"Clearly."

She levels her eyes. "I'm serious. I haven't had a single drink tonight... or this semester, period." She stares at me expectantly, like I'm supposed to understand. When the little lightbulb finally flashes on, I gasp.

"Holy shit. Do you think you're..."

"I don't know."

"Oh my God, Ex, how?!"

She sighs. "I've been throwing up and my body just feels weird. I'm freaking out, Jess. What do I do?"

"Have you missed a period yet?"

"I was supposed to have it this week, but nothing."

I curse, my hand flying to my forehead. No way. No fucking way is Erin Xander, the most angelic of all of us, pregnant. The girl doesn't party as much as we do, she hasn't had a boyfriend in I don't even know how long, and she's not exactly the hook-up kind of girl.

Actually, that's a great fucking point.

"Erin, who... um," I fade off, not sure how to phrase my question. "If there were, for argument's sake, a little bundle of joy in your belly — who would be responsible?"

She bites her lip just as the door swings open. Clinton startles when he sees us just as Erin yells something about them needing a new lock on the damn door.

"Whoa. You two okay?" Clinton asks. I ignore him, turning my eyes back to Erin.

But her eyes are still fixed on his.

And she's breathing really fucking hard.

When she looks at me once more, panic evident in her features, I know I don't need to repeat my question.

Well, shit.

Spring semester is off to an interesting start.

EPISODE 2

"Everything is Changing."

OH MY GOD, GIVE me that!"

Skyler flies through my bedroom door, kicking it closed behind her before snatching the large burrito I was just about to bite out of my hands. Her soft hair falls into her face a bit as she shoves nearly half of it in her mouth, her eyes rolling up. Moaning, she chews it slowly, like she's savoring every morsel.

I blink.

"Thank you," she says, handing me back what's left of the burrito and wiping the corners of her mouth.

"You sure you don't want to eat the tin foil, too?"

She swats at my arm before climbing into bed next to me. "Don't be an ass. This Spring Break diet is going to be the death of me, I swear."

I laugh. "Ah, it all makes sense now. Want the rest?" I offer her the burrito again but she pushes it back, shaking her head.

"I'm already going to have to do like fifty crunches and run a mile to get rid of that one bite. But seriously, who made kale a thing?" She grimaces. "I just want to eat cheese fries and lose ten pounds."

"You're beautiful," I whisper, kissing her nose. She scrunches it, so I kiss it again.

"Thank you," she murmurs, blushing a little. "Still, I'm going to be on the beach surrounded by a hundred tiny little things in thong bikinis. I need to be on my game."

Frowning, I take a bite of my burrito and chase it down with the soda on my night stand. "Don't remind me."

"Why are you all grumpy?"

I sigh. "I won't be with you that week. I'm kind of bummed about it."

"What are you talking about? Of course we'll be together."

"Did you forget what fraternity I'm in?"

Skyler's still frowning, but as recognition sets in, her brows pull inward and she chews her lip. The Kappa Kappa Betas always go on Spring Break with the Omega Chis, and being that I'm an Alpha Sigma, that pairing doesn't exactly do us any favors.

"Well, whatever. You can still come."

I chuckle around another bite. "Yeah, because that would go over well."

"I'm serious." Skyler sits up on her knees, making me look at her. She's dressed in nothing but a small Kappa Kappa Beta tank top and tiny little shorts. No make-up, hair natural and wavy. Stunning as usual. "I'm not giving you the option. You're my boyfriend and you're coming on Spring Break with me. Where's your laptop?"

"Why?"

She rolls her eyes at my question before hopping off the bed and retrieving my computer from the desk. Falling back into the covers, she flips it open without another word, clicking away at the keys.

"Done."

"What's done?"

"I just booked you for the all-day boat trip we're doing on the second day of Spring Break. And..." her voice trails off as she finishes typing off a text. Not a second goes by before her phone pings in her hand. "Perfect! You're set to go in the van we rented to take down there and you'll stay in our hotel room. All set!"

I shake my head, finishing off my burrito and chugging down half my drink. "Are you serious right now? You know the Omega Chis are going to flip their shit."

"They won't. Because if they do, I'll bitch at Bear, and he'll bitch at everyone else until they shut up. Trust me. It's all good." Smiling devilishly, she crawls up the covers and locks her lips on mine, grinding her hips against my own. My boxers, the comforter, and her tiny ass shorts are the only things separating us. I groan, tugging on her bottom lip.

"You're going to be the death of me, Skyler Thorne."

"At least it'll be a fun way to go," she whispers, nipping at the skin on my neck. Fastening my hands on her small waist, I flip her over, pinning her in the sheets.

"Can't argue that."

As I kiss my way down her neck, Skyler runs her fingers through my hair and gives it a small tug. "How are the pledges doing? You guys had a killer rush."

I move my lips to hers, snaking my tongue inside her mouth and stealing a moan before replying. "Good. We're getting ready for the camping trip before the bonfire next week."

"I always forget you do that," Skyler pants, bucking her hips up to meet mine. "Creepers. Kidnapping those poor kids."

Grinning against her skin, I slip my hands under her tank top and push it up and over her rib cage. "Trust me. It's the most fun they have in the pledge process."

"And what's the worst part?"

I pull her tank off the rest of the way, sucking the sensitive skin on the swell of her breast. "If I tell you, I'd have to kill you."

"Death by orgasm?"

"*Torturous* death by orgasm."

She smiles, biting her bottom lip as she peers down at me with heavy blue eyes. "Tell. Me. *Everything*."

Even though Skyler officially calls me her boyfriend, she never sticks around after we have sex. Sometimes she'll lie on my chest for a while or we'll talk, but sooner or later, she's out the door and it's just me alone in my bed.

And when I'm alone, I think.

About rush. About all the activities coming up. About the whispers I've been hearing around our fraternity concerning the presidency next semester.

I know I'm at the top of everyone's mind, and as fucking stoked as I am about that, I can't help but wonder if being with Skyler is going to pull me from what I need to do to make it actually happen.

I love being around her, we have fun together, but I can still tell it's not serious for either one of us. Couple that with the fact that planning events and taking on a presidency requires most if not all of my future time, it just feels like we're speeding fast toward an inevitable crash.

Sighing, I reach for my phone and type out a text to Cassie.

– Breakfast tomorrow – the usual spot? –

Letting my thoughts drift to that little redhead does absolutely nothing to soothe my stress. After what happened with Clay last semester, I knew she would need someone to lean on over break. Apparently, that someone wasn't me. It shouldn't bother me, but it does.

She came to my window that night.

I can still remember the way it felt to hold her, the way my chest ached when she told me I was right about Clay. It fucking killed me, because I didn't want to be right — not about knowing he would hurt her.

What she doesn't know — what no one knows — is that I laid that fucker out the next day. I stormed right into his bedroom while he was getting dressed, Paris having just left, and decked him hard across the jaw. I made sure he knew it was coming. Hell, I even told him to hit me back. But he didn't. He knew he was a piece of shit, even if he didn't admit it to anyone else.

But then, I didn't hear from Cassie all break, and when I finally saw her at the Omega Chi party last week, she made me feel like *I* was responsible for the hurt she endured — not him.

I can't figure this girl out.

After twenty minutes go by with no response, I sigh, plugging my phone into the charger and setting an alarm for class in the morning. Leaning back on my pillows, I tuck my hands under my head and stare up at the ceiling, brain still not getting the memo that it's time to turn off.

I'm excited Skyler wants me with her for Spring Break, but I can't shake the feeling that whatever is happening between us is going to be short lived. She's smart, funny, and gorgeous — but that's exactly it. She deserves to be with a guy who can give her all the time in his life, or at least to be able to have the freedom to do whatever she wants. I can't call her my girlfriend and then put other things before her — like the Alpha Sigma presidency.

Rolling over, I pull a pillow over my head and let out a large puff of air. There are too many "what ifs" and I don't have enough energy to figure them all out tonight. *One step at a time, Brooks.* Tomorrow starts the planning for the pledge retreat. I need to just focus on what I can control.

Except, I don't really feel in control of anything at all.

Erin

I AM FREAKING OUT.

Erin Xander does not do well with freaking out.

I am in control of all things at all times. My planner is color coordinated and scheduled through the end of the year, with very few dates to spare. I'm already three weeks ahead in my classes, and even still I'm meeting up with Cassie in less than an hour to study. Because I need to be in control, and I'm running out of things I can hold onto.

It's only Sunday, the auction isn't until Saturday, and yet I've already handled every aspect of it — the food, the drinks, the paddles, the emergency kits, the girls we'll auction and the transferring of the donations. All done. Handled. As if that wasn't enough, I've also planned half of Spring Break and hand-crafted mason jars for the sorority council meeting at the Kappa Kappa Beta house this Wednesday.

And yet, I'm still freaking out.

Because no matter what I do, I can't control what will happen after I pee on this stupid stick in my hand. The stick that will tell me if I'm carrying Clinton's child.

Oh God.

Burying my face in my hands, I drop the stick onto my lap and focus on my breathing. I need Jess, since she's the only one who knows about my... situation, but she's not answering her phone and I've barely seen her since she walked in on me vomming my brains out at the O Chi party. I can't tell any of the other girls — especially not Skyler — and yet I can't wait any longer to take the test.

Chewing my lip and knowing there's slim to no chance in hell he'll answer, I thumb through the contacts in my phone and hover over his name. Just seeing it on the screen makes my heart jump and my breath accelerate — even after all these years. Before I can talk myself out of it, I let my thumb drop, dialing his number.

Ring.

Ring ring.

Ring motherfucking ring.

Hey, you've reached Kip Jackson. Sorry I—

"Gah!" Hearing his voice springs more memories on me than I'm equipped to handle at the moment. Why did I think it was a smart idea to call the blue-eyed boy who stole my heart so many years ago? Tucking my phone into my small purse, I lift myself from my bed and stare at the pregnancy test. Sighing, I slip it in next to my phone and give myself a once over in the mirror. My eyes are tired, my skin ashen, my hair greasy. I do not look put together. I do not look in control.

At this point, I have no choice.

I need to tell Clinton.

I don't want to stress him out with thinking about the possibility of a baby if there isn't one, but at the same time, I need him right now. If there's one thing Clinton Pennington is good at, it's being a friend. We both agreed that our little hook up was just us having too much fun that night at semi-formal, and something inside me just knows he'll be calm and collected through this. He'll be able to soothe me, tell me it's okay, and make me feel like whatever the test says — we can handle it. Together.

I walk slowly down Greek row to the Omega Chi house, focusing on my breaths with every step. I'm wearing my favorite Kate Spade high heels, trying to grasp the part of me I feel quickly fading away, and I listen to them click and clack on the pavement as I near the house.

The boys welcome me in, offering me a beer even though it's only eleven in the morning on a Sunday. I shake my head. "You boys need Jesus."

"Hey, Jesus liked red wine," one of the pledges retorts.

He's got a point.

My throat swells as I make my way down the hall to Clinton's room. I try to swallow, but there's nothing there to aid in the process. My mouth is dry, my heart hammering. How the hell do I have this conversation right now?

Loud music is spilling from his room, which brings me some relief because at least he's awake. I can't imagine having to stir him from a slumber to deliver this news. Steeling myself at the door, I tap on it lightly with my knuckles.

"Bear? It's Erin. Uh, can I come in?"

No answer.

The song blaring from inside his room is slow, rhythmic — a sultry R&B song with lyrics crooning how they could fuck the subject of their affection all the time. Growing anxious, I push through the door without another knock.

"Bear, this will only take a min—"

Clinton doesn't hear me, thank God, because he's currently buried beneath a pile of sheets and blankets. A girl is leaned against his headboard, her eyes downcast at the movement between her legs. One of her hands is locked on his headboard, the other is tangled in the purple ends of her hair, and if I had to guess, the moans drowning under the loud bass of the music are courtesy of whatever Clinton is doing beneath those sheets.

My cheeks burn as flashes of our night together hit me with rapid speed. Slamming the door closed as quickly as I can, I adjust my purse on my shoulder and storm toward the exit, desperate for fresh air. The girl didn't see me, even though I was standing right in the doorway. She was preoccupied. As was Clinton.

And I was just about to tell him I need him to be with me while I take a pregnancy test.

Smacking my forehead, I start the walk back to the KKB house, mumbling under my breath the entire time. How idiotic can I be? This is Clinton we're talking about. What happened between us was a mistake, an accident, a one-night thing. Did I really think he would hold my hand while I peed on a stick?

Throwing a quick wave in the direction of my sisters gathered on the couch, I quickly sprint up the stairs and back into my room, closing the door swiftly behind me. For once, I'm actually thankful that Ashlei isn't here.

I pull the test out of my purse and make my way to our bathroom, tossing it on the counter and planting my palms to steady myself. Telling Clinton would have been a dumb move, and now that I see it more clearly, I'm thankful he was preoccupied. This is just something I need to handle on my own, even if it feels impossible. After a few deep breaths, I lift my eyes to the mirror, trying to find the courage I need.

You can do this, Erin.

Everything will be okay.

I only half-believe myself, but it's all I need to make my next move. Grabbing the test, I rip open the package, pop off the clear plastic lid, and squat down on the toilet.

And then I pee on my hand.

A smart girl would have peed in a cup and dipped the stick in, but being that all of my intelligence is wasted in the classroom, my common sense is at exactly level zero.

Luckily, I do still manage to pee on the test strip, so I set it flat on the counter and walk away.

I try playing on my phone.

I try organizing my closet.

I try laying out my outfits for the next week.

Every time I look at my phone, no time has passed.

I open my planner.

I shut it again.

I make sure I have everything I need for my study session with Cassie.

Nothing distracts me, nothing stops my mind from racing with what the results of this test could mean, but enough time finally passes that I can check it.

Everything feels numb — my nose, my ears, my feet. The house is filled with girls, yet everything seems silent as I put one foot in front of the other, making my way toward the bathroom counter. My hand shaking, I take one last deep breath, and then I lift the stick and squeeze my eyes shut.

I open one, then the other, and the tiny screen comes into focus.

"Ready, G-Big?" Cassie pushes through my bedroom door without warning, causing me to curse and fumble the pregnancy test before quickly shoving it in my makeup bag.

"Hey baby G! Yes, all set. Just let me grab my bag."

"Can we hit Cup O' Joe's on the way? I need a pick-me-up," she says, thumbing through her phone as her bright red hair falls around her.

"Definitely." I toss my makeup bag, test still inside, into the messenger bag with my books and notes before slinging it over my shoulder. "Let's go."

Ashlei

MY STOMACH ROLLS AS I step out of my car and pop open my bright pink umbrella. It's one of those dreary days in Florida — the very few we have — where it's below sixty degrees and rainy. It rarely happens, but when it does, it seems to take a toll on all of us. We're usually bathed in sunlight and donning flip flops, so rain boots and big coats don't sit well with us.

The rain seems absolutely fitting for how I feel, though, so I revel in it. It takes so much effort to smile or even just exist around my sisters right now, knowing how different my reality is from theirs. When I'm alone, I finally get to think, to feel. So, on the way here, I let myself cry — just a little — enough to let a little of the pressure out.

Xavier Rojas' club makes me feel sick every time I step foot in it, and today is no exception. My feet splash in the puddles as I make my way toward the back entrance. There are a few hours until the club opens, so it should just be me and Xavier and a few of his guards, but that doesn't make me feel any more at ease. Hands shaking, I pull my coat tighter around my small frame.

The first time I met Xavier, I had tears streaming down my face, snot running from my nose, and a thousand dollars clutched in my hands.

I had danced for money.

And it had broken me.

I can still remember the men staring at me, their hands touching me when the bouncers weren't looking, their degrading remarks, their dirty money — it's all seared into my memory. It was almost a numbing experience, being on the stage. I don't quite remember taking off my clothes, but I can still feel the cold bar grinding against my bare skin. Rock bottom is an understatement when it comes to describing that night. When I handed Xavier that first payment, I knew I couldn't stomach it again.

So, I found another way.

I sold clothes, shoes, and electronics to give him the second payment. For some reason, Xavier seemed to take pity on me. He agreed to let me pay it over time, but it always feels like his patience is thin, his timeline relative. As I give my name to the outside guard and he quietly ushers me inside the bleak building, I fist the money in my purse, hoping it'll be enough to buy me more time.

Over break, I saved every penny of Christmas money and thought of small ways to get cash out of my parents. I'm disappointed with myself, but remembering how it felt that night in the club slowly made lying easier until it almost became second nature. I'll do whatever I have to do to never be in that position again, and once this money is paid, I'm wiping my slate clean for good. Hayden and Kya have ruined pole dancing for me. I never went back to Kitty Heels and I never plan to touch another pole or another line of coke for as long as I live.

"Ashlei, baby," Xavier greets, standing long enough to wrap me in a hug and kiss both of my cheeks. He's a short man, all muscles, clean-shaved face and short curly hair. His hugs always engulf me in a scent of cigarettes, ink, and sweat. "Nice to see you again. Come, sit."

He motions to one of the chairs facing his desk before taking a seat himself, leaning back and crossing his hands over his stomach. I sit lightly, back straight, ass on the edge of the seat. I don't plan to be here long. It's always pleasantries with Xavier, but I've heard of his darker side. I know Kya has seen it up close.

I never plan to.

"What do you have for me today, sweetheart?"

I shiver at his term of endearment, reaching into my purse for the cash I brought. It's folded neatly and wrapped in a rubber band. I slide it toward him, folding my clammy hands in my lap as he counts it out.

He sighs, just barely, almost low enough for me to question whether I heard it or not. Lifting his dark eyes to mine, he offers an apologetic smile.

"Ashlei, this isn't enough."

"It's two-thousand dollars," I croak, my throat dry. *It has to be enough.*

"You owed me thirty-thousand. You've only paid five, and this makes seven. You know it isn't enough."

"Please," I beg, my voice low. My eyes water, and I hate myself for being so weak. "I'm doing all that I can."

"No!" He screams the word, pounding his fist on the desk and I jump. My heartrate spikes as I wait for his next move. His dark irises are smaller now, his face red, but he pauses, steadying his breathing and unclenching his fist. "No, you're not." He levels his eyes and I know he's referring to dancing. Swallowing, I shake my head.

"I can't."

"You might not have a choice."

"There has to be another way."

Xavier watches me carefully. "I can't keep bending the rules for you, kid. If you were anyone else, I would have already killed that pretty girlfriend of yours while you watched."

I gulp. I've tried so hard to keep Bo out of this, not even telling her why Kya showed up at our sorority house at the end of last semester. She's too pure to be sucked into my black hole.

"I don't like giving you more time, Ashlei, because it sets a precedent. Other people who owe me are looking at you wondering what it is that makes you so special." His pudgy fingers pinch the bridge of his nose. "However, I don't really give two shits what any of those fuckers think about my business, and as it stands, I think we can make a deal."

My chest is still tight.

He leans back again, tapping the tips of his pointer fingers together as he thinks. "It's safe to assume you'll be going on Spring Break with your sisters, am I right?"

"If I can afford it," I whisper, still focusing on keeping the tears from falling down my cheeks. My stomach is in knots, my eyes tired. It still doesn't feel like reality. This can't be my life.

"Tell you what. You bring me at least another five-thousand by this time next week, I'll make that your last payment."

Wait, did I hear that right?

"Oh my God." The tears finally fall, but I'm smiling. Relief — that's what I feel. "Are you serious? One more payment?" I have no idea how I'm going to come up with another five grand, but it sounds a hell of a lot better than twenty-three thousand.

Just five-thousand.

Five-thousand dollars, and then I'm free.

My heart squeezes.

"Now hang on a second," he interrupts, holding one hand up. "That will be your last payment, but your debt is still far from paid."

Sniffling, I adjust my purse on my lap. "I don't understand."

A slow grin spreads on his face, and the relief I felt moments ago instantly fades.

"You're going to sell for me, pretty girl."

"Sell?"

He nods. "During Spring Break. Weed, coke, Molly. You're going to be a one-stop-shop, my dear. I'll give you enough stash to settle the rest of your debt and then we'll be even."

"No. Absolutely not." I stand, hands shaking, bile rising. "I'm not getting anyone else caught up in the shit that ruined my life."

"Don't be so dramatic," he snarls, rolling his eyes. "Besides, what other choice do you have? You either take me up on this offer, pay me in full by Friday, or dance four nights a week at my club for the next six months." His face is stone cold, his jaw set. "I don't make exceptions like this, Ashlei. You should be fucking grateful. If you're not, we can take the route I usually take. Ask your friend Hayden how that worked out for him."

The mention of Hayden's name makes my jaw drop open. "What do you mean? Did he come back?"

Xavier's grin is menacing, his yellow teeth on full display. "He didn't have to, sweetheart. I have my ways of finding even those who try their damndest to stay lost."

I swallow. "What did you do to him?"

"Refuse my deal, and you'll find out."

Blinking, I let two more silent tears stain my cheeks.

And the helplessness sets in.

Jess is devouring her pizza like she hasn't eaten in seventeen years as I pour the dressing on my salad in Pie Heaven. Moaning, she licks extra sauce off her thumb and mumbles around the cheese in her mouth.

"Do not tell the other girls I'm eating this. Erin would kill me."

"Why? It's your love handles you're risking, not ours."

"Yeah but you know Erin. Sorority image and all that shit. She's serious about her Spring Break diets."

I laugh, shaking my head. "My lips are sealed." She throws me a *thumbs up* before folding her next slice in half and taking a huge bite. I blanch. "Even if yours aren't."

"Eat me."

I chuckle.

Pie Heaven is a small pizza joint across from campus, usually packed between the hours of midnight and 3 a.m. with drunk students. I've been holed up in my room most of the day, running over the conversation I had with Xavier on Monday, debating my options. It seems surreal, to sit here eating fast food with Jess, knowing that if I don't make a decision soon, I could get hurt. Even worse – Jess could get hurt. *Bo* could get hurt.

I feel like a weapon of destruction, harming anyone who touches me.

"So," she starts, chasing her last bite with a large drink of the extra-large Mountain Dew she ordered. "You never did tell me how your twenty-first birthday was."

Sighing, I take my first bite and grimace a little. Jess' pizza smells way better than this stupid salad tastes. "You know my birthday tends to get overlooked. Sadly this one was no different."

"Ugh, so shitty. You would think being born on the same day as Jesus would lend you some good birthday juju."

"Nope. All it lends you is a lot of combo gifts and no friends to party with. Plus it's not really the date that screws me over most."

"Let me guess. All the attention was on Abby and Amanda, as per usual?"

I offer a sour smile. "Abby was just accepted into med school and Amanda made the varsity softball team. So my twenty-first birthday wasn't exactly the most exciting thing going on."

I'm the middle child, and as much as it may be a stereotype, the whole "middle spawn is ignored eighty percent of the time" thing is pretty accurate when it comes to my family. My oldest sister is the smart one, destined to be the next family doctor, right behind my father. And Amanda, the youngest, is strikingly beautiful and incredibly talented in every sport she plays. I swear the girl could pick up a broom today and play Quidditch like Harry by the time I went to bed tonight.

And then there's me.

Crazy competitive and talented in all the things that don't matter to my parents.

Like event planning.

And pole dancing.

Funny enough, it almost feels like I'm the middle child with Jess and Erin, too. We all look so similar and hang out all the time that everyone groups us together. Except, Erin is known for running shit and Jess is the comedian. I'm just sort of there.

It's a curse.

Jess scrunches her nose. "That sucks, dude. Seriously. I wish I would have been there to take you out. Oh!" She snaps her fingers. "Let's go out this Friday before the auction. Ralph's. Break the place in before we glam it all up the next night."

"Deal."

We eat for a few moments in comfortable silence, which of course makes my mind drift to Bo. Valentine's Day is next week and I still have a few things to pick up for our date. With everything going on with Xavier, I haven't been showing her the attention she deserves, so I'm determined to make that night special.

I start to ask Jess what she's doing for the holiday but pause when I look up and see the furrow in her brow. Following her eyes, I find the sexy teacher she had a run in with last semester laughing in a booth with some hot brunette.

"Isn't that Jarrett?" I ask, turning back to Jess. She's worrying her bottom lip and staring blatantly at their booth.

"Mmhmm."

"Damn. I forgot how bangable he is."

"Ten-point-two on the bangable scale."

She makes the joke, but her eyes stay focused on Jarrett as her expression slips from confused to angry.

"Holy shit," I whisper, leaning in. "You're still messing around with him, aren't you?!"

"What?" Jess snaps her attention back to me. I waggle my eyebrows and she shakes her head, grabbing her soda and taking a big sip from the plastic straw. "I don't know what you're talking about."

"Oh come on! What's going on between you two?"

"I don't know," she snaps, her chocolate eyes hard on mine now as she crosses her arms. "What's going on with you and my Little?"

The air rushes from my chest in a whoosh.

Ears fuzzy, I swallow and force a smile.

"Bo? We've gotten a lot closer in the past few months. She's cool."

"Uh huh."

My smile falls. "Do you have something to say, Jess?"

"Do you have something to *tell me*, Lei?"

Jess is watching me carefully. I need to swallow, but I'm afraid if I do I'll give myself away. It's not that I don't trust Jess, but Bo is far from ready to tell anyone about us. Or about her, in general. And I'm the same.

"Oh thank God I found you." Erin slides into the booth next to me, planner in hand, highlighter at the ready. Jess is still eying me, but with Erin here, she knows the conversation is over for now, so she turns her attention back to Jarrett across the room. "I need you."

Finally allowing myself to swallow, I plaster on my best smile, pulling my long platinum hair over my left shoulder. "What's up, buttercup?"

"Are you busy the Monday after the auction?"

"I have class but that's it."

"Perfect. Can you please take the money we raise to the bank? I was going to after my morning classes but I have something that came up that I can't get out of."

I'm still a little too aware of Jess and her question about me and Bo, but I nod and smile wider. "Of course, no problem Ex."

Erin sighs with relief, and it's then I notice how tired she looks. Her dark blonde hair is pulled back into a tight bun and she's barely wearing any makeup, which is strange for her. "Thank you. Okay, I have to run." She stands, finally turning her attention to Jess. When she does, she frowns. "Uh, J-Love?"

"Hmm?" Jess' eyes are still on Jarrett.

"What are you eating?"

Erin points down at Jess' last slice of pizza and I cover my mouth, trying not to laugh. Jess glances at me, anger still evident in her features, but even she cracks a smile. "Um... well, it's totally *not* a five-hundred calorie slice of pizza, if that's what you're thinking. Because we're on the Spring Break diet. And pizza is not part of that diet. Therefore, that couldn't be what it is."

Erin rolls her eyes. "Whatever. I don't want to hear it when we go shopping for swim suits. See you girls later."

Jess and I wait for her to walk out the front door before bursting into a fit of laughter, which almost makes me forget that she's totally onto me and Bo. It almost makes me forget Xavier and the deal he proposed to me just two days ago. It almost makes me feel like I did last semester, before shit hit the fan and I fell into a hole too deep to climb out of alone.

Almost.

Adam

THE KAPPA KAPPA BETA auction is one of the best events of the spring semester. It always kicks off Greek events, starting a string of fundraisers, socials, and everything in-between. Fraternity brothers and non-Greek guys alike clamor into the bar, cold cash in hand, ready to buy a date with a beautiful KKB girl.

My beautiful KKB girl is currently wrapped in my arms.

And luckily, she's not for sale tonight.

"I think my Little is about to pass out," Skyler says, chuckling a little. She finishes typing out a text and tucks her phone into her small purse before leaning in closer. We're in the back of a cab on our way to the auction and Skyler is all dolled up for the occasion. Tight black dress, gold high heels and jewelry to match, hair down and carefully curled. Red, red lipstick.

She doesn't ever have to try to look sexy, but when she does, it's enough to knock a full grown man on his ass.

"She texting you?"

"Yeah. She'll be fine. Some sex-on-a-stick piece of man candy is going to buy her and take her out. Then she'll thank us."

I shift, trying not to think about why hearing that scenario made my stomach uneasy. "Yeah, I'm sure. So, you still plan on ditching me for a tournament next week?"

"Don't say it like that." She frowns.

"What? It's true. It's Valentine's Day and my girlfriend would rather hang out in a smoky room full of smelly old men than let me take her out on a nice date."

Skyler pokes me hard in the rib and I double over, laughing. "Ass. You know this tournament is too big to miss. It's a qualifier for the one this summer."

"I know, I know," I relent, pulling her in for a kiss. I know her red lipstick will be smeared all over me, but I literally have no fucks to give when she's dressed like this. I'm not stupid enough to think she doesn't feel what I feel, like what we have has an expiration date quickly approaching, so I'm going to take full advantage while I still can. "We'll have our own Valentine's Day when you're done."

"Can it include Netflix?" she asks as the cab pulls into Ralph's. I pay the driver and step out first, extending my hand for hers.

"Of course."

"How about some under-the-covers action?" She licks her lips and lowers her eyes just enough to make me groan.

"*Definitely.*"

The cab pulls away, but I tug Skyler's wrist back until she's flush against me in the dark parking lot of the bar. Grabbing her face in my hands, I press my lips to hers, tilting my hips so she feels exactly how excited I am for our date. She moans as I slip my tongue inside her mouth, letting one hand fall down the soft fabric of her dress, gripping her hip and pulling her closer.

And that's when the first flash assaults us.

Breaking the kiss, we both pull back confused, eyes trying to adjust to the darkness as we look for what caused the white burst of light. When three quick flashes follow, I pull Skyler against me, shielding her from whatever the fuck is happening.

"Skyler Thorne, is this how you're prepping for the qualifying tournament next week?"

Another flash.

"Who's this? Your boyfriend?"

Flash. Flash.

"Great dress. What do you plan on wearing to the tournament?"

Skyler's hand fists in my shirt and she buries her head into my chest. "Shit," she murmurs.

"Don't worry," I soothe, pushing through the small group of paparazzi as they try harder to talk over one another. I keep Skyler covered with my arms and she lets her hair fall in front of her face as I guide us toward Ralph's. When the bouncers notice us, they rush to help, fielding off the remaining reporters as their cameras continue flashing. When we finally break through the doors and are free from the questions, Skyler pulls back, eyes wide.

"Oh my God."

"That was insane."

Skyler nods, fingering the curls in her hair as she looks out the tinted windows of Ralph's where the bouncers are refusing to let any of the photographers in.

"You really are blowing up on the poker scene, aren't you?"

She just shakes her head. "This is unreal."

"Are you okay?"

Skyler nods, hard, for longer than necessary, her eyes still trained on the commotion outside. "Yeah. I just, I need a minute."

"Sky?" Clinton walks briskly toward us, engulfing Skyler in a crushing hug as soon as he reaches her. Her tiny hands grip his massive, dark arms and it's then that I see her shaking slightly. "Come on, follow me." He pulls her in closer. "Adam, can you go check on Cassie? She was freaking out waiting for Skyler to get here but I don't think she's going to calm anyone down like this."

I give him a curt nod, leaning in to kiss Skyler on the forehead. "Do you want me to come with you?"

She shakes her head slightly. "I'll be fine. Go help my Little. Please. I just need…" she trails off, trembling more. Clinton curses.

"Go, Brooks. I got her."

And I know he does, no one loves Skyler the way Clinton does. Still, I feel uneasy not being the one taking care of her right now. "Okay. I'll find you two in a minute."

Clinton tugs Skyler through the already packed bar and once they've disappeared, I make my way toward the stage where the KKB girls are setting up. Luckily, I run into Erin first, and she ushers me backstage to where Cassie is waiting after I tell her what happened with Skyler.

"Just don't be back here long. My Big doesn't like anyone seeing the girls before they go on stage."

"Sounds like a strip club."

Erin smacks my arm with a smile, though her face is pale, eyes watery. She doesn't look like the normal Erin Xander I'm used to seeing.

Cassie is pacing in a small space back near the bathroom, chewing her thumbnail with a contemplative look on her face. I can't help but take her in as I make my way toward her. She's not in a dress, but rather a tight, white pencil skirt and hot pink tank top with heels to match. Her bright red hair is pinned up, a few stray tendrils falling to frame her face, and her usually soft green eyes are glowing fierce against the dramatic makeup she's applied. Stuffing my hands in my pockets, I clear my throat when I reach her.

"I feel like I should save that freshly manicured nail from the wrath of your teeth."

Cassie chews for a second longer before stopping, her wide eyes finding me. She looks absolutely petrified.

And it's fucking adorable.

When she realizes it's me, I notice her face fall a bit, and I can't deny that it stings.

"Is Skyler here?"

"Yeah, but she needs a minute. We kind of got attacked by paparazzi on our way inside."

Cassie's mouth drops. "Oh my gosh. Is she okay?"

"A little shaken, but she'll be okay. Bear took her to get water and calm down."

She nods, but her eyes gloss over a bit and she goes back to chewing her thumb.

"Talk to me," I say softly, nudging her with my shoulder as I lean casually against the wall. She drops her hand from her mouth, her green irises roaming over me. I can't tell how I feel about it. She's either checking me out or questioning whether she can trust me.

Maybe both.

Sighing like I'm her last option, she leans back against the wall next to me, blowing air through her lips.

"I don't know why I let them talk me into this. I am literally the worst person for the job. I hate being the center of attention, I blush pretty much anytime someone looks at me, and on a scale of one to sexy I'm at a solid awkward turtle ninety percent of the time."

I chuckle, crossing one arm over my lower chest and bringing my opposite hand to cover my smile. Cassie glares at me, and I know she aims to intimidate me but it only breaks my resolve and makes me laugh. So, naturally, she smacks me across the chest.

"I'm serious, Adam."

"I know, I know," I say through my laughter. "It's just that all of those things are exactly why any guy out there would be lucky to win a date with you tonight."

Cassie's arms are crossed, a frown firmly in place, but she softens a bit at my words. "I beg to differ."

"Beg all you want, but I'd still never take those words back."

She chews her cheek, finally turning to face me. When I see the insecurity behind her eyes, I want to find every guy who ever put them there and kick them all straight in the teeth.

"I'm not desirable. At all. I'm going to get up there and make like twenty bucks and feel completely embarrassed."

"Listen to me." I grab her hands in mine, our shoulders still leaned against the wall, both of us hidden in our little corner of the room — of the world. "I have never, in my entire life, met another girl like you. And as much as you may think that's a bad thing, it is the exact opposite. You're intriguing, Cassie. You're light, innocent, sweet, kind, smart. I could go on and on."

"I don't think guys will buy me for my biology test scores."

Pulling her in a little closer, maybe a little too close, I bring my voice to a whisper. "It will be how fucking amazing you look in that tight little skirt that will make them want to buy you. It'll be everything else I just listed that will make them go crazy trying to keep you."

She swallows, and I watch with more curiosity than I should as her eyes flick to my mouth quickly before finding my gaze. "I should go touch up my makeup."

It's then that I realize how hard we're both breathing, how close we're standing. Dropping her hands, I shove my own back in my pockets and nod. "Okay. I'll see you out there."

Before I can think more about what the hell just happened, I turn on my heel and make my way toward the side stage exit.

"Adam?"

I pause, turning slowly, afraid she'll tell me I was over the line. Afraid I'll lose her, even though she's not really mine to keep.

"Thanks. Really." She smiles with just one side of her mouth, just for a moment, before backing into the bathroom and slowly closing the door.

"Anytime," I reply to no one. And I know even though she didn't hear it, she knows it's true as much as I do. I'd be there for her no matter what.

I just can't decide if that's a good thing.

Erin

THERE IS NOTHING WORSE than throwing up.

I usually don't even let my thighs touch the toilet seats at Ralph's, yet here I am, backstage bathroom, face resting against the dirty, cool porcelain. My head is spinning, I have to go on stage in less than ten minutes, and I can't stop vomiting.

"Goddamn it, Erin." Jess closes the bathroom door behind her and locks it. The first wave of nausea hit me so hard I didn't even have time to close the door when I rushed in. "Get your shit together, dude. You have to go on stage and you look like hell. Come here."

She helps me stand, instantly going into caregiver sister mode, which is a rare form for Jess. She's the party girl, we all know it, but when she needs to be there for someone — she pulls out all the stops. She's one of the best friends anyone could ever have.

I watch her carefully as she uses a wet paper towel on the back of my neck, whipping out her makeup bag at the same time. "Thank you."

She smiles, but her usually playful brown eyes are sad. "You have to take a test. You can't keep avoiding it." Jess shakes her head, patting my face dry with a new paper towel before applying a little cover up under my eyes. "I know it's scary, but we can handle it together. You should have already taken a test by now. Hiding from the problem isn't going to make it go away."

She keeps talking, but my ears go fuzzy, along with my vision. I feel myself slipping into a sort of numbness, a dark hole, a place where I just need to be alone.

"It's fine." I cut her off mid-sentence, forcing a smile. "I took the test, Jess. I'm not pregnant. Must just be a stomach flu."

Jess' eyes are hard on mine, like she's searching for something, but then a sigh of relief leaves her lips. "Oh, thank fuck." She shakes her head, still working on my makeup. "A stomach flu we can handle. When did you take the test?"

"Sunday."

"Why didn't you tell me? I could have been there with you."

"I tried calling, you weren't answering." Jess swallows, her eyes flitting from mine to focus on her hand where she's reapplying my lipstick. Something tells me I'm not the only one who has something to hide.

"Sorry. I think I was with my study group, now that I think of it."

"Yeah."

"Erin?" My Big knocks on the bathroom door. "You're up. Are you okay?"

"Fine! Be right out."

Kelsey is absolutely slaying it in her new position as president, and I know I can't let her down. I'm next in line. Every KKB in our family line for the past several years has held the position of president. This is my year to prove myself, and I'm not letting anything get in my way.

Pulling my shoulders back, I turn from Jess to the mirror, giving myself a once over before pulling her in for a hug. "Thank you for your help."

"Anytime, Ex. Now go raise some money for charity, you fine piece of ass." She smacks my butt as I open the bathroom door and I laugh, throwing her a wink.

I don't have time to get nervous, because Kelsey immediately leads me to the stage, helping me walk up the back stairs before Siomara, My Grand Big and last semester's president, starts speaking into the mic to begin my auction. Even though her term ended last semester, she stuck around for one more so she could graduate in the spring. Then, she'll be headed to Antigua for medical school.

Everything is changing.

"Oh boys, you're in for a real treat with this one," Siomara begins and a few whistles ring out. I shake my head, but pull on my mask, the one that lets everyone in the room know that I can handle anything — everything. "Our new Recruitment Chair is classy, beautiful, and smart. There's a reason her nickname is Ex, boys, so beware." Laughter rings out and I flash a smile at the crowd, playing into it. "And, of course, she's the one in charge of choosing the hot group of freshmen ladies that will make up the next pledge class of Kappa Kappa Beta in the fall!" The crowd cheers, and I take a mini bow before laughing softly.

"We'll start the bidding at one-hundred dollars."

A paddle flies up in the back, but I can't see the hand attached to it. Siomara keeps raising the price, and paddle after paddle goes up in response. I should be happy, flattered, but I just feel so numb. I think I'm smiling, but I can't be sure. When the amount gets up to five-hundred, I focus enough to see who's still in the race.

The paddle that goes up for five-hundred is Clinton.

He smiles at me, that heart-stopping, white-teeth-blazing-against-dark-skin smile that had me more weak in the knees than I care to admit the night he took me to semi-formal. He winks, and a sharp pang shoots through my chest. I know he's just doing it as a friend, he's just being sweet, because that's the kind of man he is.

He would have made a great father.

He *will* make a great father. Someday.

But when Siomara raises the price to six hundred, a new paddle goes up. I recognize the face below it, perfectly symmetrical like a Ken doll, defined jaw, baby face, sandy blonde hair combed over and perfectly styled. Landon Turner is practically the definition of a frat daddy. Vice President of Mu Beta Chi, pre-med with a focus in plastic surgery, dressed in coral shorts cut just above his knee, a white polo, and Sperry's — when it comes to who my parents think I should marry, he's my mother's wet dream.

Landon is standing with some of his friends, elbowing them with a wide smile as he wins the auction. He makes his way through the crowd, helping me down from the stage as a few of my sisters take his cash donation. He has light, almost crystal-blue eyes, and he's not too shy to let me know he wants me with them.

"Looks like I get the privilege of taking you out on a date," he says with a slight southern drawl. Yep, my mom would have officially lost her mind.

"Looks that way." I smile, but it's still a mask. "What do you have in mind?"

"I want it to be perfect, so I need some time to think. Can I have your phone number, Erin Xander?"

This time I smile and it's somewhat genuine. Landon is cute, sweet — he could be fun. I just need to clear my head. Hopefully I can do that before he calls for our date.

I jot my number down in his phone and he gives me a soft kiss on the cheek before returning to his friends so I can join my sisters backstage. Kelsey hands me a clipboard immediately and puts me to work, organizing the rest of the sisters going up for auction and keeping a running tab on the funds raised. For the first time tonight, I feel in my

element. Slipping into organizational mode, I push everything else out of my mind and focus on the tasks at hand.

It's the best kind of escape.

Adam

IN THE TIME I was backstage with Cassie and Skyler was behind the bar with Clinton, something changed. I'm not entirely sure what just yet, but something is different. Skyler has stopped trembling; she's smiling, talking to everyone in our group as we wait for the next sister to come up on stage. She's here, tucked under my arm, but she's not really *here*. Her mind is somewhere far away. She's thinking, and it's the kind of thinking that makes me uneasy.

I think we both feel it. We both feel something coming.

Excusing myself from the group, I slide up to the bar and get a refill on my Captain and Coke just as Cassie takes the stage.

I can tell she's still nervous, but she's much better than she was backstage. Her cheeks rosy, she's twisting her fingers together and smiling out at the crowd as Siomara talks into the mic about how great of a catch Cassie is. Paying for my drink and lifting it to my lips as I make my way back to the group, I catch just the tail end of the spiel.

"Plus, she's probably the cutest redhead Palm South University has ever seen, am I right?"

The room erupts into a mixture of cheers from her sisters and hoots from the guys crowding the bar. Cassie flushes a deep, crimson red, and I can't help but smile.

"We'll start the bidding at one-hundred dollars."

There's a lull in the noise, everyone waiting for that first paddle to go up. Only a few seconds pass, but I watch as Cassie's smile falls, worry appearing in the form of a small crease between her brows. Snatching the paddle out of my brother, Jeremy's, hand, I shoot it up into the air.

"One-hundred! Do I hear one-fifty?"

Cassie's green eyes sparkle when she sees it was me with the paddle. She mouths a *thank you*, and I just smile, handing the paddle back to Jeremy. Jeremy is one of my closest friends in the fraternity, the one brother who helped me with all the events last semester and believed in me when I said I could put our fraternity on the map. This semester, he's my right-hand man, and if we have anything to do with it, we'll be President and Vice President next year.

Skyler's arms wrap around my middle and she leans her head on my chest, looking up at me through her long lashes.

"You may officially be the best boyfriend ever. Thank you for doing that."

I shrug. "I just got the bets started."

And I did. A few more paddles go up before the bid levels out around three-hundred. Siomara is just about to call it when a last-minute paddle flies up.

"Five-hundred!"

Everyone cheers, and Cassie searches the crowd for the new bidder. When she finds him, recognition hits her eyes. She smiles, a bigger smile than I've seen on her face in some time. She knows the guy, and as he makes his way to the stage, panting slightly, like he rushed to get here and just barely made it, Cassie turns to Siomara.

"Sold!" she yells before Siomara has the chance to ask for a higher bid.

Siomara laughs, banging her make-shift gavel on the podium. "You heard the girl!"

A few laughs ring out and then everyone goes back to their conversations or to the bar, waiting for the next auction to start. My eyes, however, stay firmly on Cassie as she makes her way down the stairs. The mystery guy is waiting for her, but when she leaves the last stair, I lose sight of them just as he wraps her in a hug.

Who the hell is that?

"So, I hear you're joining us on Spring Break, Brooks. You think you can hang with a bunch of KKBs and O Chis?" Clinton clinks his class with mine and takes a drink. I sip mine and smile.

"I guess we'll find out. I am excited, though. I've never been to Key West."

"Me either," he says. "I heard Duval Street is crazy."

"I'm just ready for some sunshine and a break from classes. Homework is already killing me," Skyler adds.

"Yeah, I can't wait to see you in a bathing suit, either. Oh! I mean sunshine. Can't wait to be in the sunshine. *Totally* meant sunshine." I wink at Skyler and she elbows my side, but leans up to plant a swift kiss on my cheek.

"You two are so cute it's kind of disgusting," Jeremy says.

"Don't be jealous. I'm sure your hand looks very nice in a yellow bikini, too."

This time Jeremy slugs my arm and we all laugh just as Cassie joins our group. And she's not alone. There's a hand wrapped around her small waist, a hand attached to a long, tattooed arm.

"Hey guys, this is Grayson," Cassie introduces, looking up at the guy with a smile. He's tall, lanky but not too skinny. His hair and beard are dark, but his eyes are bright blue. He's not even remotely unfortunate looking, and for some reason, that irks me.

"Oh yeah, from the coffee shop, right?" Skyler asks, moving forward first. She gives him a hug before wrapping her arms around me again. "Thanks for donating to our cause tonight."

"Of course. I would have paid more if it meant getting Cassie to go on another date with me." He grins down at her and she flushes, just slightly, like she did the day I first met her.

"Another? I didn't know you two had already been on one," Skyler says, her arms still around my waist.

"We just went to dinner."

"She's playing hard to get," Grayson argues, but they're both smiling.

I'm highly annoyed.

"Well I guess she can't say no to a five-hundred dollar proposition," Clinton says, leaning forward to shake Grayson's hand. "I'm Bear."

"Nice to meet you, man."

"Oh! Yeah, this is my Big, Skyler, and Adam and Jeremy. They're in Alpha Sigma."

Grayson shakes Jeremy's hand first and mine last. His grip is strong, smile still in place.

"Hey, I know you. You're the one who threw that kick ass concert last semester, right?" he asks as we drop hands.

"Uh, yeah."

"Bro! That was so sick. Three of my favorite bands in the area were there. Are you doing another one next fall?"

"If I have anything to do with it, yeah." Cassie is smiling up at him as we talk a little more about the concert. He really knows his shit about local music, and before I can stop him, Jeremy is asking if he'll help scout talent next semester. The guy is nice, funny, not even a little douche-like.

I hate him.

My phone buzzes, and for the first time ever, I'm actually relieved to see a text from Clay demanding I get my ass to the house.

"Shit," I murmur. Skyler leans over to look at the text. "Clay just called an emergency meeting."

"Think it's about the retreat?" Jeremy asks.

"Not sure, but we should probably both go." I turn to Skyler, apologies at the ready.

"Don't," she says before I have the chance, holding up her hand. "It's completely fine. I'm exhausted anyway and need to call my parents about what happened tonight. I'll text you tomorrow?"

"Yeah, okay." I smile and she lifts on her toes to give me a kiss. She breaks away too soon for me, so I pull her back, running my hand up her arm to grip the back of her neck, holding her to me. She sighs a little, as if my kiss reassured her of something I didn't even know she was questioning.

"Have fun tonight."

"You too," she breathes when I break the kiss. "See you guys later. Nice to meet you, Grayson." I nod my head as he holds his whiskey up in a cheers to me.

My eyes flick to Cassie's, but just for a moment, not even long enough to read what lies behind them before I turn and make my way through the crowd with Jeremy.

Ashlei

THERE ARE TIMES WHEN our bodies warn us against the actions we choose. They make us sweat, turn our stomachs, cloud our vision, cause us to tremble. My body is sending me all the warning signs now as I clutch the donations raised Saturday night at the auction close to my chest. But I'm not walking up to the bank.

I'm walking into Xavier's office.

I know it's wrong, I'm ashamed that I'm doing it, but I don't have a choice. We raised just over five grand, just enough to buy me the time to Spring Break, just enough to move me closer to my freedom. It's selfish, it's against every value my sorority stands for, it's against everything that I am. But I know this isn't just some game I can quit and walk away from unscarred. My life is on the line.

Bo's life is on the line.

And if I want to make it out of this alive, I'm going to have to do some things I'm not proud of.

I already have.

Swallowing, I nod slightly at the body guard outside of Xavier's office as he lets me in the door. Xavier is seated at his desk, head down, looking through a folder with pictures of other men and documents I'm more than sure I don't want to know the details of.

"Have a seat, Ashlei. Just one moment."

I tuck my hair behind my ears, the ends of it sticking to my neck as I sit on the edge of the chair. Xavier shifts through a few more pages before closing the file and leaning back in his chair, steepling his fingers.

"I hope you're not here to beg for more time."

"I'm not," I say, shoving the large envelope toward him. He takes it hesitantly, his eyes on mine, before opening it and running his fingers over the money. "There's just over five-thousand in there."

He smiles, one that makes me even more uncomfortable than I was. "Does this mean you're taking me up on my offer?"

"I don't really have a choice," I squeak, my throat dry.

Xavier claps his hands together and I jump. "Beautiful! I love when it all comes together like this, kiddo." He pauses, noting my frown. "It'll be easy, I promise. You'll be on Spring Break. Everyone is looking for something."

I nod. "I just want it to be over."

He clears his throat, and I wonder if even he is uncomfortable at the position he's put me in. Then I think of how he's treated me in the past, how he's treated Kya, Hayden. There's no way this man can have a conscious.

But really, am I so different? Here I am agreeing to sell hard drugs to other students on campus. I could be starting an addiction. I could be ending a life.

"I'll call you when everything is ready for you to pick up," he says finally, dismissing me.

"Um, wait." I stand, wiping my palms on my shorts. "I, uh, I kind of need your help." Xavier cocks a brow and I close my eyes, ashamed of what I'm about to ask. I can't let anyone in Kappa Kappa Beta find out about this, which means I need an insurance policy.

"I have to convince my sisters I was mugged, that the money was stolen." I open my eyes again, hoping he'll understand without me having to explain more.

"What are you asking me, Ashlei?"

I feel it inside, a crack only I can hear as a piece of me breaks. "I need you to hit me."

Erin

I AM EMPTY.

I thought I knew what it felt like — emptiness.

The summer before my senior year of high school, I described myself as *empty*. I was searching for purpose, for something to make me feel like living, and luckily I found it in a blonde-haired, blue-eyed boy in the wheat fields of Kansas. Kip Jackson helped me find myself, and though we don't talk anymore, I still attribute a lot of who I am today to who he helped me become that summer.

But this emptiness I feel now, my hands wrapped hard around the steering wheel of Jess' BMW, white knuckles, dry eyes, tight skin, dry mouth — I've never felt anything like this before. My phone is ringing, but I can barely hear it. It's probably Landon. He's called twice today, but I'm not ready to answer. Hell, I can't even answer to myself right now.

Emptiness.

It's such a strange word.

A cup, half-empty or half-full?

I was brought up in a large, white house with light blue shutters. I went to church every Wednesday and twice on Sunday. My parents consistently donate to the Republican party, at all levels of government, and my political views are about as far right as you can go.

And yet here I am.

I wish I could cry. I wish I could feel the guilt, the shame, the pain I should feel at this moment in time. I'm angry that I'm numb, that I can't seem to wrap my mind around the word, around the act of horror I just committed.

Abortion.

Another strange word.

My right hand slides down the side of the steering wheel, dropping to my stomach, and I grip the soft cotton fabric of my t-shirt covering it. It's so flat, so hollow.

Empty.

Part of me wishes someone was here with me, but the larger part of me is thankful I didn't break down enough to ask anyone. I can barely face the facts of what I did, I'm almost sure I wouldn't be able to take the judgement from an outside party. No one knows what this feels like until they're here.

Erin Xander: College junior, pre-law, future president of her sorority, knocked up by the lovable jock in the fraternity house down the street.

That is not my story to tell.

Maybe, if I were stronger, if I were less selfish, we could have made it work. Maybe I could have given up my presidency to have the baby, put it up for adoption, still graduated and become a lawyer like I've always dreamed. Maybe Clinton would have wanted to keep it.

As it stands, Clinton will never know.

No one will ever know.

I sniff, but for no reason, because I'm not crying. I didn't cry when I read the all lowercase letters that spelled out *pregnant* on that little plastic tube in my bathroom. I didn't cry when I lied to Jess, or when I made the appointment. I didn't cry when I walked past the small group holding hand-painted signs outside of the clinic — *Choose Life*. And I know I'll never cry, because if ever there was a time, it would have been when they vacuumed my son or daughter out of my stomach like it was a mess made by an inconsiderate neighbor.

I am twenty-years-old, and yet I am a mother, to a baby I'll never have the fortune of meeting.

Except I am not a mother.

I am selfish.

I am a hypocrite.

I am empty.

Ashlei

VALENTINE'S DAY HAS NEVER been a special holiday for me. In fact, the only true valentine I ever had was in second grade when Jordan Lewis bought me a stuffed white dog and small, heart-shaped box of chocolate. He ate half of the chocolates and pushed me off the merry-go-round later that afternoon.

Asshole.

After that, I either didn't have a boyfriend during Valentine's Day or the boyfriend I had didn't celebrate it. By the time I turned sixteen, I stopped caring, and that was a relief for the two boyfriends I had in high school. Neither of them had to worry about the holiday because it meant absolutely nothing to me.

But tonight, I'm wrapped in a massive pile of blankets and sheets with Bo tucked under my arm, her small hand resting on my hip, her fingers just barely under the hem of my t-shirt. It's Valentine's Day, and I'm determined to make it one we'll both remember.

It's barely over fifty degrees tonight, one of the last cold nights we'll have in South Florida for quite a while. It's mid-February now, which means sunshine and seventies are right around the corner. Spring Break is just a few weeks away, and while everyone else is focused on their diets, I'm focused on this moment — right here — lying under the stars with the only girl I've ever truly let myself be with.

It's not that I never found a girl attractive before Bo. I've known for quite some time that I'm bisexual. Still, I never let myself be with them. A kiss here and there, maybe some nights spent together where I wondered if they felt the same, but that's where it all ended. Bo is my first girlfriend, which is part of the reason I want tonight to be so special.

"This is nice," Bo whispers, snuggling in closer. I run my fingers through her short, silky locks and sigh in agreement. "How did you even think of this?"

I shrug. "I wanted to do something no one had ever done for you before."

"You succeeded," Bo says with a giggle.

Palm South University is undergoing a lot of construction this semester, and I heard they were tearing down this parking garage to make room for a new theatre. They stopped letting students park here a few weeks ago and construction is set to pick up in March. I wanted to be alone with Bo, somewhere where we could be ourselves without anyone watching. So, I bought an air mattress, stuffed two duffle bags full of sheets, blankets, and pillows, and set up our own private bedroom under the stars. I asked Bo to bring a few candles and two bottles of wine, and now here we are.

Paradise.

Leaning up on her elbow, Bo frowns down at me, the soft flicker of the candles illuminating her face just slightly. "Are you okay?"

Her hand leaves my hip and finds the side of my face as she runs her thumb across my cheek bone. I flinch a little, the bruise still tender, but force a smile. "I'm fine."

"I can't believe some asshole mugged you. On campus, nonetheless." She shivers. "Gives me the creeps."

"Me too. But I'm okay, and I just want to move on."

She nods, but her eyes are focused hard on mine. Bo knows about the trouble I got into last semester with

Hayden and the drugs, but I never told her what Kya said when she came by the sorority house that last day of fall semester. How could I? Bo is the most special person in my life right now. I couldn't risk losing her because of a stupid decision I made.

I'm digging my way out of this hole on my own, and once I'm out, I'll stand in the sunshine with Bo.

I told Erin and the rest of my sorority that I was mugged on my way to the bank with our philanthropy money. Xavier came through with what I asked him to do, and with a smile on his face. He enjoyed it, I could tell.

"Do the campus police have any leads yet?"

I shake my head. "Not yet. But they'll find who did it. I'm not worried."

At least that's not a lie. The PSU police are the last item on my list of Shit to Worry About.

"You know you can talk to me, right?" Bo laces her fingers in mine, pulling my hand to her lips for a soft kiss. It's such an innocent touch, but my heart instantly accelerates.

"I know."

Bo seems so perfect on the outside — beautiful complexion, hair, body. She puts everyone else before herself. But over the last few weeks, I've gotten to know Bo on a deeper level. She opened up to me about her parents, the pressure they put on her to excel in life, the absolute horror she experiences at just the thought of telling them she's gay.

That I can relate to.

I've grown into my skin enough to know who I am. I like boys, but I also like girls. I just love to love, I guess. Regardless, my parents wouldn't understand — just like Bo's wouldn't. I've always thought that, maybe, they never really needed to know. After all, there's a chance I may end up marrying a guy, right? Still, I can't say I've never thought about telling them just to see their reaction. I wonder if I'd have their attention then?

But Bo doesn't have that same thought. She can't help who she loves, and she doesn't want who her parents think she should — who the bible says she should.

It's sad, and even though acceptance is spreading faster now than it ever did when my parents were my age, there are still so many who don't understand.

Our parents are at the top of that list.

"What are you thinking about?" Bo asks, sitting and pulling one of the blankets up with her to cover her shoulders. The candlelight is reflected onto the front of her face while the moon and stars shine bright behind her. It's absolutely stunning.

"Honestly?"

She nods.

I pause, leaning up to sit with her and nervously tucking my hair behind my ear. "I'm kind of scared."

Bo's face falls. "Of what?"

"Of what I want to do right now."

She swallows, pulling the blanket tighter around her petite frame. "What do you want to do?"

If I thought my heart was beating fast before, it's racing now — galloping — threatening to break my ribcage. "Kiss you."

She relaxes, just marginally. "You've kissed me before, silly." Bo leans forward, like she expects me to kiss her the way I always do, but I don't budge.

"That's not what I mean."

She halts, her midnight eyes snapping to mine. Recognition sets in and she exhales slowly, her breath just barely visible in the cool air of the night. With confidence, she drops the blanket from her shoulders as I open mine to her, instead. She crawls under, straddling me, her breath coming harder.

"Where do you want to kiss me?"

My hands shake as I frame her delicate neck in my hands, pulling her closer, our lips touching as I whisper.

"Everywhere."

Bo closes the distance, kissing me hard as we both let go of the breaths we were holding. Her hands find my hair and I trail mine down to her hips, holding her tight as I buck against her. She gasps, and the sound does something to me that I've never experienced before. Every nerve feels tight, but awake — alive.

It's suddenly no longer cold — not even close. It's scorching, too hot for blankets, too hot to touch, but we refuse to stop. Bo moves her hands to my waist, pushing my shirt up slowly, watching it roll over my curves before finally stripping it off over my head and letting it fall on the concrete. I pull her back into me, kissing her hard, my hands greedy as they roam her body for the first time. When I snake my right hand between her thighs, she tenses, moaning, grinding against the contact.

I'm breathing so hard yet I feel like I haven't inhaled once. Everything in my life is so wrong, but I only feel right in this moment. I'm scared, excited, unsure — and so fucking turned on.

Bo presses her forehead to mine, her breath labored as I find my way beneath the fabric of her yoga pants. When I find there's not another layer separating me from her, I swallow, my fingers circling her clit, my adrenaline pumping. She moans, her head falling, back arching, hips rolling. She bites her lip as her heavy eyes pin my mouth.

It's like she can't wait another moment to taste me, like her life depends on our next kiss, and when she finally presses her mouth to mine I wonder if maybe it's true.

"Lay down," she whispers and I obey. Bo winds her hips to the soft music coming from my phone as she peels my sweatpants off, lining her face up with the hem, following the fabric from my hips all the way down to my toes. I can't stop shaking, even though I'm far from cold now. I will my heart to slow down but it won't listen. I am out of control — blissfully unsteady and wild.

When Bo kisses her way back up my legs, her lips trailing a fire from my ankles to my inner thighs, my shaking becomes visible. Her eyes find mine just as she places one, feather-light kiss over my lace panties.

"Lei?"

"Hmm?" I ask, sedated, squirming beneath her.

"Is this your first time?"

My eyes widen. "No."

She smiles, crawling up my body and settling between my legs. Using her knees to spread me open to her, she slides one hand beneath the hem of my panties and I inhale stiffly.

"I mean, is this your first time with a girl?"

Oh.

Her eyes pin my own, and all I can do is nod.

Her grin turns devilish, a dominance I've never seen in her before becoming more and more prominent. She breaks our stare just long enough to pull her sweater and sheer tank top up and over her head. Wrapping her hands around my wrists, she pulls them up over my head, pressing her lips to mine and rolling her hips into me. A jolt shoots through me at the point of contact and I moan, shaking hard, breathing harder.

With her shirt, Bo ties a soft knot around my wrists, pushing them into the mattress slightly before trailing her fingers down my arms to my face. "Keep your hands there. If you move, I punish you. Understand?"

Oh. My. *God.*

My mouth opens slightly as I nod and Bo smirks, kissing my lower lip. "Good girl." Kissing her way down my neck, her hands slide under me and pop my bra effortlessly. I pull my hands down, thinking she wants to take it completely off, but she pushes them back into the mattress.

"Stay."

I gulp.

Bo just smiles, blowing on my nipple before taking it in between her teeth. When her mouth closes over the sensitive skin, warmth spreads and I gasp. She moves to the other, giving it the same pleasure as chills break across my skin. I never knew Bo was the kind to take control, and with everything the way it is in my life, all I want is to give myself to her — completely. I want to submit. I want to let go.

Her lips graze my skin as she runs her tongue down my stomach, tracing the definition there. She tugs my panties off gently, slowly, her eyes devouring me. It feels forbidden, the way she makes me feel, and yet I'm only eager for more.

She barely kisses me first, her lips touching me just enough to drive me insane, but then her tongue drags against the sensitive flesh and I moan — loud, uninhibited. She smiles, sucking my clit between her teeth and sliding one small finger inside me.

Holy hell.

Arching my back, I buck my hips against her mouth and she sucks hard, adding another finger. Every pump sends me closer to the edge, every lash of her tongue makes me cry out her name. I'm rolling, reaching, trying to grasp the release just out of reach. It's like Bo knows my body better than I do. She knows where to touch, how to move, the exact pressure to give without me saying anything.

And suddenly, the benefit of hooking up with another girl comes into view.

My hands fly to her hair and I spread my legs wider, reveling in the ache that spreads from the point where her mouth is still on me.

"I told you not to move your hands," she says, breaking contact. She withdraws her fingers quickly, leaving me empty, and her eyes light me on fire. Gripping my hips, she flips me over with ease and before I can register what's happening, her hand pops my ass. I moan as the sting spreads, my mouth falling open. Bo falls down on top of me, her fingers stroking my opening before entering me from behind. I feel her everywhere — her hair on my shoulder, her lips on my skin, her fingers deep inside me as she curls them, stroking the spot I know will give me the release I'm chasing.

"Just let go, Lei," she whispers, thrusting her hips into her hand, forcing her fingers even deeper. Sliding her free hand down my back, she wraps it around my hip and presses her fingers hard into my clit, circling with just enough pressure to make me follow her command.

As I come, I let everything go. I scream her name, flex my hips, bite my lip, and with each wave I let a tiny piece of myself float away forever.

And though the release came slow, it crashed fast, and I collapse into the sheets, completely spent. Completely hers.

"Oh my God," I breathe, chest rising and falling with effort. Bo smiles, pulling the blankets over us as she wraps her arms around my waist and brings me flush against her. She kisses my neck, my jaw before finally claiming my mouth again, and I taste myself on her tongue.

"I think it's your turn." I pull back, eyes playful, but Bo shakes her head.

"Just relax."

I frown, but Bo just bites her lip with a smile.

"We've got all night," she says, kissing my nose. "How do you feel?"

I blow out a breath. "Incredible."

Bo grins, her eyes still heavy. "Happy Valentine's Day."

Happy Valentine's Day, indeed.

EPISODE 3

"And we're just getting started."

I WATCH AS THE water breaks around my paddle, the sun warm on my face, a slight sweat breaking on the back of my neck. Each stride pushes me farther from shore and I sigh at the instant relief I feel from being in my safe space.

I picked up paddleboarding after my freshman Spring Break trip, but I never would have guessed it would become such a constant in my life. When we got back to campus, I started renting boards every weekend, paddling out on my own, fighting against the familiar aches in my muscles until they weren't even affected anymore. After a few months, I bought my own board, and now I take solace in the time I have on the water, away from the world.

There's something about being on the ocean — the wind blowing through your hair, the smell of salt in the air, the sound of the waves on the shore — that sets you free. It reminds you how small you are while making you feel invincible all at once. It's fascinating.

I try not to take life too seriously, but my mind has been bogged down ever since the auction. It's been a little over a week now, yet I still can't shake the stampede of feelings that hit me out of nowhere that night. It was like with every flash of the camera from the reporter who ambushed me and Adam outside Ralph's, a new thought assaulted me. What am I doing with Adam? Is it more serious for him than it is for me? What does it mean that I have paparazzi following me now? Is this the new normal or a one-time thing? Am I holding Adam back from getting the presidency? Is he holding me back from chasing my dreams with poker?

Though I paddle for hours, none of the answers come, and by the time my feet touch sand again, my mind is still wound as tight as the sun-kissed skin stretched over my shoulders. A loud whistle brings me back down to earth and I smile when I see Jess and Cassie sprawled out in two low-sitting beach chairs just down the beach. Hiking up my board, I make my way toward them, trying not to laugh at Jess making lewd gestures the entire time.

"You're so sexy when you lug that board around, Sky," Jess says, and I note the nasally tone of her voice. "Your leg muscles are sick."

"Are we talking sick like impressive or sick like your red nose and dark eyes?"

Jess waves me off, flicking her sunglasses back down. "It's just allergies. I'll be fine."

Cassie scoffs and pulls her bright red hair off her neck, obviously annoyed, though that's way out of character for her. "She's been coughing all morning, but refuses to go to the doctor. And she hasn't eaten since yesterday."

"Jess!"

"What?" She sighs exasperatedly. "It's fine. Good for the Spring Break diet."

Cassie and I exchange knowing looks, but don't push further as I unpack the towels from my beach bag, spreading them out in the sand.

"You seem awfully sassy today, Little. What's with the permanent frown?"

Cassie shifts, her mouth pulling to one side. "Do you guys think I'm a good girl?"

Jess and I pause, unsure of what the right answer is. I opt for the truth. "I mean, I wouldn't say you're exactly a bad girl."

"You're like Snow White, is what she's trying to say," Jess adds.

"What's that supposed to mean?"

Jess shrugs. "You're pure, innocent. You focus on your schoolwork, never really get drunk, don't hook up with random guys. You're straight-laced."

"Which isn't a bad thing," I add, scolding Jess with my eyes.

"I'm not saying it is," Jess defends. "Why are you suddenly concerned, though?"

Cassie is chewing her cheek, eyes on the ocean. "I don't know. I overheard someone saying that I was too much of a 'good girl' for something, and it got under my skin."

"Who?" I ask.

She shakes her head. "Doesn't matter."

"Well, it's not a bad thing. It shouldn't be taken as an insult."

"I'm just trying to figure out if that's the way it was intended," she says, sighing.

"I say fuck whoever said it. And, if it were me in the situation, I'd take the opportunity to prove them wrong."

Cassie perks up a little. "What do you mean?"

She shrugs. "I'm just saying if someone called me Ms. Innocent like it was a racial slur, I'd show them just how not-innocent I can be."

"Jess Vonnegut – Life Advisor," I deadpan. She smirks, tossing a half-empty suntan lotion bottle at me. I catch it with ease and squeeze some in my hands, lathering my shoulders.

"Bitch."

"You love me."

"Also true."

I turn my attention back to my Little, who now has an intrigued look on her face. "Oh God, I think you might have actually given her an idea."

"Just let me know if you need to borrow some fishnets, boo." Jess makes a kissy noise to Cassie and we all giggle.

"Where are the other girls?" I ask, flipping over to rest on my stomach. I have to mold the sand beneath my towel a bit to make a comfortable spot for my chest. Boobs are inconvenient sometimes.

"Erin was supposed to meet up with the kid who bought her at the auction and I'm not sure where Ashlei and Bo are," Jess answers. "Have you guys noticed Ashlei being weird lately?"

"I mean, she was mugged," Cassie says softly, reminding us all of what the entire campus was trying to forget. "I'm not sure I'd be exactly normal after that, either."

"Even before that, though. She seems off, like she's hiding something."

"I could say the same about my Big," I add. Jess sniffs, avoiding my comment, and I lift a brow. "Wait, do you know something?"

"No," she says quickly. "I'm just thinking."

"Well, why don't we divide and conquer. You try to talk to Ashlei, I'll see if I can get my Big to open up."

"Deal."

"What about me?" Cassie asks.

"You just worry about adding some leather to your wardrobe," Jess says and we all laugh, but Jess' face falls quickly. "Wait. Is that guy taking pictures of us?"

My stomach drops and I sit up quickly, my eyes scanning the beach for what Jess is seeing. When I spot a tall man, dressed in khakis and a polo, large camera strapped around his neck and lens focused on the three of us, I curse.

"Oh my God, he is taking pictures of us." Cassie reaches for her sundress, hastily yanking it over her head just as Jess pops up, stomping toward the man.

"Jess! Don't!" I jump up, too, grabbing her elbow and spinning her back around just as she yells obscenities at the man, his camera still fixed on us. "He's probably a reporter for a sports network or blog. We need to get out of here."

"This is ridiculous. You're a poker player and a college student, for God's sake, don't they have better shit to do?"

"Apparently not."

We gather up our stuff quickly, making our way toward the small private beach parking lot. I check my board back into the surf shop I keep it at on our way and we all pile into Jess' car, the man following us the entire way.

"Is this going to happen all the time now, Big?" Cassie asks as Jess throws the car into drive, flipping the reporter off as we pull away.

"I don't know," I murmur, my mind racing.

"What are you going to do?"

I blow out a breath. "Wear cuter bathing suits, I guess."

I try for humor but fail, the heaviness of the situation settling around all of us. My Little offers a sad smile before turning back around and Jess clicks on the radio, volume up full blast. Thumbing through the contacts in my phone, I type out a text to my dad, hoping he'll know what to do.

Jess rolls our windows down, letting the warm breeze blow through our beach-tangled hair. I drop my hand out the window, riding the wind waves, eyes blurring as the scenery races by. Something tells me this is the last calm moment before everything in my life changes, and I try to hold onto it for as long as I can.

But just like the wind, the moment is fleeting, and I know any moment I'll wake up in my new normal.

I just hope I'm ready.

Cassie

THERE'S SOMETHING ABOUT WATCHING Grayson play guitar that really gets to me. The way his hands strum the strings, each pluck so familiar to him, his rough voice rising just above the chords and combing through the warm air of Cup O' Joe's — it's enough to make a girl literally swoon. His bright blue eyes scan the coffee shop as he sings, dropping to his hands every once in a while, finding mine at the perfect times — when he wants me to really hear the words he's singing.

I just sip my coffee and smile at him, mesmerized, wondering why in the world he picked me for his muse. It's almost amusing how many girls fall over themselves trying to get him to notice them. They drop twenties in his tip jar, usually with their phone number, and sway their hips as they walk away. They cheer each time he finishes a song, they request Manchester Orchestra or other bands that they think might make him take them seriously, they compliment his beard or trace their fingers over one of his tattoos, pretending to be interested in the story behind them. Yet somehow, his eyes are fixed on mine, and I can't shake how lucky that makes me feel.

We've been a on a few dates, mostly dinners and movie nights, and each time I find myself falling a little more for him. We longboard for hours, talking about everything and nothing — laughing, existing. He took me to a local concert in the park downtown and we've even *studied* together, which usually involves less time studying our notes and more time studying each other. Not that I mind.

We're seemingly nothing alike — he's a tattooed musician with dreams of moving to New York City after graduation and I'm a freckle-faced Biology major who passes out at the mere thought of a needle going into my skin.

The stark contrast between us reminds me of the conversation I overheard between Adam and Jeremy the other night, and I frown.

They were walking toward the Student Union when I spotted them and I quickened my pace, thinking I could walk with them, but when I got close enough to hear their conversation, I slowed a little at the mention of my name. Jeremy was asking Adam which girls he thought would be good for their next philanthropy event — a B-list celebrity fight featuring two older fighters who happen to live in the Miami area. They need ring girls, and when Jeremy suggested me, Adam was quick to turn down the thought.

"She's too much of a good girl for that."

I tried not to take it personally, but how else is there to take it? He didn't say it like it was a characteristic I should be proud of, but rather like I would fail at the job. And though I've tried to strip Adam of the power he somehow holds over me, it still hurt to hear him say it. Add in the fact that my Big and Jess both agreed with him, and it's been practically impossible to let it go.

I snap my attention back to Grayson just as he finishes the last note of an X Ambassadors song, his bright smile revealing itself behind his beard, girls clapping and whistling when he blushes slightly.

"I'm going to take a quick break, and I'm taking requests when I return, so don't go anywhere," he says into the mic, tossing a wink at me that makes two girls at the table behind me nearly fall out of their chair. I just shake my head.

Grayson pulls his guitar strap over his head and props the instrument against the large metal bar stool he was seated on, hopping off the stage and making his way toward me. It's like slow motion as he walks, the muscles in his arms shifting as he shakes out his long, chestnut hair just to re-tie it in a haphazard bun again. I stand, smiling, and he pulls me in close, pressing his lips hard on mine to a symphony of groans from the rest of the girls in the shop. He knows they're here to flirt with him, yet he still makes it a point to show he's with me.

Yep, officially swooning.

"Come to the back with me? I need some water."

I nod, head still fuzzy as he grabs my hand in his and weaves us through the *STAFF ONLY* doors to a small back room. It has two faded purple couches and one long, dark, wooden coffee table along with an old stereo currently crooning out an old 90's alternative song I'm not familiar with. Grayson plops down onto one of the couches with a sigh, pulling me with him so that I straddle his hips.

"What happened to needing water?" I ask, giggling.

"I lied," he says with a grin, hands skating up my arms to frame my face and pull me into him. His beard tickles my skin as he presses his lips to mine and I fist my hands in his shirt, pulling, wanting him closer yet knowing I'm afraid of being too close at the same time.

So far, all we've done is kiss, and it's not that our make-out sessions aren't amazing — because that's an understatement — but I know Grayson wants more. Hell, *I* want more – but after Clay, I'm hesitant to take it too far too fast. I know Grayson would never push me, but I can only wonder how much longer he'll stick around if I keep holding out.

Breaking our kiss, I undo his bun and run my fingers through his long shaggy hair, massaging the scalp. His eyes close and he rests his head on the back of the couch, smiling. "That feels amazing."

"I love watching you play. You're really good, you know that?"

He chuckles, his hands gripping my hips. "Thank you. Let's hope the big wigs in New York feel the same way." He opens his eyes just enough to wink at me before letting them close again.

"They would be crazy not to."

We're quiet for a moment, my hands still running through his hair, his fingers playing with the hem of my blouse.

"Are you excited for Spring Break?"

I frown. "I'd be more excited if you were coming with me."

"Not really my thing," he says, pulling my hands to his lips. He kisses them with a smile and ties his hair back before letting his hands find my waist again. "You'll have all your sisters to keep you busy. Plus, I have to work."

"I know. Doesn't make me wish you were coming any less, though."

He smiles, blue eyes shining, the gold flecks in them playful. "You know, we could have our own Spring Break. Wear our bathing suits, grind on each other, get wasted."

"Oh?" I cock a brow as his grin widens. "And where exactly would we host this Spring Break?"

"In my dorm room, of course. I'll even put on some Skrillex for good measure."

"Well now you've thought of everything."

"Exactly. Can't turn down such a well-thought-out plan."

"Guess not," I agree, leaning in to kiss him. His hands tighten on my hips and he rocks me against him, causing my breath to hitch at the contact. Grayson deepens the kiss, wrapping his strong arms completely around me, surrounding me with his warmth. He sucks my bottom lip between his teeth and lets it go with a pop, fingers gliding just beneath the hem of my jeans, eyes hooded as he searches me for permission — permission I can't give him. Not yet.

"Can I ask you something?" I breathe and he nods, kissing me once before letting me continue. "Do you think I'm a good girl?"

His brows furrow at my question, his hand stilling. "I feel like I'm walking into a trap."

I laugh. "You're not, I promise. Just be honest."

He blows out a breath, releasing his grip around me and leaning back on the couch. "I don't know. I think you're kind and sweet, and I definitely wouldn't say you're any of the things I associate with a quote unquote *bad girl*."

I sigh, but kiss him quickly to let him know it's not him I'm upset with. "Are you busy next weekend? There's a fraternity party Saturday night that everyone's going to, and I want you to come with me."

"You sure I'll be allowed? Frats aren't exactly inviting of non-brothers."

"It's an open invitation," I assure him. "And you'll be with me. Please?"

Grayson hums, thinking, thumbs still lightly circling the exposed skin above my jeans. "How can I say no to those pouty lips?"

Smiling, I lean down and press said lips to his, letting him pull me in closer for the few minutes we have left before his next set. And though having his hands and mouth on me are my main focus, my mind drifts to everything I need to do to get ready for next weekend. Everyone has it in their mind that I'm this innocent little girl, incapable of owning the vixen inside me. Well, maybe I don't always pull her out and throw her on display for everyone to see, but next weekend, that's exactly what I plan to do.

Time to show them a Cassie McBee they've never seen before.

One they'll never forget.

Jess

MY HEAD ACHES AS I blow hard into a tissue, folding it in half and wiping at my raw nose again. "Gross," I murmur, dropping it into the light blue trash can in mine and Skyler's bathroom. Still sniffling, my dark eyes scan my appearance in the mirror. My skin is ashy white, nose like fucking Rudolph, hair greasy, eyes droopy. I look like complete shit, and regardless of how I try to act, I feel like it, too.

The most obvious thing to do in this situation is haul my happy ass to the campus health clinic, but just the thought of it makes me groan. I hate doctors — of all kinds. Dentists, nurses, vag docs — all of them. I hate the way it smells in a doctor's office, the way you have to weigh in every time, how long you have to sit before the grumpy old man waddles in to shove a thermometer in your throat and judge you for the amount of wax in your ears just to tell you you're fine and buy some over-the-counter meds. It's all an inconvenient circus and I'm over it before I even think of making the call for an appointment.

Throwing on a hoodie even though I know it's far from cold in the house, I pad down the hallway to Erin and Ashlei's room and let myself in without knocking. Erin is seated at her desk, head down, scribbling in her planner. Four highlighters are set up to the left of her hand and I sink into her sheets as she color codes her life.

"Don't bring your virus in here, J-Love," she barks without even looking up.

"Oh, shut it. I'm fine. What are you doing tonight?"

She sighs, shutting her planner and popping the caps back on her highlighters. "Landon is supposed to take me to dinner."

"Well don't seem so excited."

"I was hoping to go through my closet and make the agenda for the council meeting this Wednesday."

I eye her as I reach across her bed and rummage through her snack drawer. "You're kind of weird, Ex. Anyone ever tell you that?"

She shrugs. "I just like to throw myself into things I can control, that's all."

"Well, maybe you need to loosen up a little. You've been wound too tight since the semester started. I think this new position is putting a lot of pressure on you. Plus you had that stomach flu."

She blinks, crossing to her closet and flitting through the side with all her dresses. "Yeah. You're right. It'll be fun, I'm sure."

I shake my head, unrolling a bag of veggie chips and popping one into my mouth. Just chewing is so much effort and my appetite is nonexistent, so I huff and roll the bag back up, tossing it in her drawer again.

"Is it my turn to lecture you?" I know she's trying to joke about me being sick, but her eyes are so tired, so sad. There's something going on with her that she's not telling us.

"Erin, are you okay? Seriously. I know you had that pregnancy scare, and I'm sure even though the test was negative, it was probably pretty awful taking it on your own."

"I'm fine," she clips, stripping down to her underwear just to throw on a tight, lavender, knee-length dress. Ashlei flies through the door just as Erin bends to pull out her tall nude heels.

"Lei! What are you doing tonight? Hang out with me," I whine. That's one of my best qualities when I'm sick. I turn into the whiniest, neediest bitch ever. The problem is that what I want most right now is to either A, get drunk, or B, call Jarrett. And neither of those would be smart. Getting drunk would probably make me even sicker than I already am, and there's no way I could hook up with Jarrett with my snotty face and germy mouth, so what else could we really do? Nothing that would keep us in the safely non-defined zone we're in right now, that much I know.

"Uh, Bo and I are actually heading out to see the new Nicholas Sparks movie."

I groan. "Booooo. I don't want to go out. Can't we stay in? Sneak a bottle of wine and watch one of the other cry-inducing movies he has out already?" I don't even care that I just invited myself to crash their night. If she's lying to me about what her and Bo's relationship is, she should at least have to work to preserve that lie.

"We kind of already bought the tickets, J-Love." Ashlei frowns, tying her long blond hair up in a high pony. "I'm sorry. You can come, though. If you want. But I totally understand if you're not up for it."

As much as I want to crash what I'm *positive* is a date and make them sweat, I don't have the energy to. They'll both live to lie another day.

"Ugh. Where is Skyler? And Cassie?"

"Skyler's playing at a tournament downtown," Erin says, checking her makeup in the mirror.

Ashlei nods. "Yeah, and I'm pretty sure Cassie said she's hanging out with Grayson. They were going to check out some art festival that's in town."

I groan louder, exaggerating the noise, being as annoying as humanly possible. "Why is everyone happily living their lives tonight?"

Ashlei chuckles. "Just go to the doctor, Jess. Stop fighting it."

"I'm fine."

"Uh huh," she says, shaking her head.

"I'll *be* fine. It's just a cold."

"Whatever you say. Don't spread your germs to my side of the room."

"Oh don't worry, she's too busy rolling them around all over my pillow," Erin adds as she opens their bedroom door. "Make sure you Lysol before you leave." I toss a throw pillow at both of them just as they squeeze through the opening, laughing.

When they're gone and I'm alone, I sigh loudly, glancing at my phone and groaning again at the two missed texts from Jarrett. I've been avoiding him, which probably isn't a smart move, considering how that worked out for me last time. Although, I *really* wouldn't mind being fucked in a dark closet right about now. But ever since I saw him with that girl at Pie Heaven, I haven't answered his texts. Which is stupid. And petty.

Mrs. Stupid and Petty herself, ladies and gentlemen.

Huffing, I heave myself off Erin's bed and mope down the hallway to my own, burying myself in the covers. I tuck my phone under my pillow and will myself not to look at it again. Calling Jarrett and asking him to hang out with me while I'm sick would be crossing the line into boyfriend territory, and that's the last thing I want — the last thing *he* wants, obviously. We both understand what we are and what we are not, even if I am butt-hurt over him going to lunch with another girl, and sick cuddle buddies definitely falls on the what-we-are-not-list.

But the more time that passes, the more I want to text him — see him, be around him. The scary thing is that I don't even want to hook up, not really — not specifically, anyway. It would be a nice added feature to the package but really, I just want his company. I want to make him laugh, I want to hear him talk about his day, I want to put my feet in his lap and watch a movie. And the more that realization sets in, the harder it is to keep myself from picking up the phone — from giving into a feeling I haven't had in over a year.

I thought I could handle not putting a title on what we are, just doing what we want and going from there. But the truth of the matter is that I don't hook up with other people and when I'm not with him, he's all I think about. Toss in the fact that I get insanely jealous when I see him with any other woman, coworker or not, and the recipe for disaster thickens. I don't know who I thought I was fooling.

What have I gotten myself into?

Bear

"WHAT'S UP, BABY BROTHER?"

"About time you answered your phone!" Clayton says as I toss my gym bag into the corner of my room. I'm taken aback by the deepness of his voice. He just turned thirteen, and already I can tell he's about to hit the glorious days of puberty. "I have a serious question."

"Uh oh. Do I need to sit down?" I joke, kicking off my basketball shoes. I push the speaker-phone option on my phone and set it on the bathroom counter as I start the shower.

"Mac and I are stuck on this mission in Grand Theft Auto and can't figure it out. We've been here for hours, bro."

I laugh. "I can't believe I was playing basketball and missed your calls during this tragic time."

"I know. What a shitty big brother you are."

"Hey!" I scold as I peel my still-wet t-shirt over my head. "Since when do you curse?"

"It's not a big deal. Mac says shit all the time."

I frown. "You've been over at Mac's a lot lately."

There's a pause on Clayton's end and I still, wondering if there's something he's not telling me. "Sorry. I'll cool it on the cursing, Mom."

I laugh, asking him for more details on the mission he's on and walking him through it while the bathroom steams up. We chat for a while, mostly about school, not even a little bit about mom or Carlton. It feels good to catch up with Clayton and I can't help but feel like I should do it more often. Just because I'm not in the same state doesn't mean I shouldn't be there for him. I'm the closest thing he has to someone to look up to in his life.

That fact hits me hard. I haven't heard from mom or Carlton since I gave them enough money to get them out of whatever trouble they were in last semester, which gives me hope, at least, that they're doing okay. Still, just because I haven't heard from them doesn't mean I shouldn't pick up my phone and call Clayton more often.

"Hey," I say just as we're about to hang up. "Why don't you come down for family weekend? I'll book the flight. We can hit the beach and go go-karting."

"Really?" Clayton asks, excited.

"Yeah, really. I'll even let you get your ass kicked in Halo if you're lucky."

"Hey, what happened to no cursing?"

"I'm twenty-one. I'm allowed to curse."

He chuckles. "I really would like to. I feel like there's a lot we never get to talk about with all the distance, you know?"

I run my hand through my fade, catching my own eyes in the mirror. "Yeah I know. It'll be fun. I'll text you later with the flight details. If mom is upset or has questions, just have her call me," I add, jaw tensing at the mention of her.

"I doubt she will, but yeah, I'll tell her. Love you, big bro."

"You too."

We end the call and I thumb through my music, pressing play on a J Cole song and setting it to shuffle through my playlist. I take my time in the shower, letting the hot water soothe my aching muscles from playing hard at the courts. My knees are tight, arms sore, and I'm ready to collapse in bed and watch ESPN. But as I step out of the shower and wrap a towel around my waist, I see a completely different option presented.

"Your clothes smell, dude." Shawna says, her small frame leaning against the bathroom counter. "Like, bad."

"Hi to you, too."

"Hi," she says, kissing me swiftly before propping her ass on the bathroom counter, shamelessly watching me dry off. "There's an art festival in town. You should take me."

I chuckle. "You have absolutely zero fucks to give about the normal way people do things, huh?"

"Normal is boring."

"What do I get out of this deal?"

"My company, of course. Plus we can knock out that extra credit assignment for our art class. It's a win-win."

I brace my hands on either side of her legs on the counter, boxing her in, watching as her eyes follow the beads of water gliding down my chest. "Hmm... so what you're saying is you want me to do homework with you. Sounds like a favor of sorts."

She grins. "Okay, I'll bite. What do you want in exchange, Bear?"

"Come to Key West."

"No."

I laugh. "You're so exhausting. Just come with me. I want to bang you in at least four places on Duval Street."

"So romantic."

"It's your kind of romantic and you know it."

"Touché."

"So you'll come?" I ask, hopeful.

Shawna leans forward, her bright green eyes playful behind her black frames. "Nah."

I drop my forehead to hers. "You're impossible, woman." She just giggles, but the sound is cut short when I press my hips forward, meeting hers. She wraps her legs around my waist, pulling me closer. She's in a simple, strapless black dress, and with only my towel and her panties separating us, it suddenly feels a lot hotter in the bathroom.

"Well, if your persuasion tactics weren't so awful, maybe I wouldn't be so impossible." She bites her lip, rolling her hips just enough to stir up the friction between us.

"You're saying I'm not bringing enough to the table?" I ask, sucking her bottom lip between my teeth and reaching my hands into her jet black hair. When I reach the purple ends, I grip harder, tugging with just enough force to expose her neck to me. She gasps, arching her back.

"That's exactly what I'm saying," she breathes.

My hands still in her hair, I kiss across the swell of her breasts. "Well, let me sweeten the deal, then."

In one fluid motion, I drop my towel to the floor, push her panties to the side, and slide inside her, pulling her hair harder as she cries out. She's so wet, so ready, and I pull out before rocking back into her again, slowly this time, letting her feel every inch.

"Oh fuck," she breathes, letting her legs fall open wider as she takes me in. My hands snake up her thighs, bunching her dress just above her hips as I flex mine again. I grow harder with each thrust, hitting her deeper every time, and she rewards me with nails digging just as deep in my back.

I work her slow at first, watching her mouth hang slightly open, her eyes focused on where we meet. It's so hot that she loves to watch, and when she lifts her legs to rest on my shoulders, I find a new depth that makes us both moan. I know she loves when I work her clit, but this time I want her orgasm to come from the spot only I can reach inside.

Grabbing her ass in my hands, I lift her, just slightly, just enough to push deeper. Her head falls back, hair sticking to her back, and I take advantage of the access to her breasts. Using my teeth, I pull the top of her dress down and say a silent prayer that she's not wearing a bra. Sucking her nipple ring between my teeth, I pump harder, the steam circling around us, our breaths shallow.

Suddenly, Shawna bucks against me, pressing her hands into my chest until I stumble back a bit. She hops off the counter, spins around, and bends at the waist, pressing her chest to the cool counter, hooded eyes finding mine in the mirror. I take my cue, stroking myself as my free hand finds her center. Slipping two fingers inside, she moans, and the sound jolts straight through me as I place myself at her entrance. When I rock into her, my hands gripping her waist, she gasps.

I start slow again, savoring the feel of her warmth around me, but before long she's demanding harder, faster, more — and I deliver on all accounts. She comes first, her breath clouding the mirror, her eyes wide open and staring at me. It's the sexiest fucking thing I've ever seen to watch her fall apart so unabashedly. I follow right after, cursing under my breath at the electric release only she can bring.

For a moment I stay inside her, resting my chest against her back, my arms around her, our breaths leveling out. When I finally pull out, Shawna stands, shimmying her dress down and adjusting the top in the mirror.

Moving her hair off her neck, I press my lips to her salty skin. "So, Key West?"

She grins. "Valiant effort, but it's still a no." She spins in my arms, kissing me once before smacking my ass playfully. "Now get dressed and take me to this art festival."

I laugh, because what else is there to do? Shawna is unlike any other girl I've ever known, and even though she drives me mad, I wouldn't have her any other way.

Well, let me rephrase that: I wouldn't have her any other way *characteristically*.

There are countless ways I'd *have* her. Take her. Own her.

And we're just getting started.

Skyler

IT'S EIGHT O'CLOCK ON Friday morning, and I have yet to sleep. The downtown casino has had back to back tournaments, and I'm raking up enough to pay off the rest of spring semester and hopefully to pay my entry fee for a larger tournament this summer. I'm on the leaderboard right now, but an opponent delivered a nice little blow to my mental stability this morning in the form of a printed out blog article.

Skyler Thorne: Poker's Hottest New Player

At first, it sounded flattering — and, some of it is — but most of it details my physical features, complete with a center photo of me in the small red bikini I was wearing on the beach with Jess and Cassie. Of the entire article, only one tiny paragraph mentions my skills at the table.

Entering the code for the Omega Chi house into the keypad, I let myself through the front door and make my way back to Clinton's bedroom.

"I brought bagels," I say, louder than I expected, as I kick his door closed behind me. "Coffee, too."

Clinton peeks at me through his heavy eyelids before reaching for his phone, noting the time. When he sees the look on my face, I sigh, setting the bag of bagels and coffee on his bedside table and retrieving the article from my pocket. I unfold it and drop it on his chest.

Squinting, he reads the headline, but his eyes widen at the slew of photos. I don't even think he reads more than the first paragraph. Sighing, he crumples it, tosses it across his room, and scoots over, lifting the covers. "Come here."

I crawl in, snuggling close to him as he tucks the covers around us. "They're such assholes."

"I know," he says, his voice groggy as he kisses my forehead. "Did you talk to President Whittington about the paparazzi on campus yet?"

"Yeah, but so far everything they've taken of me has been off campus, technically. He assured me that if they tried anything on school grounds, he would step in and take legal action against them. But off campus, I need to watch out for myself."

"I swear, if it ever happens when I'm around I'll pummel their asses."

I smile, resting my head on his chest. "Tell me about your life so I can stop thinking about mine for a while."

Clinton blows out a breath, his fingers lazily tracing circles on my shoulder. "Well, I've been steadily banging someone since my birthday."

"The random-birthday-kiss girl?"

"Indeed."

I nod. "Huh. That's kind of a big deal for you."

"Tell me about it." He reaches over me for the coffee I brought him. It's probably a good thing I don't drink coffee, otherwise I'd be even more wired than I am already. "She's cool, though. Different."

"Is she coming to Key West?"

He frowns. "No. I tried to convince her, but she's not having it."

I sigh. "Is it awful of me to feel like maybe I made a mistake inviting Adam?"

"Uh oh. Trouble in paradise?"

My stomach aches and I curl my legs into my body. "No, we're amazing — perfect, even. He's so sweet, funny, charming. We always have a great time when we're together."

"But?"

"But... I just feel like we maybe jumped into the whole boyfriend and girlfriend thing too fast. I never expected it to become as serious as it has. And I feel like Adam is really starting to feel things — real things. But he needs to be focusing on becoming president. Alpha Sigma needs him as president. And me, I feel like I'm on the precipice of something with my poker career — like there's something big coming. And every time I'm at a tournament, I feel bad for not spending time with him."

Clinton is quiet for a moment, sipping his coffee, his arm still around me. "I don't know, Skyler. Maybe the timing just isn't right for you guys right now. I think Adam is a cool guy, but — if I'm being honest — I've always felt like you two were meant to just hook up and hang out. It became more serious than a lot of us expected. And not that that's a bad thing or means anything, but if you feel it, too... well, maybe there's some truth to it."

Sighing, I sit up in the bed, pulling my knees to my chest. "I don't want to make any decisions right now. I think the reporter stuff is just getting to my head. I need to think for a while."

"Fair enough."

"Have you heard from your mom?"

Clinton clears his throat. "No. But I did talk to Clayton. I'm flying him down for family weekend."

"That's awesome, Bear! I can't wait to meet him!"

Clinton rolls his eyes. "Oh God, he's going to *love* you. I'm sorry in advance for the inappropriate comments he's guaranteed to make. Kid just started going through puberty and can't help himself."

I laugh. "So, don't hate me, but I won't be at the Fratalina Wine Mixer tomorrow."

"What?!"

I cringe. "I know, I'm sorry. This tournament isn't over until Sunday."

"Damnit, Skyler. It's the fucking Fratalina Wine Mixer!" he screams, exaggerating the words like the guys in Step Brothers where the event idea originated from. It's one of the best parties during spring semester and I'm more bummed than I admit to miss it.

"I'll make up for it. Promise. I'm not doing anything poker related at all during Spring Break."

"Fine. I'm making you do a beer bong as soon as we get there."

Laughing, I extend my hand and he shakes it firmly. "Deal."

My smile stays intact as I stare at my best friend who I can always count on — no matter the situation. There aren't many people in this world I can be completely honest with. Tugging the covers with me, I bury myself in his chest and squeeze him tight. He abandons his coffee on the table and wraps both arms around me, pulling me in as close as he can.

"Bear hugs really are the best," I say with a sigh.

"Good thing you have them available whenever you need them."

"Always?"

He smiles, giving me a noogie as I squirm against his firm grip.

"Always."

Cassie

IT'S TIMES LIKE THESE when I wish my life had a soundtrack.

I totally need a bad ass rock chick ballad playing right now as I strut up to the Omega Chi Beta house, bottle of Maker's in hand, looking completely unlike the normal me but in the best way possible.

When I was younger, I used to love to play dress up — it's part of the reason I enjoyed theatre so much when I did it in high school. For a while, you get to step out of your skin and be anyone you want to be. Tonight, I'm a too-hot-to-touch vixen with a mission to prove everyone wrong.

And there's something incredibly powerful about letting yourself be everything you're not.

My black, strappy heels click on the sidewalk as I take my last step before pushing my way through the door, but then it's too loud to hear my steps anymore. The house is packed, music blaring, students crammed in every open space. Hoisting the bottle of whiskey over my head, I snake my way through the crowd searching for the girls. The weird thing is, people don't ignore me this time. In fact, it's almost like the sea is parting as I maneuver through the crowd. Those who know who I am are staring, mouth open, while those who don't assess me with a mixture of curiosity and desire.

I smile.

When I spot Ashlei and Bo dancing, I adjust my path and clear my throat just as I reach them, popping a hip and holding out the bottle. "Who's up for a shot?"

It's Ashlei who reacts first — jaw dropping, eyes bulging. "Oh. My God."

Bo is still somewhat dancing, but she halts when she realizes it's me. "Holy shit. *Roomie*?!"

I give a little twirl, letting their eyes run over my exposed skin. I wasn't naïve enough to think I could pull this off with anything in my own closet, so I let Jess dress me before she finally gave in and went to the doctor. Even with a red, runny nose — the girl has style. I watch as Bo takes in my carefully teased hair and dramatic makeup, complete with smoky eye, winged eyeliner and bright red lips. Ashlei focuses more on the outfit — painted on black jeans ripped from the knee to the upper thigh, black sweetheart crop top and my personal favorite touch — sick black leather jacket. Black on black on black.

"Holy fuck. I kind of want to lick you. Can I lick you?" Bo asks and Ashlei smacks her arm, almost as if she wishes she was the one Bo wanted to lick. *Weird.* "What?! Look at her!"

"I am. Jesus, Cassie. What's the occasion?"

Confidence is not a virtue I possess, but it's almost like it came along with the heels and makeup tonight. I know it'll be gone again in the morning, but I'm rocking it tonight.

Cocking a brow, I smile wider. "It's the fucking Fratalina Wine Mixer, am I right?!"

They both throw their fists in the air and cheer.

"Fuck yeah it is!"

"Not sure if your intention was to make little boys cry tonight but if it was, you're spot on." Ashlei shakes her head. "You're going to be fighting them off all night."

I smirk. "My only goal right now is to finish this handle. You two want to help me get started?"

"You know this is a wine mixer… meaning you're supposed to get sloshed on wine," Ashlei points out.

Shrugging, I twist the top off the bottle and tilt it to my lips with a wink. "Whiskey works faster."

Bo and Ashlei exchange looks as I take three hits from the bottle without flinching, even though the shit burns like hell. It's not that I never drink, it's just that I usually stick to a few beers. Tipsy is about as far as I've ever gone, but that all changes tonight.

Realizing Grayson isn't anywhere near them as I wipe the corners of my mouth, careful not to smear my lipstick, I frown. "Did Grayson not show?"

Ashlei chews her cheek, her fingers twisting in her long blonde hair. "Sorry, Cassie. We waited an extra twenty minutes before leaving the house but we didn't hear from him."

My heart sinks a little. I set Grayson up to get here with Ashlei so I could finish getting ready and surprise him, too, tonight. Before the disappointment can wash in too much, I take another shot and offer the bottle to the girls, but they both decline and hold up their red plastic cups filled with white wine.

"Wine pong?" I ask, nodding toward the tables set up outside. This jacket is just as hot as it makes me look, and luckily it's chilly outside tonight. It's probably the last cold night we'll have until after fall, so we might as well enjoy it.

The girls agree and we set up quickly, reeling in some random Omega Chi pledge to be my partner against Bo and Ashlei. I sink the first cup without even hitting the rim and that's when I feel the whiskey settle in, the warmth spreading from my stomach to my toes.

I can feel it, tonight's going to be a good night.

Math and science have always been my strengths in school, which means I should have seen this coming.

Half a bottle of whiskey plus countless plastic cups of wine equals a very drunk, very smiley Cassie McBee.

Still, my makeup is holding up and I'm keeping myself together, heels and all, like a champ. The random Omega Chi pledge is actually a freshman like me. His name is Todd and we've been running the pong table ever since we stepped up to it. When we win our eighth straight game in a row, I climb onto the table on my knees and swing my hair around to the music, thumbing the strings of an air guitar like I'm Jimi Hendrix as the crowd gathered around us cheers.

The moment his skin touches mine, I freeze.

I don't even have to turn around. I don't even have to look down at the hand hooked around the crease of my elbow. I think I felt him before he even touched me, and that's even scarier.

Slowly, I climb off the table, fixing my hair as I come face to face with deep, chocolate brown eyes — eyes that are absolutely on fire.

"What the hell are you doing?" Adam asks, scowling, his hand still on my arm. I shake it off and hang a hand on my hip.

"Running the table. Want downs on the next ass-kicking?" I try my best not to slur my words, but I'm eighty-seven percent sure I fail.

His frown deepens. "You're drunk."

"And youuu are a buzz kill," I say sweetly, booping his nose with my pointer finger before prancing off to my spot behind the table.

Adam follows, hooking my arm again and pulling me away from the crowd as I protest.

"Hey!"

"You need water."

"I'm fine," I argue, ripping my arm from his grasp once more. This time I stand firm, crossing my arms over my chest, trying hard to focus on his slightly-blurry face. "And, once again, I need to remind you that you're not my boyfriend. Or my father, for that matter."

Adam sighs, pinching the bridge of his nose. "I didn't realize I had to be either of those to care about you."

I scoff, rolling my eyes as he lifts his to stare at me with more questions than I care to answer right now. "Whatever. Is this not enough, Adam? Am I not ring girl material yet? Want me to strip off this jacket and hold it over my head like a *round three* sign?"

"What are you talking about?"

"Hey, there you are." Grayson slides up beside me, wrapping an arm around my waist and pulling me into him for a panty-melting kiss. My brain fuzzy from the alcohol, I let the kiss sink in, feeling it weakening every limb.

"You came," I whisper against his lips.

Grayson pulls back, smiling, his blue eyes hot on mine. "I came." Adam clears his throat and Grayson turns to shake his hand, but his other arm stays fixed around me. "Hey man, nice to see you again."

"Likewise," Adam says, but his eyes don't move from where they've pinned me. "Cassie, please, drink some water. Just a little and I'll leave you alone. You don't need to be stumbling around in this with all these horny pledges around." He gestures toward my outfit, pain etched in his forehead for reasons unbeknownst to me.

"I think she looks hot," Grayson says, grip tightening on my hip. "And I'm pretty sure I can handle any asshole who even thinks about touching her. And I do mean *any* asshole." With that last line he glares pointedly at Adam. Adam's jaw tenses and Grayson stands taller.

And now we're in a pissing contest.

"Grayson, can you grab me a cup of water from the kitchen? I'll meet you in there." I say the words softly, but it does nothing to pull his icy stare from Adam. Framing his face in my hands, I press my lips to his and make him look at me, instead. "I'm right behind you. Promise."

With that he relaxes, kissing me back with purpose before finally letting me go and making his way inside. When my eyes find Adam again, a sharp, tiny pang shoots through my chest. *Why is it so hard to breathe?*

"I'll grab a water, and then I need to get back to the table."

I make to turn, but Adam stops me, gripping both my arms in his rough hands. "Cassie, look at me." I don't. Tucking my hair behind my ear, I look down at my freshly manicured toes, instead. "Look. At. *Me*," he demands again, but the moment I do, I wish I wouldn't have. I've never had eyes look straight through me before. Adam takes a breath, one that takes mine with it, and then he says what we both know to be true.

"This isn't you."

Swallowing, I stand as straight as I can. "Don't act like you know who I am."

"Oh, but he does?" he gestures to where Grayson just disappeared in the crowd without taking his eyes off mine. "I call bullshit."

"Well, he doesn't confuse me."

"And I do?"

My ears fuzzy, I answer only the way an intoxicated, uninhibited girl can.

"No one confuses me more."

Adam's hands drop from my arms, and I watch as the number of questions in his eyes multiplies at my words.

"Goodnight, Adam."

With that, I spin on my heels and walk with shaky ankles into the house, wondering if it was the leather jacket or the alcohol that gave me the balls to say what I just did. Maybe it was both.

Or maybe I had just lost the resolve to hold it back any longer.

It's just after four in the morning by the time Grayson and I crash through the door of his dorm room, all tangled arms and heavy breaths. The alcohol still buzzing through me intensifies every touch, every kiss, and I try as hard as I can but I can't seem to take a full breath.

Grayson pulls me back to his room, pushing me against his door to close it behind us before dragging his tongue along the skin of my neck. I moan, tiny alarms sounding in my head to no avail — his touch is too loud for me to hear anything else.

Breaking from our kiss, Grayson leans his forehead against mine. "You are so sexy in that outfit," he breathes and my confidence disappears, a blush breaking on my cheeks. "But I bet you can't wait to change."

I laugh. "These pants are the worst."

Smirking, Grayson pushes off the door and yanks open the first drawer on his tall dresser, tossing me a pair of boxers and a t-shirt. Rolling the fabric in my hands, I chew my bottom lip, trying to decipher my next move. My hands trembling, I drop the clothes on the edge of his bed and slip out of my jacket, letting it fall to the floor where my eyes are fixed. Slowly, button by button, I undo my pants, finally finding the nerve to flick my eyes to Grayson. His blue pools are on my fingertips, nostrils flaring. When my hands find the hem of my crop top and I pull it up and over my head, my hair falling against my naked back, he pushes a long breath from his lips and squeezes his eyes shut.

"God, why do I have to be a gentleman?"

I pause, my voice just above a whisper. "What do you mean?"

Grayson opens his eyes just enough to grab the shirt and boxers on the bed and press them into my hands, covering my chest, though his hands hover there for a moment while he tries to steady his breathing. "Cassie, I want nothing more than to take you right now. Right here. In my bed, on this floor, in that shower..." he trails off, releasing his grip on the clothes to run a hand through his hair. "But you're drunk. I'm drunk. And I don't want my first time with you to be tainted with alcohol."

My first instinct is to be upset, but the way he's looking at me, blue eyes paincd, heart beating hard enough for me to hear it — I know it's as hard for him to say no as it is for me to hear it.

"My bathroom is right there," he says, gesturing to the door behind me. "Get changed and then come back in here so I can hold you."

My heart leaps and I smile, stepping up on my toes to kiss him quickly before escaping to the bathroom. I don't catch my breath as I change, so when I join him again, crawling into his sheets as he turns down the lights, I feel like I may explode if he doesn't touch me.

As if he can sense it, Grayson pulls me into him, my back against his chest, and a flash memory of being in Adam's bed assaults me in the darkness. Twisting in his arms to face him, I shake the thought, focusing on the man with his arms around me, instead. We lie with our eyes locked, his fingers lazily tracing the hem of his boxers on my hip bone.

"I think I might really like you, Grayson Anderson," I whisper in the darkness.

He swallows, taking his hand from my hip just long enough to run it back through my hair and pull me in for a kiss. "Likewise, Cassie McBee."

And just like that, another player is added to the game.

Bear

MY FIRST THOUGHT IS that it's hot as balls in my room.

Kicking the covers off, I blindly reach for my phone and squint through the sunlight filling my small room to peek at the time.

Two o'clock.

PM.

Mouth dry, I pull a pillow over my head to block out the light, groaning. When a small, warm body snuggles up next to me, my eyes fly open. Peeking under the pillow, I spot bright purple tendrils sprawled on my chest and I sigh, smiling, pulling Shawna in closer.

"Morning," she says, her voice hoarse.

I chuckle. "Morning."

"I stayed the night."

"You stayed the night."

She pauses for a moment, thinking, then plants a kiss on my chest. "I'm hungry."

I laugh just as my door swings open and Skyler bounds through.

"Scoot over," she says, crawling into bed on the other side of me before I have the chance to say otherwise. When she notices the other girl in the bed, she smiles, blue eyes bright. "Oh my God, you must be Shawna! I'm Skyler, Bear's Little. I've heard so much about you!"

"Same here, chica!"

"I brought bagels again," Skyler says, tossing the bag in my lap. I'm still trying to process the fact that I have two girls in my bed right now.

"You da real MVP," Shawna says, rummaging through it like a raccoon, hair a mess, mascara smeared from having my dick rammed down her throat last night.

Again, still processing here.

"How was the tournament?" I ask Skyler, propping my pillow up behind me.

"Long, but I won." She waggles her eyebrows and I throw her a high five. "More importantly, how was the fucking Fratalina Wine Mixer?! Tell me everything."

"Well, let's see." I rub my chin, the pieces of last night slowly coming together. "We had slap the bag tournaments. Ashlei and Bo actually won, believe it or not."

"Those girls can drink some wine."

"Indeed. And your Little showed up with that dude who bought her at the auction. She was dressed way differently than she usually is — all black, leather jacket, crazy makeup. Turned a lot of heads."

"*My* Little?"

"Yep."

"Cassie."

"Cassie."

Skyler chews on that for a moment. "Interesting."

"Yeah. Your boyfriend was here, too," I add, shifting a bit.

"Really? That's awesome. I was afraid he wouldn't come since I didn't."

"I think he enjoyed himself."

She smiles. "That's good."

What I don't tell her is that I didn't just see Adam. In fact, I had a pretty drunken heart-to-heart with him after seeing the scene between him and Cassie unfold. I don't know where the kid's head is at, but I know for fucking sure that I'm not going to sit back and watch him dick Skyler or Cassie around — and I told him that. He assured me he would never hurt either of them, but I could see it on his face — confusion. Adam Brooks is caught up in a game I'm not even sure he knows he's playing. By the time he left, I know I had his wheels spinning. I just hope he takes the time to think about what he wants right now.

"What about Ex?" Skyler asks as Shawna passes her the bagel bag, licking cream cheese spread off her fingers.

Focus, Bear.

"Yeah she was here for a while. She mostly hung around that dude from the auction."

"She's been weird lately. Distant. More controlling than normal."

I laugh. "Is that possible?"

Skyler shakes her head. "I wish I was joking."

The girls start talking about how Skyler got into poker and I take my opportunity to relieve myself. When I'm behind the bathroom door, I remember the interaction between Erin and me last night. She practically avoided me all night, which isn't anything out of the normal, really, but when we did end up in the same place and I tried talking to her, she teared up, running out of the room without so much as a word.

And she was worried about *me* after we hooked up.

There's a reason everyone calls her Ex.

I wash my hands and make my way back into my room, casually picking up the random trash from the night before. Skyler and Shawna are cuddled up, staring at something on Shawna's phone and laughing.

"Are you cleaning?" Shawna asks.

"Just picking up a little."

"Oh, can you put on a little apron?" Shawna sits up in bed, excited.

"Maybe use one of those little feather dusters?" Skyler adds.

"Yes! And talk with a French accent."

They high five and I just stand there gaping.

"Shit," I murmur, scrubbing my hands down my face. "I'm in real trouble with you two, aren't I?"

They both giggle and settle back into the sheets, their direction fixed on the phone again. I shake my head just as a loud knock sounds at the front door.

"No making out while I'm gone." I say pointedly, mostly to Skyler.

"No promises." She winks and Shawna holds up two fingers, lewdly waving her tongue between them.

Lord help me.

I can't quite shake that image from my head as I walk down the hall, but when I wade through the brothers sleeping on the floor and the trash spread everywhere and find Alec on the other side of the peep hole, my stomach drops.

Squinting at the sun as I open the door just a fraction, hoping to hide the mess inside from the one alumni who's managed to shut us down for half a semester, I force a smile.

"Hey, Alec. What brings you by?"

His jaw is set, mouth in a thin line, and it dawns on me that I probably don't want to know the answer to my own question.

"We need to talk."

Jess

I'M DYING.

Death by sinus infection.

Rest in peace. And mounds of tissues.

When I woke up yesterday morning with a stiff jaw and heavy head, I knew I couldn't push off going to the doctor any longer. If my voice wasn't an indication that there was way too much mucus happening in my head, my puffy cheeks definitely were. So, after I helped Cassie channel her inner Christina Aguilera circa 2002, I dragged my snotty ass down to the health clinic and faced my verdict.

Severe sinus infection.

And, because my luck is just the best, I made it to the campus pharmacy six minutes after they'd closed for a *mid-semester celebration*, whatever the fuck that means. So not only did I have to miss the Fratalina Wine Mixer because I felt like shit, but I also couldn't even get the meds started to make me feel better.

Perfect.

But, finally, here I am — in line to pay for my antibiotics and a can of condensed soup so I can start getting my life back on track. Spring Break is in a week, and I'll be damned if I'm going to be a snot head in a bikini come then.

"Jess?"

Shit.

Shit shit shit.

I don't even want to turn around, but at this point, I'm busted. Moving slowly as if I'm in the presence of a poisonous snake, I force a smile, cringing simultaneously at the thought of what I look like right now just as Jarrett's face comes into view.

Pissed is an understatement.

I wait for him to yell, scream, ask me why the hell I've been ignoring him — but instead, his eyes rake over my body, catching on the pharmacy bag clutched in my right hand.

"You're sick."

I chew my lip in response and he blows out a breath, closing his eyes for a short moment before springing into action. Snatching the soup from my hand, he walks it back to its place on the shelf with me trailing behind.

"What are you doing?"

"You don't need to eat that processed shit if you're sick."

"It's just a sinus infection."

Setting the can back on the shelf with more force than necessary, Jarrett takes a breath before turning to face me. "Don't argue with me right now, Jess."

I swallow.

"I'm sorry I've been avoiding you."

"Is this why?" he asks, his expression pained.

"Mostly, yes."

"Mostly?"

Ugh, this is the last thing I want to do right now. I was so close to soup and Netflix.

Jarrett runs a hand over his bald head before grabbing my hand. "Come on."

"Where are we going?" I ask, not really minding as long as I can have this view of Jarrett's tight ass in the basketball shorts he's wearing.

"We're paying for your script, going to a real grocery store, and then back to my place."

"Wait," I interrupt, tugging my hand out of his grip. "Jarrett, I'm sick. I don't want to..." I trail off. How do I say this lightly?

Hey Jarrett, can we lay off the fucking until I can breathe through my nose again? Kay thanks.

"We're not going to," he says as we reach the counter, taking my script from my hand and plopping it down in front of the cashier. She's a student, probably a senior, with dead eyes that light up just marginally when she sees Jarrett.

"I don't understand."

Jarrett pays for my script and then grabs my hand again, leading me out the door without another word.

I've been in Jarrett's apartment several times — hell, it's practically the only place we can hook up outside of his truck or my car or some random public place. I've slept over, we've made breakfast together — but no matter what, it always began or ended with fucking each other senseless.

So being wrapped in his goose down comforter on his couch, homemade soup in hand while he finds a movie on Netflix and pulls me close to him, I'm a little uncomfortable.

My appetite has been virtually nonexistent for weeks now, but when I take the first bite of Jarrett's homemade potato soup, I moan at the creamy deliciousness.

"This is amazing," I mumble around my next bite. "Thank you."

"It's my mom's recipe."

I pause, spoon halfway to my mouth. "Really?"

He nods. "She, uh," he pauses, sniffing. "She gave me the recipe before she passed."

The air in his apartment takes on a heavier weight and it's too much to even hold my spoon up. Letting it drop back into the soup, I reach out and gently touch his arm. "I didn't know. I'm so sorry."

Jarrett covers my hand with his own and squeezes. "It's all good, I was young. She had cancer. Classic kid-with-a-dead-parent sob story."

I frown. "Don't be like that."

"Sorry. I'm fine, really. Honestly, I came to peace with my mom's death a long time ago. What I can't understand in this moment is why you've been ignoring me." His dark eyes are hard on mine. "You said it's *mostly* because you're sick. What else?"

I take another bite, mainly to buy myself another minute to think. "Well, remember how you fucked me into admitting I was jealous over Spencer?" He nods. "I, uh, I saw you two together. At Pie Heaven."

Jarrett sighs, rubbing his face. "I told you she's just my boss' daughter. We surfed that morning and grabbed lunch after."

I shake my head. "Stop. You don't need to explain yourself to me. I know we're not together, and that's why I've been avoiding you, because I shouldn't feel jealous over who I see you with, Jarrett. Jealousy is dangerous. It leads to more intense feelings."

He watches me carefully, chewing the inside of his cheek. "Come here."

"Ew, I'm so gross right now."

Jarrett fights a smile. "Jess, come here."

I'm hesitant, but eventually comply, setting my bowl on the coffee table and maneuvering until we're both lying on the couch spooning. Jarrett wraps his arms around me, tight, pulling me into him and kissing my bare shoulder. "You are the most stubborn woman I have ever met."

I snicker, pulling the blanket up under my chin. "How long before I chase you away?"

He's quiet for a moment, his free hand running through my hair, lulling me into a sedative state. "You can't chase someone who's not running."

My heart accelerates at his words, but before I have the chance to call him out, he pushes play on the remote and we fall into a comfortable silence.

And that's how the rest of the afternoon and night go. We cuddle, watch movies, talk, eat when necessary, and eventually crawl into bed around midnight. Jarrett tends to my every need, making sure I'm comfortable, bringing me my medication with a fresh glass of water when the time comes and making sure I eat. When he flicks off his bedroom light and slides into the sheets next to me, pulling me until I'm resting on his chest, and kisses my forehead sweetly, I feel it all press in around me.

I thought I would feel the fall. I thought I would crash on the cold hard ground and look around wondering what the hell happened. But the truth is, I fell slowly, softly — like a feather floating down, down, down into an undiscovered world.

And now, I'm scared there isn't an option to go back to the person I was before.

EPISODE 4

Adam

"It's Spring Break, Bitches!"

IT'S ONE OF THOSE perfect South Florida nights.

Skyler's hand is in mine, the wind blowing through her hair as we cruise around campus. She rented a hot yellow Ford Mustang convertible for Spring Break but asked me to break it in with her tonight first, and with the moon bright in the sky and Skyler's short skirt, I should be ecstatic. I should be thinking of all the ways I'll have her tangled up in the backseat once we put this car in park.

Instead, I'm thinking of the right words to break up with her.

The thought brings on another surge of nausea and I shift in my seat, pulling my hand from Skyler's grasp to grip the steering wheel. She doesn't seem to notice, just pulls out her cell phone and clicks through a few messages while her right hand surfs the air waves out the window.

I watch her for a moment, taking a silent inventory of all the things I'll miss — her electric blue eyes, her almost-too plump bottom lip I love to bite, her contagious laugh and easy banter. The list is long — too long — but the list of reasons we should end things ran out of paper a long time ago.

The semester is flying by, spiraling me faster and faster toward elections. If I want the presidency, now is crunch time. I only have a little over a month to prove why I deserve the position and Clay seems hell-bent on finding anyone but me to move in. I've barely had time for Skyler this semester and it's only going to get worse. It's not fair to her, and to be honest — I know she feels the same when it comes to her tournaments. Whether she's ready to admit it or not, she's not a small-time poker player anymore. People know her, she has a strong reputation forming and more and more tournaments piling up, which means less and less time for me.

The fact of the matter is that we're both young and we both have more we want to accomplish before we can give ourselves to anyone else.

The timing isn't right.

I've tried to ignore it, but Clinton all but handed my ass to me at the Fratalina Wine Mixer, telling me I needed to make a decision that was best for the both of us. He's right, I just hate admitting it. Add in the hot mess of confusion that is my relationship with Cassie and it all points to Disasterville. Still, I can't help feeling like I'm about to do something I'll regret later.

Sighing, I roll the volume knob between my finger and thumb until the car is silent but for the light wind. Skyler turns to me, smiling, and I run a hand through my hair.

"Sky, we need to talk."

"Well that's not ominous or anything," she jokes, kicking off her sandals and propping her feet up on the dash. "Let me guess — you want to break up?" She giggles, sticking her pink tongue between her teeth in a teasing manner. When I just grip the steering wheel tighter in response, my eyes fixed on the road ahead, Skyler's smile fades in my peripheral. "Holy shit. You do, don't you?"

"Honestly, not really."

"But?"

I cut the wheel right, steering us toward the small road that circles the campus lake as the realization of what's happening settles in my stomach. "But I think we both know the timing isn't right."

Skyler wets her lips, turning to the windshield. "We've both been avoiding this moment, haven't we?"

"I'm still kind of wishing I'd stuck with that plan."

She sighs, wrapping her arms around her thighs and resting her chin on her knees. "Do you have some big speech planned?"

I shake my head. "I'll skip the stuff you probably already know because you've been thinking it, too — like how I'm in line to be president and you're blowing up on the poker scene — and tell you what I think you probably don't already know." Pulling the car into a parking spot in front of the lake dock, I cut the engine, reveling in the silence as I turn to face her. "I like you. A lot, Skyler. More than I've liked any other girl since I've been at PSU. And if I was a selfish asshole, I would stay with you as long as I could and let the pressure and the bad timing slowly tear us apart. I'd make you feel like shit for blowing me off on Valentine's Day for a tournament and I'd make you sound needy for being upset that I skipped out on the auction for a fraternity meeting. I'd hold onto you and what we could potentially be even though I know it'd hurt us both in the long run." I lean down in her line of vision, lifting her chin so that my eyes catch her blue irises. "But the truth is that I care about you too much as a person to become your enemy when I know I could be your friend."

Skyler smiles, her hand folding over where mine is on her face as she leans into the touch. "I really like you, too." Laughing a little, she shakes her head, pulling my hand into hers. "I almost broke up with you the night of the auction."

"Really?"

She nods. "Yeah. Everything you've said is right and I saw it then just as clearly as we both see it now. Things are only going to get busier for both of us, and as much as we have fun together, I think we're at the point where if we don't stop the train now, we could land at a much more serious station than we ever intended on reaching."

I can't help but feel a small sense of relief. Skyler isn't the kind of girl to lose her shit, but I had no idea how she would react to any of this. Knowing that she feels the same way about everything stings just as much as it soothes.

"I still want to be friends. And not in the cliché, asshole way. In the legit way."

"Me too. And you're coming to Spring Break. Don't think you can get out of the trip just by breaking my heart."

"Breaking your — "

She laughs, cutting off my mild panic attack. "Kidding! I'm kidding, Adam." Her smile is wide, genuine. "But seriously, you're coming."

"Don't you think it'll be weird?"

"Not if you don't make it that way," she sasses, still grinning. "Besides, the cars and hotels and activities are already booked. It's two days away. You're coming."

"Well, not yet, but we could change that," I throw back, waggling my eyebrows. Skyler smacks me across the chest and rolls her eyes, but then she pauses, her stare leveling, a fire lighting. She bites her lower lip just slightly.

"Actually, I really wasn't kidding about breaking this bad boy in."

"We have, haven't we? I can drive around a while longer," I say, starting the car and checking the time on the dash. Skyler just keeps her eyes on me, wicked smile in place. When the intention behind her words sinks in, I shake my head at my slowness. "Wow. Can we pretend like I didn't just miss that cue and you still want to bang?"

"Ex sex is the best sex, right?"

"That's what they say."

Skyler raises the volume on the stereo as loud as it can go before leaning over the console, her lips finding mine for what may be the last time as a strong electronic dance beat courses through the small space of the car.

"Let's prove them right."

Erin

"COME ON, JUST ONE hit," Landon coaxes me, waving the joint in front of my face, eyes low. His goofy grin is on full display, Ken doll hair styled, teeth almost too white against his tan skin.

Giggling, I push his arm away and twist the top off my water bottle. "Not tonight. I still need to pack and I don't want to forget something because I'm high," I lie. The truth is that I packed this morning. I've never smoked before and I certainly don't plan on trying it now. When you're high, you don't have full control of yourself — and I'm not letting that happen again.

"It's Spring Break, Ex!" He takes another pull before passing to his brother on the other couch. The Mu Beta Chi house isn't the top party house on campus, since that title is firmly held by Omega Chi Beta, but it is a strong contender. The Mu boys are known for their involvement in student government mostly, though they do throw pretty solid ragers. "At least have a beer. Or a fruity cocktail. I'll even make you a vodka water so you don't break the diet."

"I think the Chinese food we ate earlier kind of ruined that already," I point out, pulling my legs up on the cushion to sit Indian style and dodging the drink offer. Again, alcohol equals stupid decisions. I've learned my lesson.

In probably the most excruciating way.

"You can't say you didn't thoroughly enjoy teaching me how to use chopsticks."

"You were pretty adorable."

"Almost as adorable as you in that sundress," he says sweetly, kissing my cheek.

Landon has been nothing but a gentleman since our first date. He took me to coffee first, but not in the morning. Instead, he picked me up at nearly midnight, driving us to a swanky coffee shop downtown that stays open until 2:00 a.m. with live acoustic music. We spent the night talking, and for the first time since I made the most horrific choice of my life, I smiled. And laughed. And had a good time.

Since then, we've been to the beach together, studied in Greek library, and he even went shopping with me to pick out my Spring Break swimsuits — not that he found that a particularly boring date. He's picked up the bill at every event, and though I haven't let him move even a hair past first base, he seems content with what we have. He reminds me a lot of the men my mom read about in her historical romances. He takes his time, he's patient.

Still, I'm not naïve enough to think Landon is anything but a numbing device, a distraction, a flimsy umbrella fighting against the storm inside me. When I'm by myself, the storm rages so hard I feel every gust of wind all the way to my core. But Landon is almost always available, and he's the storm shelter - at least for now.

The Mu house is buzzing, filled with brothers and sorority girls kicking off the first night of Spring Break. Landon pulls my legs into his lap and absentmindedly rubs my calves as he and his brothers chat over the music. Tomorrow, most of us will go our separate ways, including Landon and me. I'll be headed to Key West with the Omega Chis while he jets north to Panama City Beach with his brothers and the Zetas.

The realization that I'll be spending a week in close proximity to Clinton is one I've been trying to grasp unsuccessfully. I can't for the life of me figure out why he makes me feel so out of control. I keep trying to convince myself my head is just messed up from what happened, because what else could it be? It's not like I *like* him. I mean, this is *Clinton* we're talking about. I mean sure, I invited him to semi-formal with me, but only because his fraternity was on lockdown. I was being nice. And yeah, his sex appeal was comparable to Chris Hemsworth with his Thor hammer that night and we had a good time, but we were drunk — wild — and things just happened. Neither of us wanted them to. It's all just some sort of twisted fluke.

Still, every time I see him, my body does weird things — things it hasn't done in what feels like forever — and I can't get a grip.

The alarm on my phone sounds and I silence it quickly, pulling my feet from Landon's grasp and standing. "That's my cue. Time to finish packing and help my sisters decide on bathing suits."

"Tough job," Landon mocks, pushing to his feet. He grabs my hand in his and walks me out the front door, pulling me into his hard body as soon as the fresh night air hits our skin. "Are you sure you don't want to stay a while longer? Kick Spring Break off the right way..." He trails off, his lips just barely brushing the skin of my neck.

Uncomfortable, I shrug away from him and pretend to be teasing. "You'll have plenty of girls on the beach more than willing to take you up on that offer."

"I'd rather wait for you," he whispers, tucking a strand of hair behind my ear. His smile is so kind, glass-like eyes sincere, and for some reason I believe him when he says he'd wait. Part of me feels awful for even letting him think he has a chance, because I know in my heart I'm nowhere near ready to sleep with another man — I may never be.

Some girls my age see accidental pregnancy as a curse, a mistake, a run of "bad luck". I see it as a privilege, one that I threw away so carelessly for selfish reasons. If I can ever find it in me to forgive myself, I'd still have to push past my fear of landing in the same situation again.

Nope, control is my only option.

"Goodnight, Landon," I say softly, lifting up on my toes to kiss his slightly-chapped lips.

"Want me to walk you?"

"I'll be okay. I like the time to think." I smile through one of the only true sentences I've uttered all night.

"Have fun, but not too much," he adds, winking.

"You too." With one last wave, I adjust my purse strap on my shoulder and start down Greek row toward the Kappa Kappa Beta house.

It only takes a few steps for the loneliness to sink in. The front door opens and closes behind me, letting the laughter and cheers escape for just a short moment before the silence of campus on Spring Break blankets me completely.

I listen to my sandals clack against my heel with each step, trying my best to keep the dark thoughts at bay, but like monsters they creep in through the night and settle in around me. In the past weeks, I've trained myself to choose numbness over feeling, having yet to shed a single tear or scream or sigh over what happened. It's in the past, I tell myself, and the only thing to do now is move on.

The Kappa Kappa Beta house is alive with laughter and music as I make my way up the hardwood stairs to my room. All the doors are propped open, sisters bouncing from room to room with bathing suits and bottles of alcohol in hand. Mom Cindy doesn't even bother checking on us tonight because she knows she'd have to suspend the whole chapter if she did.

Ashlei is in Bo and Cassie's room when I get to ours and I take what's likely to be the only alone time I get in the next week and slip into our bathroom, shutting the door behind me. My palms braced on the pearl white sink, I close my eyes and inhale deeply through my nose, steeling myself for the challenges coming my way. Splashing water on my face, I dab my eyes and cheeks dry with a fluffy yellow hand towel and catch my dark eyes in the mirror.

For the next week, I'll have to be around the father of a child I never gave birth to.

A sharp pang rolls through my stomach and I double over, my palms finding the sink again as I grit my teeth through the ache. I'm so disappointed with myself, so disgusted. It seems utterly impossible to move on from who I am in this moment.

I'm hoping Spring Break will help me get past this, but inside my heart I know the chance is slim. The truth is, there are some challenges we face in our lives that completely change us. We step into a moment in time as one person and emerge in new skin, with a new, slightly-battered heart that doesn't beat the same. I'm still getting used to my new self, and the only way I know how to deal is to exert power over everything I can. I'm unsteady, trying to find balance at the edge of a cliff I've never been on before.

I just hope I don't fall in the process.

Cassie

JESS AND SKYLER ARE still shoving the last bags in the trunk of Skyler's bright yellow convertible rental as Grayson's thumbs run the hem of my tank top. Jess takes four steps backward before running full speed at the car and jumping on the bags, which only makes her fall flat to the ground and the rest of us die laughing. Her blonde hair is splayed out on the pavement as she curses. When one of my make-up bags tumbles out and hits her square in the gut, Skyler doubles over, laughing so hard she can't breathe.

Turning in Grayson's arms, I thread my fingers together behind his neck and squint against the sun's rays into his bright blue eyes. "Are you sure you don't want to come? Save me from my sisters?"

He chuckles, sweeping my red locks to the side long enough to kiss my forehead. The heat from the sun mixed with the warmth of his touch is just enough to make a film of sweat gather on my forehead. "You're going to have an amazing time."

"I would have a better time if you were coming, too."

"I know, Cass, I know," he says with a sigh. Running a rough hand over his beard, he glares at the space behind me. "I wish I could. You know I have to work," he explains again, his hand gripping the back of his neck. "I don't really fit in with this crowd, anyway."

"What?" I ask, shaking my head slightly at his assumption. "Everyone loves you."

"Not everyone."

I pause as his eyes harden right along with his jaw. Following his line of sight, I find Adam, and his eyes flick down to the ground as soon as I do.

"He's just protective over me," I say with a shake of my head, turning and forcing Grayson's gaze to me again. "We're friends."

"That's not what he thinks."

I scoff. "Trust me — Adam is *well* aware that we are friends." *He put the title there first*, I want to say, but I don't.

"If you honestly think that, then your pretty green eyes are more closed than I thought."

My mouth snaps shut, my mind suddenly racing with what he sees that I don't. The last thing I want is for Grayson to feel like he needs to compete with Adam. This semester was supposed to be about leaving all that drama in last semester — Adam, Clay, all of it.

So, I'll prove to him that I mean what I say.

"Is he looking at us?"

Grayson looks up and nods. "Of course he is."

Smiling, I slide my hands up into his hair and pull him down to me, pressing my lips to his, pushing my hips forward. He stiffens slightly, but when I moan softly and slide my tongue inside his mouth, he breathes a sigh of relief and tightens his grip on my waist.

When I finally pull back, panting just slightly, I smile. "Good. Now he knows I'm yours."

Grayson grins, breathless, his forehead to mine just as Skyler calls out after me.

"Come on, Little! Key West awaits!"

Jess does some sort of banshee call and Erin, Ashlei, and Bo join in from where they've already piled into one of the huge buses the Omega Chis rented out. I giggle, kissing Grayson once more.

"I think the time has come."

Grayson watches as Skyler slides behind the wheel of the Mustang and Jess finds her place in the passenger seat, leaving my only option right next to Adam in the small backseat.

"Ugh, I hate this," he breathes, his hands gripping at my shirt as he pulls me as close as he can. "But I trust you."

"It's less than a week."

"Barely."

I smile, pulling him in for a long, heated kiss before finally backing away. Grayson holds my hand until it pops out of his grip and I turn, jogging toward the car and hopping into the backseat. When I'm settled next to Adam, I blow a kiss back to Grayson and he catches it, tucking that hand into his pocket and using his free hand to push his shades back down. I watch him, still mesmerized by the tattoos on his arms as they flex beneath the hot Florida sun.

"I think you found a winner there, Little," Skyler says, eying me in the rearview mirror.

"Me too," I agree, and I know it's true. Grayson came when I least expected him, when I had sworn off boys completely, and every day with him since then has been amazing.

As we pull out of the Kappa Kappa Beta driveway, a string of cars, vans, and buses, horns blaring, voices cheering, I keep my eyes fixed on Grayson until we turn the corner out of campus and he fades from view. Flipping back around in my seat with a sigh and a smile, I type out a text to him on my phone, telling him once more how much I'll miss him.

"It's Spring Break, bitches!" Jess screams, blasting the music at the highest volume. Skyler lets her head fall back with a loud battle cry and Adam laughs, nudging me. When I don't move, partly from the unwanted shock of his skin on mine, he grabs my wrist and throws my hand into the air, waving it around with his own. My eyes are still trained on him, his dark eyes hidden behind black Ray Bans, hair disheveled and blowing in the wind, white t-shirt hot against his blazing tan arms. He joins in with the screaming, moving my arm more frantically, and I can't help it, I burst out laughing and thrust my other arm into the air with a yell, which makes all of them hoot louder.

It's Spring Break.

It's my *first* Spring Break.

And something tells me the KKB girls are about to take me on the ride of my life.

It;s only about a five hour drive from Palm South University to Key West. The first little bit is highway, but then it turns into the two-lane US 1 that runs all the way down the Keys. Skyler and Jess traded spots with Adam and me in Key Largo and passed out soon after, the long night of packing finally getting the best of them. This was after copious amounts of Backstreet Boys, Spice Girls, and Britney Spears, of course. Still, sleep caught up with them in the end.

I, on the other hand, am wide awake — mesmerized by the bright blue and sea green water surrounding both sides of the highway as we drive. Adam is drumming his right thumb on the steering wheel while the left rests comfortably on the door, a wide grin on his face.

I've been to the beach plenty of times since my move to Florida for school, but this is the first time I've seen water this clear — this beautiful. It never gets old. Every clearing of trees exposes a new patch of bright water that I can't keep my eyes off or capture with my camera phone.

"So, how awkward is this? Be honest." Adam rolls the dial between his fingers until the music is only playing softly. I turn to the backseat, expecting it to be Skyler or Jess he's speaking to, but they're both passed out — Jess's head on Skyler's shoulder while Skyler leans hers back against the seat. Both of them have sunglasses on and headphones in, their music now louder than the tune coming from the Mustang speakers.

Is he really asking me to rate the awkwardness of being in the same car with him after what happened at the Fratalina Wine Mixer?

What's the correct number for somewhere between *conversation with old, distant relatives* and *waving back at someone who wasn't really waving at you in the first place*?

"What do you mean?" I ask, facing Adam again.

He shifts to hold the steering wheel with his left hand and drops the right to the console between us. "I don't know. I mean, she begged me to still come — swore it wouldn't be weird — and I guess I'm the only one making it that way. It's just like the closer we get to Key West, the more I wish I would have fought her on it."

Blinking, I push my sunglasses up into my windblown hair. "What are you talking about?"

"Me and Skyler?"

"What about you and Skyler?"

"She didn't tell you?"

My frustration climbs and I huff. "Tell me what?!"

Adam laughs a little, shaking his head. "Sorry, I just figured she would have by now." His smile fades. "We broke up the other night."

I try not to let the words slam into me. I try to run from them, brace for them, take them as a small wave — but they crash into me all at once. "Oh."

He runs his right hand through his hair, his shaded eyes still on the road ahead. "Yeah."

"I'm sorry."

"Don't be. We both agreed it was best."

I don't know why I have no idea what to say. There are millions of words out there, yet all I can do is face the windshield again and mutter the same one. "Oh."

Adam chews his cheek, silent for a moment. I almost reach for the radio dial when he speaks again. "Listen, I'm sorry about the party. I shouldn't have tried to tell you what to do. I learned my lesson on that last semester at semi-formal," he adds with a chuckle, and I blink at the thought of him warning me about Clay that night. I didn't listen to him then, and he ended up being right. "I don't know, I just saw how drunk you were and I've never seen you like that before. I was worried. And I know you're with Grayson and he can take care of you. I was out of line." He turns to me for just a moment and I scan his face, looking for a hint of jealousy, a molecule of dishonesty. I don't find either. "I was. I admit it. And I'm sorry."

"It's okay," I breathe, just barely over the music. I watch as he finally takes a breath.

"Can we just start over?"

I laugh. "You're so cliché."

"I'm serious." His hand finds mine and he gives it a firm squeeze — a friendly squeeze — but for some reason my heart still stammers. "I really do care about you, Cassie. I just want to be there for you, however you need me to be. And I'm sorry I ever... I'm sorry I confuse you." His tongue jets out to wet his lips just as one of the Omega Chi vans speeds around us. I let my eyes follow it just so I have somewhere — anywhere — to look other than at Adam. I almost forgot I admitted to Adam that he confuses me. *Stupid alcohol.* "I never intended to. For what it's worth."

"Gah," Jess yelps as she wakes, startling us all. "I need to piss and then we need to crack some roadies."

"Oh my God, J-Love," Skyler smacks her. "You scared the shit out of me!"

Adam drops my hand and I pull it into my lap, the skin still hot from his.

We pull into a gas station a few minutes later and as the girls climb out of the car and head inside, I stop Adam, holding him back.

"I agree."

"You agree?"

I nod, though I'm not entirely sure what I'm doing. "Let's start over."

He smiles, one of those dazzling smiles that makes it hard to breathe. "I think it's time for our first shot of Spring Break." Jumping out, Adam pops open the trunk and digs around before retrieving a small bottle of Jack. "If I remember right, you like whiskey." He winks and my cheeks heat, memories of the Fratalina Wine Mixer hitting me.

Adam rips open one of the packs of red plastic cups and pours us each a shot.

"What are we toasting to?"

He fixes his gaze on the console between us, tasting the words he's about to speak before lifting his eyes to mine. "To a second chance — for a boy who didn't deserve the first one." He offers a weak, half-smile. "And to the girl sweet enough to give it to him."

Our plastic cups click together as his eyes pin me, purpose in their gaze, and we lift the liquid to our lips. It burns on the way down, and I can't help but think it isn't the only thing.

"We come bearing snacks!" Skyler yells as she and Jess fly through the small gas station's doors, multiple white plastic bags swinging from their arms. We all pile back into the car as they pass around chips, candy, and drinks. Skyler and Jess both pop open Bud Lights but I pass, the whiskey is still settling in my stomach as Adam pulls back onto US 1.

He called me sweet.

But I think *stupid* might be the more accurate term.

"OH FUCK YES, I see a pool!" Jess yells as we all pile through the door of the suites we booked, bags over our shoulders and sweat already gathering on the backs of our necks. She scoots past me and jogs up the stairs to where the two bedrooms are, no doubt taking claim to whichever room has the largest bed. I just smile, dropping my bags to the floor and immediately hooking up my iPhone speaker. Turning on my Avicii radio station, I pump up the volume and finally take in the surroundings.

Cassie and Adam are slowly making their way up the stairs where Jess is and I take the opportunity to check out the kitchen. It's full service — dishes and cooking utensils stocked — with a bar area and a dining room table set. The living room connects and everything is decorated just like a Key West suite should be — bright coral couches, light aqua-blue rugs and accents, beachy paintings hung on the wall, bamboo and light wood finishes. There's a sliding glass door that leads out to a back patio area, complete with a small hot tub that I'm sure will be occupied at the end of the night.

Slinging my bags back over my shoulders, I make my way upstairs and toss them into the room where Jess has set up camp.

"So, what's the sitch?" I ask, wiping the sheen from my forehead. Jess is spread out on the king size, pillow-top bed with a huge grin on her face. The bedrooms seem to embody the same beachy-vibe from downstairs, paintings and all. There's a huge mirror just above the master bedroom bed and I stare at my reflection. "Side note — I totally want to watch someone bang me in that mirror."

"Well, obviously you and I are in here. So I mean if you want to swing that way for a night, I'm totally down." She smirks and I cross my arms, rolling my eyes. "It's a king, so we can fit one more."

"Dibs!" Erin yells behind me and I jump. The Omega Chi bus must have arrived.

I chuckle. "Okay, well that's figured out."

"I'm calling the other room, then," Cassie says, propping herself against the doorframe and thumbing over her shoulder. Everyone's eyes fall to Adam standing behind her then.

"Uh, I can sleep on the couch." He rubs the back of his neck and offers a shy grin. I hate it, because I know he feels awkward, and as much as I swore it wouldn't be — I think everyone feels like it's a little weird that he's here.

"Actually, can we take the couch?" Ashlei asks, rounding the corner from the stairs, her wind-blown hair tossed into a messy bun. Bo is just behind her. "It folds out, so it would make sense that two people sleep there. And we don't mind."

"There we go. All settled. Adam, you can just crash in the other room with my Little." I smile, clapping my hands together as Adam and Cassie exchange glances. I know they go to breakfast sometimes and they seem to get along, so it shouldn't be too strange for them to sleep together. Definitely better her than me. "And now — we drink!"

Everyone cheers and we funnel down the stairs and into the kitchen, retrieving alcohol, cups, ice, and everything else we grabbed at the grocery store on our way to check in.

"Wait! I made us something," Erin says, heaving one of her bags onto the dining room table. It's a glass top, and whatever is inside her bag settles with a clink. When she unzips it and pulls out the first Bubba Keg, bedazzled with jewels and her name, I can't help but smile. My Big is one of the most thoughtful people I know, and any chance she has to make her sisters feel special, she takes.

"These ought to keep our drinks cold on the beach," she says, passing them around. Bubba Kegs are essentially giant mugs that keep cold beverages chilled and hot beverages warmed. For our purposes, they'll play home to our mixed drinks under the Key West sun. Each one is decorated with personal flair, including poker chips and dollar signs for me and glittery curse words for Jess. They're huge — holding about seventy-two ounces — and they're thermos-style with a silver middle and different colored tops and bottoms. Perfect for beach day drinking.

"Well shit, I made something, too. Hang on." Jess runs up the stairs while the rest of us fill our cups with our liquor of choice. When she rounds the corner again, she starts hurling neon balls of cloth at our heads. Cassie tries but fails to snatch hers out of the air, so it wraps around her face and falls to the floor as we all laugh. "Suit up, bitches!"

I catch the one she throws at me and unfold it, my eyes scanning the bold black letters on the neon yellow tank top.

OUTRAGEOUS? ALWAYS.
OUT RAGE US? NEVER.

"Fucking right," Ashlei says. "We're wearing these tonight. All of us."

"Wait! Can't forget these," Bo adds, passing around the custom trucker-style snapbacks to match. They're all black with bright neon letters that read **KKB**.

"Hold on a second, did you two coordinate these?" I ask, adjusting the back of my hat and throwing it on backward.

Bo nods, smiling at Jess. "It was a Big/Little bonding sesh."

"The idea was hers," Jess adds, tossing her tank top over her shoulder. "Clearly. We all know I'm not that thoughtful."

Everyone laughs and once Jess and Bo finish filling up their cups, we cheers them together.

"Time to fuck Key West up, ladies." Jess turns to Adam. "And gentleman."

Chuckling, Adam shoves his free hand into his pocket and shakes his head. "I'm a little scared for my life."

"As you should be," I add with a wink. "Let's do this!" We clink our glasses together and throw back the first drink of Spring Break, dance music filling the room around us, our skin already sun kissed from the drive down.

And then, it begins.

I've been to Key West before, but less than an hour on Duval Street and I already never want to leave. This place is *alive*. Every bar is packed, students from campuses all over the nation spilling out onto the streets, drinks in hand. The music is loud, the personalities colorful, the feeling — wild. These are the future business men and women, parents, doctors, lawyers, dropouts, travelers, teachers — but tonight, we're just young.

We started our night at Fat Tuesday, filling our Bubba Kegs with frozen deliciousness and an extra shot to kick off the night right. We managed to run into Clinton and some of his brothers there and now we're all cramming our way into the Coyote Ugly bar. Jess and Erin are hand in hand, arms swinging, voices carrying the tune of a popular country song as they head straight for the bathrooms. Breaking the seal, already.

"We're heading to Irish Kevin's right after this," Clinton says, pointing his finger in my face as he slides by. "Car bombs, baby!" We high-five as he continues down the bar with his brothers, nearly all of them dressed in the same white frat tank. **Omega Chi Wasted** is in bold letters like a dictionary entry, complete with the definition: *intoxication level – attempted by many, reached only by the elite.*

"You know what I love about these hats?" my Little asks me as we slide up to the bar. "They hide the effects of drinking in Florida." She lifts the snapback, revealing her crazy, slightly damp red hair underneath it. I laugh and tip mine up, showing the same hot mess beneath.

"And they're perfect for selfies," I add, pulling my phone from my pocket. I slide the camera icon up and flip the lens, my cheek touching Cassie's as I push the shutter button.

"Love it!"

"We need one with the whole group," I say, looking around for someone I could flirt into taking the photo for us.

"I can take that for you," a southern voice twangs from behind me. When I turn, ready to hand my phone to a stranger, I stop mid-pass. Key West is crawling with attractive men right now, especially fraternity brothers, but this one just might take the cake. His dark blonde hair is hidden beneath an orange University of Tennessee hat, his teal-green eyes bright even in the dark bar. The first thing I notice is how his smile is almost too big for his face, but in the most charming way. His jaw is wide-set, his face clean-shaven, his body thin but toned. I don't even care that he's watching as my eyes scan him from head to toe and back up again.

"Go Vols," I say, cocking a brow and finally handing him my phone. Then, I turn back to the bar and shout out, "Get together, everyone!"

We're all a little past drunk at this point, so it takes a minute to get everyone paying attention and lined up in a way that doesn't hide any faces. Hot Tennessee Guy takes several pictures, of which I'm sure only one is social media appropriate, before we all disperse and he slides the phone back into my hand.

"I'm Trevor," he says, holding the phone between our hands for a moment.

"Trevor from Tenneesee."

He nods, blushing slightly. I can't stop staring at his All-American features.

"Skyler, from Florida."

Trevor releases my hand and crosses his arms over his chest, his glorious arm muscles on full display. "You're a little far from home, huh?"

I chuckle. "A whole five hours."

"Well, I guess I'm lucky you decided to stay in your home state for Spring Break."

"Who said you're getting lucky?" I ask, crossing my arms to mirror him.

He shrugs. "The universe. When I happened to walk through that door over there as soon as you started scanning the room for trouble."

"I see. So, Trevor, the trouble from Tennessee, what now?"

"Now," he says, voice thick with a southern accent as he takes his place at the bar next to me. "I buy you a shot."

A smile finds my lips just as Ashlei hops up on the bar behind Trevor. I shout out her name, beating my fists on the bar, and everyone else joins in once they realize what's happening. The coyote girls are inviting other girls up on the bar to join them for a dance, but when *Pour Some Sugar On Me* starts playing and Ashlei whips out moves that put every single other girl to shame, all of our jaws drop. She's owning the hairography, dropping down to her knees on the bar and crawling across it, even going as far as kissing Bo for show. The guys, of course, go absolutely ape shit at that. When she bites her bottom lip, swollen from her kiss with Bo, and turns around to twerk, the entire bar erupts in a frenzy. All I can do is shake my head — that girl is full of surprises.

"Looks like you found the sexiest girls in Key West," a guy says to Trevor with a similar accent, clapping him on the back. I assume it's one of his brothers, especially as more of them filter in around us.

"You read my mind," Trevor agrees, holding out a liquid cocaine shot to me. I take it between my fingers with a wink before turning back to my sisters.

"Hey KKB! This handsome man just bought me a shot!"

All of my sisters in the bar cry out before starting a low, rumbling "Ohhh" that stretches out into the beginning of one of our chants.

Take a shot, take a shot, take a goddamn shot!
If you can't take a shot like a KKB can,

Then you shouldn't have a fucking shot in your hand!
Take a shot, take a shot, take a goddamn shot!

Everyone cheers and Trevor and I knock back the Jager and Bicardi 151 concoction. When we slam the glasses back on the bar, I use my thumb to wipe my bottom lip, my eyes finding his brothers all gaping behind him.

"Buckle up, boys."

I FUCKING LOVE SPRING Break.

As I guzzle down my second Flabongo in nothing but a cheeky, hot pink pair of bikini bottoms and black strapless top, I remember what all the dieting and gym time was for. In a way, I guess it's kind of a blessing that I've been sick the past couple of weeks. I feel completely back to my old self now, though, and I clear my bong well before the Omega Chi pledge opposite me. He's still struggling, holding the plastic Flamingo upside down trying to guzzle the beer inside it through the opening at the mouth while I'm passing mine off to the next contender. When his brothers start shoving him, teasing, I just wink and wipe my mouth with the back of my hand.

"Nice try, champ."

He grins, his dark eyes scanning me slowly. They remind me a little of Jarrett's, except this kid can't be much older than nineteen and therefore his eyes are missing that bit of confidence — the assurance of a good time. He's scrawny, cute, but just not Jarrett.

The sun is hot on my shoulders, no cloud cover to shield the rays, and I wiggle my toes in the hot sand as I make my way through the tents set up on Smathers Beach. There are students from all over the nation here for Spring Break and each tent has a university, fraternity, or sorority flag flying high. My eyes drift from the chaos to the bright blue, almost aqua water and I sigh, wishing more than before that Jarrett was here.

If this were any other Spring Break, I would have at least made out with five guys by now. There are so many eyes on me, so many easy targets, and yet I don't feel compelled to aim my dart at a single one. I almost want to take a frat daddy back to our suite just to prove to myself that I can, but then I think about Jarrett, and the truth comes to light — I can't.

Not now that I've had him.

"Hey sexy," Skyler says, words slurring slightly as she smacks my ass. Her all black sunglasses reflect my messy bun and the bright water backdrop behind me. I smile, eying her brand new, bright coral and rhinestoned bikini. She's catching a tan quickly, which makes it seem even more electric against her skin. "Tell me this isn't the best Spring Break ever."

"It's pretty epic so far," I agree, though I know something that would make it better. Or rather, some*one*.

"I'm hungry."

"Let's get some street meat," I say, hooking my arm in hers and steering us toward the hot dog stand set up on the other side of the boardwalk.

Skyler scrunches her nose, leaning her weight on me. "That sounds dangerous."

"There's only like a forty percent chance you'll get food poisoning."

"Well when you put it like that... YOLO!"

My eyes scan the beach where our crew set up camp, stopping abruptly when I find Ashlei and Bo cuddled up on a blanket together. They're sitting shoulder to shoulder, legs tangled, laughing. Ashlei occasionally plays with Bo's short hair and Bo lazily runs her fingers along Ashlei's freshly tan leg.

"I can't fucking hold this in anymore," I say suddenly, pulling Skyler to a halt just before the sand meets boardwalk. My hand flies up in the direction of Ashlei and Bo. "Sky. They're fucking. Look at them."

Skyler's eyes follow my hand and she blanches. "Cassie and Adam?"

I frown, noticing Adam and Cassie leaned over Adam's phone on the other side of the girls. Adam's hand is resting casually on Cassie's lower back and her cheeks are flushed, probably more from the heat and her day drinking buzz than him touching her. From what I can tell, it looks like they're laughing at a cat video or something else equally uneventful. Cassie is about as prude as they come and Adam is still up Skyler's ass as far as I'm concerned, no matter how he tries to deny it.

"Oh please," I say, rolling my eyes and grabbing Skyler's jaw in my hands. I squish her cheeks together and steer her eyesight toward Ashlei and Bo, who are now leaning so close I'm almost positive they're going to kiss. "Those two."

"Ashlei? And your Little?" Skyler's brows shoot up. "No... you think? I mean they hang out a lot, but wouldn't we know if they were... well... you know?"

"Skyler. *Look* at them."

She does, even taking the effort to lift her sunglasses over her wavy brown locks for a minute. She has drunk eyes to the max – slightly smeared mascara, glassy surface – but I know she still sees it.

"Shit," she murmurs, flicking her sunglasses back down.

"Yeah."

I grab her by the elbow and drag her toward the hot dog stand. "I saw them kiss at semi-formal."

"What?!"

I nod. "I didn't tell anyone because I thought it was a fluke – a drunken kiss or something. I mean, shit, you and I have shared a few of those."

"True. I saw Ashlei kiss her on the bar last night, but I thought it was just for show."

"Maybe. But I've been seeing them together all the time, always touching, always sneaking off," I add just as we reach the food stand. Skyler crosses her arms and eyes the menu. "I don't care. I mean seriously, I don't. But why won't they just fucking tell us?"

"I don't think it's that easy, J-Love," she says before leaning into the window of the food cart. "I'll just take a hot dog and French fries, please." She glances back at me. "Want anything?"

I shake my head.

"Anything to drink?" The man inside asks. He's short, balding, light blue t-shirt covered with grease. Every inch of his exposed skin is tan and leathery, but I guess you can't live in Key West and *not* be tan.

Skyler chuckles. "I think we've got the drinks covered."

The man eyes the rowdy scene behind us and nods, taking Skyler's wet cash. "Ain't that some true shit."

He ducks back inside and I chew my lip, still not wanting to let the subject go. "Look, Bo is my Little. She knows I'll understand. And Lei is one of my best friends! It just doesn't make sense."

"Do you know one other girl in our sorority who's a lesbian?"

I scoff. "I can think of at least three."

"*Openly*," Skyler adds, rolling her eyes. "Think about it. It's not something you see often in Greek life, especially not at Palm South. Maybe they're just taking their time. Or maybe they want to see if it's serious before they say anything." She shrugs just as too-tan man hands her a small cardboard box with her food. "Or, maybe, there's nothing to tell. They could just be friends, Jess."

"I highly doubt that," I grumble, snatching one of her French fries and popping it in my mouth.

She chuckles. "Just chill. If they are together, they'll tell us – when *they're* ready."

I'm still not satisfied, but I let out a long breath, conceding for the moment. "Fine."

Skyler looks proud. "Great. Now that we've got that out of the way..." she trails off, her tiny hand cupping the rather large hot dog out of her box. "Wanna suck my wiener?"

"I'd rather bite it."

"Oh, feisty!" Skyler waves the encased meat in my face. "Okay, fine. I'll let you eat my wiener."

"I bet you'd rather I eat something else, you cheeky bitch."

"Hey, don't post an offer you can't come through with." Skyler winks just as our feet reach sand again and someone chokes behind us. When we turn, two guys with pasty-white skin and University of Kansas tank tops on are staring wide-eyed right back at us.

Stealing Skyler's hot dog, I carefully take nearly half of it in my mouth and bite slowly, letting my eyes flutter back. "Mmmm... so tasty," I mumble around the mouthful.

The guys swallow, eyes shifting from me to each other before they scurry off.

Skyler bursts out laughing. "Oh my God, they're going to have nightmares."

"Or wet dreams," I combat, sucking ketchup off my index finger.

"You're such a bitch. I really am hungry," she pouts, inspecting what's left of her street meat.

"We can sixty-nine if you want?"

She shoves me just as we reach our spot on the beach and I fall easily into my lounge chair, still laughing and stealing another French fry on my way down.

"I love you," I coo, blowing drunken kissy faces at her.

Skyler eyes me, fighting back a smile. It's moments like these when I realize that maybe it doesn't matter who's hiding what. It's not about my future with or without Jarrett, my tests next week, or the career path I should probably be shaping. Sometimes it's just about living in the moment with your sisters. It's about being young, and silly, and wild and carefree.

With a content sigh, I lean back in my chair and let the sun rays soak in, lifting my freshly filled Bubba Keg cup to my lips and tasting the fruity cocktail inside.

It's good to be a KKB.

Bear

"CAR BOMBS!" MATT, THE President of Omega Chi, yells as we burst through the open doors of Irish Kevin's. Skyler and her sisters weave past us and make their way to the front of the stage where a small band is set up. They're doing covers of popular songs and taking requests in the form of cold hard cash, and Skyler is the first to pull out a twenty.

She waves it in the air and calls out, *"Sweet Caroline!"* The bar cheers and the tall, lanky guy behind the mic starts flirting with her as she drops it in the jar. When he takes note of all her sisters filing in around her, I just shake my head.

He has no idea what he's in for.

"I can't believe so many of us are still hanging in after day drinking at Smathers all day," I say to Matt as we slide up to the bar. The bartender is already pouring up our car bombs.

"Shit, you know how it is when Omega Chi and KKB get together."

"Fucking insanity?"

He waggles his eyebrows, handing me a car bomb and tipping his toward me. "Damn straight."

Matt's sporting a sunburn along with the rest of us, though his shows as lobster red and mine as dark choco-late. The tightness of my skin only reminds me what a kick ass day it was as we drop the shot of Bailey's into our mugs of Guinness and chug. Slamming them back down on the bar, Matt throws me a high five and wades through the crowd to where Skyler is. Poor guy, he's been trying since we got here to move in on her since she's not with Adam anymore. The thing is, I don't think she plans on giving Matt another round in her bed — especially not with literally thousands of other choices on Duval Street.

I whip out my phone to check for texts from Shawna, frowning when the screen is blank. We were writing back and forth all day today, but she stopped responding a few hours ago, making me realize just how much I wish I would have dragged her ass with me. Trying not to dwell on it, I tuck my phone back in my pocket and lean against the bar. When I notice Erin a few barstools down, eyes low as she watches the rest of her sisters in front of the stage, I pay the bartender for two beers and slide down next to her.

"You should go join them," I shout over the band singing *Wagon Wheel.* Erin's eyes flick to mine, her brows pinching together before she turns away again. Her make-up is flawless, her dark blonde hair pin straight beneath the snapback she and her sisters are all wearing. On the outside she seems put together and fine, but all it took was that one second of looking into her eyes for me to know she's not. I already feel like walking over to her was a mistake.

"I'm just hanging back for now," she says softly, forcing a smile. "How are you, Bear?"

"Fan-flipping-tastic. Here," I say, thrusting the beer I've yet to drink from toward her. "Special delivery."

She eyes the glass in my hand, readjusting to lean her opposite elbow back on the bar. It's then that I notice she's shaking slightly. I internally groan, cursing myself for thinking she would be able to keep it cool after our hook up last semester. I still don't even know how that shit happened, but Erin clearly can't let it go. It's like she thinks I'm going to jump on stage, steal the mic from the band and shout out to everyone that we fucked like porn stars in the KKB house.

"Thanks, but I'm not really… I don't want to drink." Her honey eyes find mine as she tucks a strand of hair behind her ear. "I tend to lose control when I do."

Pursing my lips together, I fight the urge to roll my eyes and shrug, instead. The girl is fucking ridiculous. "Whatever you say, peach. More for me." I tip back the glass I was holding out for her and drain it, popping it back onto the bar next to her.

"Bear!" Skyler bounds toward us, an infectious grin on her face. "I have a surprise for you." She drags out the last word, her buzz clearly still in effect.

"I feel like I should run."

She laughs, grabbing me by the wrist and dragging me through the bar back to Duval Street. "Trust me. You're going to *love* this surprise."

I follow her, my eyes on the neon KKB letters on the back of her hat as she steers us through the crowd. When she finally tugs me out into the warm night air, she drops my wrist and plants her hands on her hips, victorious smile still intact.

"Why are you grinning like you shit in my bed?"

Skyler just wrinkles her nose, but then her eyes jet to the space behind me. I barely have time to turn around before I'm tackled. I hold the offender tight as their legs wrap around me, and that's all it takes for me to realize who it is.

I'd know those legs anywhere.

"Surprise!" Skyler yells behind me as I grip Shawna tighter, inhaling the floral scent of her black and purple locks. She squeezes me tight in return until I drop her gently to her feet.

"What the hell are you doing here?"

She shrugs, tucking her hands into the pockets of her tiny ripped jean shorts. "I got tired of texting you, so

I called Skyler and she told me where you're staying and helped me set this up. Hope you don't mind me crashing your bed."

She winks and I pull her under my arm, kissing her temple before whispering in her ear. "As long as you don't plan on getting any sleep, I think we'll be fine."

Shawna shivers under my touch and I grin against the skin of her neck.

"Uh, okay, looks like my job here is done. Have fun, you two!" Skyler quickly hugs Shawna and steps up on her toes long enough to kiss my cheek before skipping back inside, her beachy waves swinging behind her.

"Should we head in?" Shawna asks, thumb pointed toward the bar.

"I have a better idea."

Shawna is still blushing as we wander the empty streets of Key West, dawn just within reach. She's not exactly one who blushes lightly, but I kind of like the way the rosiness sets on her cheeks. I'm not sure if she's blushing from the heat we built up dancing or the fact that we just stripped down to our Birthday Suits and partied with a bunch of old naked men and women in the Garden of Eden.

Either way, I like that I put that blush there.

"I cannot believe we just did that," she breathes, still giggling. "I will never get helicockter guy out of my head."

"Hey! That's the best part about having a dick," I defend, swinging my hips to mimic the motion of the skinny sixty-year old biker from the bar. The Garden of Eden is a rooftop bar above a country bar on Duval Street and it's clothing optional. There are no phones or cameras allowed, but it still took three shots to get either one of us comfortable enough to take our clothes off. We were the hottest people there, and as soon as we lost our underwear, all the attention was on us. I expected Shawna to be shy or embarrassed, but she danced with me and flaunted her shit in front of everyone like she was the most confident woman on earth.

I'm starting to think she might actually be.

Shawna rolls her eyes and shoves me but I bounce back, pulling her under my arm. She sighs, content in my grasp. The night air has cooled down significantly, blanketing our hot skin in a relieving reprieve.

"What a wild place."

I nod, taking in the brightly colored houses on either side of the street. We're not really walking anywhere, just strolling, and we're the only ones left, it seems. Occasionally, a cab will blow buy, rowdy Spring Breakers hanging out the windows, but for the most part it's just us. "It's amazing." I kiss her temple, smiling down at her bright green eyes. "Even better now that you're here."

She's quiet for a moment, and we fall into a rhythm, her sandals and my Jordan's thumping the pavement with each step.

"You know, when we first started hooking up, I thought that's all you'd be to me," Shawna says, wrapping her arm around my waist and hooking her finger into my belt loop. "It made sense. You were hot, we had amazing sex, and it was fun." She shrugs. "But I didn't expect you to be a great listener. Or a protective friend. Or an amazing big brother. It's like everything I never thought I'd feel with you actually came easily — effortlessly, without even thinking about it." She smiles softly, biting her lower lip as her eyes stay fixed on her feet. "Somewhere along the way, I think I started falling for you."

My throat constricts at her words, the darkness of night just before dawn surrounding me. I swallow, wondering why I'm not laughing, or shaking my head, or planning my escape route. I never wanted anything serious with Shawna, and even now, it feels like a bad idea. But the truth is, I think I'm falling for her, too.

I halt, pulling Shawna into my arms. She wraps hers around my neck, eyes fierce as she stares up at me, not the least bit ashamed of what she just admitted out loud.

"Me too," I say simply.

She smiles, the black frames of her glasses lifting on her cheeks. "I really want you to nail me on the beach."

I choke out a laugh, snaking my hand up to brush one of her purple locks aside. "Hmm... I could possibly be persuaded to oblige."

Shawna's eyes sparkle as she lifts up on her toes, pressing her lips to mine. I pull her into me, hands gripping her shirt at the hem, slipping my tongue inside her mouth only to be rewarded with a moan.

We're all hands and lips as we stumble our way onto a private beach of a hotel, breaking contact just long enough to jump a fence or strip off clothing before collapsing into a beach cabana bed. The soft blue hue of morning battles with the dark night just as I sink inside her, her nails dragging down my sunburned back. I hiss at the sensation and she takes my mouth with hers. When she flips us over, her hips straddling mine, I watch with fascination as bright pinks and oranges light the sky behind her arching back.

By the time the sun breaks its kiss with the horizon, we're completely spent, skin slick, legs tangled. And for a while it's just the sound of our breathing and the waves on the shore that exist in the world. Shawna falls asleep on my chest and I let her rest for a while, knowing I'll have to wake her soon before we're caught. A strange emotion washes over me, one I've never felt but don't feel compelled to fight.

With my fingers in her hair and my heart on my sleeve, I let myself fall a little further.

Ashlei

I THOUGHT DOING COCAINE would be the highest high I would ever feel.

I still remember the first time, the night we won first place in four categories at the South Florida Pole Dance Event. Hayden pulled me into the bathroom, we got high, and then we had the best sex I'd had up until that point. I thought that was it. In my head, it couldn't get better than that feeling right there — the ultimate high.

But right now, stuffing the last bit of cash I needed into my small Vera Bradley backpack and handing off the final bag of Molly, a new kind of high sets in. It's the kind that can only be obtained when the optimum feeling passes over you.

Freedom.

The girl who bought the last bag from me is young, maybe a sophomore, from a small private college in New York. She's dressed in cut off, high-waisted jeans and a frayed top with a flower headband wrapped around her huge, bouncy blonde curls. She looks like she's ready for a music festival, and with her new possession courtesy of me, she might as well be.

"Thanks," she says sweetly, tucking the baggy in her pocket and skipping off to rejoin her friends standing outside of Sloppy Joe's. I pull my backpack over my shoulders again and tighten the straps, hiking it up to my upper back. Most of the money I've made this week is stashed back at our suite, but today's portion — the final portion — is finally resting right in the center of my back. Funny, it's the lightest my shoulders have felt in months.

It's only the third night of Spring Break.

I thought it would take so much longer.

Bo slides up beside me, her pinky hooking around one of my belt loops. Even though it's hot and humid tonight, her fingers are icy as they graze my skin. "Who was that?"

It's such a simple question, but her words chase away my momentary high of freedom. Because the truth is, I don't know who that girl is. I don't know if she's a druggie or if this is her first time. I don't know her apart from any of the other kids I've sold coke or Molly or marijuana to over the past few days. I knew going into this that I'd have to disconnect my personal feelings. I can't think about them and save myself, too. I had to make a choice.

I chose me.

Still, what if someone gets hurt because of me? Would I even know? Hundreds of kids get too stupid on Spring Break and hurt themselves. But until now, I never had to make peace with the fact that I could, potentially, be the one responsible for that.

But they would probably find a way to get the drugs with or without me, right? It's not like I'm the only one with a stash. And it's their choice to take the drug, not mine.

Sighing, a bit defeated, I realize it doesn't matter how I put it — I still did a shitty thing. But when I glance over at Bo's wide eyes sparkling in the bright lights of Duval Street, knowing she's safe from Xavier, knowing I'm free from his grip on my life, I don't feel sad. I don't feel guilty.

I feel relieved.

"No one. She just asked to borrow a hair tie," I reply. Sliding my hand up Bo's arm, I hook my fingers around the nape of her neck and pull her into me, pressing my lips hard on hers in the middle of the sea of Spring Breakers. For a moment, it feels like everything around us is muted — the harsh lights, the shrieks from tipsy girls, the bar chants from rowdy boys. Bo freezes, fighting the urge to moan, her hands gripping my waist before pushing me away.

"What are you doing?" she hisses, her eyes searching the busy street. "Someone could see us."

I grin, knowing she's right but not really caring at the moment. "Let's go fucking crazy tonight. I mean like let's take it to an entirely new level."

Bo's eyes light up and I feel my energy transfer to her. We're tied together like that — if she's low, I feel low. If I'm high, she feels high. We feed off each other.

"What do you have in mind, Ashlei Daniels?"

Grabbing her hand in mine and tugging her toward The Lazy Gecko, the excitement I felt building all day burns faster, consuming me inch by inch.

"Let's start with shots and go from there."

Bo giggles, bouncing with me. "Deal!"

A few hours later, Bo and I are closing our tabs at the fifth bar of the night. It's late, or should I say early, but Key West doesn't shut down until the patrons let it. Every bar stays open as long as they feel like it, and with the bass still thumping hard and bodies still pressed together on the dance floor behind us, I know they'll be here a while.

Bo is signing her check when I spot him.

I'm not the kind of person who finds attraction to a person slowly. I know from the first time I meet them whether I'll be into them or not. With Bo, the connection was instant, even if I didn't voice it out loud. And right now, staring at a tall, dark-haired, dark-eyed guy just down the bar, I feel it — that instant assault of flutters in my stomach.

"Bo, what if I told you I wanted to do something *really* crazy tonight?"

She eyes me, letting her pen drop to the bar. "What do you mean?"

I swallow, unsure of what her reaction will be when I pose my next question. But the adrenaline is coursing through my veins right along with the alcohol, my freedom from the hell that's been binding me for months making me feel more alive than ever. Taking her hands in mine, I kiss her knuckles and level my eyes with hers. "Have a threesome with me."

"What?" she balks, her mouth hanging open. "Ashlei, I don't... I just want you."

I swallow, nodding. "I know, and you know I want you, too. I love you," I say the words before thinking better of them, but I don't take them back. It's true. I do love her.

She closes her mouth, her brows pulling inward as her hands squeeze mine. "You do?"

I nod. "I do, Bo. You pulled me out of a darkness I didn't think I would ever survive. And now that I'm here, in a better place than I've been in months, with you — I want to celebrate by doing something wild. But only if it's with you. I want this with *you*." She frowns, but I pull her closer. "Please."

Bo studies me, chewing her slim bottom lip. "Have you ever done it before?"

I shake my head, and that seems to reassure her. "I just... I feel so alive right now, Bo. I feel spontaneous. It's Spring Break, I'm here with you, I'm free from all the shit that's been holding me back," I trail off, not wanting to get into details since Bo isn't aware of what I had to do to achieve said freedom. Tucking a strand of blonde hair behind my ear, I ask again. "Please. Let's experience this together."

For a moment longer, she keeps her bottom lip pinned between her teeth. But then, slowly, she nods, and when I smile, she does, too.

"Come with me."

I wrap my arms around her waist and walk her with me, straight up to Mystery Man, whose eyes are just as fiercely attached to mine as mine are his.

"Hi," I say softly, not even attempting to hide how my eyes are devouring every inch of him.

The corner of his lips tilts up in response, and he takes it as permission to do the same. "Hello, ladies," he replies, his gaze finding Bo next.

Bo swallows, flushing before she asks me, "Is he the one you want?"

I nod and she takes a deep breath, giving me a small smile that lets me know to make my next move. Excitement burns through me, its source at my core as I turn back to the guy.

"What's your name?"

"Alex," he answers smoothly.

"Alex..." I try it on, tasting it as my eyes skate over his muscular forearms. "Take us back to your place."

Bo's hand shakes in mine and I squeeze it gently, trying to soothe her nerves as the cab drops us at the large gate of a private home.

"I thought you said you were here with your fraternity brothers?" I ask, referencing Alex's conversation in the car ride over. It turns out, he's an Omega Chi. I have no fucking idea how I've never seen him before now.

He unlocks the large wooden door and gestures for us to walk in first. "I am."

I shoulder off my Vera Bradley bag and toss it into a small chair near the front door as Alex shuts it behind us, my eyes on the lavish surroundings and my hand still latched onto Bo's.

"A little high-end for a house full of fraternity brothers, don't you think?" I ask, glancing back at him. He runs a hand through his dark hair and grins, his eyes heavy from the alcohol. "It's my uncle's place. He rents it out most of the year, so when I found out this is where we were going for Spring Break, he blocked it out so I could have it."

"Wait, so you guys get to stay here for free?" Bo asks, now letting her own eyes wander the no-doubt expensive paintings lining the walls. Alex nods and I trail my fingers along the smooth, polished wood surface of the long dining room table before my eyes catch on something shiny in the next room.

"Oh my God, your uncle must be a bachelor." Dropping Bo's hand, I cross quickly into the other room, empty save for a few air mattresses blown up along the far wall and one, lone pole in the middle. One wall is made up completely of floor-to-ceiling mirrors and I note my wild blonde hair and dark, mascara smeared eyes.

Alex chuckles. "Yeah, I guess you could say that." He slides up next to Bo and watches me carefully as my hands find the pole. When the cool metal hits my palms, I exhale long and slow, a rush of emotions hitting me — fear, excitement, longing. I've missed being on the pole, and I'm just drunk enough to not let the dark thoughts creep in as I grip it hard and swing my legs, hoisting myself up into an easy spin and high kick hold. I drop back down to the ground gently, balancing on the balls of my feet as I circle the pole, one hand still attached, my eyes finding Bo's.

Suddenly, she doesn't seem so nervous.

She seems mesmerized.

Alex's eyes are on fire, one arm crossed over his chest while the opposite hand covers his mouth. They're both watching me, enamored, and the power of their stares sinks deep in my center.

There's no music in the room, but there's always been music in my heart, and I let the passion I feel move me. Climbing my way back up the pole, I start with a few more beginner moves, spinning and holding flexes before dropping back down to the floor each time, circling, arching my back, sinking low to the floor only to climb back up the pole again. I'm not sure how long I dance before Bo crosses the room to me, her chest rising and falling with heavy breaths as I press my back to the pole and wait for her. She steps closer and closer, dark eyes hard on mine. When she reaches the space in front of me, she bites her bottom lip.

"You are so fucking sexy."

I don't smile, I don't respond, I just slowly reach my hand out until I find her waist and then I pull her into me, pressing my lips to her neck and sucking her tender skin between my teeth, my back still flush against the cool surface of the pole. She hisses, letting her head fall back, and I kiss around the swell of her throat before finding her mouth. Her hands are in my hair, mine crawl her body as my tongue slides between her lips. When Alex steps into the space beside us, she stiffens, but I keep my touch calm and sure.

"It's okay," I whisper, my forehead to hers. She nods, concern still written in her features as I kiss her again. It's so strange seeing Bo this way, so nervous and unsure. She's the confident one in the bedroom — commanding, strong. As Alex's hand snakes its way into my hair and he pulls my mouth from Bo's to his own, I wonder if he'll be taking the captain's chair tonight.

My heart hammers beneath my ribcage as I taste him, new and exotic. Bo's lips trail down my neck to my cleavage as she palms the space between my thighs. Moaning into Alex's mouth at the touch, he pops the button on his jeans without breaking our kiss. I hear his zipper next, and then his shorts are on the floor. He kicks them away, just as Bo pulls me from him, her hand tugging at my tank top. I lift my arms and she rips it up and over, tossing it to the side before making quick work of my bra.

It's almost too much. We're all hands and mouths — stripping, kissing, touching, stripping more. Somewhere along the way we find the stairs, which lead up to a master bedroom Alex is clearly occupying. The four post bed is built with dark wood and lined with deep red accents that match the comforter Bo and I slide onto easily, feeling the cool fabric against our skin. Alex makes his way between us, propping himself up against the headboard and taking each of us by the waist as we kiss over him.

Bo's breaths are still shaky, her arms trembling as she holds herself steady on the bed. We're leaning over Alex, our tongues tangled, while he slowly strokes himself and watches. I massage her tongue with mine, each kiss an attempt to bring her energy back to mine. Just when I have her there, Alex's hand moves from my waist to behind my thigh. It hovers there for just a moment before I feel his fingers penetrate me, and from Bo's reaction, his other hand is doing the same to her.

"I don't know if I can do this," she whispers between our kisses. I pull back, panting at the feel of Alex's fingers inside me and how turned on I am by Bo's kisses.

"You don't have to do anything to him. Or vice versa. Just focus on me."

With that, I break contact from Alex and pull Bo with me, rolling over until I'm on my back and Bo's straddling me. I love the way the skin stretches across her petite hips as she rubs against me, building a friction that will drive her to the edge. Alex takes my cue, moving between my legs and spreading my thighs open to him as I maneuver Bo up my body. When her knees are on either side of my head, I slide my hands down her neck, her arms, until I lace my hands in hers. Placing them on the headboard above us, I curl her fingers, locking them in place.

"Hold on tight," I whisper, licking my lips. Bo's breaths are heavy, her eyes hooded as I grab her ass in my hands and invade the space between us, flicking my tongue out to stroke her clit. She moans, letting her head fall back as her knuckles whiten with her tightening grip.

Alex groans from somewhere behind Bo and then there's the sound of a condom package ripping. My view is blocked, my face completely owned by her, but I feel him. His hands — one on my hip, the other I can only assume palming himself as he places himself at my entrance. And then, with one, strong thrust, I'm filled.

I gasp against Bo, sucking her clit between my teeth to make her moan with me. My nails dig into the smooth skin of her thighs as she rocks her hips, her pelvis grinding against my mouth. Alex is so big, and it's been so long since I've felt a man between my legs that the sensation is overwhelming. Each time he pushes into me he reaches a new depth and I feel myself climbing, higher, higher.

My hands snake up Bo's frame to palm her breasts and she cries out as my fingers pinch her nipples. She's grinding harder now, and I know she's close. Wrapping my hands around her small waist, I flip her, her short hair blowing out in a whoosh against the sheets as it frames her face. Alex pulls out long enough for me to change positions, taking my place between Bo's legs, a grin on my face.

"Do you know how turned on I am by you?" I whisper against her neck before sinking my teeth into the flesh. "I have never wanted anyone more than I want you right now."

She moans, dragging her nails through my hair and pulling my mouth up to hers just as Alex sinks down over us. I'm sandwiched between them — Alex's hard chest and abs against my back, Bo's soft body below me. When Alex enters me from behind, I arch my back and Bo bucks her hips up to meet mine. One arm holding me steady, I glide the opposite hand down her navel, pausing at the small birth mark above her left hip before settling between her thighs. She's still shaking, but now I know it's because she's close. When I thrust two fingers inside her at once, moving them in time with Alex's pulses, her hands fly up to grip the headboard again.

"Oh God," she moans, sucking her lips between her teeth. She's fighting it. "Oh fuck!"

"Come," I demand, and she does, her wetness soaking my fingers as her moans echo off the walls. Alex moans, cursing under his breath. I'm so incredibly turned on, I can't imagine how he feels right now.

I lower myself for just a moment, kissing Bo softly, letting her ride the wave down. Her eyes flutter open to meet mine and she smiles. "You're amazing."

I just kiss her in response, but then Alex's hands grip my elbows, pulling them together behind me. He pins them at my middle back, forcing an arch in my back as he plows harder, deeper, his mouth on my neck. He's kissing, sucking, biting, and then he shares a look with Bo. They seem to agree on something not spoken aloud, because Bo leans up, taking my mouth with hers as her hand shoots between my legs. When she starts circling my clit, I break our kiss, crying out at the sensation. Her free hand grips my neck with just enough pressure to heighten my sensitivity.

Holy fuck.

Alex's hands are gripping me so hard, I know I'll be bruised in the morning, but I love it. Bo intensifies the pressure on my clit, biting my bottom lip, leaving my mouth open to scream as my orgasm shoots through me. Alex takes it as permission to come with me, and he flexes into me once, twice, deeper, three times, so fucking deep, his groans mixing with mine. It's the highest ecstasy I've ever known. Every touch is amplified, every movement too much yet never enough.

Bo's hands don't leave me until I collapse against her, Alex rolling off of us and sprawling out on the sheets beside us, his chest heaving. My head against Bo's chest, I watch him smile and shake his head before his dark eyes turn to us, flicking between the two.

"You girls are fucking wild."

Bo giggles, her fears shattered now that the experience is over. "I blame her."

Alex grins wider, baring his bright, beautiful teeth and I just shrug.

"I love Spring Break."

Cassie

AFTER ALL THE CRAZINESS of the first few days of Spring Break, it feels amazing to just lay on the top deck of a sail boat, sun rays hot on my skin, sea breeze blowing over me. We're all in a line — Bo, Ashlei, Jess, Skyler, Erin, and then me — our bright, matching beach towels beneath us. The few Omega Chi brothers who dragged their asses out of bed early enough to make our all-day excursion are on the bottom deck, getting boozy on the free drinks. For the girls, I think we're finally taking the time to soak in some silence.

It's already been a long day. I've applied sunscreen every hour on the hour just to be safe, and yet still I know I'll go back to our suite with a burn. It will eventually turn into a slight tan, but I never get as dark as the rest of the girls. Skyler always seems to catch the darkest tan, probably from paddleboarding all the time.

We started at eight this morning and we've already been snorkeling, parasailing and had lunch. Add that to the fact that I'm getting practically no sleep because I'm too self-aware of how close Adam and I are in our bed, and you could say I'm a little tired. Now, we're parked at a floating dock with plenty of activities at our disposal, but I'm not the only one who doesn't seem eager to jump on them. We're all catching our breath. Tonight, we'll be back on Duval Street, so for now, we're taking it easy.

Zack Brown Band croons from the speakers on the boat and I tap my toes to the beat, smiling as I recount all the memories we've already made this week. I was warned that my first Spring Break with Kappa Kappa Beta would be wild and crazy, but no one told me how amazing it would be, too. I've literally been having the time of my life, and we're only halfway through.

"Hey," a voice whisper-shouts right above me. My eyes fly open to a dark silhouette haloed by the sun. I shield my eyes with my hand and Adam's goofy grin comes into view, along with his abs and the hard V that leads right down to his dark red swim trunks. "Come ride the jet skis with me."

He looks like a little kid, grinning ear to ear, a small speck of sunscreen that hasn't been rubbed in resting on the bridge of his nose. His tan shoulders are starting to freckle, and a sheen of sweat has gathered across his pecs.

Scanning the rest of the girls, I realize he's talking to only me. Jess is snoring, mouth hanging open, while Bo and Ashlei lean together over a book. Skyler and Erin are both on their backs, eyes closed, and I assume since they're not stirring, they're probably sleeping, too.

I look back up at Adam, hand still over my eyes. "Yeah. Okay."

He smiles wider, holding out his hand to help me up. I take it, ignoring the dull buzz that always hums through me each time our skin touches. When I'm on my feet, Adam watches as I pull the straps of my light green top up and re-tie them at my neck.

"Um, they're parked over here. Come on." He leads the way down the stairs and over to the starboard side of the boat where ten wave runners are parked along the same dock as we are. We listen to one of the crew members go over safety and speed reminders before each climbing onto our own and pushing off the dock. We wade out a safe distance and then hit the gas, speeding off into the waves.

We ride side-by-side for a while, laughing as the waves spritz us with cool ocean water. Adam breaks off and goes wide left, jumping the wake of another boat and doing donuts. I just shake my head and speed off, pushing the jet ski as fast as it will go. The wind flies through my hair, my eyes shielded only by my sunglasses as I tear through the water. It's an amazing sound, an incredible rush, and I only slow down when I reach the distance the crew member warned was as far as we could go.

Releasing my thumb off the gas throttle, I let the engine hum and stare off into the distance, taking it all in. Adam rumbles up beside me and does the same and for a few moments, we just exist.

"My grandpa used to water ski," he says after a while. I turn, watching as he leans forward and crosses his arms on his handlebars, his eyes still off in the distance. "It was so amazing to watch. I was young, but I still remember it. He was one of those men who excelled at everything he did. It wasn't just on the water, either. He was like that in his job, as a friend, a parent, a grandparent. Everything."

I nod, smiling, getting the sense that maybe I'm just supposed to listen right now. Adam chuckles softly, as if he's recalling a memory as he leans back again.

"He raised me, you know?" he asks, turning to me with one eyebrow raised.

"Really?"

"Yeah. My mom and dad traveled a lot for work. They're both in sales for a technology company, so it's their job to schmooze the clients, keep them happy, and sell them on new products and services. They were gone at least ten months out of the year if you added it all up."

I blanch. "Wow. That's a lot, Adam."

A short laugh escapes his lips, the wind blowing his dark hair back. "I know. But I had my grandpa. I stayed with him most of the time or he would come sleep at our house. Either way, he was the one always there, teaching me the things I needed to know, helping me with homework, showing me how to throw a punch the first time I got bullied. He used to have this one, long patch of hair that he would comb over his bald head" He crosses his arms over his chest, still smiling, the waves rocking us gently. "I miss him every day."

A sadness washes over me. "He passed, didn't he?"

Adam gives one curt nod. "When I was a junior in high school. I had to stay with my aunt a lot after that, until college, anyway. But it wasn't the same." He blows out a long, slow breath. "He's the reason I do what I do, you know?" He turns to me, black sunglasses misted from the sea salt. "He never half-assed anything. So when I came to PSU, when I rushed Alpha Sigma, I knew I had the chance to take an organization that everyone underestimated and really make something of it — and maybe of myself, in the process."

My heart squeezes and I fight the urge to reach out to him. Adam and I have talked a lot since we met, especially when we were doing breakfast on a normal basis, but I never questioned why he cared so much about Alpha Sigma and the direction it was headed in. I always just assumed that was part of who he was, and I guess in a way it is — but it's not just a part of him, it's a part of his grandpa, too.

"That's really beautiful, Adam," I finally say, my voice low. He crooks a smile at me, his left dimple making an appearance as his hands find the handlebars again. But then he pauses, lifting his sunglasses, eyes wide.

"Cassie! Look!" I follow his finger and strain my eyes against the bright blue water.

"What?!"

"Do you see them? Dolphins!"

I scan the water, waiting, and then two fins break the surface followed by a third and fourth one.

"Oh my God!"

"It looks like an entire pod of them."

"Wow," I breathe, watching them as they come closer. "They're so close!"

"They're probably curious about us."

They're not alone there.

The dolphins play around us for a while and we just watch, pointing, laughing, talking. It's easy and relaxed, and for once, I don't feel awkward or afraid of my feelings around him. For once, it feels like maybe we really can have a real friendship.

As we ride back up to the dock, I think of Skyler and Clinton, how they are together. It's clear they love each other, but not in a way that crosses the friendship line. I wonder if maybe Adam could be that friend for me. The thought of it twists my stomach just as much as it makes me smile.

Adam helps me off my jet ski once we dock and I unzip my life jacket, tossing it to the crew member as Adam does the same. We both head straight to the bar on the first deck of the boat to grab water, taking our plastic cups to the back of the boat and leaning our arms against the railing.

"If I ask you something, do you promise to answer me honestly?" Adam asks, sipping from his cup. I nod, though something tells me I might regret it. For a moment he's quiet, but then he drains the rest of his water and turns to face me, one elbow still propped on the white railing. "What happened with you and Clay last semester?"

Yep. Instant regret.

I clear my throat. "You know what happened."

"No I don't."

I shift my weight to my other hip, chewing at the chapped skin on my top lip. "I don't know, Adam. I liked him. I thought he was nice. And honestly, I just wanted to have fun. We fooled around and stuff, and I didn't expect it to go as far as it did, but that night after semi-formal, I was just so upset with you and he was treating me so kindly, even though you told me he was an ass. And I don't know, I just trusted him for some reason. So we..." I trail off, shaking my head. "Well, I don't think I really need to say it."

Adam winces. "You slept with him because of me?"

My heart kicks in my chest. "Oh God, that didn't come out right." I know I'm blushing furiously, trying to save my ass but coming up with absolutely no words that help me achieve that. "I just mean that I was in a weird head space. I wasn't thinking. Normal me, in her right frame of mind, would have remembered that I have always wanted my first time to be special. I wouldn't have let some frat daddy take it after seeing each other for less than a month."

I chuckle, but when I lift my eyes to Adam, his fist is clutched around the empty plastic cup, crushing it, his other hand still gripping the bar. His nose flares, murderous eyes hard on mine. "He took your virginity?"

Oh God.

Now I'm *really* blushing.

Covering my face with my hands, I shake my head, peeking through my fingers. "This is so embarrassing."

"He took your virginity and then dumped you for your ex-best friend in front of everyone." It's not a question. His jaw is ticking beneath the strained skin. "Unfuckingbelievable."

Dropping my hands to my side again, I offer a sad smile, the scars from that night stinging a little. "It's okay,

Adam. I mean, that's what college is all about, right?" I shrug. "Lessons learned and all that."

I force a smile, but Adam is still glaring at me like I took my own virginity. Finally, he sighs, blowing the breath out hard and loosening his grip on the cup in his hands. He doesn't say a word, just takes my cup, too, and walks them to the trash can nearby. I watch him, wondering if I should have lied about what happened. When he reaches me again, he doesn't stop in the space next to me. He pulls me into him completely, wrapping his arms all the way around me, his naked chest on mine, his abs pressed against my navel, his arms hard around my shoulders.

"I'm so sorry, Cassie," he whispers into my hair and chills race from the point of contact all the way to my toes. He doesn't break our hug, just holds me, and each second kills me and fills me with hope all at once. Hesitantly, I wrap my arms around him, too, and my eyes water.

When he pulls back, he sees, and he wipes at the corner of my eye with the pad of his thumb, catching the tear before it even had the chance to fall.

And it's in that moment I know for sure.

We will never be like Skyler and Clinton.

Skyler

MY MOM IS A huge Ernest Hemingway fan. She has all of his books on her shelf at home and loves to quote him frequently. So, of course, I couldn't come to Key West without visiting his old-home-turned-museum for her.

"That was amazing!" mom squeals as I take a seat on one of the benches in the back yard area of the house, holding the phone so mom can still see my face on our video chat. I had her on video the entire tour, showing her every nook and cranny of the house. A cozy, black polydactyl cat is curled up on the bench next to me, and it doesn't stir in the slightest when I sit. Apparently, the six-toed Hemingway cats are pretty famous, and therefore, pretty immune to all the petting and picture-taking that happens to them every day.

"That was pretty cool. Hey, maybe I could be a writer," I joke, pulling my damp hair away from my neck. Still, the thought isn't too far off. I've been trying to figure out what I want to do after college, and the truth is, I was really fascinated by the tour. Ernest Hemingway was an interesting man. Oddly enough, even though he was one of the most prolific writers of his time, he was better known in Key West for his hunting, fishing, and fighting skills. And of course, his love for whiskey.

Sounds like my kind of lifestyle.

"You think so, baby?"

I scrunch my nose. "Nah, probably not. At least half the words in any book I write would be offensive."

Mom giggles, roping her dark hazelnut hair around her fingers and draping it over one shoulder. "Oh gee, I wonder who you get that from."

"Not me!" Dad calls out in the background and we both laugh.

"Well if it isn't Skyler from Florida," a voice twangs above me. Squinting against the rays of light streaming through the trees, I grin when I find exactly who I thought I would.

"Trevor, the trouble from Tennessee."

"Who's that?" Mom asks and I flip my phone, making Trevor blush and offer a half wave as my mom nearly falls out of her chair. "Oh my! Aren't you handsome."

"Thank you, ma'am."

Mom scoffs. "Did he just call me ma'am? What am I, eighty?"

I choke out a laugh and mouth a *sorry* to Trevor, turning my phone back to my own face. "Got to go, Mom. I'll call when we're back on campus."

"Don't get into any *trouble*!" she teases just as I blow a kiss and end the call, standing to join Trevor.

"Your mom is hot."

"Ew," I laugh the word, adjusting my purse strap across my chest.

He barks out a laugh, loud and strong. "You are the last person I expected to find here."

"What? I don't look like the literature loving type of gal?" *Did I just say gal?*

"I guess I shouldn't assume, huh?"

"Damn straight," I say, crossing my arms. "But I only came for my mom, so in this case, you were right." I wink and Trevor smiles. "You here alone?"

"Yeah, not exactly what my brothers had in mind for Spring Break."

"My sisters neither. They're at Smathers again."

"You heading there now?"

I shrug, reaching down to run my hand over the black cat's silky fur as she slumbers through our chat. If I remember right, the tour guide said this one is named Betty Grable. "I was, but I could be persuaded." Glancing up at him through my lashes, his tongue darts out to wet his lips and his eyes fall to his feet as he catches on.

He's so goddamn cute.

"I was going to be super touristy today. Want to join me?"

Betty mewls as my hand leaves her fur. "Sounds like Betty is on board, so I'm in, too."

He extends his arm, showing off those glorious bicep muscles I fell for our first night in Key West, turquoise eyes sparkling. "I'll guide the way."

I didn't realize when I agreed to being a tourist with Trevor all day that my feet would want to murder me for it. Luckily, that southern charm translates into some pretty stellar foot rubs.

"God, I don't know whether to scream or moan or pass out or cry," I spout, words running together as Trevor pushes his thumb into my heel. My feet are propped in his lap on the back porch of our suite and he just shakes his head, rubbing the arch next.

"I had a lot of fun today," he says and I nod in agreement, still watching as his hands move over my skin. "You're nothing like I thought you were, Skyler Thorne."

"Hey now," I warn, pointing my index finger at him. "Don't go falling in love on me. We go to different schools, remember?"

His eyes still on his hands, he just laughs. "I don't

know. I'm not scared to fall in love. I think we should fall in love with as many things as we can."

"I think I read that on a pillow once."

"You're impossible," he says, squeezing my ankles once more before letting me drop my feet to the warm concrete. The sun is sinking lower, which means the girls will all be back soon, ready to start the nightly shower cycle and get ready for Duval Street.

"Tell me, Trevor," I say, leaning forward to rest my elbows on my knees. "Do you have any of those sexy country songs saved on your phone?"

He knows where I'm going with this, but he pretends he doesn't. "Indeed I do. I have an entire playlist, actually."

I nod, looking around the back porch, silent for a moment before meeting his eyes again. "How many times do you think we can get through the playlist before you make me come?"

He swallows, the Adam's apple in his throat bobbing with the action. Without another word, I grab his hand and pull him upstairs to my room, locking the door behind us. He turns on the playlist as promised, and when he kisses me for the first time, his hands framing my face, it's as if he's transported me to a wild field in the middle of nowhere.

He fucks me the way I thought he would — steady, strong and sure. His touches are gentle but firm and confident, and when we're done, I let him cuddle with me for a while, because I know he's the kind of guy who loves that sort of thing. But, before the sun sets, I walk him back downstairs and out the front door. Leaning against the frame, eyes heavy and limbs sedated, I offer him a soft smile.

"See you around, Trouble."

He grins, bringing my hand to his lips. He almost walks away, but thinks better of it, bringing me into him for one last kiss.

Click.

"Oh, who's this, Skyler?" *Click.* Trevor and I both turn, eyes wide, and the moment I take in a middle-aged woman with a tight bun, a camera, and *Star Poker Florida* badge slung around her neck, my stomach drops. "Latest flavor of the week?"

Well, shit.

Erin

I WISH WE WERE still on the beach.

When we're on the beach or out on the boat during the day, I have fun. I don't have to drink to soak up the sun or paddleboard or read or talk to the girls. But when the sun goes down and we all invade Duval Street, the intoxication levels increase as my patience decreases. Alcohol intensifies everything, so half of my sisters are loud and crazy and the others are blubbering messes. I was finally able to talk Skyler down after being ambushed by a stupid reporter earlier today, but now, Jess is the new patient in my office.

"You can't tell anyone," she slurs for the seventh time, her elbows propped on the bar at Sloppy Joe's as she lifts her rum and Coke to her lips. Her lips pucker a bit as she sips it down. "He could lose his job."

"I won't say anything. I promise. But I still don't understand why you're so upset."

Jess has been going on and on for the past hour about Jarrett, her ex-teacher-turned-not-boyfriend. She was dancing with the girls earlier, but eventually made her way over to the bar where I set up camp, and it was like she was coming to the confessional. She unleashed all of her anxiety in about two full breaths.

"I'm upset because I *like* him," she draws out her words, as if I should already know this is a huge issue.

"And? Isn't that the point?"

She shakes her head, chocolate eyes on the stirrer in her drink as the bass from the live band thumps through the bar. "I just have a feeling I'm setting myself up to get hurt. Remember how I got my nickname?"

I make a face, thinking back to our freshmen year when Jess told every single guy she hooked up with that she loved him. She used to fall hard and fast and with abandon. She wasn't afraid of being hurt, she wasn't afraid of them not loving her back, she wasn't afraid of anything. I guess the same could be said about her now — about not being afraid — but the truth is, I think her tough, I-don't-give-a-shit attitude is a mask over the fear she developed the moment she became known as J-Love.

"I think Jarrett is different. I mean, I haven't really had the chance to get to know him, but I do know you. And it's been years since you've had feelings for a guy. Maybe it's okay to let them happen. Maybe there's a reason."

"Maybe," she says softly, hiccupping.

I laugh. "Give me this." Pulling her half-empty glass from her hands, I nod toward where Skyler and Cassie are dancing in front of the large stage in the middle of the bar. "Go dance and have fun. Relax. It's Spring Break. You can figure everything out with Jarrett when we get back."

Jess smiles, her eyes glossy, hair wild. "Mmkay." With that, she slides off her barstool and stumbles over to the dance floor, throwing her hands up and shouting something I can't quite make out as soon as she reaches our group.

I watch them all dancing and laughing, stirring the remains of Jess' drink on the bar. Skyler starts moonwalking when the band plays the first notes of *Smooth Criminal* and Ashlei pops off her snapback, tipping it over and holding it out to the crowd like she's taking tips for the performance. I can't help but smile.

In a little while, I'll get up and go dance with them. I enjoy dancing, whether drunk or not. Right now, though, I'd rather sit and watch Clinton and Shawna grinding on each other, because torturing myself is apparently a favorite pastime of mine.

I don't know why seeing them together upsets me. Is it because I have feelings for Clinton? I chew on that thought, assessing my heart rate and stomach knots.

No, I don't think that's it.

I mean, I care for him, but I never wanted to date him. I never expected us to be more than a friendly date that night at semi-formal. Still, seeing his hands tangled in Shawna's purple locks and her lips on his neck makes me feel... something.

Jealous?

Angry?

Sad?

All of the above?

As I'm ticking through the possibilities in my mind, Clinton's eyes lift to mine and I'm caught staring. I snap my attention back to Jess' drink and lift it to my lips, sucking down the smallest sip, just enough to look like I wasn't being a creep without making me want to drink the rest.

But Clinton stops dancing, kissing Shawna's temple and leaving her with Skyler before crossing the room to me.

Shit.

"Thought you weren't drinking," his voice booms as he reaches the bar, his eyes on the bartender instead of me. He nods his head once to the short, dark-haired pixie with tattoos and she gets to work on two drinks that I assume he's been ordering all night — one for him, one for Shawna.

"I'm not." He glances at the drink in my hand from the corner of his eye, brow cocked. "It's Jess'. I'm just holding it."

"Ah."

I stir the drink faster, nervous, before dropping my hands into my lap and clasping them tight. "Having fun?"

"Yep. You would be, too, if you'd loosen up a little bit."

I wince. "I'm having fun."

"Clearly," he scoffs. Sliding a twenty toward the bartender, he takes the drinks from her hands and shakes his head when she asks if he wants change. "Come on. Take this drink and come dance with us. It's Spring Break, Ex."

"Isn't that Shawna's drink?"

"She still has one," he says, holding one of the mixed drinks toward me. It's clear, something with Sprite, I imagine. "Here."

I bite my lip, wondering if maybe he's right. I can have a few drinks and be okay, right? But when my eyes flick to his and a flash of smaller, younger eyes assaults me, I squeeze my own tight.

Would our baby have had his eyes?

His nose?

His skin?

And I realize that maybe that's why I feel something when I see him with Shawna – because he is supposed to be a father. *My* child's father.

The child I killed.

I shake my head, hands clasping tighter. "Thanks, Bear, but I'm okay."

For a moment he watches me, jaw set. He turns just a fraction like he's going to let it go, but then he whips back around. "This is fucking ridiculous, Erin. We hooked up, okay? We had sex. It's not the end of the world and I'm not going to tell anyone. And, whether you stay sober as a judge or get shitfaced tonight, I'm never going to sleep with you again, okay? So stop looking at me like you have to worry about ending up in my bed tonight." His words slam into me like a Mack truck and my mouth pops open as he scowls, rolling his eyes. "Get over yourself."

My nose burns, but I stand before the sensation can reach my eyes. Pulling my purse over my shoulder, I straighten, chest to his. "Fuck you, Bear."

With that, I turn on my heel and push through the crowd of drunk college students to the street. I don't slow down, I don't apologize, and I don't look back at him or anyone else who might have seen the exchange.

I'm done.

Less than an hour later, I'm tossing my bag into the back of a Cadillac Escalade sent by my father. I told him I was terribly sick and I needed to get back to campus and he called out a driver from the airport without another question. After shooting a text to Skyler with the same bogus excuse, I let the driver help me into the backseat and sigh as he shuts the door behind me.

Sinking into the cool leather seats, I cross my arms tight over my chest, not even bothering to brush away the few strands of hair falling into my eyes. My chest feels like it's being squeezed by a boa constrictor and no matter how I focus on my breathing, I can't steady it out. Clinton's words slap me over and over again, the anger behind them washing over me in treacherous waves.

I should have told him.

He doesn't understand because I never did. I never will.

Clinton thinks I'm upset that we hooked up, that I'm ashamed or scared or embarrassed by it to the point that I refuse to drink again. He doesn't know that I'm terrified of letting another drop of alcohol hit my system because it could mean losing a part of myself again. It could mean having an amazing night with a great guy without being smart enough to use protection. It could mean one night of fun in exchange for one day of anguish, my back sticky on a paper-covered bed, my feet propped up on cold, unforgiving stirrups.

My heart races, the emotion I've been fighting so hard to keep down threatening to break the surface. Hands fumbling, I rip my phone from my Michael Kors purse and dial his number before I can stop myself. My knee bounces as the phone rings over and over, sending me closer to voicemail.

But then, he answers.

"Hello?"

I stop breathing, stop shaking, stop everything. Eyes wide, I clutch the phone tighter at the sound of his voice.

"Hello? Anyone there?"

Now that I have him on the phone, I don't even know what to say. All I know is that Kip Jackson was the only boy to ever make me feel truly loved. Even though it was years ago, he's the only person I want to call when life gets too hard to handle. But I haven't talked to him since that summer, the one when we fell in love and then I chased him away just as quickly.

There's a shift on the other end and then the line goes dead with a soft, quiet click. I let the cool device drop into my lap, bringing one trembling hand to my lips. And then, I stop fighting. Taking one last breath, I let the pressure rumbling through my chest and up into my throat break through. Loud, ugly, and painful, as so often hidden hurt is, I allow it to consume me.

I finally let myself cry.

Bear

I FEEL A LITTLE shitty when I wake up on the last day of Spring Break. Even after taking a long, hot shower, popping a couple of Advils and drinking an entire Gatorade, I still feel the effects of our week weighing on me. For once, I'm actually looking forward to a day without boozing. I know we'll all go hard one last time on Duval Street tonight, but today, I'm spending time with Shawna.

Away from everyone else.

But, the hangover and dehydration aren't the only reasons I'm feeling like a particularly ripe ass today. Skyler called me this morning to tell me Erin left last night, so Shawna could ride home in our van instead of trying to find a flight home. I should have been happy that I would get to be next to her on the way back, but instead all I felt was an insufferable amount of guilt. Erin wasn't sick, she was hurt.

Because I was a giant bag of dicks.

Sighing, I pull another Gatorade from the fridge and take a few swigs before splaying my palms out on the counter. I didn't mean to lash out at her, especially knowing how sensitive she is, but I was tired of feeling like I did something wrong by hooking up with her. I know I remember the night of semi-formal a little better than she does, but she wanted me. *She* was the one who asked me back to the house. *She* peeled my clothes off. I definitely didn't stop her, hell — I enjoyed myself. But she's making me feel like a criminal and it needs to stop.

Still, I could have waited until I wasn't shitfaced to talk to her about it.

Maybe she caught feelings. Maybe she's jealous seeing me with Shawna. I actually laugh out loud at that, knowing there's no way in hell Erin would ever want to actually *be* with me. She's got her eyes set on a doctor or a lawyer, I'm sure, and even that won't be until after she's reigned as president of KKB.

A loud chorus of laughter from the other room shakes my thoughts and I grab my Gatorade, making my way toward the noise. Several of my brothers are gathered around my Little's laptop, pointing and talking over each other. Josh is furiously typing and clicking away, almost like he's playing a game.

"What are you guys doing?"

Half of them go sheet white and they all stop talking. Instantly, I know they're up to no good.

"Nothing. Just watching YouTube videos," Josh lies. I know it's a lie, I can see right through his blushing ginger cheeks, even if he did bake on the fake tanner this week. I narrow my eyes.

"Do I need to remind you guys about the warning Alec hand-delivered to us before Spring Break? If any of you fuckers get us suspended, I'll personally kick all of your asses."

One of the pledges gulps and Alex, a sophomore pledge who seems to be the leader of the new class, salutes me. "Aye aye, captain." He's a cocky son of a bitch, that's for sure, but he's the only reason we're all in this swanky house for Spring Break, so I can't exactly bitch at the moment.

Everyone fights back laughter just as Shawna slides up next to me, pulling my arm around her shoulder. "Hey, you ready?"

My eyes still hard on my brothers, I give them one last pointed look before turning and pulling Shawna with me.

I don't have time to deal with their bullshit today. "Yeah, let's do this."

"So where are we going?" she asks when we're outside. I pat down my pockets, checking to make sure I have my phone and wallet.

"Anything but Smathers Beach."

She giggles, pushing her sunglasses up the bridge of her nose and lacing her hand in mine. I'm so used to seeing her in her regular glasses it almost feels weird to see her in shades. I much prefer having full visibility of her green eyes. "Can we start with breakfast? I'm starving."

"Breakfast it is," I oblige, kissing her hair as we walk.

We don't even look up anything on our phones, just stroll into the first brunch place we find, which just so happens to have unlimited mimosas until noon. And that's how the rest of the day goes. We don't plan, we don't rush — we just take our time and enjoy a little of everything Key West has to offer. We rent bikes, riding them through the shaded streets between colorful houses and stopping at the major tourist spots, like Mile Marker 0 and the Southernmost Point. At sunset, we park our bikes by Mallory Square and find a place on the edge of the water right behind where a man dressed like Captain Jack Sparrow is collecting tips for photos.

As the sun sinks over the water, musical performers serenading us as it does, I pull Shawna in closer, wrapping both arms around her middle and resting my chin on her shoulder. For once, I kind of just want to stay in tonight, take her back to the house, take her slow and steady between the sheets all night long. The crazy thing is that I'm not even scared of the way she makes me feel.

"I'm not ready to go back to reality," she says with a sigh, leaning her head back against me. I rub the smooth skin on her arms with my thumbs as the sky breaks out into a red glow. I feel the same way. When we go back, it's tests and homework and social events. Family Weekend is right around the corner, which means I have to get everything figured out for my brother's stay. But here, in Key West, we don't have any responsibilities. We get to be who we want and do what we want, even if just for a week.

"Stay with me in paradise for a little while longer," I whisper into her ear, my nose in her hair. She smells like tequila and pineapples, my little island girl for at least a few more hours.

Shawna twists in my arms, pulling off her sunglasses to look me in the eyes. We don't say anything, but that one look between us tells me we're both completely out of our element here.

"Maybe we can bring paradise back with us." A smile curls at the left side of her mouth and I slide my hand into her hair. She leans in, pressing her lips to mine just as the square breaks out in applause, the last of the sun sinking away.

Jess

"**ARE YOU SURE YOU** haven't seen it?" Jess calls out again, this time tossing the same pillows she just rummaged through on one side of the room to the other. "It's Vera Bradley, Can–"

"Canyon print, small backpack, with your name embroidered in yellow I know, Lei, and no, for the one-hundredth time, I haven't seen it," I cut her off. "Jesus, just chill. You can get another Vera bag."

She huffs, standing with her hands hooked on her hips, her hair in a crazy bun as she sweeps the corners of the room with her eyes. "It's not the bag I'm worried about."

"Was your wallet in it?"

"No."

"Your phone?"

"No, it was just something important," she says, frustrated, digging through Skyler's bag now. I roll my eyes, still thumbing through social media on my phone.

"God, if I didn't know you better I'd say it was stashed with drug money." I laugh, shaking my head.

"Could you at least fucking pretend to help me find it?" she snaps, her eyes wild. "You're just sitting there being a giant bitch, which usually I don't mind, but for once in your life can you help me without making me feel like shit in the process?"

"Excuse me?" I scoff, uncrossing my feet on the bed and sitting up straighter. "I am always there for you. If anything, you're the one who always holds me at ten-foot-distance. So don't take your period out on me because you can't find a fucking backpack."

"Whatever, Jess."

"Yeah. Whatever," I repeat, snatching my drink off the nightstand and walking my happy ass downstairs. "Let me know when you're ready."

Everyone else is already on Duval Street, but I agreed to stay back with Ashlei so she could look for her bag without everyone being there. Now, I'm wishing I would have let her do it on her own. She's already being dishonest about whatever is happening with Bo, and now I get the feeling she's hiding something else. At this point, I'm tired of trying to step around the fact that she's being secretive. She knows it, I know it, and I'm sure she can feel that I'm getting tired of it.

Just as my foot hits the bottom step, my phone screen lights up with Jarrett's number.

"Come get me," I answer and he chuckles.

"Over it, are you?"

"Beyond. What are you doing?"

"I just got out of the shower, have to work at the bar tonight. But I was... thinking of you."

The way he says the words flips my stomach. "Were you now?"

"Let's just say I'm more than a little worked up at the moment," he replies, his voice husky. "Are you alone?"

Ashlei curses from upstairs and a loud clatter breaks out. Clearly we're going to be here a while, might as well get my kicks.

"Not right now, but I could be."

"Find a room. I'll call you back." Jarrett ends the call before I have the chance to ask why he needed to end it. Confused, I keep my phone in my hand and duck inside the small half-bathroom downstairs, flicking on the light and checking my appearance in the mirror. If I'm going to be sending him pictures, I definitely want to make them drool-worthy. Luckily, there are about a million makeup bags lined up on the counter, so I reapply my red lipstick and darken my lashes. As soon as I pop the lid back on Skyler's mascara, my phone buzzes.

This time, with a video chat request.

Oh.

"Hi," I say as Jarrett's blurry face slowly comes into view. I almost forgot how incredibly sexy he is. The only view I have is of the top of his shoulders, covered with tats, and his heart-stopping, demanding dark eyes. He's still in his bathroom, the mirror fogged up behind him and small beads of water from his shower gathered on his neck.

"Goddamn, I miss you," he breathes, his eyes searching mine. "Take your clothes off."

I almost laugh, but he's not joking, there's no playful tone to his voice — he meant what he said. His eyes hooded, he bites his lip as I set up my phone on the counter, my hands pulling my hair down from the loose hair tie I had it in.

I shimmy out of my jean shorts first, letting them drop to the floor and eying him through my lashes as I hook my thumbs in the band of my panties and pull them down next. My blouse is light, and I peel it off with ease, unhooking my bra and shaking it off each arm quickly. Jarrett's eyes never leave me, his breaths coming harder.

He moves from the bathroom to his bedroom, propping himself up against his headboard. The camera blanks for just a moment before the view switches and I see him sprawled out in his sheets, his hard body still damp from the shower. Slowly, he unwraps his towel and lets it fall to the side, and I moan when I see how hard he is. He grips himself, stroking slowly as he grows even harder, and suddenly I can't breathe.

"I want you so bad," I whisper, palming my breasts and imagining his hands on me, instead. Each time he strokes, he grows harder, longer, thicker, his fist opening around his shaft as his thumb grazes the tip. I drop to my knees in front of the phone and insert two fingers between my lips, eyes on the lens as I suck my own flesh. Jarrett groans, flipping the camera and adjusting his phone so that I have the most glorious view — his hard cock in his hand, his slick abs and chest, his bottom lip pinned between his teeth as he strokes and watches me.

"Take those wet fingers and fuck yourself with them," he demands, his forearm muscles flexing under the tattooed skin. Grabbing my phone, I lean back against the door and spread my legs wide, taking my time dragging the lens down my body until it lands between my legs. Slowly, my eyes still on his dick, I spread my lips and slide one finger inside, my head falling back at the sensation.

"Oh fuck," Jarrett breathes. "You're always so tight."

"You're always too big," I moan, dipping another finger inside as Jarrett quickens his pace.

"I want to bury my face in that pussy," he husks and the filth turns me on. I let my legs fall open wider, moving up to circle my clit before plunging my fingers back inside. "Taste yourself."

I pull my fingers out and slowly trail them up my stomach, pausing to work my nipples between the slick tips before sliding them in my mouth. Jarrett groans and the guttural noise sends a jolt through me. I'm so fucking hot it's uncomfortable. Squirming, I bite my lip and fuck myself with my fingers again, this time steadying my rhythm, reaching for the orgasm I feel mounting.

"Do you even know how sexy you are?" Jarrett asks, his voice raspy as he pumps. When his hand rolls over the tip of his cock it grazes the abs just above his naval. His every inch is on full display, and all I want is him inside me right now. "You make me so weak, Jess. So fucking weak."

I try so hard to stay quiet, but I know Ashlei must hear my screams as I tumble over the edge, pulling my fingers out to circle my clit and lengthen the ride. Jarrett comes with me, flexing his hips into his hand one last time before grunting out his release. I never thought it would be so seductive to watch him shudder and hear him moan my name as he busts on his abs. I keep my eyes glued on the screen, fascinated, feeling powerful and sexy as hell.

Our breaths are both loud, our limbs weak as we clean up. Jarrett brings the screen to his face, biting his lip. "Hurry home tomorrow."

"Cancel all your plans until Monday."

He chuckles, his eyes low and sedated. "Have fun to-night."

I blow him a kiss and end the call, staring at all my clothes on the floor and laughing to myself. *Did I just video sex my boyfriend in a bathroom?*

Oh my God, did I just call him my boyfriend?

Shaking my head, I quickly dress and burst through the bathroom door, ready to storm upstairs and drag Ashlei down to Duval Street. Instead, I find a sticky note on my purse.

Left without you. Didn't want to interrupt. ;) – Lei

"That little bitch," I whisper with a laugh, wondering if she's still mad at me. I hate fighting with her, and now that I've worked off some tension, I realize I was a little harsh upstairs. Locking up behind me, I scamper down to the street and flag down the first cab I see to shuttle me down to the bars. I'll make it up to Ashlei tonight. Our *last* night. Spring Break is almost over.

My phone pings and when I slide the screen, a full photo of Jarrett in just his board shorts pops up. He's holding the phone to show his reflection in the mirror and my eyes stick hard on the area where his lower abs meet his hip flexors, forming that glorious V.

– A little something to get you through the night. –

I drag my teeth over my bottom lip, shaking my head before tucking my phone away. For once, I can't wait to get back to campus.

Adam

MY FAVORITE TIME TO be on the beach is after midnight, when the water is calmer, the sand cooler, and the conversation deeper. Leaning back on my palms, the heels of my feet just barely touching the sand at the edge of my blanket, I listen to the waves roll in.

The last night of Spring Break is coming to an end.

I thought it would be weird, coming with Skyler, her sisters, and Omega Chi Beta without a single other brother of my own. Somehow, though, I managed to have the best time of my life. It was never weird, it was a constant high. Funny enough, I'm one of the last ones standing tonight. It has to be at least three in the morning and the only other people on the beach that I recognize are Cassie, Ashlei, and Bo. They're all gathered around the last beer pong table set up on Smathers Beach, playing against three Omega Chis I don't recognize.

We started our night on Duval Street but moved the population from half the bars to the beach around midnight, wanting to take over the Key West sand one last time. Skyler and Jess turned in pretty early, both exhausted from the week, and Clinton dragged Shawna off not too long after. But I'm still buzzed, not ready to give up vacation just yet.

"Hey." Cassie's voice catches me off guard, I didn't realize she'd stopped playing. Lifting my eyes up her long, lean legs, I note the way the beach fire makes the edges of her silhouetted hair glow a fierce orange. She points back at Bo and Ashlei. "I think we're about to head out."

I frown, nodding. "Okay. I have a key."

"You're not coming with us?"

I shrug, rolling my neck a little and turning back toward the water. "I don't know, I'm not really tired."

"Me either," she says.

"Hang out with me?"

Even with the fire light behind her and her face hidden by the dark night sky, I see the faintest smile. "Okay. One sec." She jogs back over to the girls, saying something I can't quite hear before hugging them both and watching them leave. The last straggling Omega Chi brothers follow suit and then it's just me and Cassie. As she makes her way back across the sand, a familiar ache settles in my chest. It's the same one I've been dealing with every night sleeping next to her — like heartburn, but worse.

I slide over, making more room on my blanket for her to sit. She plops down, pulling her knees up to her chest and threading her arms under her thighs. "I can't believe it's over."

"It's not," I correct. "Not yet."

She grins, laying her cheek on her knees, her green eyes curious as she watches me. She's quiet for a while before she bursts out in a fit of laughter. "I still can't believe you danced on stage at the Red Garter."

"Hey, I got a few dollar bills in the waistband of my boxers that night," I tease, throwing her a wink.

"Yeah. Until the security guards threw you out." She laughs harder, her lightly-tanned cheeks flushing.

"I love how I'm getting picked on by the girl who took fifty-seven seconds to do a beer bong."

"It was my first one!" She smacks my arm and I grin, pulling her head under my arm and ruffling her wild red hair. She pokes me hard in my chest until I release her, both of us still chuckling.

"It really was an amazing trip," she breathes, stretching her legs out on the blanket, her eyes on the waves, mine glued on her. I've never seen her look so free before. Even with her pink lips chapped from the sun and fresh freckles on her cheeks, she's absolutely beautiful in the low glow from the half-moon. Crossing her arms over her chest, she shivers slightly.

"Are you cold?"

"A little."

I smile, opening my arm. "Come here." Her green eyes assess me, as if she's afraid of my touch. "I radiate heat like a werewolf. Seriously, come here."

Cassie hesitates, but slides over, letting me wrap my arms around her. She settles into my grasp and sighs. "Wow. You really are warm."

"Told you."

A small curve meets her lips and she rests her head against my chest. The moment she does, I feel the energy change. I can't explain it. It's like the ocean blanketed us in an electric mist the minute her skin met mine. My throat constricts as I battle with what I should do and what I want to. I don't know if it's the moonlight or the sand or the energy from the night, but I give up trying to fight my urge when it comes to her. I don't want to fight it tonight. I want it to consume me.

Attempting to swallow the lump in my throat, I lift my hand from where it was holding tight to her middle and trail it up her arm, rendering chills in my wake. She stiffens when my fingers graze the bottom of her chin and I lift it, just slightly, tilting my own down toward her. My thumb grazes her jaw and her emerald eyes flick to mine, pupils large and dark. She holds my gaze, her breaths as hard as mine when she lets her eyes fall to my lips.

"What are you doing?" she breathes, so quiet against the sound of the waves that I almost don't hear her.

"Kissing you."

I feel her heart stop and start again with a kick beneath my forearm as I lean in closer, my hand sliding into her hair.

"Adam," she starts. "You're drunk."

"Just because I'm drunk doesn't mean I'm stupid, and I'd be stupid not to kiss you right now."

My hands frame her face and I pull her into me, our lips barely touching before her hand finds the center of my chest. "I have a boyfriend."

I rest my forehead against hers, breaths sharp as they escape my open lips just centimeters from hers. "So tell me to stop."

I wait, expecting to hear the word and praying I won't. My hands slide back into her hair, tilting her mouth up to mine, and her eyes plead with me for something I'm not sure I can give before she lets them flutter closed. Permission granted, I close the distance, pressing my lips to hers as the energy band snaps around us.

Our first kiss flashes through my mind and I let my hands fall to her hips, pulling her closer, knowing it will never be close enough. It's then that I realize Cassie took a piece of me with her that night and she never gave it back. I never asked for it back. And something tells me she'll always have it, no matter what happens after this.

Her fingers weave into my hair, tugging, her back arching toward me as my tongue glides between her lips to meet her own. She whimpers, soft and sweet, and I'm thankful we're sitting because that sound alone would have brought me to my knees. I tug at the belt loop on her shorts and she takes the cue, straddling me, every inch of her shaking as everything we've held back for so long breaks through the fog we've tried to cover it with.

I take my time, massaging her tongue with my own, peppering her neck with kisses, her jaw, sucking the skin behind her ear before finding her mouth again. My hands are everywhere, holding her while she trembles beneath each new touch. She flexes her hips against mine and I wince, my fingertips gripping her hard to stop her from doing it again. It's too much. I know we can't take it there, not tonight, not when she's technically someone else's. Tonight, I'll kiss her, for as long as she'll let me, and hope that, eventually, she'll be able to give me all of her. I'll be able to give her all of me.

Tomorrow will come, and neither of us can stop that. But for now, on a blanket in the sand, beneath a sky of stars, we have tonight.

We have tonight.

I'M SO FUCKING SICK.

I wish it was from the alcohol, or sun poisoning, or anything else in the world except the true source. I've tried talking myself down, soothing my nerves, sourcing my options but the truth is I have none.

I lost the backpack.

My chest stings as the realization sinks in and I press my forehead to the bus window. I misplaced my ticket to freedom like it was a spare set of car keys. I looked everywhere, I called everyone, I retraced my steps and dug through every bag in our suite. It's gone. The money is gone.

Xavier is going to kill me.

I mean he might *literally* kill me.

Bo's head is heavy on my shoulder, her breaths long and steady as we pull back into campus. The entire ride home was silent, save for the old 80s rock music keeping the driver of our bus awake. When we stop in front of the Kappa Kappa Beta house, I shrug Bo awake and she wipes at the corner of her mouth, scrubbing her hands down her face.

"I'm so tired."

"Come on, we can take a nap."

She smiles sweetly at me before we shuffle off the bus behind the rest of our sisters. Every step feels weighted as my mind races with what my next moves need to be. I was so close, *so* close to being done with Kya and Hayden and Xavier and every fucking nightmare that's been wrecking my life for months. My only saving grace is that I didn't lose all of the money, but I still lost over a third of it, which is enough to get me into an even deeper hole with a very dangerous man. Every new thought drives the knife in deeper and tears sting my eyes. I suck my lips between my teeth, fighting them back, just as several of my sisters' phones ping all at once.

A chorus of varying ringtones surrounds us on the front lawn of our house and glances are exchanged as we pull out our phones. Mine is in my bag, so I lean over Bo's as she slides the notification. It's a group text from a short-code number.

– OMEGA CHI BETA SPRING BREAK CONQUESTS. CLICK TO VIEW. –

Bo eyes me with a bent brow before tapping the link. When she does, her hand flies to her mouth.

It's a website.

With photos and videos of every girl fucked inside Alex's Spring Break mansion.

My stomach sinks deeper and deeper as our sisters turn one by one, their eyes landing hard on us as a sweat breaks at the nape of my neck. I catch the betrayal beneath Jess' hurt expression and feel the knife twist once again.

Because right there on the homepage is a looping video of their top conquest.

Me and Bo.

EPISODE 5

"What Are Sisters For?"

IF EVER IT WERE true that Bear hugs are the best hugs, right now would be that moment. Wrapping my arms around my baby brother, I clap him hard on the back, holding him longer than usual and fighting back the sting of emotions threatening to form as tears. We're in the middle of the airport and I know I'm probably embarrassing him, but I don't give a shit. It's the start of Family Weekend and my baby brother is here.

My baby brother is *here*.

"Nice to see you too, loser," he mumbles into my chest, voice cracking a bit less than our last long phone call. He weaves his way out of my grasp and I ruffle his hair.

"Don't act like you're too cool to hug your big bro."

"Well, if you didn't hug like Aunt Shonda at Easter," he teases and I sock him hard on the arm, making him yelp and rub the spot with a smile on his face. My little brother is not-so-little anymore. At just thirteen, the top of his head reaches my shoulders and he's started to bulk, though his frame is still pretty lean in comparison to mine. His curly hair is medium length and unruly, his skin as dark as mine, eyes and nose virtually identical. Anyone who looked at us would know we're brothers, and I catch Skyler ogling our similarities from the corner of my eye.

"Clayton, this is Skyler Thorne. She's the one I'm always telling you about."

"Damn," he draws out the word, eyes devouring Skyler in her small, tight white shorts and loose tank top. "Please tell me I'm bunking with you this weekend, sweetheart."

I thump him on the head and he shoots me a glare, but Skyler just laughs.

"You couldn't handle a night in my bed, Baby Bear."

He grimaces. "Ugh, please tell me that's not going to be my nickname."

"What? I think it's cute," Skyler defends. Clayton's shoulders fall and Skyler fights back a smile as I grab his duffle bag and throw it over my shoulder.

"Come on," I say, steering us toward the large automatic doors that lead out to the taxi cabs. "Your big brother is taking you to a college party."

"What?! No way!" Clayton's dark eyes light up and he holds his hand out until Skyler smacks it with a high five. "Time to get wasted. Make sure you call up all the hottest sorority babes because Baby Bear is looking for someone to hibernate with tonight." He howls and it echoes off the concrete walls of the parking garage.

"Going to get a thirteen-year-old drunk?" Skyler asks me quietly, cocking a brow.

"I bought some non-alcoholic beer. What he doesn't know won't hurt him." I wink and she shakes her head, a few strands falling from the messy bun she's paired with her casual appearance. I love her like this—no makeup, hair up, wearing the first thing she found in her closet. Skyler Thorne in her natural element, ladies and gents.

"I smell trouble."

"Nah, he'll be fine. He's a Pennington."

I beam at Skyler before hailing a cab and climbing in the back with her and Clayton. I throw my arm around his shoulders and tease him about girls and video games and everything else simple in his life because it makes me feel like home. *He* makes me feel like home. The good part of home that I miss.

When we get to the Omega Chi house, I give Clayton the tour while Skyler sets us up for a game of beer pong, complete with cups filled to the brim with Clayton's special beer on one side.

"This place is amazing," he says with wonder as we finally drop his bag off in my room. "No wonder you never come home."

I frown, trying not to read too much into that assessment. "Ready for your first game of beer pong?"

He laughs. "I'm ready for *a* game of beer pong."

"Wait, you've played before?"

Clayton shrugs, like it's no big deal. "Maybe."

It honestly doesn't surprise me that he's already played, because that's the way it was where I grew up in Pittsburgh—where he's growing up right now. I was exposed to drinking and drugs well before my pre-teen years—mostly courtesy of our own family—and I know he's no stranger to it, either. I can only hope he's smart about his choices, and judging by the way he looks up to me, I feel confident that he is.

Smirking, I grab a fresh pack of pong balls out of my dresser and break it open, tossing one up in the air. "Fine. I guess I don't need to take it easy on you, then."

He grins back just as cockily and I wonder how much of myself I've rubbed off on him over the years.

We play three back-to-back games before Clayton realizes his beer isn't doing what it should be. Skyler and I are playing on a team and I paired him with a hot little Zeta, but she's probably doing more to distract him than help him. Her name is Jazmine, though everyone around campus calls her Jazzy, and she keeps running her long manicured nails through Clayton's tight curls and touching his arm over the table. If his skin wasn't so dark, I'd swear he was blushing.

I finally concede and let him drink a little Bud Light, but not in beer pong, because after a few games he'd probably be shitfaced. The last thing our fraternity needs is to get caught with a drunk minor at our house. Frowning, I realize I haven't been able to talk to Skyler much about how her sisters are handling everything with the Spring Break debacle, so I leave Clayton where he's set up on a bean bag playing video games with Josh and go search for her.

It's a Thursday night and everyone is still recovering from Spring Break, so the house is surprisingly dead. Well, for our house, anyway. I can hear Clayton's laughs over the video game sound effects as I round the corner into our kitchen and lean against the counter next to Skyler.

"Tequila?" I ask, eyes on the shot glass pinched between her fingers.

She nods, her blue eyes dull and tired. "It's been that kind of week."

"The blogs?"

She throws the liquid down her throat, eyes squinting against the burn as she reaches for a lime slice. "Partly. I mean, I can't say I'm exactly thrilled to be gaining the reputation as a heartbreaker, but it's not the biggest thing on my plate right now."

"The website?"

She nods, quiet as she refills her shot glass. I push off the counter long enough to retrieve one for me and slide it up next to hers to fill, too. "We kicked him out, you know? Alex." I blow out a long breath through my nose, my hands gripping the edge of the counter as I think about the website he made from Spring Break detailing all his conquests and a few of our other brothers'. I knew I didn't like that cocky son of a bitch, but I didn't know he was a fucking idiot. He's lucky Florida doesn't have laws against "revenge porn" yet, though our alumni brothers made sure to warn us that those laws are well on their way to being passed. Even though it was only one brother's idea, several were involved, and it reflected on our entire chapter as a whole. So, naturally, Alec already called a meeting with nationals, and now, we await our fate. "Thank God he hadn't been sworn in as a brother yet. He doesn't deserve our letters."

"That's the fucking truth." She clinks her glass to mine and we toss them back, hissing through our teeth as we slam them back on the counter. "It was fucked up what he did, but I think our sisters are a little more shocked by Bo and Ashlei. No one knew. I mean, Jess suspected but . . ." She shrugs. "We've never had this situation before, you know? At least not openly. They're our sisters, but they're dating each other. Let's just say some are handling it better than others. And Jess has already almost fought the half of our chapter stupid enough to be vocal about their disapproval."

"Shit, I didn't even think about that."

"Erin is going crazy trying to figure out what to do. Everyone on the executive board is."

I feel a pang of guilt chase the tequila at the mention of Erin's name, remembering how I lashed out on her on Spring Break. I haven't talked to her since. "It's not like they can kick them out, right? They didn't do anything wrong. They couldn't have known he had a camera set up in that room."

"No, they didn't do anything wrong, but some of the girls on exec don't think it's okay for them to date. It's a big ordeal." She sighs. "I don't know. I just hope it doesn't tear any of us apart."

"It won't," I assure her, wrapping her in my arms. She inhales a deep, shaky breath as I rest my chin on her head.

"I know my KKB girls, and the bond you guys have is too strong to be broken by something like this."

"I hope you're right."

"I am." I kiss her forehead before we make our way back to the living room, joining Clayton and the rest of my brothers around the television. For the rest of the night, my brothers tell Clayton stories about me and give him tips on how to score girls, like they have any credibility in that area. It's all laughter and good vibes, and in so many ways it feels like a piece of me that I've been missing is finally in the same room again.

I never want to let the feeling go.

I'm not sure what times it is when I feel her crawl into bed with me.

I left my window open, knowing she would want me tonight since we haven't seen each other all day. Clayton is sleeping on the giant bean bag in the Omega Chi loft, and as soon as he passed out, I shot off a text to Shawna to let her know the offer was open.

As if it ever wasn't anymore.

She doesn't speak when she climbs under the covers, already undressed, already panting with need. She just slips her warm hand beneath the band of my boxer briefs and drags her tongue along the edge of my jaw until I meet her mouth with my own. She inhales stiffly when our lips touch and her grip on me tightens, intoxication flowing through the point of contact straight into my blood stream. Shawna always brings me to the best kind of high, but having her hands on me when I'm balancing on the edge of sleep is fucking incredible.

My hands find her hips and I grip her hard, pulling her to straddle me without my mouth breaking contact with hers. She pulls my briefs down just enough for me to kick them the rest of the way off and then she pushes off my chest. Palming me, she places me at her wet entrance, pausing for just the smallest second. It's long enough for me to peek up at her through heavy eyelids and see her bathed in the dim moonlight streaming through my window, reminding me of our first night together on my birthday. She arches her back as I flex my hips and push inside her, my hands still holding her firmly in place.

We moan together, the same numbing electricity rolling over each of us. I let her work me slow, her thighs tensing beneath my rough fingertips as she does. Her hands are on my chest, balancing, her head is back, hair falling down her back, the purple ends catching the light in a metallic glimmer. I slide my hands up to frame her small waist, trail them over her hard, pierced nipples, and hook them behind her neck before pulling her down to me.

I kiss her softly, her hair falling all around us as I gently take the lead. Rocking my hips deeper, soft whimpers escape her lips and find refuge on mine. My hands on the move again, chills break in their wake as they snake down her lower back to grip her ass firmly, controlling her movements. She willingly lets me take the reins. Her teeth bite the sensitive skin on my neck just below my ear and I hiss, pumping into her harder, driving us both toward the apex.

When I know we're both close, I pull her forehead to mine, eyes searching, breaths coming hard as I keep our rhythm steady. There are words suspended between us in a space they may never escape, and though neither of us dare speak them out loud, our bodies scream them between the sheets as I rock once, twice, three times, reaching new depths. We hold each other tighter, nails in skin, eyes still wide as the final spark ignites and burns us to the core. We ride out the flames, scorching together, caught in the fire.

A blistering inferno rages in my bedroom, and we gladly go down together in the blaze.

Skyler

IT'S SUCH A CONTRAST to see the same sisters who were barely clothed and completely sloshed just over a week ago completely sober, dressed in our school colors, ribbons in their hair as they greet the constant stream of parents entering our house. I'm on the front line, handing out programs to smiling faces as they file in out of the Florida heat. My parents aren't among them, since last minute work issues kept them from making the trip down for Family Weekend, but Erin has volunteered her mom as tribute to keep me company—almost too eagerly, actually.

I find out very quickly why.

After an introductory speech from my Grand Big, Kelsey, the parents get tours of the house while sipping lemonade and Erin introduces me to a thin, older version of herself.

"Mom, this is Skyler, my Little," Erin says, gesturing to me.

"Elizabeth Xander." I take her dainty hand in my own and attempt a shake, but she stops me short with a tight, brief squeeze. "Pleasure, I'm sure."

"I've heard so much about you," I volunteer, my eyes catching Erin's. She rolls them behind her mom's back and I grin. "Would you like to see our rooms?"

Elizabeth shakes her head, scouring the living room of the house with an upturned nose. Her dark blonde hair looks just like Erin's, especially since it's pulled back into a tight bun, throwing more attention to the strand of pearls draped over her collar bone. She and Erin are both in brightly colored Lily Pulitzer dresses and wedges, and suddenly I wish I'd let Erin dress me this morning. I'm in jean shorts and a white tank top with our letters on it.

"No need, I had the full tour last year."

"We should probably head over to the tailgate, any-way," Erin adds. Her mother nods and they link arms, leading the way.

Family Weekend is packed with random events for students and their parents, including everything from guest lectures to fraternity parties. The biggest event, how-ever, is the baseball game tailgate. The grassy event area right beside the baseball stadium is transformed into the ultimate tailgate experience, food and booze included, and we all pack the stands for the night's game. Well, those of us who make it past the day drinking, anyway.

Elizabeth talks the entire walk over, chatting with us about her latest shopping trips and Botox treatments. Any-time Erin attempts bringing up her position in the soror-ity or her classes, her mother loses interest immediately, tapping away on her phone or changing the subject back to something superficial. It's clear she doesn't approve of Erin's major or career choice.

"Oh my, am I seeing double?" A smooth voice drawls from behind us just as we reach the edge of the tailgate yard. Bright orange, teal, and white tents pepper the grass and our Student Government President speaks loudly over the microphone system, welcoming the parents to PSU. When we turn, Erin smiles at Landon, her latest fling and the owner of the smooth voice spitting out clichés. Still, her smile seems bleak, the same way it's been for weeks, and I wonder how badly the stress of the Omega Chi web-site is getting to her.

"Hi," she says sweetly and Landon grasps her gen-tly by the elbow, pulling her just close enough to kiss her cheek before turning to Elizabeth. His blonde hair is almost too perfectly styled and his freshly tanned skin from Spring Break contrasts harshly with the pastels of his polo and frat shorts.

"You didn't tell me you had a sister, Ex," he flirts, reaching for her mom's hand. She's all smiles as he lifts it to his mouth for a kiss. Erin and I exchange glances. *Is this guy serious right now?*

"Aren't you sweet as pie. I'm Elizabeth Xander, Erin's mother. And you are?"

"Landon Turner, ma'am."

"What a strong name," she says, giggling, eyes bright. "Are you Erin's boyfriend?"

"Mother," Erin scolds, cheeks blushing a light shade of pink.

Landon doesn't miss a beat. He pulls Erin in under his arm and smiles a bright, charming, country smile—all toothy and genuine. "Just friends for now, ma'am. But I'm working on her."

Elizabeth's brows shoot up and she grins at Erin. "Well heavens, child, give in already!"

We all laugh, me mostly to ease the awkwardness, and Erin leads us to a shaded picnic table near the alumni tent. It's a little too warm today, the sun shining high in the sky without a cloud to block it. I'm already sweating slightly from the walk over and gladly take the fresh bottle of water offered to us by the volunteers as we sit down.

"So, Landon, what's your major?" Erin's mom asks, sipping from her own bottle. She's leaning over the dark teal picnic table, ready to devour whatever he says. Of course, when he tells her he's pre-med with a focus in plastic surgery, his Ken doll smile locked in place and his hand running through his blonde hair, she practically sits in his lap.

She lets him ramble on and I lean in to whisper to Erin. "You okay?"

"Fine. This is actually tame for her, believe it or not."

"I think she's planning your wedding."

"Like I said, tame."

We both giggle but neither Landon nor Elizabeth notice us. Draining the rest of my water, I tip the empty plastic toward Erin. "I'm going to get a refill and see if I can track down the other girls. Find me later?"

She nods and I don't even bother interrupting the conversation between Landon and Erin's mom to excuse myself. After tossing my empty bottle in one of the recycling bins, I snatch a turkey wrap off the alumni table and walk the tents. It's kind of funny seeing the parents on campus. Some of them are starry-eyed, possibly setting foot on a college campus for the first time while others look comfortable as they chat about the "glory days" of PSU. I smile, realizing my parents belong to that first group. Skott, my older brother, never went to college. He just left straight for the Peace Corps after high school. I'm the first and *only* one in our family to ever attend a university, which makes me feel strangely like a pioneer for the Thornes.

I wouldn't even be here if it weren't for poker, and now that I'm getting noticed by big poker blogs and reporters, the two worlds are crossing more than I ever thought they would. Adam was right to call it off with me before this summer, because there's no way I'll have time for him. Or anyone else, for that matter. I feel like I'm at the precipice of something huge, and now is my time to make a name for myself, so I'm filling my schedule with tournaments all summer long. If I have it my way, I'll have next year's tuition paid off by July so I can start focusing on bigger and better things.

Like the American Poker Club Tournament.

A light breeze rolls across the tailgate yard and blows my hair back as I round the second row of tents, mind still wandering. It's a tempting thought, entering the APC tourney. I'm not prepared enough to enter it this year. Hell, I don't even have a third of the entry fee. But if I play my cards right, I just might be able to enter the one next May, and if I won or even placed in the top three, I'd be set. No more having to work tournaments at night and be a sorority girl during the day. I could get my parents completely out of debt and then some, tuition for the rest of my time at PSU would be paid, and I could focus on my major and figure out what I want to do with my life.

The thought makes me giddy.

"Hey heartbreaker," Adam says, bumping into me from the side and stirring me from my thoughts. His signature goofy grin is firmly in place, his dark hair a little unruly and a light sweat is breaking on his forehead.

"Oh God, not you, too. I really hope that's not my new nickname."

He shrugs, falling in line with my rhythm. "I don't know, I think it fits pretty perfectly."

"Says the one who broke up with me."

"That's not what the tabloids are saying."

I blanch. "What?"

Adam's shit-eating grin grows wider and when I realize he's joking, I shove him hard into the pole of a passing tent. He laughs, dodging it easily and scooping me up into a hug from behind. "You should have seen your face!"

"You're an asshole."

He drops me back to the ground easily and we walk the yard until we find my sisters, talking the entire time about Spring Break and his upcoming chapter elections.

It's nice to know we can still be friends with no awkward feelings between us. Adam Brooks is a nice guy to have in your corner, and I'm glad I didn't screw that up by tagging him as my boyfriend for a few months.

I realize it may be quite a while before I let anyone hold that title again, because the truth is, my heart is already taken. Poker is my boyfriend, and we're taking our relationship to the next level this summer. It's getting serious between us, and Poker is one jealous son-of-a-bitch who hates the idea of sharing me. Probably smart, since the last thing I want to be known as if I make it to the tournament next May is a slut or a man-eater. If I'm going to get my name out of the headlines for my dating lifestyle and into the limelight for my skills, I've got some work to do.

I feel some big changes on the horizon.

And I've got my game face on.

Ashlei

THEY SAY AVOIDING YOUR problems won't make them go away, but what happens when you have too many problems to face them all at once?

That's the question I've been battling with since Spring Break. First and foremost, I had to deal with the Omega Chi website—there was no running away from that. Once we hit campus, the website was texted to virtually everyone, and those who didn't get the original text eventually found out from the masses. Gossip like that spreads like a wildfire at PSU, and with a threesome on the front page, there was plenty of juice to fuel the flames.

So, like my mom always taught me, I focused on one thing at a time—starting with Bo and the website. As I ignore yet another text from Xavier and slip my phone back into my pocket, I try to reassure myself that mom's philosophy will pull through. If it's one thing at a time, I'd rather start with Bo than Xavier.

Ralph's is more packed than usual, but with a rather different crowd. The baseball game is over and all the students and parents have migrated north to everyone's favorite bar. As they do every year, the owners of Ralph's have set up karaoke on the same stage where we held the KKB auction just a couple of months ago and my dad is currently belting out *Paradise by the Dashboard Light*. His dark curls sway a bit as he animates the Meatloaf hit and Mom loops her arm through mine, bending over in a fit of laughter at our table. We're the same size, twins by practically every feature, and I can't help but mirror her laugh when my dad dramatically dips the microphone at the end.

"Bravo!" Mom yells as the bar erupts into whistles and catcalls. Dad takes a bow and hops off the stage, strutting back over to our table with a Cheshire grin. He kisses my mom's forehead and flops down on the bench across from her, taking a long swig from his beer mug.

"Well now I see where Ashlei gets her performance skills from," Skyler jokes, throwing my dad a high five. They've been buddied up all night, like two peas in a pod. In fact, my parents have been getting along with everyone—even Bo's parents. Erin and her mom went out to a late dinner with Landon after the baseball game and Cassie took her parents to watch Grayson play at Cup O' Joe's, but Skyler, Bo, her parents, my parents and I all came out to Ralph's to continue the night's festivities. I have yet to see Jess or her family, but that's been normal lately.

It's strange. Jess has been sticking up for me and Bo more than anyone in the chapter, yet she hasn't said one word to me since the day the news about the website broke. I can't say I blame her, because I know she feels betrayed. We're best friends and Bo is her Little. For many reasons, we should have told her, but we didn't get the chance. She'll come around, she just needs time. Jess is the kind of person who has to go through her own process, and she can't be swayed by anyone else.

"You're up next, sweetie," Dad says, nodding at Mom. She snorts.

"You wish. I wouldn't get on that stage if you paid me."

"Oh yeah?" Dad rubs his chin, bright green eyes lifting to the dingy ceiling of the bar. "What if that Michael Kors watch you've been wanting was up for grabs?"

Mom's eyes widen. "Don't play with my emotions."

"Come on, Mom!" I coax her further. "We can do a duet. Spice Girls or something equally as cliché."

She chews her lip, contemplating. Her eyes find Dad again and she points a freshly manicured finger in his direction. "You swear about the watch?"

Dad holds up two fingers. "On my honor."

Mom jumps up and skips to the stage and I follow. She selects *Turn Back Time* by Cher and we sound absolutely horrible together, but it's the first time I've done something with my mom, just the two of us, in longer than I can remember. I'm always hidden behind my sisters, and as shitty as it is, part of me is thankful that neither of them could make it this weekend. For once, the attention is on me, and I don't care how petty and immature it is to want that because I do. I need it right now.

I told my parents that I'm bisexual last night.

I expected Dad to scream and Mom to cry, but instead they gave each other a knowing look as if I didn't even have to say the words out loud. They both hugged me and we talked all night, each word making me feel more and more okay. I even told them about the website, though I begged them not to say anything to Bo's parents until she felt comfortable enough to tell them herself—if that day ever even came.

So maybe it's the fact that I finally opened up to them that makes me feel like I'm part of the family again. Still, I didn't tell them everything—I conveniently left out that I'm indebted to a drug lord and I lost a third of what I owe him a little over a week ago.

Baby steps.

I've been so caught up dealing with the website scandal that I really haven't had time to figure out what I'm going to do about Xavier. If I know him as well as I think I do, his patience is wearing thin, and it's only a matter of time before he shows up at my door demanding his money.

After my parents leave, I'll have to face the music and figure it out.

I just have no idea where to even start.

Dad pays up just like he said he would, ordering Mom's watch right on his phone once we're back at the table. Bo's parents have the same look on their face that's been there all night—a cross between amused and terrified. Apart from her skin tone, Bo looks nothing like them. Her eyes are wide, pinched just a bit at the corners, her smile big and bright, hair sleek. Her parents, on the other hand, rarely smile, their narrow eyes always surveying the surroundings like they're looking for escape routes.

"Well shit, looks like I missed the invitation to the party."

We're all mid-laugh when we turn and find Jess, solo, her eyes glossy and low, a half-empty beer bottle in her hand. I don't have to look at her longer than two seconds to know she's shitfaced. And, judging by the sneer on her lips, she's still pissed at me.

"Jess!" My dad jumps up first with Mom right behind him and they each wrap her in a hug, but her eyes don't leave mine. "It's so nice to see you. Are your parents here? I'd love to buy your dad a beer." Jess and I have spent a lot of time at each other's houses on breaks, and our parents are close because of it. I wonder if Jess told her parents about me and Bo. For some reason, the thought of them disapproving upsets me more than anyone else.

Dad looks around Jess' shoulder like he expects them to appear, but Jess just tilts her bottle to her lips and sloshes it back. "Nah, they went back to the hotel. Maybe you'll see them tomorrow."

Bo shifts in her seat, uneasy under Jess' glare. Her parents seem to pick up her vibes, too, because they're assessing Jess like she's a threat rather than a sister.

"They didn't drop you at the house on their way?" Skyler asks, and I know she's picking up the same cues I am. Jess is swaying, even with one hand firmly propped on the edge of our table, and she simply shakes her head no. Skyler smiles, but with caution. "Well I was just about to get a cab, so we can ride back together."

"We should probably get you guys back to the hotel, too," Bo says to her mom and dad as she stands. Her parents do the same but Jess stumbles over to them quickly.

"Oh no, I just got here!" She trips over the leg of a chair just as she reaches them and I eye Skyler, silently making a plan to get her out of here—and fast. "Are these your parents, Little? You have to introduce me!" But instead of waiting for an introduction, Jess throws her arms around Bo's mother first before fist bumping her father. They don't even try to hide their shock, they just let their mouths hang open before pinning Bo under a disapproving glare.

"Māmā, Bàba, this is Jess. She's my Big Sister in the sorority."

Bo's mother bows just slightly but her father narrows his eyes further before spouting off something in Chinese to Bo.

"Please, at least join me for one drink before you leave. We've just met," Jess says, motioning for them to take a seat. Bo looks to me for help but I just shrug, feeling as helpless as she does. Painting on a forced smile as everyone sits back down, Jess turns to my mom. "How was your day? What did you do?"

"Oh we had a wonderful time! We toured the house and sat front row at the game. Oh, and then Ron did karaoke!"

Dad smacks her leg playfully. "So did you! Should I pull up the video on my phone, Cher?"

Mom cackles, reaching out to touch Jess' arm, clearly oblivious to the tension at the table. Jess just listens patiently, sipping from her beer intermittently.

"Ashlei sang with me. She was actually kind of amazing. Who knew our little princess was keeping her singing talents a secret?"

Jess laughs with Mom, waving her empty beer bottle at a passing waitress. "Oh, she's quite good at keeping secrets."

"Jess," Skyler warns, silently signaling to the same waitress not to bring her another damn drop.

"What?" Jess scoffs, balancing the bottle between her forefinger and the table. "The girl should get an award. Do they have one for that sort of thing? We could always make one." Her lazy eyes find mine again. "*Most Likely to be a Lying Bitch*—Ashlei Daniels."

"We're leaving," Bo snaps, pushing her chair back again as her parents lift themselves from the bench.

"I think I know what this is about, Jess, and I understand why you're upset," my dad says, his hands up just a bit. When I filled my parents in on the website last night, I told them my suspicions that Jess was far from okay with the whole situation. He's talking to her like she's about to jump off the ledge of a building. Right about now, I wish she would. "But maybe we should talk about this later."

"Huh," Jess surmises, chewing on Dad's words. "I don't know. Now seems like the perfect fucking time to talk about it, actually. Especially since we've got the whole fam damily here." She gestures to Bo and her parents and suddenly my entire body is alert. I feel it—something bad is about to happen.

"What is she talking about, Bo?" her mom asks, brows bent inward in confusion.

"Nothing, Māmā. Let's go."

"What, you don't know?" Jess interjects before barking out a loud laugh. "Oh, please, let me be the one to fill you in."

"Jess!" Skyler hisses just as I warn, "That's enough, J-Love." My parents and I stand together, ready to escort Jess out to a cab.

"You see, your lovely daughter here, my precious, *sweet* Little, has been keeping a secret from me. From all of us, actually."

"You don't know what you're saying," my mom tries, but Jess just keeps talking louder.

"Don't worry, she's not alone, because Ashlei was part of all of this, too."

"Big, please," Bo pleads.

"But now, their secret's been leaked—because they're all over a website. And wasn't *that* just the peachiest way to find out that two of my best friends are lesbians." She pauses and my stomach sinks through the floor. "Together."

Everyone is silent for a stretched moment and as Jess' face crumples, I know she regretted the words she said before they even left her mouth. But now it's too late. And after just three quiet seconds, chaos erupts.

Bo's hand flies to her mouth as her parents start screaming at her in Chinese while my parents scream at Jess in English. Skyler pinches the bridge of her nose and I flop back down into my seat, feeling the weight heavy on my chest. I can't breathe, I can't speak, I can't think.

"What the fuck is wrong with you?!" Bo yells so loud her voice cracks and tears break on her cheeks. Her parents are still screaming, fingers waving, faces red with anger. Bo snatches her purse off the table and I shake myself out of my trance, jumping up to pull her into me.

"I'm so sorry."

When I touch her, her parents go absolutely ballistic and she rips away from my grasp.

"Not now." Bo snaps as her parents shove her toward the door.

"Just call me later, it'll be okay," I lie, calling out after her. She turns just enough for the light to catch the fresh tears on her cheeks and I suck my bottom lip between my teeth, knowing in my gut that nothing is okay, least of all this.

Whipping around, I pin Jess with my glare, chest heaving as what she did finally settles in. "Are you fucking happy, Jess? Is this what you wanted? You aired our dirty laundry so now you can feel better about yours?"

Jess' face is sheet white and her palms grip the edge of the table hard.

"We all know you're still fucking your teacher, but guess what? We're your sisters. And we know you'll tell us when *you're* ready, just like Bo and I would have told you. It's not our fault that website happened, but thanks for making an already shitty situation ten times shittier."

"I think I'm going to be sick." Jess gags into the back of her wrist and takes off for the bathroom, parting the sea of drunk parents on wobbly ankles.

Skyler's shoulders sag and she lets out a long sigh. "I'm so sorry, guys."

"It's not your fault," my dad assures her, running a hand through his thick hair, the curls bouncing right back into place. "She was hurt and upset and she acted irrationally. It happens."

"She's a bitch," I correct him and he scolds me with his eyes, but I just cross my arms over my chest.

"You better go check on her, sweetie." My mom motions toward the bathroom and Skyler nods, giving my arm a squeeze on her way.

Dad lets out a breath through his nose before crossing to me and pulling me into his arms. He wraps me in a tight hug, the one he used to save for the bad days, and I fold into him, squeezing my eyes tight against the pain.

"It'll be okay, baby girl," he whispers into my hair, rocking me gently. "Her parents will understand. That's their daughter, and they'll support her. No matter what."

I sniff, shaking my head against his chest. "Nice speech. Now tell me what you really think they'll do."

Dad just pulls me closer and Mom rubs my back, her sad eyes connecting with mine. He doesn't have to say a word.

The answer is in the silence.

Bear

THE BEST THING ABOUT going to school in Florida is the spring weather. While the rest of the country is still battling with cold fronts and snow, we're sitting pretty at eighty-five degrees under a partly-cloudy sky. There's a light breeze rolling through the palm trees and Clayton inhales a deep breath, letting it go with a grin on his face. It's the last day of Family Weekend, and as my little brother and I walk across campus to the College Showcase, I can't help but smile along with him. It's been amazing having him here.

"We should do this more often," I say, tossing my arm over his shoulder. "Maybe you could fly down for Shark Week this summer."

"That would be so awesome!" He shakes his head, eyes hidden behind Omega Chi branded sunglasses. "I can't wait to go to college . . . to get out of Pittsburgh."

I squeeze his shoulder firmly before dropping my arm and tucking my hands in my pockets. "You'll be out of there soon enough, little brother. Just try to stay focused on your grades and sports while you're there. Set up your future."

He nods, squinting slightly as the sun peeks around a cloud. "I will." When he turns to me, his expression is hard. "Once I leave, I'm never going back, Clinton."

I swallow, knowing exactly where he is right now. I remember the feeling. I thought the longer I was at Palm South, the more it would fade away, but I can still remember every minute of hating life when I was waiting for high school to end. "I know, baby brother. I don't blame you. I only go back because you're there."

Clayton's brows furrow as we round the fountain and make our way toward the Student Union. "Our family sucks."

I offer a short laugh. "Yeah, unfortunately you can't choose your blood family, but you'll always have me." Smiling, I nudge him. "And when you rush, you get to pick a whole new band of brothers—ones who also don't suck. Then, one day, you'll find a girl, and she'll make all the other girls feel so obsolete. You'll marry her, you'll have kids, and then before you know it, you have your own family." I adjust the backpack of beer on my back, pulling the straps down so it adjusts higher on my shoulders. "And it'll be up to you, then, to make sure that family doesn't suck like ours did."

Clayton smiles up at me, just a slight tug at the corner of his lips, but enough to let me know he needed to hear that. I pull him in for a noogie just as we reach the first row of tents outside the union. The fraternities and sororities always make up the entire first row, and when I spot Adam at the Alpha Sigma tent, I whistle through my teeth.

"Glad to see you're still alive after Spring Break, Brooks." I clap him on the back and he flips me the bird, but with a smile. "This is my little brother, Clayton."

Adam shakes Clayton's hand, lifting his sunglasses up into his hair. "Oh shit, there's another generation of you? President Whittington is going to have a heart attack when your name comes across the admissions desk."

I chuckle. "Just wait until he realizes Clayton is rushing, too."

"God help us all."

We all laugh for a second before Adam breaks the conversation long enough to talk to the mom of a pledge. He hands her a few pamphlets about their founders and heritage and runs over their philanthropic events before she nods and smiles, letting her son lead her to the food set up behind the tent. When Adam turns back to us, his smile fades, his eyes adjusting on something behind us rather than on our faces. He flicks his sunglasses back down and I spin to see what he's looking at. When I find Cassie, her parents, and Grayson laughing as they make their way down the line of tents, I turn to Adam again, narrowing my eyes.

"Hey guys!" Cassie says cheerily when they reach us. I watch as her face transforms from ecstatic when she sees me to curious when she notices Clayton to absolutely terrified when she realizes Adam is behind us. Or maybe that's nervous I'm seeing. Maybe both.

Something is weird between those two.

"Hey," I greet, pulling her in for a hug. "Cassie, this is my little brother, Clayton."

Clayton reaches out for her hand, sliding his sunglasses down his nose just enough to peek at her over the top of the shades. "Well hello, Beautiful. You can call me Baby Bear. How do you feel about younger men, sweetheart?"

Cassie's mom blushes and covers her smile as her dad lets out a loud belly laugh. Her dad is odd-looking, sporting the same fiery red hair that Cassie has except with bronze skin and not a freckle in sight. Her mom, on the other hand, has light blonde hair and green eyes with pale skin, the apples of her cheeks peppered with freckles. It's like Cassie is literally the perfect mix of the two.

"Damn, I need to step up my game," Grayson says, reaching out his hand to shake Clayton's next. "Sorry, Baby Bear, but this little lady is taken at the moment."

Clayton shrugs. "We'll see what the story is in four-and-a-half years when I turn eighteen." Cassie's parents laugh again, but Adam's mouth is still in a thin line, his eyes hard on where Cassie's hand is grasped firmly in Grayson's.

I introduce myself to Cassie's parents next and then they turn to Adam, expectant. He shifts, gripping the fliers in his hand a little too tightly as Cassie finally clears her throat. "Mom, Dad, this is Adam Brooks. He's going to be the president of Alpha Sigma next year."

Adam forces a smile, one that's all teeth and charming as fuck. The kid is good, but I can still see that he's hiding something. I knew the night of the Fratalina Wine Mixer. He's lucky he was smart enough to call it off with Skyler. "Well, we'll see. Elections haven't happened yet."

"We all know it'll be you," Cassie says again with a sweet smile, but her eyes look stressed, too, as they connect with Adam's.

We chat for a while in what feels like a pleasant manner, though Adam, Cassie and I feel the awkward tension that lies beneath it. After Grayson tells Cassie's dad how he works to pay for his tuition and everyone leans in for more, Adam excuses himself to go talk to a group of Alpha Sigma parents, but not until he and Cassie share another glance that says nothing but screams something fucked up all at once.

I catch Cassie's eyes with my own after Adam's gone and she flushes, tucking a strand of hair behind her ear and looping her arm through Grayson's, her attention snapping back to him. It's then that I notice a familiar face at a tent two rows over behind Cassie.

A familiar face, but that's all that's familiar about her.

Shawna's once-purple hair is now all black, falling straight down to her shoulders where it curls in soft waves. Her glasses are replaced with contacts, her normally casual and grungy style opted out in exchange for a knee-length white skirt and light yellow, button-up blouse. She's even wearing wedges, which I didn't realize she owned at all. Still, even with the changes, she's fucking gorgeous, and a shit-eating grin spreads on my face at the sight of her.

"Be right back," I murmur to Clayton before sprinting across the union to the tent she and who I assume are her parents are gathered around. I'm light on my feet, careful to watch the angle at which I approach. When I know I'm safe and she hasn't seen me, I close the distance and scoop her into my arms from behind, spinning her around. She squeals, but not in the way I wanted, before wriggling out of my arms. I drop her gently to the ground and kiss her cheek, but she backs away quickly, her cheeks hot, a nervous smile on her face.

"Hi, Clinton," she says, her bright green eyes darting to her parents before reconnecting with mine. "It's nice to see you."

"It's nice to see *you*," I respond with a chuckle. She must be joking, I don't think I've ever seen her be so formal. Realizing maybe it's her parents, I throw her a wink and slip on my professional face. "Sir, ma'am, my name is Clinton Pennington."

I extend my right hand to her father first, but his eyes don't leave his daughter and my hand remains empty. Her mother reaches her dainty hand across her husband to give mine a light squeeze. "Pleasure, dear. And how do you two know each other?" She phrases the question to her daughter, not to me. Neither of them will look at me.

"Oh we're just project partners in art class, Momma. Clinton is actually really great. He's got a lot of talent."

Her parents' brows shoot up in synchrony, their lips tight, but satisfied at their daughter's response. It's as if their eyebrows have a direct connection to my stomach—they rise, my stomach falls.

What the fuck is happening.

"I have a lot of talent, do I?" I don't even bother hiding my sarcasm as I snap the question at Shawna. All the little pieces are clicking into place as my heart rate accelerates, my nose flaring along with the beat.

"Momma, Daddy, I'll be right back. Clinton and I need to discuss an assignment that's due this week. Why don't I meet you at the alumni tent?"

They both nod, their eyes raking me disapprovingly once more before Shawna pulls me in the opposite direction. I barely let them get out of earshot before I rip away from her grasp.

"What the fuck was that, Shawna?" I seethe. "Your *project partner*? Are you fucking kidding me?"

"Bear, please."

"Oh, *now* I'm Bear to you. What, that didn't sound as impressive to say to Mommy and Daddy? I guess I can thank my deadbeat dad for his last name, at least."

"Stop!" she screams, her eyes glossing over. She's never seen this side of me before. "You don't understand."

"Clearly. Although, I'd love to hear your explanation. Please," I scoff, motioning my hand toward her before crossing my arms over my chest. Her bottom lip quivers as I close myself off to her, and it's almost enough to make me apologize.

"My parents are old-fashioned . . ." She trails off, eyes on her fingers as she wrings them together. "We're from Mississippi, and where I grew up, there weren't many . . . there wasn't much . . . diversity."

She peeks up at me through her lashes, brows furrowed, eyes guilty and ashamed. It takes me a moment to understand as I squint at her, the sun beaming behind her black hair, framing her in a silhouette. When the anchor drops, pulling my chest along with it, I have to force a breath.

"It's because I'm black."

Shawna cringes, one arm crossing her chest as the other lifts her hand to cover her mouth. I watch as her eyes fill to the brim with tears, but I feel no urge to soothe her.

"They hate me already because of the color of my skin, don't they?"

Shawna just shakes her head, refusing to answer my question and answering it all the same.

I lick my bottom lip against a manic smile, clenching my fists where they're still crossed over my chest. "And you?"

"What about me?" she asks softly, her brows pinched in confusion.

"Do you have an opinion about me based on my race?"

"What? No!" Two tears stream out of her left eye, one after the other, the stream falling vertically before breaking right at her jaw line. "I thought that was obvious."

"Then tell them." I point two fingers straight over at where her parents are standing at the alumni tent, not even bothering to see if they're looking at us. "Walk over to them right now and tell them what you told me last week. Tell them you're falling in love with me. Tell them I'm not your project partner, I'm your boyfriend."

She chokes on a sob, biting her lips together. "I can't." She hiccups the words, just above a whisper. "Please, just let me explain."

"I think I've heard plenty." I don't look at her again before walking straight past her back to the Alpha Sigma tent. I *can't* look at her. Still, I hear her calling my name as I stride, her tears breaking on the one harsh syllable.

"Who was that," Clayton asks as I hook my hand around his elbow, pulling him away from the A Sig tent. I'm on a mission to find my own brothers now. It's been a long time since I've drowned myself in a bottle of liquor to find the numb I used to crave so often, but I feel that same want creeping into my bloodstream now.

"No one."

"No one," Clayton deadpans, struggling to keep up with me. "So, you ran up and wrapped your arms around her, but you don't know her?"

His words dig into my chest like a rusty butter knife and I suck in a breath, desperate for air, for relief.

"Not anymore."

Skyler

I'VE ALWAYS THOUGHT OF Erin as the mom of our group. She's the one who has her head on straight, the one with the conscience, the one who knows what to wear and what to say and what not to drink. But she's been absent since Spring Break, tied up in executive board shit half the time and tied up in Landon the other half. I've barely seen her, other than the awkward twenty minutes with her and her real mom, and I'm not even sure she knows what happened last night between Jess and Ashlei. Which means it's my turn to step up to the plate and put on my mom pants.

Jess hasn't moved out of her bed all day, so I'm not surprised when I push through our bedroom door and see her still buried under the covers. It's just after five in the evening, the campus slowly draining itself of parents. Jess' didn't even bother sticking around for today's events, they just left me some cash for Jess and told me to send their love. They assume she's hungover, but I know the truth—she's feeling guilty.

As she should.

I leave the big light out, but click on the small lamp on my bedside table before climbing into bed next to Jess. She doesn't fight me, just lets me slide under the sheets until we're nose-to-nose. I'm silent for a moment, noting the smeared mascara around her tired brown eyes.

"I brought wine," I finally say, reaching into the bag I pulled under the covers with us. The brown paper crinkles as I reveal a sweet moscato.

Jess cringes. "Get that away from me."

"Oh, so you don't want to drink anymore?" I nod, twisting off the top. Buying a bottle that needed a cork popped would have alerted Mom Cindy. I lift the bottle to my lips, shrugging. "I was so sure you were hell-bent on drinking yourself into stupidity."

"I think I already hit that town last night."

"I think you stayed in a hotel overnight and they named the city after you."

She sighs, sniffling as her eyes connect with mine. "I get it, okay?"

"I don't think you do, Jess."

She throws the covers off of us in a huff, the cool air rushing in. "If you came here to lecture me, you can get the fuck out."

"It's my room, too."

"Don't be a bitch."

"*Me?*"

She groans, snatching a pillow up and covering her face with it. "You're not going away, are you?" she mumbles. I just wait, taking another pull from the wine bottle until she tosses the pillow back down. She exhales like a horse, her lips flapping dramatically. "I fucked up."

"Mm hmm."

"So now what?"

"I was going to ask you the same thing."

Jess flips over to rest on her left elbow, her greasy blonde hair falling over her eyes. She brushes it back behind her ear slowly. "I was pissed, Skyler. They both hid that shit for who knows how long and then they get busted, on camera, and act like nothing happened. I've had to stick up for them against all of our sisters who are calling for them to be kicked out of KKB meanwhile I'm pissed at them, myself. And meanwhile, they've been like two fuck-ing mice, not saying a word, not apologizing. It's bullshit."

"What exactly are they supposed to be apologizing for?"

"For lying! For, for . . ." she trails off, her hands wav-ing wildly as she grasps for something else to be pissed about. "All of it!"

Pressing my lips together, I lean up against the head-board of her bed and take another sip of the wine. When I offer it to Jess again, she grimaces and pushes it back toward me.

"Listen, they don't have anything to be sorry for. So what if they're in a relationship? It's no different than you being in a relationship with your teacher and not telling any of us about it."

"We're not in a relationship. And that's different."

"You so are, and no, it's not. And what, they're sup-posed to be apologizing for getting caught on camera hav-ing sex with one lucky son-of-a-bitch on Spring Break? I hooked up last week, too. I could have been taped just as easily. They're not at fault here, Jess."

"Oh, so I'm just some crazy mean bitch, then?"

"Don't be dramatic."

She eyes the bottle in my hand like she's almost tempted to take a drink, but thinks better of it. Squeezing her eyes shut, she covers them with the heels of her hands and blows out a long, slow breath. "I was wasted."

"That's still not an apology."

She huffs. "Fine, I was wrong."

I nod, satisfied, tipping the bottle back once more. "I'm glad you see it now, but I'm not the one you need to be saying that to."

She whimpers, falling forward until her head is in my lap. I run my fingers through her hair as she speaks into the covers, her voice muffled. "She hates me. They both do. Where do I even start?"

"Just be honest with them, J-Love. And apologize, don't make excuses. That's all you can do. They'll either forgive you or tell you to go to hell. Either way, you have to say you're sorry—and mean it."

She swallows, but nods, leaning up to face me again. "I should go find Ashlei."

Wrinkling my nose, I eye the shirt she was wearing last night paired with underwear that could have that same reputation for all I know. "You should shower first."

Jess laughs, smacking me with a pillow, but then her mouth pulls to the side. She leans into me, wrapping her lean arms around me and leaning her head on my shoulder. I hold her for a minute, trying to be the strength she needs. "Thank you, Skyler."

Petting her hair, I offer a reassuring smile. "What are sisters for?"

An hour later, Clinton is unloading Clayton's bag from the cab as we stand on the curb outside of the departing flights terminal. They've both been joking around the entire cab ride, but Clinton filled me in on what happened with Shawna just before we piled into the car, so I'm itching to talk to him more about it. Though judging by his forced playfulness with his brother, I can tell he isn't. I wonder if it's one of those situations where I'll need to let him come to me again, the same way I had to wait with his family drama last semester.

It's not that I think racism is dead—I'd be naïve to honestly believe that. Still, I've never been so up close and personal to it before. Shawna seemed so into Clinton, she seemed like a down to earth chick. The fact that she let her prejudiced parents break them apart throttles me.

I can only imagine how Clinton feels.

"I think that Zeta wants me," Clayton says with a sly grin as the cab pulls away and we make our way inside. "She gave me her phone number."

"Oh yeah? Let me see." I hold out my hand and Clayton places his cell phone into my palm, a number pulled up on the screen under the name *Ass-tastic Jazzy*. I chuckle at the name, but full on laugh when I see the number. "Oh, Baby Bear."

"What?!" He looks alarmed, snatching the phone away like I've deleted the number.

"That's the Loser Line."

His brows tug inward over his chocolate irises. "What's that?"

"It's a phone number the local radio station gives out to girls so they can blow off losers. If you call that number and leave a voicemail, they'll probably play it on the air," Clinton explains.

Clayton narrows his eyes and snaps his fingers together. "What a minx. She's playing hard to get."

Clinton nudges him with a grin as I roll my eyes.

The Penningtons are something else.

We check Clayton's bag and make our way toward security, the mood shifting. There's something about seeing boys express emotion that really gets to me. I've never seen my father cry, nor have I stuck around long enough to see any of my exes cry, either. But I feel the weight of Clayton's departure, and Clinton keeps pressing his lips together and chewing the skin next to his thumb nail, fighting back what I'm positive would be tears if he'd let them fall.

"Well, I guess this is it, little bro," he finally says as we reach the security line. Clayton adjusts the small backpack he's using as a carry-on over his shoulder, his eyes on his shoes. "Did you call to make sure Mom would be there to pick you up?"

"Nah, Mac's mom is coming to get me."

Clinton frowns. "Are you staying there again tonight?"

When Clayton twists his mouth and lifts his eyes to mine, my heart stops before he even says a word.

Uh oh.

"I'm sort of staying there every night . . ."

It takes two-and-a-half seconds for Clinton to catch on, and when he does, I watch his nose flare as his fists tighten at his sides. "What are you talking about?"

"Don't be mad," Clayton pleads, holding his hands up. "Mac's family is cool with it. They think of me like a son, and I'm doing chores and stuff to help out around the house."

"Mac's mom I understand, but I have a really fucking hard time believing *our* mom is okay with this." I remember Clinton telling me over Winter Break that his mom never let him leave when he wanted to, even the time his aunt offered her spare bedroom up. His mom needs to feel in control of her kids' lives, no matter how dangerous that may be.

"Well, I wouldn't know."

Clinton and I exchange questioning glances. "What do you mean, Baby Bear?" I ask.

He sighs, his dark fingers fidgeting with the straps of his backpack. "She never came home in December. Neither did Carleton."

Shit.

Clinton's anger disappears as all emotions drain from his face. It's the palest I've ever seen him. "Are you telling me you've been living with Mac since December and you haven't told me?" Clayton doesn't dare answer and I don't dare move. I'm almost afraid to breathe.

For a moment, Clinton just nods, short little nods as his eyes scan the airport, looking everywhere but at Clayton. He chews the insides of his lips and I see the wheels spinning.

"I'm coming home with you. Right now."

"No!" Clayton yells at the same time as I grab Clinton's arm.

"Bear, just relax a second."

"Skyler," he warns and I pull my hand away. He turns his attention back to his brother. "I'm coming. End of story."

"Please, don't." Clayton's eyes brim with tears, his age showing more than it has all weekend. I keep forgetting he's only thirteen. That realization only makes my heart ache more. "You're the only one in our family who has their shit together. I can't wait to get out of Pittsburgh and be with you. If you come home and throw this semester away, you'll fall back and have to take extra classes to catch up or stay another year, and that's *if* you even ever come back. I don't want that for you, for me, for either of us."

"I'm not going to let you live by yourself. Without a mom, without any fucking family."

"I have a family," he pleads. "Mac and his sister and their parents. They make dinner every night, did you know that? I didn't think anyone did that anymore." He smiles, his eyes still glossy, his movements animated as he tries to make his big brother see his side. "And we play video games and go do fun things on the weekend. There's no smoke in the house, no drugs, no fighting."

Clinton crosses his arms, still staring somewhere behind his little brother. Suddenly, his eyes grow wide. "Where are the boys?"

I snap my attention back to Clayton, the realization that Carleton has two sons hitting me as hard and fast as it hit Clinton.

"They're with Tara. They're okay, she's taking care of them. I see them on the weekends."

Clinton exhales a breath, letting me know it's okay I do the same. I think Tara is the mom, but I'm not sure. My eyes find Clinton again. Noting his steadier breathing, I take the opportunity to give my input.

"Bear, he's right. You can't just leave Palm South. I know this isn't easy to hear, but look at Clayton." I point in his direction. "He's fine. He's better than fine."

"I should be there for him."

"You *are*," Clayton emphasizes. "By being here and being the man I hope to be, you're there for me. That's what I need from you right now."

I nod, still not believing how wise Clayton is for such a young kid. "Listen, let's plan a trip home to see him this summer. You can see where he's staying and if you decide then that it's not good enough, then you can stay. I won't even ask you twice to come back." The words sting as they leave my lips, but I know they're necessary. Clinton needs to hear that he has options, especially when it comes to the last family member he really cares about.

"I'll have Mac's mom call you as soon as I get home so you can talk. She's been wanting me to tell you."

"But you didn't," Clinton throws back.

"And this is why."

Clinton shakes his head, his arms still tight over his chest. When his eyes turn to mine, they ask me for permission I'm not sure I can really give. But I smile, giving a short nod to let him know I think it's okay—and truly, I do.

Blowing out a long breath, he pulls his little brother into him and crushes his arms around the smaller version of himself. They hold each other tight and I lean in long enough to ruffle Clayton's curls.

"I'll give you two a minute. Catch you later, Baby Bear. Don't grow up too much before I see you again."

"Afraid you'll want to date me, Sky?"

Clinton finally laughs and I just shoot Clayton a wink before excusing myself. I wait on a small bench as they say their goodbyes, pretending to look through my phone, though I'm too aware of the moment being shared between them to really do anything else. After a while, Clinton makes his way back toward me and I stand to meet him, his eyes still not meeting mine.

Clayton waves at us once more as he hands his ID to the TSA agent and Bear sighs. Sliding my hand into his, I lean my head on his shoulder and he tightens his grip around my fingers.

"Everything is falling to shit, Skyler."

I kiss his arm, squeezing his hand just once. "We'll get through it together. We always do."

He peeks down at me, the smallest smile curving over his lips as he tucks me under his arm. When Clayton finally disappears from view on the other side of security, Clinton pulls me all the way into him, his large frame folding into me. He doesn't sob, but he clutches me tight, using me to steady himself.

"I don't know what I'd do without you," he finally

whispers, sniffling as he straightens once more. The left side of my mouth quirks up and I tug him toward the exit.

"Ditto, Bear. Ditto."

Ashlei

MY EYES ARE CLOSED, the sand cold on the back of my thighs as I face the ocean and listen to the waves crashing on the beach. They're not gently rolling in tonight, they're slapping the wet sand, rolling over one another in a race to meet their demise. I don't see or hear her take her place in the sand next to me. I just feel her. Our souls are at war right now, and it's as if my entire body is set on alert just from her nearness.

"How'd you find me?" I finally ask with a sigh. It's not like the beach is a normal place for me to go when I need to get away, that's more Skyler's thing than mine. I'm usually at the gym or, when I danced, at the studio. Even now as I try to find solace in the quietness of the beach at night, I'm mostly annoyed by the sand sticking to my ass and the salt water spritzing my hair.

"Bo told me," Jess answers, her voice quiet. She's sober.

"I'm surprised she's even talking to you."

She offers a short laugh and I open my eyes, letting them land on where her fingers are tracing the sand. "I'm not sure that 'fuck off' counts as talking."

"So she didn't tell you?"

"She didn't have to. I saw the sand on her feet and guessed. Or hoped, rather."

I'm torn between the urge to cry and the overwhelming want to slap her hard across the face. Before Bo, Jess was my best friend in the sorority. I thought she still was. Yes, things have been tired and tense between us since my situation all started last semester, but I never questioned that she would ever hurt me. Now I don't just feel blind-sided, but I feel betrayed, too.

"Are you two okay?" Jess asks, and I can tell the question feels strange on her lips.

I shrug, picking up a small shell and using it to carve through the soft sand. My heart aches as I ask myself to answer her question honestly. Bo was just here, maybe two hours ago, and as much as I want us to be okay, we're not. Not even close.

"She's hurt. She's scared. The website hit her hard and this . . . *you* nearly killed her."

Jess swallows, pulling her knees up and tucking her hands under her thighs. "I am so, *so* sorry, Lei. I know that's not enough. It wasn't enough when I told Bo tonight, either, and I'm not really asking for forgiveness. I'm just letting you both know that I regret what I said and how I said it and if I could take it all back, I would. But I can't. So, I'm sorry. And I hope that in time, I can earn back your trust. Both of you."

I don't look at her yet, I can't. I just nod along with her words, tears blurring the line where the light sand meets the dark water. I'm waiting for it—the *but*—the part where she says it's my fault she exploded the way she did. In a way, I sort of agree with her. In another way, I think she's completely full of shit.

After a few moments of silence, I get impatient. Pulling my knees in to mirror her, I finally turn my head, resting my cheek on my knees and connecting my eyes with hers. I find more remorse there than I thought I would. "But?"

Jess breathes out slowly. "No buts. I was wrong."

"Yes you fucking were," I spit out, my voice shaky as the tears break down my cheeks. Her lip quivers, too, and I squeeze my eyes shut against the pain, pulling my arms up to my knees and burying my head between them. Sobs rack my body as the waves rack the shore and I cry with them, both of us losing a part of ourselves, both of us struggling to begin once again.

Hesitantly, Jess' hand touches my back. She waits, ready for me to jerk away, but when I don't, she pulls me flush against her and I cry harder.

"Shhh," she whispers, her fingers running through my hair. She's crying, too. "I'm sorry. I'm so sorry. You're right, I have been hiding Jarrett from you—from all of you. I saw you and Bo kiss at formal and instead of being an adult and asking you to talk to me about it, I figured two could play that game. So we've been shutting each other out for months now, seeing who could be the most secretive. But I don't want to play anymore, Lei. I love you. I miss my best friend."

"I miss you, too," I cry, my hands fisting in her loose t-shirt. My ribs ache with the force of my sobs but I let them hurt me. I let it all sink in.

"Ashlei, let me in. I know there's more you're battling with. I've known it since last semester. First, I pushed you, but you kept it all locked away. So then I gave up asking, and then I saw the Bo thing and I just got so angry. I'm sorry I did that, I wasn't a good sister. But I'm here, right now, and I can help you—with whatever is happening. But you have to let me in, first."

I think I understand why Skyler goes to the ocean when she's struggling, now. It feels like a place where you can be reborn—where you can change. The only person I've let in is Bo, and I haven't even let her all the way in. I've been so set on handling it on my own, afraid of what everyone would think of me, afraid of being a failure. But now, the website has already done that for me. Some of my sisters are judging me, the entire campus has seen me at my most vulnerable, and no matter what happens to the asshole who videotaped us, I'll never have that peace of mind back again. Our secret was no longer ours to keep after that night. And no matter how I try to avoid Xavier, I have to face him eventually—soon. I may not have been ready to come out as a bisexual yet, but that wasn't even my biggest demon. Xavier is.

Wouldn't it be easier to face him if I weren't alone?

Straightening, I wipe my nose against my bare wrist and pull my eyes to Jess'. I inhale a shaky breath that doesn't quite reach my ribs and then, with her hand squeezing mine, I tell her everything. I tell her about pole dancing, how much I loved it, how much I miss it now because of a stupid decision I made with a stupid boy. I tell her about getting shoved out of the car and waking up that night, realizing I was making a mistake, but I was too late. Jess still holds tight to my hand, not an ounce of judgement in her eyes.

I tell her about the first payment, how I lied to my parents, how I let Bo help me and we thought we figured it out together, but then Kya showed up and blew up my entire world. Every word leaves me feeling more broken and somehow fixable at the same time.

I can't look at her when I tell her I did dance for money—once—just enough for me to realize I couldn't do it. I still can't lift my eyes to hers as I tell her about the deals I made with the devil—the payments, the stolen money from our auction, how I asked him to hit me, how I sold drugs on Spring Break. By the time I'm completely caught up, telling her how I lost over a third of the money I owe him and I know any day now he's going to give up trying to call me and send someone to bring me to him, I can't place how I feel. Relieved? Terrified? I'm not sure.

I don't know how long I've been talking. My voice is scratchy, my throat sore, my eyes puffy. Jess' hand is still firmly holding mine.

"I don't know what to do anymore," I whisper, shaking my head as my eyes stay fixed on our hands. "I've tried for so long to figure this out on my own. I was afraid of the judgement, afraid of the consequences. I was so ruled by fear that I kept digging deeper and deeper into a hole I fell into accidentally but stayed in by choice." Realization hits me like a freight train. "This is my fault, Jess. This is all my fault."

"Hey," she says as I start to cry again, her free hand finding my chin. She lifts my head, but I keep my eyes shut. "Look at me, Lei."

Shaking my head, I force a breath and finally crack my eyes open, her blurred face coming into view slowly.

"It's okay. Do you hear me?" She leans in closer, her chocolate eyes connecting hard with mine. "It is *okay*."

It's like those words are all I've been wanting for months now, I just didn't know I needed them. I didn't know what to even ask for. Now that she's said it, my heart finally realizes.

I just want to be okay.

"I wish you would have come to me sooner, Lei. I can't believe you've been going through this on your own." She hugs me close to her chest again and I wrap my arms around her shoulders.

Sniffling, I stare out into the dark ocean, feeling better but not saved yet. "Jess, what am I going to do? He's going to come looking for me. He's killed people before." I choke on the words, gripping her shirt between my fingers. "He could kill *me*."

Everything is heavy—the air, my arms, those words. Jess peels me off of her and frames my arms with her hands, holding me tight, forcing my eyes to hers. Though the mascara stains under her eyes and her body shakes with mine, she no longer looks remorseful or sad. She looks determined—fierce—the Jess I know slowly rising to the surface again. Her eyes narrow, her lips pursed, and slowly, she nods.

"I have a plan."

EPISODE 6

Jess

"Time to Kiss Spring Semester Goodbye in Style."

HYSTERICAL LAUGHTER.

That's what's coming from my mouth right now as Jarrett stares at me from his side of the bed, brows furrowed, lips pressed together in a thin line. He's not amused, and nothing he said was funny, but I can't stop laughing.

It's a nervous habit I've always had. I'm not good with handling serious situations. Anytime I'm uncomfortable or freaked out, I crack a joke or laugh uncontrollably. In both situations, I piss someone off.

And Jarrett is the last person I want to make mad.

Throwing the covers off, he shakes his head and leaves the bed. I instantly miss him, especially as his tight ass stalks toward his closet. Reaching out, I try to fight the giggles. "Wait, Jarrett." Still giggling. "I'm sorry."

"This isn't fucking funny, Jess. Not anymore," he snaps, hastily stepping into a pair of boxer briefs and yanking them up to his hips. My eyes are glued to the deep V of his lower abdomen still left exposed, the one I was dragging my tongue across just moments ago. Before Jarrett asked me—in all seriousness, my hands grasped in his as he kissed my knuckles—to be his girlfriend.

His legit girlfriend—not a fuck buddy, not a friend with benefits, not something we don't title. He wants it all.

And I don't think I can give it to him.

"I know," I say, clearing my throat. The early morning light is trying to break through the navy blue curtains of his bedroom, bathing us in the cool glow of dawn. Another fit of laughter threatens to break loose but I twist my face to fight it down. "It's a nervous habit. I can't really control it."

He sighs, pulling a pair of jeans off a hanger and throwing them on just as quickly as his boxer briefs, the metal hanger still flailing against the others. "I don't understand why you even hesitated when I asked. Are you not essentially my girlfriend already?"

"You know it's not the same."

"Oh? It's not?" He fastens his belt and then slowly crosses the room to me, sitting on the edge of his bed and framing me with his fists pressed into the comforter. "Do you want anyone else? Do you want *me* to be with anyone else? Do you think about me every minute you're not with me? Do you see me in your future? Do you want me here with you in your present?" His dark eyes drink me in, begging for me to argue with him. I can't. "Can you honestly answer 'no' to any of those questions? Even one?"

I'm not laughing anymore.

My breath leaves my chest in a slow exhale along with one word. "No."

"Then fucking *be* with me," he pleads earnestly, the veins in his arms protruding. "I'm tired of this game. You're mine. I'm yours. I want every fucking person in our lives to know that. And I don't want to have to watch you leave my house every morning wondering if you'll come back again."

My breathing accelerates and I pin my bottom lip between my teeth. He makes it sound so easy. *Just be with me.* But it's never that easy. What if the whole reason he loves being with me is because he doesn't have me—not really, not all the way? Or what if, just like how I gained my nickname, I tell him yes, then tell him I love him, and eventually he's gone—just like all the others. Jarrett is possessive over me now, I can't imagine how that would transfer into him being my actual boyfriend. Would he let me go to fraternity parties without him? Would he want to meet my parents?

"You'll lose your job," I try, knowing it's the bottom line from my list of excuses.

Jarrett scoffs. "The semester is all but over, Jess. I'll have a new job within the next few weeks."

"Still, this could damage your reputation."

"It won't. We started dating after I was your teacher, not during that semester. And I wasn't even technically your teacher. I'm a student. A grad student."

"But I'm still here. I have years to go. Don't you want to find a successful woman with her shit together?" Even suggesting he be with someone else makes my stomach lurch.

Jarrett pushes back from where he was angled over me and runs his hands over his bald head, his eyes on the bathroom door. I watch as the tattoos on his arms flex with the movement. They seem angry at me, too.

"Fucking Christ, Jess. How many times do I have to tell you?" He drops his hands to the bed, exhausted. His chest is heaving as he connects his eyes with mine. Suddenly, I'm too aware of my messy, freshly-fucked hair and what I'm sure is smeared makeup. I tuck my knees up to my chest. "I want *you*. I haven't looked at a single other fucking woman since the moment you strolled into the bar looking for me. You didn't know it that night, you didn't know it was me you wanted, but I did. I knew it when I saw the look in your eyes and the determination in your walk. I wanted you then, I want you now, and if you just fucking *let me in*—" His voice cuts off, his fists tightening.

An unfamiliar sting hits my nose and eyes but I sniff it away. *Am I about to cry?* Oh hell no. I'm Jess Vonnegut and I do *not* do emotions—not like this. I have too much shit going on with Ashlei right now as it is. I should be focusing on how I'm going to help her out of the disaster she's found herself in, not on this. Why do we have to figure all of this out right now?

"I thought we were fine the way we were. The way we *are*. Why isn't this enough for you?"

He pauses, a long, slow breath expelling from his lips as he stands. "I don't know. I thought I could do this, not put a title on it, just be whatever we are. But I can't anymore." He crosses back to his closet and tugs a long-sleeved button-up down, shrugging it over his shoulders. On the third button, he stops, peering up at me with a pained expression. "I love you, Jess."

I swallow.

"I do," he continues, his fingers working the buttons again. "And it's okay if you don't feel the same. But I need this from you. I need you to be mine—completely." He's still getting dressed, as if the words slipping from his lips in the process aren't life-changing. He snaps on his watch and grabs his nice shoes, the ones he often wears to class. It's Friday, so he's a little more casual than usual, but just barely.

"And if I can't?" I sit up on my knees, pulling the sheets over my still-naked chest. "Would you rather not have me at all if you can't have me as your girlfriend? Does the title really make that much of a difference to you?"

He halts at his bedroom door, his back to me, shoulders taught.

"It's not just a title. If it were, you wouldn't be fighting it as much as you are."

He's right. I know he's right. Somewhere, deep inside my gut, I feel my own soul screaming at me to tell him yes. But I can't.

"You didn't answer my question."

He sighs, snatching his keys off the small table just outside his bedroom door. "I don't have to, you already know the answer." With that, he crosses the apartment and swings open the front door. His hand gripping the knob, he lifts his eyes to mine again, the space between us deafening. "So?"

My heart races so fast I have to balance my palms on the bed to keep myself upright. I'm not ready to be his girlfriend. I can't be his girlfriend. It's too much, it's too fast, it's too uncertain. I want what we have now, but he's saying that's not an option any longer. Why? What changed? My head is spinning, the room following suit. When my wild eyes find his again, I know I don't have to answer his question, either.

He bites his bottom lip, eyes falling to the floor as one, short laugh echoes through the apartment. Jarrett shakes his head swiftly and turns, calling out behind him. "Lock up before you leave."

He doesn't slam the door. He doesn't need to. It's there, sitting naked in the sheets still warm from sex, that I realize I've been fooling myself all along. Jarrett and I have always wanted different things. How stupid could I have been to think we could just avoid our questions simply because we already knew the answers?

I almost call out for him but stop myself, thinking better of it. Instead, I whisper to myself.

"He loves me?"

A smile touches my lips before reality chases it away. Jarrett loves me, but he's asking me to love him back. He's asking me to give more than we agreed on. We made a deal last semester, and that was working for me. I thought it was working for him. And now, because I won't be his girl-friend, I can't have him at all.

My stomach lurches and I sit up, planting my bare feet on the floor, letting the sheet fall to the side. I need a clear mind today and I know I'm not going to get it. I'm meeting with Ashlei in an hour to finalize our plan for Xavier, and yet now, there's only one thought in my head.

Can I really let Jarrett Locke walk out of my life?

Adam

"AND THAT'S WHY I'M proud to announce that the newest president of Alpha Sigma by an overwhelming vote is Adam Brooks."

The chapter room erupts in cheers, Jeremy going especially wild and hooting loudly over everyone as I stand and make my way to the front of the room. It feels like I'm walking in slow motion, trying to take it all in and feeling like it's impossible to do.

Ever since I rushed Alpha Sigma, I've been busting my ass to make us a top fraternity on campus again. We once were, especially in the 90s, but we fell off along the way. It hasn't been easy and the job is far from done, but now, I'll have more resources to make the difference I want to make. I finally let myself smile, wishing my grandfather could be here to see me. I'm doing it. I'm making something of my organization, of myself.

Clay forces a smile as he shakes my hand. I know he hates this, passing the crown to me, but in a way I think he saw it coming. He had to. He's graduating in just a few short weeks, so it really shouldn't bother him, but it does. I grin smugly, pulling him in to clap him on the back as the cheers continue. I hold him there a moment, squeezing his hand tighter than necessary.

"If you ever so much as fucking look at Cassie McBee again, you'll need reconstructive surgery to get back that fake ass smile of yours. Understand?"

Clay is normally cocky, but I catch the swallow he forces down as he pulls away. He doesn't meet my eyes, just motions toward me with both hands and a smile facing our brothers, making the room go crazy once more. Something tells me I won't have to warn him twice.

After a short speech and photo of me along with the new executive board, my brothers disperse, slipping back into finals mode as we all prepare for the end of the semester. I should feel elated, I should want to go get celebratory drinks, I should be making calls—but there's only one person I want to talk to right now. One person I *need* to talk to.

Pulling my phone from my pocket, I type out a quick text to Cassie, praying she'll actually respond. We've barely talked since Spring Break. I came back on such a high, which makes no sense because all I had done was complicate whatever relationship we have further. We kissed, it was amazing, but what does that really mean? Apparently, to her—nothing. She was back in Grayson's arms as soon as we returned. I wondered why she wasn't returning my calls, but Family Weekend answered that question for me. I may not deserve to know what that night meant to her, but I have to ask anyway.

My phone pings with a text from her saying she's at the KKB house and to come to the back kitchen door. Steeling myself, I tuck my phone back in my pocket and start the walk down Greek Row, words I want to say scrolling through my mind like movie credits the entire time. But when I knock softly on the back door and she lets me in, her soft red curls pulled in a low ponytail over her shoulder and her legs exposed in a tiny pair of plaid sleep shorts, everything I planned to say leaves me instantly—like a candle flame snuffed out by a lid.

"Congrats," she says first with a genuine grin before pulling me in for a hug, like she hasn't been ignoring me for weeks. I'm almost too shocked to hug her back, but slowly, my arms wrap around her and I hold her tight against me, inhaling the tropical scent from her hair. She always smells like paradise.

"News travels fast."

She giggles, pulling back and crossing her arms over her chest, framing the small bit of cleavage exposed by her tank top. "Come on, how long have you been at PSU? You know better than I do."

"True story."

"Well, I wish we could have a shot to celebrate, but, you know, house rules and all." She points a thumb over her shoulder. "Want a root beer?"

I laugh. "Do you *have* a root beer?"

Cassie rolls her eyes as if it's obvious. "Of course. It's my favorite drink."

"Interesting. Well in that case, make it a double." I like that it's easy between us right now, especially after the tension during Family Weekend. Still, I'm not just going to slip back into the friend zone. I have to talk to her about what happened.

She chuckles, arms still crossed until she reaches the refrigerator. Pulling out two tall glasses and filling them to the top with the foamy dark liquid, she slides one down the counter to me as she lifts the other to her own lips. The bubbles stick at the corners of her mouth for just a moment before she licks them away.

"I forgot how much I love root beer," I say, taking a sip myself.

Her eyebrows shoot up and she points at me over her glass. "See? You're welcome."

As our smiles settle, I grip the glass a little tighter. "I didn't come here to celebrate."

"I figured," she responds, eyes on her own hands. "Listen, I get it. It was Spring Break, we were both drinking. It's all good."

I cock a brow, setting my glass down on the kitchen island. It's Sunday night and the house is mostly quiet, save for the faint sound of giggling coming from the rooms upstairs.

"It wasn't a mistake, Cassie. It wasn't an accident or a drunken decision. Ever since I kissed you at the concert last semester, I've wanted to do it again."

She wants me to apologize for the kiss. She thinks I regret it. I don't.

"How can you say that?" she asks, green eyes wide. "You were with Skyler."

"I know, I know." I pinch the bridge of my nose, not really knowing how to explain what I need to. "It's not that I didn't care for her—that I don't *still* care for her. But I also care about you. And that night on the beach, it was like the biggest moment of clarity for me."

Cassie drops her glass to the counter and brings her fingernails to her teeth, nibbling, eyes on the tile floor.

"You can't do this, Adam. I mean, what are you even asking me?" Her voice is shaky when she finally speaks.

"I don't know." I sigh, knowing none of this is coming out right. But what do I really expect? I was dating her Big Sister just a few short weeks ago and now, what? I'm going to ask her to be with me? "I guess I'm just saying that I get what you said at the Fratalina Wine Mixer now." I shrug, lifting my eyes to hers. "You confuse me, too."

"I'm with Grayson."

She says those three words like they won't puncture my lungs, stealing my breath. "Let me take you to formal. Please. Give me . . . I don't know, give me one night."

"One night for what?" She stands straighter, tucking a loose strand of hair behind her ear. "Didn't you hear me? I'm with Grayson. *He's* taking me to formal."

I wince, inching toward her. She's basically telling me to eat shit and die but I can't let it go. Grabbing the crook of her elbow, I force her to look at me, hoping my eyes will be able to say what my words can't. "Shit, Cassie. Did it mean nothing to you? Was this all one-sided?"

She chews the inside of her cheek and I can see her debating whether she should tell me the truth or not. I already know it meant something to her, too, but I need to hear it. I don't want the lies between us anymore, the secrets, the hidden thoughts. I want it all on the table. I want her exposed.

"It doesn't matter. You just broke up with Skyler because you knew you were going to get president. You weren't going to have time for her, so what makes you think you'll have time for me?"

I open my mouth to respond, but snap it shut again. I don't have an answer for that. And as I'm trying my damndest to find one, someone rounds the corner into the kitchen.

"Where's my beautiful redhead?"

I drop Cassie's arm and grab my glass, quickly lifting it to my lips and keeping my eyes on her as she gazes behind me at Grayson. For a moment she just stares at him, but then slowly, she forces a smile. "Hi. I didn't know you were coming over."

"Clearly," he snaps and I grit my teeth. This isn't good. "Brooks." He says my name as a greeting and a threat all at the same time.

Turning in place, I tilt my glass toward him and take another drink. I don't feel like pretending to give a shit that he's here.

He runs a hand over his beard and looks to Cassie once more. "Can we talk?"

She nods, eyes flicking to me quickly before following him out of the kitchen. I think this is where I'm supposed to leave. Or apologize. Or do anything but what I'm actually doing, which is leaning up against the kitchen counter, straining my ears to hear their conversation in the next room.

It's all muffled voices, but every now and then Grayson's voice will boom out loud enough for me to hear. Mostly, when he's saying my name.

This isn't good.

Sighing, I dump the remains of my glass down the drain and flatten my palms on the counter, eyes closed. She wants him. She doesn't want me. Do I even have a right to be upset about that? I've been with Skyler all this time, not realizing that I wanted Cassie, too. Or did I realize it and just ignore it? I'm not sure. It's not fair for me to ask her for anything now, not when she's right about my time. And even if I did have the time, do I deserve hers?

"Can you even deny it?! Look me in the eyes right now and tell me you feel nothing for him." Grayson's voice echoes into the kitchen and I'm sure I'm not the only one in the house who hears him. I strain my ears for her answer, but hear nothing until the front door slams.

Shit.

After a moment, Cassie shuffles back into the kitchen, the skin under her eyes red and puffy. Seeing her like that breaks me.

"Cassie," I breathe her name, crossing the room in two full strides to pull her into me. But the moment my hands find her waist, she shrugs away like I'm a flame set to burn her. She crosses her arms tight over her middle, shielding herself from me—the threat, the danger, the problem.

"You need to go."

My chest deflates. "Just—"

"Adam." She cuts me off, her voice loud but laced with uncertainty. "You need to *go*."

Everything in me screams for me not to leave, to force her to talk to me, but I've pushed her enough this semester. I didn't realize the pain I was putting her through, and now that it's all come to the surface, it's all I can do to not kick my own ass. I may want to hold her right now, but it's not what she wants. It's time to let me be the one who hurts if it means she gets what she needs.

"I'm sorry," I whisper, as if it's enough, as if I really know what I'm apologizing for. Am I sorry I kissed her? Hell no. Am I sorry she's hurt right now? That I'm part of the reason? An ache in my chest answers that question for me.

I pause when my hand is on the back doorknob, words still left unsaid, but I push them back down and force myself forward through the door.

It's not the first time I've left her without saying everything I wanted to, but it's the first time I've worried I may never get the chance again.

Bear

RAIN POUNDS HARD ON the pavement as I run, chest tight, legs burning across campus. I've been going for hours now. I stopped tracking after the first three miles. Every inch of my body is screaming for me to stop but I need the pain right now, I need it to consume me until it numbs me from my thoughts. I didn't even bring my headphones. I don't want the distraction, I just want the pain.

Though the rain is cold, the evening air is still warm from another spring day in Florida. My sneakers rub new blisters on my heels with every push, adding to the collection I've been building in the last week and a half since I last saw Shawna.

I'm not stupid enough to think racism doesn't exist. I know it does. I've been the subject of it more times in my life than I care to recall. Still, Shawna was different—or so I thought. She opened me up in a way no one ever had before. She was everything I'd been looking for in a girl, everything I thought I'd never find. To find out all of that was an illusion, a dream shattered by reality in the form of her parents, killed me. Skyler tried to convince me I should give her a chance, let her explain. But what is there to explain, really? This is exactly why I don't let myself get caught up in the girls I fuck. If I hadn't learned my lesson before, I damn sure won't forget now.

My hoodie is soaked, so I rip the zipper down and toss it in the yard of the Omega Chi house as I run past. Through the downpour, a faint voice calls out my name.

"Bear! Wait!"

I stop, squinting through the rain until Shawna's

frame comes into focus. She's sprinting toward me, the rain assaulting her along the way. Her long hair sticks to her neck and chest as she reaches me, chest heaving. The ends of her jet black hair are purple once again and rain drops gather at the top of her glasses before sliding down the lenses.

For a long minute, she just stares at me, her breaths coming hard as she peers up at me through the rain. She's so goddamn beautiful it takes every ounce of control left in me not to crash my mouth to hers and claim her as mine, even though she clearly isn't.

"I prefer to work out alone," I finally say, speaking loud enough to drown out the weather. A soft rumble of thunder sounds in the distance and I shift from one foot to the other, feeling the aches settle in every inch of my body the longer I stand there.

"I'm sorry!" She screams over the rain. "I was a complete asshole at Family Weekend. You were right to leave. You're right to hate me right now. But you don't understand my parents, you don't understand my family. It's complicated, Bear."

"It doesn't have to be. You're your own person, Shawna. Man the fuck up and tell them what matters to you. *Who* matters to you."

She rakes her fingers back through her soaked hair, squinting up to the sky. "Can we go somewhere to talk?"

"Depends. Are you going to call your parents and tell them we're together?"

"It's not that easy."

"Actually, it is. It really fucking is," I correct her.

"I don't want to lose you over this. Please," she pleads, her icy hands reaching out to grasp my forearms. "I just need some time."

"Do you know how fucking hard it is to hear the first girl I've ever come close to loving tell me she needs *time* to not be ashamed of me?" I ask, ripping my arms away from her. "It's simple, Shawna. You either care about me enough to stand up to your parents and stop giving two shits what they think about the color of my skin or you don't. There is no in-between."

"I can't just tell them like that! They'll cut me off, they'll disown me. Didn't you see the way they looked at me when you were there? How do I look them in the eyes and tell them their only baby girl is dating a black man?"

My neck snaps back as if her words slapped me hard across the face. "Wow. I didn't realize that was something so devastating."

Her lip quivers and as much as I probably should feel sorry for her, I don't. I've been cut off from my parents since before I was old enough to make money on my own. In the downpour, it becomes clear to me just how different Shawna and I truly are.

"I didn't mean it like that," she tries, wringing her hair over her shoulder. "I just . . . I need time. I can't tell them yet, but I will."

"And I'm just supposed to wait around until you find the courage?" I ask incredulously. "Well, that's something *I* can't do. We're done, Shawna. It's over."

Her face twists, but I can't tell if tears fall or if it's just the rain. I may have a weak spot for women, I may want to take care of everyone around me, but there comes a point where I have to shut others out to take care of myself. With my little brother living on his own, my mom and older brother nowhere to be found, and my fraternity under strict watch from nationals, I don't have any room left to deal with racist assholes—especially if the girl I would consider putting up with them for doesn't have the nerve to stand up to them with me.

"Take care of yourself." They're the last words I say to her before my feet are pushing off the pavement once more, my body finding its rhythm. I don't know if it's something I should be proud of, but I have the innate capability to shut people out of my life at the flip of a switch. With every drop of rain that hits my skin, I feel Shawna wash away, leaving nothing but memories behind.

Less than an hour later, I push through the doors at Ralph's, still soaking wet from the rain. I'm sore, I smell like complete ass, but I have zero fucks to give as I slide up to the bar and order my first drink. A few girls at a high-top table in front of me are giggling, their eyes glued to where my tank top is stuck on my chest. Crazy how I have *go fuck yourself* written all over my face but all they notice are my swollen muscles. I'd be terrified of me right now if I were them.

The male bartender slides me my beer and my check, not even asking if I want to open a tab. He eyes me under his backward hat with disgust before turning to the other end of the bar where a small crowd is gathered. I throw back half the beer when I realize who's drawing all the attention.

Alex.

"If you thought the video was hot, you should have seen it in person," he says loudly, a bit of his drink flopping out of his mug and onto the floor. The crowd of guys around him is eating up every word. I scan them, making sure none of them are brothers, and breathe easier when

I don't find a single one. It's a good thing, because then I would have had to kick their asses, too.

I stand, my bar stool scraping the floor as I push my way around it toward him.

"I mean, she was just straight up finger-banging the Asian chick while I pounded her from behind. Fucking Spring Break man." He high fives some douchebag behind him right before his eyes connect with mine.

He gulps. I smirk.

"Hey, whoa, Bear. I'm just kidding. We're just having a little fun, right guys?" He looks around for help, eyes wide, but everyone just clears out. I don't even have to say a word. He knows. They all do.

"You've got a lot of fucking nerve showing your face here," I snarl, snatching him by the collar of his Omega Chi shirt. "And these letters? You don't *ever* get to fucking wear them. Ever."

"I'm sorry. I'll leave." He's shaking. It only fuels me more. My entire body comes to life as adrenaline soars through my veins. I need a release, and Alex's face seems like the perfect way to get it.

"It's a little too late for that." I hear the bartender from before holler something out to his manager just as I throw the first punch, my fist connecting with Alex's jaw with a sickening crack. I throw another into his stomach before shoving him to the ground and pinning his arms down. Each punch is for someone new—Ashlei, Bo, Skyler, Erin, Omega Chi. My knuckles sting as they split open from the force, but I welcome the pain.

"Jesus Christ, Bear, that's enough!" I'm finally tugged back, but my hand around Alex's shirt collar rips it with me. I expect to find my brothers behind me, but it's Adam and Jeremy, instead. I use the shirt to wipe the blood from my hands, chest, and face before tossing it over my shoulder.

"If you show your face again," I start to threaten, but Alex is unconscious. I don't even know when I knocked him out. Bouncers grab my arms but I shake them loose and walk myself out, Adam and Jeremy on my heels. No one in the bar says a word, the crowd parting like the red sea with every step I take.

When I'm outside, the rain still dripping from the trees as the clouds clear, Adam approaches me hesitantly. "Hey, you okay?"

Shawna may have been the reason I walked into this bar, but with every punch I threw, I felt her leave my system. It's the end of the semester, the promise of summer so close I can taste it. Alex deserved to have his ass kicked, and the fact that he served as the perfect release for me was only a bonus. I may get knocked down, I may walk through hell, but no one can ever say I don't handle my own. I'm Clinton Fucking Pennington, and though Shawna is the one with the phoenix inked into her skin, it's me rising from her ashes this time.

The left side of my mouth quirks up just marginally. "Never better."

Ashlei

"LISTEN, LET'S JUST GO cut the balls off this motherfucker and then we'll go dress shopping, okay?" Jess says, squeezing my hand once before climbing out of the cab in front of Xavier's club. I follow, but stay frozen in place as the yellow car pulls away, letting the gray, rainy day surround me.

"I can't believe you did this for me," I whisper. I've been trying to talk her out of her plan the entire ride over, but unsuccessfully. I know my freedom is just minutes away, but I can't shake the overwhelming feeling of guilt for letting Jess help me reach it.

"Lei," she says my name with a smile, not an ounce of nervousness apparent as she frames my shoulders with her hands. Her blonde hair is pulled into a tight, high ponytail, accenting her cheekbones. "Dude. I'm your sister. I'm your fucking *best friend*. You shouldn't be struggling to believe I'd do this for you. If anything, *I* can't believe you waited this long to ask me to help. You put yourself through hell trying to handle this on your own when I was literally right down the hall."

"It's dangerous, Jess. I didn't want to get anyone else involved. And I was ashamed," I respond softly. "I still am."

"You wanted to do it alone. I get it," she says. "But that's the best thing about being in a sorority. It's like having an entire army of lipstick-wearing badasses behind you." I laugh a little, though my eyes blur with tears. "You're a Kappa Kappa Beta, Ashlei. You never have to face anything alone again."

She pulls me in for a hug and I squeeze her so tight she coughs, tapping my shoulder like a wrestler tapping out of a match.

"Come on, the mall closes in four hours. Let's get this over with."

Jess checks her lipstick on her phone camera as we cross the parking lot to the same bouncer who's always guarding the backdoor. He doesn't even ask who I am this time, just shakes his head as if he knows I won't be coming out alive. Xavier has been looking for me—he knows that just as well as I do.

Jess takes in our surroundings as I lead her back to Xavier's office, my hands still trembling even with her by my side.

"You danced here?" she asks softly, her eyes wide as she meets mine. I just nod in response. Jess reaches out for my hand and squeezes it tight as we reach Xavier's office door. He's bent over his computer, a cigar in his mouth as he hammers away at the keys.

"What?" He hollers out, eyes glancing up at us quickly before going back to the screen. Once realization hits, he pauses, a slow smirk growing above the stubble on his chin. He sits back, lacing his fingers together and propping his elbows on the armrests of his chair as his pulls his eyes to us again. "Well, well. Look who finally decided to show up."

Jess rolls her eyes, clearly not affected by a man who has killed before. Who could easily kill again. "Here's your money, asshole. All of it." She slaps the thick envelope down on his desk, unimpressed. "Now call your watch dogs off Ashlei and take a good look at her tight ass because the last time you'll see it is when we turn around and walk out of this shithole of a club."

Xavier's brows shoot up to his forehead and he barks out a laugh. "I see you brought your bull dog."

"I'm more of a pit bull, actually." She smiles with her eyes, hooking me by the elbow and steering me toward the exit. "Do you want to count that before we go or no?"

"I don't have to count it to know it's not enough. It's a late payment, which means I need interest."

"All the money she owed you before you made your disgusting little deal is in there, plus an additional ten-thousand." Jess spouts off the numbers like they don't affect her, like she didn't sell her prized possession to get that money. Her BMW now belongs to some Botoxed-out bimbo in South Beach, but Jess didn't even flinch when she handed over the keys.

I've never felt so loved in my life.

"And what makes you think that's enough, princess?"

Jess grits her teeth together, dropping my arm and crossing the room to plant her hands on his desk. She leans over and Xavier sneaks a look at her cleavage before his eyes lift up to hers, a sneer still firmly in place.

"It's plenty. And in case you don't know who I am, my name is Jess Vonnegut. That last name ring a bell?" She waits as Xavier files through the names in his head. "My family has won in court before and we can do it again. You forced a young college girl to dance in your club and pay you every penny she earned for drugs she wasn't even responsible for losing. Your death threats might have scared her for this long, but let me assure you—I don't feel one ounce of fear when I look into your beady little eyes." Standing, she presses her finger into the envelope. "The money is here, and unless you want to find out what a crazy son of a bitch my father can be when his little *princess* is fucked with, I suggest you take it and let us go."

Xavier sniffs, clearly more familiar with Jess' family lawsuit than I am. In fact, I don't think anyone really knows how Jess came into money. Whatever it was, Xavier doesn't taunt her further.

"Get the fuck out of my club."

"Gladly," she sings sweetly. "Come on, Lei."

She holds my hand the entire way out, and once we make it to the parking lot, the heavy metal door slamming shut behind us, I take a breath. It fills my lungs to capacity, overwhelming me with oxygen I feel like I've been deprived of for months. Sensing my emotions, Jess calls a cab quickly before pulling me into her.

"Shhh," she whispers into my hair. "It's okay. It's over. It's all over now."

I feel like I should cry, but instead, I laugh. Hard. Uncontrollably. Jess laughs with me, and before I know it, tears do leave my eyes—but not from sadness. I'm elated.

I'm free.

"I don't even know what to do right now," I squeak out between giggles. "This feels so unreal."

"It's real, babe. And now, we hit the mall and buy some sexy dresses and killer heels to match." She smiles, but it's tight. Now that my situation is resolved, I think she's finally letting herself think about her own. She hasn't spoken to Jarrett in almost a week.

"Jess," I start, but she shakes her head.

"Not today. Let's just shop, okay?"

Sighing, I nod. "Okay. Deal."

The same yellow taxi cab pulls in and we climb inside, the leather seats sticking to the back of my thighs just a bit. Folding my hands in my lap, I shake my head, still unable to stop smiling. The last eight months of my life have been ruled by monsters, and now, finally, I'm free of their claws. Finally, I can be me again—Ashlei Daniels—sister, friend, girlfriend.

My smile falters at that last thought. *Hopefully* girlfriend. Now that Xavier is behind me, I can focus on Bo and what comes next for us. As much as I've been through this semester, I've dragged Bo through the gutter with me. I convinced her to have that threesome when it was clear she was only doing it for me, and now, the consequences of my selfishness have stolen her smile that I loved so much.

Jess helped me rid myself of one demon, but now it's up to me to chase away the other one still lurking around. I'm going to make it right. I have to.

"Ready?" Jess asks me when the cab comes to a stop in front of the food court. She reaches a few twenties over the seat into the cabbie's hand before turning to me with a reassuring smile.

Taking a deep breath, I nod. "Ready."

Skyler

"I SWEAR, I'M GOING to gouge my eyes out before this semester ends," Cassie says, flopping her head down on my desk. "Studying is hard."

I laugh. "Formal is tonight, Little. Just put your notes away and work on it tomorrow."

"Says the communications major."

"Hey! I have tests, too," I defend, but she peeks up at me through her red locks with a smirk. We both know her classes are harder than mine, even if she is a year younger. I toss a highlighter at her. "Whatever. I'm changing my major anyway." The truth is I have no idea what I want to do with my life. Right now, I'm trying to focus on poker and paying my tuition. The American Poker Club tournament pops into my head again and I let myself daydream about what it would be like to not have to worry about money again.

Could I really win it? Could I really take home the grand prize of the largest poker tournament in the nation?

Part of me thinks I could, but the larger part wonders if I'll ever be good enough. I've stacked my summer with tournaments, some bigger than I've ever done before, so I guess the time to show up or shut up has arrived.

At this point, I feel like I'm on the edge of something . . . something I can't quite grasp yet. I can either keep pushing through the fog to find out what it is or I can stay in my comfort zone and go along like I have been.

I've never been one for comfort zones.

Cassie smiles and closes her textbook with a snap, tucking it inside her messenger bag along with the fifty neon-colored notecards she's been reciting all afternoon. Jess swings through the door at the same time and bounds toward me.

"I just realized you and I are going stag to formal tonight." She bounces on the bed excitedly. "Girl fucking power, bitch. I packed us each a flask. Let's get wild!"

"Except I'm not going stag." I point out.

Jess' face falls. "What? I thought you and Adam broke up!"

"We did. Which means . . ." I wait for her to fill in the blank.

"Ugh," she groans. "You're bringing Bear. Of course you're fucking bringing Bear." Waving her hands, she dismisses me quickly. "Fine. More alcohol for me."

"So because I have a date, I don't get booze?"

"Your date can buy your booze, hussy."

Cassie laughs, shaking her head as she pulls her messenger bag over her shoulder. "If it helps, J-Love, I'm going alone, too. I just want to spend time with my sisters. Maybe I can finally take my sister's advice and stay away from boys."

"I hear you on that one," I chime in. The only boy I plan on having anything to do with for quite a while is Bear. He needs me right now after the whole Shawna Shit Show, not to mention his family. For now, my best friend is the only guy I need. No more *Skyler the Heartbreaker* headlines. If I have anything to do with it, those tabloids are going to start to notice me for my talent, not my dating life.

"Wait, what happened to Grayson?" Jess asks.

Her pale fingers fidget with the strap on her bag as her eyes dart toward the door. "It's complicated. I'm going to go grab my makeup bag. Be right back."

She's out the door before I can ask anything else and Jess and I share a glance. "Wonder what that's about."

Jess shrugs. "No clue. That tatted up man-bun piece of sex candy is definitely not one I'd let get away easily."

I cross my arms over my chest and cock a brow. "Funny. I seem to recall you giving up a pretty hot tatted up piece of sex candy yourself."

"Don't, Skyler," she warns, pointing a finger in my direction as she crosses to her closet. She pulls out the clear plastic bag housing her formal dress and lays it across the bed with her back still to me.

"Jess, just call him."

"And say what? He wants me to be his girlfriend or nothing at all."

"So be his girlfriend, you idiot."

She sighs. "He's my teacher."

"*Was*. And technically, he was the Graduate Assistant, which isn't even the same thing."

"I don't do boyfriends."

"And? That's a personal choice, which means you can change it."

Jess rolls her eyes, yanking her dress out of the plastic bag forcefully. "He's about to graduate and have a job. I'm still in college. It'd be weird."

"Says who?"

"Says me. It's not like I could bring him to socials or frat parties."

"Actually, you could. Sisters bring their boyfriends from other schools and stuff all the time. No one would care that he's a couple years older. You act like he's fifty." I grab a pillow and hug it close to my chest, resting my chin on the edge.

"I'd probably hurt him. Or he'd hurt me."

"Again, that's a choice. And you could literally hurt anyone around you at any point in time. Need I remind you of Family Weekend?"

"Which is exactly why I need to keep him in the little box I have him in now. He knows what to expect and so do I."

"Except that he's not trying to live in that box anymore," I argue.

"Ugh you're so exhausting!"

"Well, are you done yet?"

"I'm scared, okay?!" she screams, her hands flying into the air. She holds them there for a moment, her chest heaving, wild eyes searching mine. Finally, she lets them fall, raking her nails back through her messy bun. It falls with the force and she ties it up again before crossing her arms. "I haven't had a boyfriend since the day I found out why everyone calls me J-Love. I've embraced the name, turned it from an embarrassing one to a badass one. Everyone thinks I fall in love too fast and chase guys away? Fine, I'll make *them* fall in love and chase *me*, instead. I flipped a switch, Skyler, and I don't want to go back to where I was before. I was pathetic. I was weak. I was—"

"Normal, Jess," I breathe, hopping off my bed. "You were a normal girl. We all fall in love, sometimes too fast, sometimes not fast enough. We get reputations, we go for the wrong guys and we survive on heartbreak diets when it all goes wrong. We lean on our sisters and we pick ourselves back up just to do it all over again because if we don't, what's the point? It's okay that you love Jarrett."

"I—"

"Yes, you do. And you should. What's more, he should know how you feel because he feels the same way and you guys are just being stupid trying to be together without actually *being* together."

Her face crumples and she buries it in her hands, standing in the middle of our room, exposed. "I do love him."

I pull her in for a hug, squishing my cheek to her head. "I know."

"I'm just so fucking scared."

"That's okay, too."

She sighs, shaking her head against my chest before standing tall again. "He put his feelings out there so easily when I know it wasn't that easy for him to do. We both thought we knew what we were getting into and somewhere along the way we just . . . I don't know. We fell deeper."

"Listen, you've spent this last semester hiding him from us while trying to figure it all out on your own. Before that, you were both hiding because he was your teacher. You've spent all this time feeling like being together was something to be ashamed of when really it should be celebrated."

She sniffs, wiping her nose with the back of her wrist. "You're right. You're so right. God, he probably feels so fucking rejected right now when really he's everything I want. He's *all* I want." Her eyes lift to mine. "I'm going to go tell him. Right now."

"Right now?" I ask as she sprints for her Keds, yanking them on one foot and then the other.

"Yep. Right now."

"What about formal?"

She laughs as she swings our bedroom door open. "Fuck formal."

But before she can exit, Erin and Cassie usher in a red-faced, snotty-nosed Ashlei. She's sobbing, using both my Little and my Big to hold her steady.

"Oh my God, what happened?" Jess asks, dropping the purse she'd just picked up and rushing to help them.

"No idea. I just found her in our room like this," Erin answers. They help Ashlei into Jess' bed and she curls up into a ball, pulling the comforter up to her chin, eyes still squeezed shut. Erin sits on the edge of the bed and pets her hair, murmuring soothing words for a while as the rest of us stand around watching, waiting.

Slowly, Ashlei's cries soften, until she's not crying at all. None of us push, we just let her take the time she needs. Every now and then when we think she's going to speak, she closes her eyes tight again and fights back another wave of tears.

"Bo left," she finally whispers, her voice dry and croaky.

"What do you mean she left?" Jess asks from behind Erin. Cassie and I share concerned looks as Erin rubs Ashlei's back, coaxing her forward.

"She left. She dropped. She's going back home, or to another college, I don't know—she wouldn't really say. But she's gone. She's leaving KKB, she's leaving Palm South. She's done."

We all gasp, questions flying from everyone.

What? Why? When?

Ashlei cringes away from the noise, burrowing herself into the covers more before Erin snaps her fingers and glares at all of us to shut up. Ashlei takes a deep breath, exhaling it shakily. "It was too much. It was all too much for her. The website, Family Weekend, me, us, all of it. And her parents are on her ass. She just can't take it anymore." Ashlei laughs, though nothing is funny right now. "I can't even blame her."

Jess's brows pull inward and she connects eyes with me, guilt evident in her features. Suddenly, Jarrett can wait.

Because when your sister is hurting, you drop everything to be whatever she needs in that moment.

No one says sorry, because Ashlei already knows we are. Jess jumps up into the bed with her and scoots between the wall and Ashlei's back, tugging her close and wrapping her arms tightly around her middle. Erin leans her head down to their shoulders as Cassie and I crowd our way in, too. For a long while we just hold each other, a KKB shield around Ashlei as we let her grieve her loss. Jess cries with her, knowing she was part of the reason for the loss and also mourning herself. Bo was her Little, and she didn't even say goodbye.

"Let's blow formal," Cassie says finally. "We can rent movies and get wine and junk food."

Ashlei shakes her head, sitting up slowly as we all disperse from her like a flower's petals falling back.

"I want to go." She chews her lip, grabbing Jess' hand in hers. "I'm going to miss Bo, but it was her decision to leave and I respect it." Ashlei sniffs, looking around at each of us with a small smile. "Tonight is about more than her. It's about celebrating another semester with my sisters, who I learned recently care about me more than anyone else." Jess squeezes her hand. "We may go through hell when we face life on our own, but together, we can build a bridge over that bitch."

We all laugh and I wipe a tear from the corner of my eye, knowing her words are true. The Kappa Kappa Beta girls may get into trouble. We may try to handle the world on our shoulders and party hard all at the same time, but we're a force to be reckoned with. We're a unit. We're a family.

"On that note," Jess says, popping out of her bed with a bright smile. "I've got the liquor, who's doing our make-up?"

"On it!" Erin chimes, thrusting her finger into the air before speeding out of the room to grab her giant makeup case. And just like that, the room is alive again, everyone talking and laughing, wiping tears, pulling out dresses.

Time to kiss spring semester goodbye in style.

Erin

AS THE KAPPA KAPPA Beta house fills up with sisters and their dates, everyone dressed to perfection, I can't help but feel displaced. It's almost as if I'm under water, the sounds muffled, vision slightly blurred. I'm here, but I don't feel *here*.

The past few weeks have been exhausting. I finally let myself break on the way home from Key West, and I guess in a way it's good that I got it out of my system then because I've had no time for myself since. With the Omega Chi website and recruitment preparations, not to mention studying for finals, I haven't had time to breathe let alone think.

Still, Bo leaving so unexpectedly has me shaken. Did she feel the same way I do right now—like an outsider? Was the website combined with her parents just too much for her to handle? I wonder if her shoulders feel lighter now. I wonder what would happen if *I* just packed up my room after this semester and never came back. Would I feel better?

I know the answer before my mind has even finished the question. I can't quit, it's not in me—it's not who I am.

Besides, now is the time for me to shine and prove I'm ready to be president next year. I'm the Recruitment Chair, which means all summer I'll be focusing on planning our fall rush. I'll be responsible for the clothing, the music, the food, the entertaining—everything. And more than that, I'll be responsible for the next pledge class of Kappa Kappa Beta.

That makes me smile.

As shitty as the semester has been, Ashlei was right when she said the KKBs are a special family. Eventually, this fog I've been living in will clear and I'll be back to having fun with my sisters. It may take me a little time, but something tells me spending the summer planning recruitment will put me back in the spirit. We already have an amazing organization, one of the best on campus, and I look forward to being a part of what makes our family grow even stronger.

"Ready, gorgeous?" Landon asks, his hands framing my upper arms from behind as he plants a kiss on my cheek. I jump a little, stirred from my daze, but smile back at him over my bare shoulder.

"Yeah, I just need a minute."

"I'll go grab us a seat on the bus," he says sweetly, leaning in for a longer kiss on my lips. He looks handsome tonight, his blonde hair styled perfectly in a swoop, his jaw freshly shaven. He selected a beige tuxedo with light blue accents to match my dress and I can't help but feel a little like Cinderella with her prince.

When Landon's gone again, I scan the room for the rest of the girls, knowing we'll all want to stick together tonight after what happened with Ashlei. When I find them at the photo booth, my heart stops and kicks back into rhythm quickly at the sight of Clinton standing with them. He's just off to the side, his eyes on me as Skyler, Jess, Ashlei, and Cassie crowd around the green screen with silly props.

I don't know why I can't look away from him.

Maybe it's because he's looking at me, *really* looking at me, for the first time since Spring Break. Maybe it's because he's absolutely mouthwatering in the light gray tuxedo he's wearing. Or maybe it's because the anger I felt behind his eyes last time we spoke is completely gone, replaced instead by something else. Sadness? Curiosity?

Remorse?

He grabs one of the speech bubble props and a marker and scribbles something out before holding it in perfect position, so that it appears the message is coming from his lips.

Sorry for being a giant bag of dicks.

I laugh out loud, covering my mouth with my fingertips as I shake my head from across the chapter room. He quirks a smile from the left side of his mouth and shrugs. I shrug, too. Then, I mouth, "It's okay."

Skyler loops her arm through his, tugging him toward the bus, so he throws me one last wink before following her. Slipping into our downstairs guest bathroom, I check my makeup one last time. My lips are nude but glossy, eyeshadow natural yet complementing. My hair is pulled up off my neck and twisted into a side bun held together with bobby pins, accenting my bare collarbone from my strapless gown. The light blue sequins sparkle in the low light of the bathroom and I turn, checking the back one last time before shutting off the light and making my way out to the buses.

There are three large charter buses ready to take us all to the location for formal. Landon taps on the back window from the third one and I smile up at him, waving to the girls who are already climbing onto the one in front of us.

"See you guys there!" I call out and they all smile and wave back. It's then that I notice Adam is here, too. I didn't realize anyone had invited him.

When I reach the back of the bus, I slide into the seat next to Landon and he greets me with a longer, steamier kiss than before. If we keep on this track, I know exactly where this night will lead.

And I'm not sure I'm ready for that.

"Whoa, easy," I say with a giggle, pulling back from his kiss. "At least let me take a few pictures before you smudge my lip gloss."

Landon grins, his eyes low from pre-gaming. "Fine. On one condition."

"And that is?"

His grin widens. "Turn around."

I do as he says, tucking my knees up slightly as I turn my back to him. When his strong hands find my shoulders and he begins to massage my tense muscles, I moan out loud.

"Oh my *God*," I breathe. "That feels amazing."

"Mmm," Landon groans with me, kissing the soft skin just below my ear. "You've been so stressed lately, Ex. I know you've had a lot going on with the website and with recruitment, but for tonight, even if it's *just* for tonight, you should let loose. Try to enjoy yourself. We're only young once, you know." He plants another kiss and it spreads warmth through my chilled skin.

"I don't know, I'm on the executive board. I don't want to get too crazy . . ."

"You won't. Just relax. Here," he says, squeezing my shoulders once more before removing his hands. I turn in my seat to face him as he pulls a leather-bound flask from the inside of his jacket. "This should help."

Chewing my bottom lip, I eye the flask before lifting my gaze to Landon. He looks so happy, so content, and he's been a complete gentleman to me all semester. I'm not even sure why he's stuck around for as long as he has. Maybe he knew I needed someone to lean on. Maybe he's a sort of gift from the gods for putting me through such hell lately.

"You know what," I concede, taking the flask from his hand. "You're right. I think I should loosen up a bit. The semester is almost over and I feel like I haven't had one ounce of fun this entire time." I cheers to him and he pulls a different flask out, tapping the lip of mine with his.

"Cheers, baby."

We both knock back a few swigs, me cringing as the liquid burns my throat. I shake it off quickly and plaster on a smile, throwing my fist in the air. "Let's party!"

The entire bus erupts with my declaration and Landon's eyes devour me, lighting my insides on fire more than the alcohol. Maybe I have been too uptight lately. I tried the whole staying-sober-to-maintain-control thing during Spring Break and look where that got me. Is it possible I've been going about this all wrong?

It's time to let go of everything that's been plaguing me. What's done is done, and Clinton's apology somehow made me feel like everything will be okay. For the first time this semester, I'm going to enjoy myself.

Landon tips his flask once more and I follow his lead, this time pulling him in for a long kiss once the liquid settles in my stomach. His hands find my waist and grip tight as I snake my fingers into the back of his hair, pulling him closer, needing his escape. With each stroke of his tongue against mine, I feel the water clearing. With each brush of his skin against mine, I feel less and less stressed. It's like my mind and body are screaming together for me to let go, to live life tonight. So, when Landon pulls back, his brows pinched together and his eyes on my mouth, I answer his question without him having to ask it.

"Screw the lip gloss."

Cassie

I CAN STILL FEEL that night.

If I close my eyes, like I am right now, I can go back there so easily, as if I never left. The sand between my toes, the damp ocean air in my hair, the hot night sticking to the skin of my thighs just below the hem of my dress. And if I run my fingertips across the same places he touched me in the sand under the stars, it's like he's still here. My thumb brushes my bottom lip and I feel his teeth biting the same spot. My fingers slide shakily to grip the back of my neck and I feel his handprint, instead.

And when I open my eyes again, just before my vision clears, I swear I can still see his eyes.

"You okay, Little?" Skyler asks just as I pop my eyes open. Warm brown eyes flash in the mirror before being chased away by reality. "You have a headache or something? I think I might have some Advil."

Skyler starts sifting through her clutch and I force a smile, shaking my head. "No, no, I'm fine, Big. Just a little sore from . . . yoga," I lie.

"Well, at least the soreness paid off. You look amazing tonight." She smiles before leaning forward in the bathroom mirror to fix her lipstick. I follow suit, smoothing my hands over the sleek black fabric of my dress. My arms are covered with thin lace that trails up to my shoulders before breaking into a conservative top. Everything is covered, the black framing and slimming me all the way down to the middle of my thigh where it breaks for one, long slit— just enough for my pale leg and strappy gold shoes to peek through. My normally frizzy, crazy red hair is tamed, softly curled, and falling lightly over one shoulder. Erin did my makeup, and whatever eyeshadow she used sets my emerald eyes ablaze against it. I feel beautiful, yet at the same time, inadequate.

Because I'm here alone.

Grayson should be here, waiting for me on the dance floor, tattoos covered by a tuxedo jacket. But he broke up with me, and I can't even blame him for it. How do you stay with someone when they can't deny they have feelings for someone else?

Skyler and I finish our touchups and rejoin our group in the ballroom. I thought the semi-formal venue was beautiful, but this? This is absolutely breathtaking. Our executive board rented out a private plantation, and the fact that this house used to entertain one family and their guests is mind blowing. It's huge and regal, the grand architecture giving off a royal feel with just a hint of southern hospitality. The ballroom is fit for a princess or a wedding, which I imagine it's probably played home to both at some point.

Skyler runs off to Erin as soon as we get back inside, who, surprisingly, is having more fun than any of us. She must have pre-gamed pretty hard on the bus because when she piled off it, her eyes were low, hair mussed, and she was clearly ready to party. She was the first on the dance floor and hasn't left since. She may be a little tipsier than the rest of us but I don't think anyone is even judging because she deserves this. It's nice to see her smiling, dancing, letting go.

"Hi." His voice is low, timid, hesitant. I consider ignoring him, since that tactic has been working in my favor all night so far, but with him so close, it's nearly impossible now.

"Hi, Adam." I keep my eyes on the dance floor, watching as Erin and Skyler captivate everyone around them.

"Need a drink?"

As much as I don't want him to be the one to get me a drink, I really do need one right now, so I concede. "Sure."

We walk in silence over to the bar and Adam slides up first, ordering us two Maker's & Cokes. I almost open my mouth to argue with him, to ask him why he thinks I'd want to drink that, but the truth is whiskey is necessary to get through tonight. Apparently, he gets that. Besides, any words I had on my tongue disappeared when he looked back over his shoulder at me and crooked that signature smile of his. Adam in board shorts or a frat tank is one thing, but seeing him in a perfectly-fitting tux, complete with bowtie, makes my knees weak, no matter how loudly I yell at them to hold it together.

"Having fun?"

I clasp my hands together and stare down at my fingers, noting how the light reflects off the gold polish. "Mm hmm."

He hands me my drink and I take it without looking up, sipping from the skinny black straw and letting the liquid burn, just like it did before Spring Break.

"Cassie . . ." he starts, but I cut him off.

"So who are you here with, anyway?" I ask, snapping my head up to look him in the eyes. His brow drops low as he swallows, shifting.

"No one."

I scoff. "What do you mean, 'no one'? You can't just come to the Kappa Kappa Beta formal without someone inviting . . ." my words trail off as I note his nervous eyes watching those close enough to us to overhear. "Oh my God. Did you sneak into formal?"

He pauses, a guilty grin spreading on his lips. "Maybe."

"Why? To try to get me to talk to you?"

"No," he says quickly, but his eyes drop to his drink. "Yes. Well, kind of." He blows out a long, slow breath before lifting his gaze to me once more. "I just had to apologize. I want you to know I'm sorry, for whatever that's worth."

"For?"

"For . . ." He clearly hasn't thought that far. Maybe he didn't think he'd get the chance to say he was sorry, and now that I let him get it out, he's wondering what exactly he apologized for in the first place. "I don't know, Cassie. I'm not sorry for kissing you," he says the words easily, like they don't rob my next breath. "I probably should be, but I'm not."

"So then what are you apologizing for?" I ask again, softer this time.

"Hurting you. Confusing you. Making you cry." He shrugs. "Should I go on? I'm sure you could help me build the list of things I should be sorry for."

My brows pinch together as I study his face. I find nothing but sincerity. My eyes flick down to the water beading on the outside of my glass and I laugh a little before peeking up at him through my lashes. "I can't believe you snuck into my formal."

He smiles with me, relief exhaling from his chest. "How else could I dance with you?"

Adam holds out his hand just as the slow melody of a familiar song starts to play. I chew my cheek, debating if I should, and just as I reach my hand out to place it in his, I pause, sucking in a breath when my eyes focus behind him. It's not the DJ playing the acoustic tune.

It's Grayson.

"Good evening, Kappa Kappa Betas," his gruff voice speaks into the microphone and my sisters all cheer, half of them visibly swooning as Grayson's eyes scan the crowd. I've only seen him play in the coffee shop, but he always looks comfortable there—confident. Right now, he's plucking away at the strings, missing a few notes here and there, finding his footing, cheeks slightly flushed behind his beard.

He's nervous.

But when his gray-blue eyes finally find me, he smiles, radiant, as if he found exactly what he was looking for. "I'm sorry to interrupt your formal, and I promise to let the DJ get you back to dancing, but first, I have a little story to tell you. Is that okay?"

More cheers. I abandon my glass on the bar and slowly walk toward the stage, eyes never leaving his.

"Some of you already know that a certain redheaded sister of yours played hard to get the first time I saw her in Cup O' Joes." A few giggles break out and all eyes turn to me. "I almost gave up on her, I almost took no for an answer. But something inside me wouldn't let me let *her* walk away." A collective *aww*. "Now I knew that she would be sweet, that she would be fun. But I never could have known that she would bring a light to my life that no one else ever could." He swallows and stops strumming just long enough to run a hand over his beard. "Sorry, nervous habit." More laughs.

He starts again, the chords stronger, more sure. "Cassie, I knew letting you walk away that first time would be a mistake, and yet I made the even bigger mistake of walking away from *you*. And I regret it. Because here's the thing . . ." His strums turn even more familiar and I can't fight the smile on my lips when the tune of Train's *Hey Soul Sister* comes together. "I don't want to miss a single thing you do tonight."

With that, he kicks the beat in and starts crooning out the first set of lyrics, everyone in the room singing with him. All the girls rush around me, their arms enclosing me and making me sway but I can't stop staring at Grayson and he won't stop staring at me. His smile is bright, his eyes hopeful as he puts his heart on the line in front of my entire chapter. Each word he sings, each note that finds my ears sends me even higher. I'm light, almost too light on my feet and I grab ahold of Skyler's arm so I don't float away. When the last note plays, Grayson jumps down from the stage, landing hard on both feet before pulling his guitar overhead and leaving it behind. He stands there in front of the stage, heart open, and I don't waste one second before crossing the space between us and throwing my arms around his neck, pressing my lips against his to the sound of applause.

"I thought," I try, but he stops me.

"I know. I did, too." He kisses me again, hands fisting at the lower back of my dress as mine slide into his beard. "I just decided that he can't have you. Not yet. Not until I do everything in my power to prove to you that I deserve you more than he does."

It's like his words have a direct connection to my heartbeat. It hammers hard against my chest, ringing my ears as I try to focus on his words. *He can't have you.*

But what if he already does?

Grayson wraps me in his arms as the DJ plays the next track, kicking the room back into action. When he pulls back, a crowd of my sisters engulfs us, all wanting to talk to Grayson. He just smiles his charming smile and answers all their questions as I hang on his arm, wondering how he's so perfect. But my stomach sinks a little when I catch sight of Adam's back as he pushes through one of the exits. He just apologized to me and I walked away without so much as an *apology accepted.*

"I'll be right back, going to grab us drinks," I say to Grayson, lifting up on my toes to kiss his cheek swiftly. His brows pull inward for just a moment before he smiles and nods, listening again to one of the sisters in my pledge class as she tells him she's been looking into guitar lessons.

My hands are shaking slightly as I push through the same door Adam just did moments ago, finding myself alone with him in the large, fully-stocked house library. He's facing the far bookshelf, hands in his pocket, eyes focused straight ahead like he's picking out his next read. The door shuts softly behind me, blocking out the noise until only our breathing can be heard.

"Adam . . ."

"Don't," he says, back still to me.

"What?"

He turns, dark eyes determined. "Don't. Don't say my name like that. Like you're about to tell me I'm too late. Like you're about to look me in the goddamn eyes and tell me you're back with him."

My lips quiver as I press them tightly together. "Adam, we talked about this."

"Just wait for me," he pleads, louder this time, his feet moving toward me. "Maybe it won't be crazy as president. Maybe I'll have plenty of time. Maybe all that shit was just me grasping at something to break up with Skyler because I knew deep down that it's *you* I should be with." His breaths are labored, chest heaving.

I close my eyes tight. "It's not the right time, Adam."

"Why? Because of him?" He gestures to the ballroom.

"It's not fair of you to ask me to give him up when I never asked that of you with Skyler!" My voice cracks. "You're *president* now. You can't ask me to wait for you to figure out if that means you'll have time for me or not. It's not fair."

"Of course it's not *fair*, Cassie!" Adam scoffs. "Is anything with us? How the hell do you ever expect me to not be selfish when it comes to you?" His tongue jets out to wet his lips and his hands find his waist. He hangs his head, shaking it just slightly.

"The timing isn't right," I whisper again.

He snaps his eye to mine again. "What if you fall in love with him?" His hands fly up. "Don't answer that." And I don't, because the truth is, I could.

The truth is I might already be on my way.

For a moment, we just stand there, Adam's fingers pinching the bridge of his nose while mine grip the edges of my dress like it'll somehow hold me steady.

"I should probably get back out there," I say softly and he just nods, too much, as if he's trying to convince himself of something. I make to turn, but stop myself. "I still want to be friends, Adam."

He winces, a low groan leaving him as if I just threw a punch straight into his stomach. I guess in a way I did.

There's nothing more to say, so I make a move toward the door.

"Cassie," he calls out, his hand catching the crook of my elbow as I turn. My eyes focus on the point of contact, noting the slight tremble in his hands as they glue me to this spot. "Just because the timing isn't right for us now doesn't mean it never will be."

I squeeze my eyes tight as he leans forward, pressing his lips to my forehead before letting me go. He crosses the room quickly, not looking back once, and when the door closes behind him and I'm left alone, the skin his lips touched burns almost as much as my heart.

Bear

EVERYTHING'S GOING TO BE okay.

It's taken me a while to get to this point, but I know it's the truth. I'm finally feeling lighter, laughing and dancing with Skyler to an old 90s hip hop song as I celebrate the end of another semester. We're on the brink of summer, and in just a couple of weeks I'll be on my way home to spend time with Clayton.

Shawna hurt me, I can't deny that. I won't act like I'm too tough to be affected by a girl. The truth is, I cared about her—a lot. But at the end of the day, I look out for number one—me. So, I let her go that night in the rain, and this summer, I'll focus on my family and come back to PSU regrouped, centered, and ready to take on whatever new challenges may come.

"Shit, Bear," Skyler says, grabbing my arm. "You're bleeding." She holds up my fist where the cuts from Alex have split open.

"Fuck," I murmur, pressing my other hand over the wounds. "Be right back."

I weave through the crowded dance floor and head straight for the bathroom, pushing the door open with my back and flipping the water on with my elbow before submerging my hand under the faucet. When the blood flow is under control, I wrap a paper towel around my knuckles and apply pressure, the stinging a reminder of the trouble I caused by fighting Alex.

Omega Chi has been under watch for a while now. It's one thing to party hard, but to get busted for the website and then put the kid responsible for it in the hospital?

That's something nationals won't tolerate, even if the little bastard did deserve every hit.

I was called into a conference call with Alec, several other alumni brothers and the president of our national chapter earlier this week. I've never really taken anything they said seriously before now, but they all made it clear that this is it—we're on our last chance. One more strike, and we're out. They told me to take the summer to cool off and figure out what's important to Omega Chi as an organization. Matt just handed over the presidency to my Little's close friend, Taylor, and as much as I like him as a beer pong partner, I'm worried about him as president. I hope we can team up to get our fraternity back in line, but I'll worry more about that later. Tonight, I'm going to dance with my best friend and take shots and say goodbye to spring semester.

One of the workers with the plantation helps me find gauze and we wrap my knuckles before I make my way back toward the ballroom. A loud burst of laughter from down the hall catches my attention on the way and I slow, watching as Landon and two of his Mu Beta Chi brothers exit a room at the far end. His brothers share a high five as Landon takes a long pull from his flask, checking over his shoulder for something in the room they just exited. When another brother joins them, sweat on his forehead, hands adjusting his dress shirt back into his pants, my stomach drops.

Something isn't right.

Landon sniffs, eyes catching mine just briefly before he nods toward the exit and his brothers follow quickly. Before I know what I'm doing, I let my feet carry me toward the room. Every step feels weighted, slow, like I'm walking through quicksand. My heart is hammering in my ears, adrenaline coursing through my veins and telling me I should walk away. Those primal instincts deep within me are screaming *danger* but I can't stop walking. My hand finds the hard wood of the door and I pause, waiting for permission that never comes. Then, slowly, I push it open with a creak.

What I find knocks the breath from my chest.

That's the only thing that happens quickly, and in the next few moments where I'm not breathing, everything else comes slow in a steady rhythm with my heartbeat.

One beat, Erin, face down on a pool table. Another beat, her mascara stained on her cheeks, brown eyes wide open, staring at me like I'm not real. A third beat, her light blue dress, torn in the back, bunched above her waist. The fourth and final beat, her lacey white panties around her ankles, strained against her silver heels still planted firmly on the floor.

One breath, inhaled slowly and exhaled like fire through my nose as my fists clench, breaking the cuts on my knuckles open once more.

"I'll fucking murder them."

I turn fast, eyes searching for Landon and his brothers as Erin calls out my name.

"Bear!"

"I'll fucking murder them!" I repeat, running in the direction I watched them leave, but Erin's voice stops me.

"Bear, don't leave me!" she cries, and the sound rips through my chest like the sharpest blade. I choke on my next breath, torn between chasing after them and staying with her. A soft whimper is all it takes to make my decision for me.

"Fuck!"

I rush through the door, shutting it quickly behind me before crossing quickly to Erin. She hasn't moved except for to squeeze her eyes shut tightly as fresh tears mark her cheeks. My hands gently find the edge of her dress on the table and I pull it down, covering her shaking legs, closing my eyes along with her and forcing another breath to stop myself from leaving her again.

I'll fucking murder them.

I rip my phone from my pocket.

"I'm calling 911."

"No," she says softly, quickly.

"Yes, Erin."

"Bear, please, stop," she says a little louder, her palms finding the table as she tries to push herself up. The bruises already forming on her arms fuel the fire searing my chest. Erin was having fun tonight, she was smiling, she was dancing, she was wild.

And that's when it hits me.

"They drugged you," I whisper. She pauses, stomach still to the table. Her hesitation is answer enough. "I'm calling, Erin."

"No."

"Yes, goddamn it."

"No!" she screams it this time, standing straight, fresh tears falling with the force. "It's my body, Bear! And I said no!"

A sob breaks through and she doubles over, clutching her stomach as she sinks down to the floor, ankles still bound together by lace. I go down with her, trying to lessen the fall with my arms as I pull her into me. Slowly, I slide her underwear up, but she stops me.

"Take them off. Get them off of me."

I rip the fabric and quickly tuck them inside my jacket, wrapping my arms around her again. I don't know what to do. I don't know what to say. All the skits from PSU freshman orientation and years of sex education come flying at me but none of it feels right. "We have to call 911, Erin."

"And what?" she asks, lifting her tear-stained face to me, blue dress crumpled around her. It's the most heartbreaking thing I've ever seen, like I'm holding a princess broken beyond repair. "This isn't a movie or a fucking seminar, Bear. This is real life. And in real life, rich boys with even richer parents and lawyers don't go away for raping a sorority girl." The word *rape* spits from her lips like poison. "They'll say I wanted it, they'll say I planned it, they'll say I consented, they'll say I was drunk on my own, they'll say whatever they have to because it's four of them against one of me. You weren't here, you can't say without a doubt that you saw them do anything. It's me versus them. And in this world, when the *me* is a girl known for being emotionally unstable and the *them* is a group of privileged white men, they win, Bear." She sniffs, leaning her head against my chest. "They win."

My hand finds her hair and I pull her close, as close as I can, trying to protect her from a monster I was too late to fight. "Erin, you're still . . . you're not thinking right."

"Please," she begs, fists curling in my dress shirt. "Just take me home. Please, Bear. Please. *Please*." She says the word over and over, each time softer, her frail body rocking in my arms. "Please."

"Okay," I finally say, letting myself feel her pain. I take it in, take it as my own, let it overtake my urge to do what I've been taught is the right thing. "Okay."

Erin asks me to take her to my room, knowing her house will soon be flooded with sisters soon, so I do. She asks me to help her undress, so I do. She asks me to burn her dress, so I do. But when she turns on my shower, I quickly turn it back off, keeping my eyes on hers.

"If you're going to shower, if you're really not going to tell anyone, then I need you to promise me something."

Her eyes are so tired, so red, yet tears still pool and spill over. She doesn't ask me what the promise is, she hasn't said much at all.

"Erin, you have to get tested. They could have given you something." I feel weird saying it, but I can't just let her wash away all evidence without a promise that she'll take care of herself. I'm already going against every principle in my being. "A disease . . ."

"A baby?" she finishes for me, laughing a bit. I can't understand why. She shakes her head, leaning over to turn on the shower again. "They used condoms."

"I don't care." I shut it off. She turns it on again but my hand covers hers. "I'm serious, Erin. Promise me."

She swallows, and the way her eyes connect with mine makes me feel like our souls are tied together in a way that can never be undone from this day forward.

"Okay."

I nod, dropping my hand and leaving to let her shower in peace but she reaches out for my arm. "Wait." I pause. "Can you . . . will you . . ."

I turn, brows pinched together as the realization of what she's asking settles in. But I won't leave her, not if what she needs is for me to be here right now. I peel my shirt off in response and Erin watches me for just a moment before stepping behind the curtain.

The water is scalding, almost too hot to bear, but I let it burn us both as she scrubs their hands off her skin. The bruises are really starting to show now and her pale skin turns redder and redder as she scrubs, her tears mixing with the water from the showerhead. Tentatively, I take the rag from her hands and slowly run it over her tender skin. My touches are gentle, and she closes her eyes, lips quivering as I try to help her shed the last few hours.

I'm not sure how long we stay in the shower together. The water runs cold and still we stay, shivering together, crying as one. When her tears stop, I turn the water off and wrap her in a towel, carrying her to my room. I find a t-shirt and boxer shorts and she slips them on, crawling into my sheets and reaching out for me again.

So I hold her, all night, through the tears and the silence and the nightmares and the pain. I hold her close, tight, and I whisper the same words over and over and over again until we have no choice but to believe them, until I have no choice but to never rest until they're true.

"Everything's going to be okay."

Erin

HOW MUCH WEIGHT CAN one girl hold before she crumples beneath it, spent, too tired to even care if it crushes her?

I've been strong before. I've held myself together through experiences that should have killed me. But now, it's as if that girl is a distant memory, or as if she never really existed at all. I'm just a shell now. A cracked, rusted shell.

I can't shower enough. I can't scrub enough. I can't cry enough. *Nothing* is enough to cleanse me of that night. Nothing ever will be.

I think I broke Clinton, too.

He brought me back to life just enough to let me breathe on my own, though anything else feels impossible, and I asked him to go against everything he stands for. But he did it. For me. And I wonder how much of himself he gave up just to let me hold tight to the last little shred of what was left of me.

I've been holed up in my room since the morning after when I walked in a daze back to the house. I left long enough to take my last final and that's it. The girls think I'm sick, and I let them think whatever they want to. Clinton checks on me from time to time but I ignore him for the most part, only responding enough to let him know I'm alive, though maybe that's a lie, too.

But today, like a child, I called my mother. I showed her my scraped knees and asked her to bandage them. I asked her to fix me. Instead, she cried. And I cried with her. Now, we sit quiet on the phone together, both still sniffling as I curl into myself under my sheets.

"Are you packed?" she finally asks.

"I am."

She sniffs, clearing her throat. "Good. I'm sending a car now. Listen to me." Her voice cracks a bit and a new wave of tears rush in on me. "You are a strong, brave, incredible young lady. You have way too much ahead of you to let four spoiled little punks take your life away." I tuck my knees up closer to my chest and exhale loudly to ward off a sob. "So you're going to come home, and we're going to figure this out together. Do you hear me? You are not broken, Erin Xander. You need to harden your heart, baby girl. Take everything you feel right now and hone it, use it to push you toward what you want most in life. *Take* what you want. Take what you need. Right now, you feel like you've been robbed, right?" I nod, even though she can't see me. "So, take back what's yours."

"I don't know how," I whisper, wanting to believe her but feeling the exact opposite of her words. Is this what bravery looks like? A scared little girl curled up in sheets like they'll be her saving grace?

There's a weighted pause on the other end before Mom's voice comes through again, stronger than before.

"I do. And I'll teach you. Just come home, baby."

So I do.

And going home isn't the hard part. I go willingly, hopefully.

It's coming back to PSU that won't be easy.

And *if* I do make it back, the truth remains that I won't be the same girl everyone knew before. That girl is dead.

Can a new one be reborn?

Jess

I'VE BEEN PRACTICING.

I've been working every word over and over in my head for the last week since formal. I want this to be perfect, I want this moment to be as big as I feel like it should be. So when Jarrett opens his door dressed in nothing but relaxed, navy blue sweat pants that hang low on his hips, I close my eyes to stop myself from getting distracted.

"Jess?"

"Don't talk," I say quickly, eyes still closed. "I just need to get this all out, okay?" I crack one eye open just long enough to make sure he's still there. And he is, in all his sexy, tattooed glory, brow cocked, an amused look on his face. I close my eyes again, blowing out one long breath.

"I've been stupid. I've been fighting you on this whole relationship thing and giving you every excuse I could think of because the truth is that I'm scared. I'm terrified, actually. That I'll hurt you, that you'll hurt me, that we'll fail miserably or worse—actually make it together." I'm rambling. I'm an idiot. I keep going. "Because if we do make it together, then that means we give each other even more power to break one another. And that's fucking scary, okay? So, I'm sorry I've been a little crybaby bitch. I sucked on a pacifier for a few weeks and pulled up my big girl panties and now I'm ready. I'm still scared," I clarified. "But I'm ready to do this. I want to be your girlfriend." I wait, chest heaving, but no response comes. "Jarrett?"

When I open my eyes to make sure I'm not talking to a closed door, Jarrett comes into view slowly, one arm crossed over his chest and the other holding his hand over his perfect mouth as he fights back laughter.

"This isn't funny, Jarrett!" I scream, my hands flying up. "I'm serious! I love you! I fucking—"

Jarrett's mouth crashes down hard on mine, stealing my next words along with my breath. His hands wrap around my hips with ease and he yanks me inside his apartment, slamming the door closed behind us before throwing me up against it. A picture frame on the same wall falls to the floor, glass cracking as I wrap my legs around his waist and lock ankles. I tug him closer, my nails digging into his bare back, our breaths heavy and desperate.

His mouth is eager as he tastes my lips, my neck, the swell of my breasts. His hips pin mine against the door and he lifts my arms, pulling my tank top up and over my head before flinging it to the side. His expert fingers snap my bra off quickly, letting it fall to the floor as he lifts me once more and carries me to the bedroom. We barely reach the bed before he tosses me onto it, the comforter expelling around me in a *whoosh*.

Jarrett makes quick work of my jean shorts, stripping them off my legs and yanking his own pants to the floor as I lean up to kiss his abs. I take him in my hand, stroking him from the tip all the way down to the base and back, my tongue still tracing figure eights on his chiseled abdomen. Jarrett groans before pushing me back into the bed, his hands gripping my skin as he drags my panties down my thighs, my calves, all the way to my ankles. He lets them drop before wrapping his long fingers around my ankles once more, pulling my legs up one by one to rest on his shoulders. Planting one soft kiss on the inside of my left ankle, he smirks, the tug of his lips tied to the longing building inside me. My thighs tense and tingle as he flexes his hips forward, his hard on pressed against my slit, teasing.

"Jarrett," I breathe his name as my hands find my breasts. He watches as I frame my nipples, tugging each of them gently. Groaning, his hands grip my thighs hard and he pulls me to the edge of the bed, answering my call, filling me with one solid thrust.

"Fuck," he drags the word out, his hands sliding up my ribs, my breasts before holding tight to my shoulders and pulling me toward his second thrust. With my ankles on his shoulders, he hits me deeper than I've ever felt him before. He works me slow and steady, letting me feel every inch as he pulls all the way out before sliding back inside.

His hands slide up higher, cradling my neck and stretching my legs further as he leans in close to my chest. Jarrett's pace intensifies, his eyes dark, wide, and locked on mine as his slides the thumb from his right hand in to hook the corner of my mouth. I suck hard, letting it go with a pop and his eyes roll back as his hips roll forward.

"I want you to come like this," he demands, trailing his hands down my body as he straightens his stance. The same thumb that was just in my mouth finds my clit and I reward him with a sharp cry of pleasure.

"Only if you come with me."

He smiles, biting his lower lip as his thumb applies more pressure. Every circle sends a jolt through me, my need pulsing in time with his movement. "Always so fucking stubborn."

"You love it," I shoot back and he slows, his smile falling.

"I love *you*."

I eye him through heavy lids, my sexy, bald, tattooed boyfriend.

Boyfriend.

Yeah, I could get used to that.

"I love you, too."

He stops, dropping my ankles off his shoulders and pulling me up to meet his lips. His kiss tells me more than his words do, and I let it speak freely, wrapping my arms around his neck and tugging him closer.

"Turn around," he demands, smacking my ass. I giggle, doing as he says, but when one hand grips the bend at my waist and the other positions him behind me, the laughter is gone, replaced by a carnal need only Jarrett makes me feel.

He rocks in slowly, but picks up speed quickly, his hands pulling my hips back to meet his own again and again. When his palm finds the center of my back and he presses me face down into the sheets, I grip them with my fists and hold on tight as I find my climax. I call out his name, chest tight as I ride the wave for as long as I can. Jarrett comes right behind me, and hearing him moan sends an aftershock through my core.

When we're both spent, Jarrett falls into the sheets with me, pulling me to straddle his waist. His hands slide into my hair and he kisses me, softer this time, longer kisses followed by short ones, like the most beautiful cadence.

"Mine," he whispers between kisses, smiling. "Thank *fuck* you're finally mine."

"Well, looks like another semester bites, girls," I say, tossing the last of my bags into my rental car. It feels weird to not be loading up the Bimmer for my trip home, but I don't regret giving her up one bit. I would do it all over again, if it meant Ashlei's freedom from Xavier. Even with Bo leaving, she still seems so much happier—lighter—and I look forward to her getting back to the old Ashlei.

Cassie shakes her head, squinting under the bright beams of the Florida sun. The first day of summer may be over a month away, but it's sweltering already. "I can't believe I'll be a sophomore when we all come back."

"THEY GROW UP SO FAST," Skyler fake blubbers, pulling Cassie into a crushing hug.

"I'm not ready to go home," Ashlei says with a sigh as Skyler and Cassie break, still laughing. "It doesn't feel like it's time yet. So much has changed, it feels anti-climactic to just pack up this semester in a duffle bag and head home for three months."

"Tell me about it. I turn twenty-one in two weeks and I won't even have anyone there to celebrate with, unless you count my grams. Which, I mean, the lady can party but . . ."

Ashlei and Cassie laugh but Skyler is just staring at me.

"What?" I ask. "Why are you looking at me like your dad just found your vibrator?"

"What if we just don't go home?" Skyler asks, looking around at each of us. "I mean, not yet. Jess' birthday is in two weeks. What if we . . . I don't know, what if we went somewhere? My place, or anywhere, really. Two of us are newly single while the other two are freshly wifed up. I feel like we should celebrate, kick the summer off in style." At first I shake my head, but the more she talks, the more I think she might have a brilliant idea. "I mean come on. It's J-Love's twenty-first birthday. We can't just *not* be there for it."

"I have a flight in like three hours," Cassie points out.

"So? Cancel it," Skyler challenges.

"Well, I'm in no rush to get home. I say let's do it." Ashlei smiles and Skyler throws her a high-five before turning to me.

"Oh come on, like you even have to ask me," I scoff. "Jarrett already left for his summer internship, so it's not like I have the possibility of getting banged anytime soon. Therefore, I'll need lots of alcohol."

They both grin and then it's just Cassie left. She bites her cheek. "What about Erin? Did she leave already?"

Skyler frowns. "Yeah, she was pretty sick, I guess. I feel like she was just ready to get out of here after all the executive board drama."

Cassie nods, debating. "Well . . . I'm sure my parents can change the flight."

"Yes!" Skyler and I cheer together and we all grab Cassie in another hug. She laughs, throwing her head back as we crowd in around her. She has so much fucking hair that I cough on a strand of the red beast and everyone laughs harder.

"Fuck yes! Pile in, bitches. Let's take this thing back to the rental car place and trade it in for something with more room. Then, we're calling my parents and telling them not to book the beach house in New Smyrna for the next three weeks."

"Shotgun!" Skyler yells, hoisting her bag over her shoulder and running toward the car. Everyone is talking all at once, cramming bags into the trunk and fitting extras on laps. The girls start making phone calls as I pull out of the KKB house, adjusting my rearview mirror when we pull away.

"Someone text Erin. Tell her to meet us there," I say, rolling our windows down to let the warm breeze fill the space between us.

"On it!" Ashlei replies, ending the call with her dad and typing out a text immediately.

As I flick my shades down over my eyes, I take one last glance at campus fading behind us, watching how the bright orange of the setting sun casts it in a fiery glow. My eyes find Cassie's in the rearview and I take the time to look around at my sisters, all of us smiling, all of us leaving Palm South University different than we arrived.

Each and every one of us has climbed a mountain this semester, some with less equipment and rougher paths. But here we are, standing together at the top, and suddenly it feels like there's nothing that can stop us now.

It's going to be one hell of a summer.

Tweet as you read using #PalmSouth and join the Facebook Discussion Group here (http://bit.ly/PSUDiscussionGroup).

Read Book 3: Pledge (Palm South University 3) now! (http://amzn.to/2vLkDXN)

More from Kandi Steiner

The Red Zone Rivals Series
Fair Catch
As if being the only girl on the college football team wasn't hard enough, Coach had to go and assign my brother's best friend — and *my* number one enemy — as my roommate.
Blind Side
The hottest college football safety in the nation just asked me to be his fake girlfriend.
And I just asked him to take my virginity.
Quarterback Sneak
Quarterback Holden Moore can have any girl he wants.
Except me: the coach's daughter.
Hail Mary
(AN AMAZON #1 BESTSELLER)
I used to love Leo Hernandez, but that was before I hated him. And now, I have no choice but to move in with him.

The Becker Brothers Series
On the Rocks (book 1)
Neat (book 2)
Manhattan (book 3)
Old Fashioned (book 4)
Four brothers finding love in a small Tennessee town that revolves around a whiskey distillery with a dark past — including the mysterious death of their father.

The Best Kept Secrets Series
(AN AMAZON TOP 10 BESTSELLER)
What He Doesn't Know (book 1)
What He Always Knew (book 2)
What He Never Knew (book 3)
Charlie's marriage is dying. She's perfectly content to go down in the flames, until her first love shows back up and reminds her the other way love can burn.

Close Quarters
A summer yachting the Mediterranean sounded like heaven to Jasmine after finishing her undergrad degree. But her boyfriend's billionaire boss always gets what he wants. And this time, he wants her.

Make Me Hate You
Jasmine has been avoiding her best friend's brother for years, but when they're both in the same house for a wedding, she can't resist him — no matter how she tries.

The Wrong Game
(AN AMAZON TOP 5 BESTSELLER)
Gemma's plan is simple: invite a new guy to each home game using her season tickets for the Chicago Bears. It's the perfect way to avoid getting emotionally attached and also get some action. But after Zach gets his chance to be her practice round, he decides one game just isn't enough. A sexy, fun sports romance.

The Right Player
She's avoiding love at all costs. He wants nothing more than to lock her down. Sexy, hilarious and swoon-worthy, The Right Player is the perfect read for sports romance lovers.

On the Way to You
It was only supposed to be a road trip, but when Cooper discovers the journal of the boy driving the getaway car, everything changes. An emotional, angsty road trip romance.

A Love Letter to Whiskey
(AN AMAZON TOP 10 BESTSELLER)
An angsty, emotional romance between two lovers fighting the curse of bad timing.
Read Love, Whiskey – Jamie's side of the story and an extended epilogue – in the new Fifth Anniversary Edition! (https://amzn.to/3FB1B7E)

Weightless
Young Natalie finds self-love and romance with her personal trainer, along with a slew of secrets that tie them together in ways she never thought possible.

Revelry
Recently divorced, Wren searches for clarity in a summer cabin outside of Seattle, where she makes an unforgettable connection with the broody, small town recluse next door.

Say Yes
Harley is studying art abroad in Florence, Italy. Trying to break free of her perfectionism, she steps outside one night determined to Say Yes to anything that comes her way. Of course, she didn't expect to run into Liam Benson...

Washed Up
Gregory Weston, the boy I once knew as my son's best friend, now a man I don't know at all. No, not just a man. A doctor. And he wants me...

The Christmas Blanket
Stuck in a cabin with my ex-husband waiting out a blizzard? Not exactly what I had pictured when I planned a surprise visit home for the holidays...

Black Number Four
A college, Greek-life romance of a hot young poker star and the boy sent to take her down.

The Palm South University Series
Rush (book 1) FREE if you sign up for my newsletter!
Anchor, PSU #2
Pledge, PSU #3
Legacy, PSU #4
Ritual, PSU #5
Hazed, PSU #6
Greek, PSU #7
#1 NYT Bestselling Author Rachel Van Dyken says, "If Gossip Girl and Riverdale had a love child, it would be PSU." This angsty college series will be your next guilty addiction.

Tag Chaser
She made a bet that she could stop chasing military men, which seemed easy — until her knight in shining armor and latest client at work showed up in Army ACUs.

Song Chaser
Tanner and Kellee are perfect for each other. They frequent the same bars, love the same music, and have the same desire to rip each other's clothes off. Only problem? Tanner is still in love with his best friend.

About the Author

KANDI STEINER is #1 Amazon Bestseller and whiskey connoisseur living in Tampa, FL. Best known for writing "emotional rollercoaster" stories, she loves bringing flawed characters to life and writing about real, raw romance — in all its forms. No two Kandi Steiner books are the same, and if you're a lover of angsty, emotional, and inspirational reads, she's your gal.

An alumna of the University of Central Florida, Kandi graduated with a double major in Creative Writing and Advertising/PR with a minor in Women's Studies. She started writing back in the 4th grade after reading the first Harry Potter installment. In 6th grade, she wrote and edited her own newspaper and distributed to her classmates. Eventually, the principal caught on and the newspaper was quickly halted, though Kandi tried fighting for her "freedom of press."

She took particular interest in writing romance after college, as she has always been a die hard hopeless romantic, and likes to highlight all the challenges of love as well as the triumphs.

When Kandi isn't writing, you can find her reading books of all kinds, planning her next adventure, or pole dancing (yes, you read that right). She enjoys live music, traveling, playing with her fur babies and soaking up the sweetness of life.

CONNECT WITH KANDI:
NEWSLETTER: kandisteiner.com/newsletter
FACEBOOK: facebook.com/kandisteiner
FACEBOOK READER GROUP (Kandiland):
facebook.com/groups/kandilandks
INSTAGRAM: Instagram.com/kandisteiner
TIKTOK: tiktok.com/@authorkandisteiner
TWITTER: twitter.com/kandisteiner
PINTEREST: pinterest.com/authorkandisteiner
WEBSITE: www.kandisteiner.com

Kandi Steiner may be coming to a city near you!
Check out her "events" tab to see all the
signings she's attending in the near future:
www.kandisteiner.com/events

Note from the Author

I'M WRITING THIS NOTE with shaky hands and a heavy heart. This season of *Palm South University* covered a lot of serious topics, including the sexual assault of Erin Xander in this episode. While this was an important part of Erin's journey and story to tell, it's equally important for you, as a reader, to understand that there are options if you ever find yourself in this terrifying situation or one similar to it.

If you become a victim of sexual assault, call 911 or RAINN at 1–800–656-HOPE immediately.

Just like Erin's situation, four out of five rapes are committed by someone known to the victim. Similarly, 68% of rapes are not reported to the police, and 98% of rapists never spend a day in jail or prison. And unfortunately, a college campus isn't always a safe place, as women 18–24 who are enrolled in college are 3 times more likely than women in general to suffer from sexual violence.

If you're like Erin, you may feel that it's useless to tell anyone—no one will believe you, they'll say it was your fault, they'll embarrass you and end up winning in the end, anyway. But no matter what, you must understand that it is **not your fault** and **there is help** available.

I hope you never find yourself in this situation or never have in the past, but if you're reading this and you feel isolated and alone, please, reach out to someone. Reach out to *me*. I am always here, and I care about you—every single one of you.

Take care of your mind, your body, and your soul. You're the only one who can.

For more information and resources, please visit *www.rainn.org*.

Acknowledgments

FIRST AND FOREMOST, I want to thank you, the reader, for continuing the wild ride at PSU with me. Serials aren't easy to give yourself to—you have to wait between episodes, you have to wait between seasons, and each week is as much a gripping story as it is a tease—so just know that I appreciate you so much. Thank you for posting in the *discussion group* (https://www.facebook.com/groups/712042985606913/) every week and in the off months between seasons, fan-casting your favorite characters, and fangirling at the moments that meant the most to me, too. PSU is a passion project of mine and so close to my heart, and I hope you feel the same.

This season was especially pressing on me physically and emotionally, so thank you Hubs, Mr. Steiner, for holding my hand through it all. I know my time was tied up and my stress level was through the roof, but you rubbed my shoulders and fed me whiskey to keep me going. I love you!

Staci Brillhart and Becca Hensley Mysoor—where do I even begin with you two? I could probably write an entire season thanking you for all the invaluable advice, writing wisdom, plot points and character motivations. I could write another listing everything that makes you both such incredible women and friends. You constantly see a potential in me and do everything in your power to help me achieve it, and that is both a rare and special thing. #Tribecycle for life, homies.

Mom, thanks for always being my best friend and believing in my writing. I couldn't do this every day without your support.

As always, to "the girls" who these characters are named after—the *real* Cassie (Graham), Jess (Vogel), Ashlei (Davison), and Erin (Spencer), thank you for being a constant circle of trust I can depend on. You inspired some pretty kick ass characters and I love you for every one of our memories.

An even bigger thank than usual to my beta readers, who put up with tight deadlines and fussy nights of me feeling inadequate to help me crank out an even better season of PSU than last year. Kellee Fabre, Sasha Whittington, Ashlei Davison, Jess Vogel, and Staci Brillhart—you are the wind beneath my beat up, crusty wings.

Sasha—I'm sorry these deadlines took away from bestie time. Thanks for understanding and supporting my dreams. I've got Chinese food and a girly movie night with your name on it whenever you're ready.

Big ups to Kash Monay, AKA Betsy Kash for still finding time in your life to edit my stories. Your notes literally make my day. And to Elaine Hudson York for the beautiful formatting that brings the tropical feel of PSU to life.

To my #Tribe—thanks for the good vibes and endless support. I love you.

Shout out to my fan group, Kandiland, #KandisChasers, for being the reason PSU even became a thing in the first place. You helped me see I wasn't ready to leave these characters, and I can't thank you enough for helping me get their story out. Plus, you push me daily with your love notes, and I'm convinced there's no better place in the world than Kandiland.

A notable thank you goes out to Jessica McBee, Beth Hurley, Trish Mint, Mykayla Morgan Wilson, Kiersten Hill, Trinity Snyder, Tina Lynne, Sylvia McCormick DiBlasi, Gladymar Hernandez, Andrea Britton, and Jess Rivers for sending me special notes during this season and writing reviews that made my heart smile.

I also want to give a special shout out to Shawna Broadstock, who won the character name giveaway last season and inspired one of the quirkiest and most amazing characters I've had the privilege of writing. I know you're beginning to tell your own stories now, and I wish you nothing but the best!

And as always, I'm forever thankful to my God in heaven who continues to bless me with a writer's heart and a dreamer's soul.

www.ingramcontent.com/pod-product-compliance
Lightning Source LLC
Chambersburg PA
CBHW020904060726
47591CB00004B/1077

9 781960 649096